# ASK ME SOMETHING

## AUBREY BONDURANT

Text copyright © 2015 by Aubrey Bondurant
ISBN: 9781523216529

# CHAPTER ONE

 $\mathcal{M}$ y perfectly manicured nails flew across the keyboard with the intention of sending one last email out this evening before I left to meet my friend Catherine. If I hoped to take the next week off, flying out first thing on Christmas Eve, I needed to ensure everything was in order. Not that I wouldn't be working over the holidays. I never truly turned it off as Vice President of the New York branch of Gamble Advertising.

The direct line lit on my desk phone, and I smiled at the number that flashed.

"Sasha Brooks here," I answered.

"Are you working late tonight?" Brian's smooth baritone came over the line.

Brian Carpenter was the East Coast Regional Vice President for our company. We'd known each other almost eight years. Over that time, we'd developed a relationship that was a combination of colleagues and friends. When I'd been promoted last year, however, he'd become my boss. Our working relationship was going through some growing pains, but the biggest change had been my move from Charlotte up to New York City, where I no longer saw him every day.

"Actually, I'm finishing up right now." Glancing at the clock, I saw it was only five-thirty. Early, for me.

"Good. Are you free for dinner tonight?"

My heart beat faster. "Wait. You're here in the city?" Brian traveled up here at least once a month. When he did, we tried to get together outside of the office for dinner or drinks. These occasions didn't happen as often as when we'd both lived down in Charlotte, so when he was in town I tried to rearrange my plans to see him.

"I am," he chuckled. "Otherwise it might be awkward."

Shit. I couldn't get out of my commitment. "Cute. Uh, I wish I'd known. I have this thing tonight."

"Oh, yeah? Hot date?"

I groaned and decided to come clean even though he would give me a hard time. "I promised to go with Catherine to a speed dating night."

"Uh, I wasn't aware you were into that sort of thing."

"Believe me, I'm not. I'm doing it for Catherine. You should feel sorry for me."

"Honey, I don't know who to feel sorrier for: you or those poor bastards you're going to meet. Why in the world is Catherine speed dating to begin with? She shouldn't need that type of thing to meet a man."

I couldn't help smiling when he called me honey. It always got me in my sweet spot. "I tried to tell her that, but I think she's anxious ever since her ex got engaged. I'm accompanying her for support."

"That's rough, but you're being a good friend. I know this type of thing is outside your comfort zone."

Yes, it was. He knew I had apprehension with new social situations. "What about drinks afterwards? If you're okay with the both of us, we should be finished by eight o'clock."

"Sure. Text me when you're done and let me know where. I'll meet you."

"Okay, sounds good. See you later." At least my evening was looking up now.

---

*WHY THE HELL had I agreed to this?* I'd asked myself that question ten times over since arriving but had yet to come up with an answer that didn't have me scoping out the exit signs in this eclectic little coffee shop decorated for the holidays. The scene in front of me was like a bad dream, but in all reality here I was at my first and hopefully last Manhattan speed dating night.

Damn, the perky woman in charge of the evening was talking to us ladies, and I hadn't been paying attention. I took in her big hair, heavy makeup—and were those shoulder pads? Huh. It was like I was looking at Miss Texas circa nineteen eighty-five. Considering she'd preserved her signature style while living in fashion-centric New York City spoke volumes. The woman obviously had some impressive self-confidence.

"Are you nervous, Sasha?" Catherine asked, interrupting my wandering thoughts.

Observing her barely contained enthusiasm, I realized I'd need to fake it tonight in order to be a good friend. Right. That's why I was here: to be supportive. Deep breaths and think about how much fun I was going to pretend to have.

I gave Catherine a wan smile. "No, this is less intimidating than a one-on-one blind date."

She beamed, and I knew that I'd done the right thing in agreeing to accompany her tonight. Catherine's divorce last year had taken quite a toll on her self-esteem when it came to dating and men. Since we'd become good friends, she'd confided in me about trying to venture out. Being single, I'd agreed to come along so that she wouldn't have to do it alone. It was my own fault for getting into this situation. Upon meeting Catherine, I'd gone out with her like I'd written the book on how to meet men. This was the image I'd created for myself, and I was too invested to back down now.

Taking a deep breath, I glanced at my watch. If all went according to plan, we'd be done in less than two hours. I'd text Brian and we'd meet for drinks. It had been three weeks since I'd last seen him, and I was looking forward to it.

Catherine handed me a chai tea and I wished it was something stronger. Amongst the twenty women attending, I wondered how many of them were regulars to this type of thing? Is this what females over the age of thirty did to meet men in this city? I was slightly north of that aging milestone, but I felt more pressure in imagining a romantic relationship than in worrying about a biological clock ticking.

I observed the men file in and take their seats. The women assessed them with quiet whispers, practically giddy with anticipation over the potential to meet the man of their dreams.

"Remember, ladies, you only get one chance to make a good first impression," Ms. Texas advised us.

Like I needed a reminder about the importance of a good first impression or the fact that I wasn't the kind of girl known for making one. Initially, I came off as unfriendly, but the truth was wrapped around my wrist in the form of a hair band. I snapped it discreetly: once, twice and a third time, telling myself that I wouldn't let my anxiety control me.

"The gentlemen are getting their nametags and sheets together, so only five more minutes, ladies," our MC of Love offered up.

For a moment it was so laughable that someone like me was here trying to make a good first impression that I knew I had to fire off a text to Brian.

*"About to start. Lady in charge said to be sure to make a good first impression."*

*"Your specialty. Remember no RBF."*

*"Haha, very funny."*

RBF was an acronym for Resting Bitch Face. I had it. I couldn't help it. And I'd refused to believe it until he'd essentially proven it to me years ago. Our professional relationship wasn't without its challenges, considering I wasn't always the easiest person to manage. But the one thing I could always count on was him being honest with me even if it meant telling me I had a resting bitch face.

*"I'd wish you luck, but I wouldn't really mean it,"* he texted back.

I wondered if he'd intended it the way it sounded. We were always flirting like this, with neither of us actually making a move beyond the platonic.

Bracing myself, I downed one final gulp of my tea before Ms. You-Can-Find-Love-In-Five-Minutes told us to stand in front of a chair along the line.

The bell sounded, and we each took a seat in front of prospective mates with the clock ticking.

Raising a brow at the man across from me, I tried very hard to keep my face from sliding into RBF. My mind wandered to why Brian was up in New York in the first place. He hadn't mentioned it when we'd spoken yesterday on the phone.

Crap. I was still thinking about Brian, and the man in front of me at the small table had been talking for two full minutes. I shifted my focus to him.

He wasn't unattractive. And that was pretty much the only description I could give as he finished up.

"That's me in a nutshell. How about you?" he asked.

Er, okay. "My name is Sasha—"

"Yeah that's on your nametag," he teased.

Before I could help it, my eyes narrowed. I watched him shift uncomfortably. Oh, hell. I'd gone from resting bitch face to full-on active bitch face. "Right, sorry. I'm nervous," I fibbed, trying

5

to recover. I took a deep breath. "I'm thirty-two, and I work a lot of hours in the advertising field. Um, I moved up here from Charlotte, North Carolina, last year."

"Do you like your job?" He appeared genuinely curious.

"Yes, absolutely." There should be no reason why I shouldn't enjoy it. My career was exactly where I'd always dreamed it would be. So what if my level of anxiety had increased with it? It was to be expected, right? The higher the paycheck, the larger the responsibility, my dad had once told me.

"That's good. Not many people can say that. I'm currently between jobs and trying my hand at Broadway auditions."

Uh, yeah. I could officially add that statement to my virtual list of instant turnoffs. *Be nice,* I reminded myself. "Is there any particular part or show you're interested in?"

He nodded enthusiastically. "My dream would be one of the monkeys in the Wicked production."

For a moment, I entertained the idea that I was on some type of reality television show where I was being punked. I even looked up for the hidden camera or for some celebrity to come out. Who the hell said their Broadway dream was to be a monkey? After thirty seconds, it became obvious this was for real, and even though my mind was saying, *I've got nothing*, my mouth mercifully managed, "That's nice."

Thank God I was literally saved by the bell. But as I scanned down the long line of nineteen more men, the panic started to well up.

Catherine caught my eye and gave me a wink. She was enjoying herself. Undoubtedly she would make a great impression in the small allotted time. We might both be polished and professional career women who were single in the city, but that was about it when it came to the similarities between us. Her blonde hair was soft and framed her heart-shaped face flawlessly. My chin-length hair was black and cut in a chic bob. She was fair with blue eyes and classic features, whereas I had my biological mother's brown eyes, olive skin and full lips from somewhere else in my family gene pool. Despite being the editor for Cosmo Life magazine, Catherine was down-to-earth and genuinely sweet. Sweet would never be a word to describe me. I snapped my band under the next table three more times, willing myself to stay calm. I could do this.

Five guys later, I was ready to feign a minor medical emergency. The next candidate, however, interrupted my thoughts on what appendicitis might look like. He was very attractive. Since his eyes were running over me with frank interest, I could tell he might be thinking the same thing.

"I'm Bradley, and you must be lost. A woman like you definitely doesn't need a speed date to find a man," he theorized.

He was clean-cut, and professional in a suit and tie. But he still wasn't as handsome as Brian.

Jesus. Where had that thought come from? Giving Bradley a smile, I confessed, "I'm here with a friend who wanted to come. What about you?"

"I'm in the same situation. Can you believe some of the losers at this tonight?"

My smile faltered. Sweet might never describe me, but I wasn't mean-spirited. "Uh, I don't know that I'd go that far."

"That blonde two down had promise, but then she started talking about her divorce. Like a prospective date wants to hear about that kind of baggage. Completely pathetic."

Active bitch face came out in full force. "That blonde happens to be my friend. And I've learned all I need to about you, *Bradley*."

"Come on, don't you believe in second chances?" he cajoled, leaning forward. The practiced look he was giving me suggested that Bradley had probably enjoyed his share of second chances with women.

"Not when they need to happen within the first five minutes, I don't." I smiled tightly and took out my phone to google symptoms of acute medical emergencies.

---

THE REST of the evening was a blur. In addition to being soured on bachelor number six, by the time I got to number twenty, I could barely manage a smile. Since bachelor seven had been a doctor, I'd abandoned the idea of feigning an episode of anything medical. The man was creepy enough that he'd most likely perform mouth-to-mouth for a sprained ankle. Ugh.

Catherine, on the other hand, was thrilled with the evening and the results. Our hostess-of-human-torture-otherwise-known-as-speed-dating passed out the contact information of the men who'd been interested and Catherine had garnered fourteen of them.

Was there no other female participant here tonight who was indignant that they'd polled the men instead of us women? I folded my paper and tucked it into my purse wishing I could throw it away without hurting Catherine's feelings.

"How many names did you get?" she questioned.

"Uh, only a couple and I'm not interested in them unfortunately," I supplied, not wanting to let her know I'd also gotten fourteen. For the life of me, I didn't know why. Perhaps my numbed responses and pained face came off as an attractive quality in New York City.

Eager to see Brian, I took out my phone and typed. *"On our way to Evan's Grill. There were no casualties."*

*"Oh, I'm certain plenty of hearts are breaking. See you there in about twenty."*

"Who's the reason for the smile?" Catherine probed, catching me off guard as we slid into the back of her sedan.

"Uh, it was a funny text from my boss, Brian. He's in town,

and I told him we were out for drinks. Hope you don't mind if he joins us later?"

"No, I don't mind at all. The couple times I've met him, he's seemed like a fun guy."

He was good fun and could maybe talk Catherine into better ways to meet eligible men. "Yeah, he is. We should have some time to recap the bachelors before he shows up."

After arriving at the bar, we got a table and ordered some drinks. I loved Evan's old wood and romantic lighting and knew it was a favorite of Brian's as well.

By the time Catherine and I recapped the men from earlier, laughing at some of conversations we'd had, I spotted Brian come through the door. He was dressed in slacks and a sweater, complete with his long wool jacket. My heart skipped a beat when his warm brown eyes found mine, and he started walking toward us.

"Hi, Sasha. Hi, Catherine." He kissed both of our cheeks and took the empty stool next to me. "Catherine, nice to see you again. It's been awhile."

She smiled. "Nice to see you again, too. Are you up here for Christmas?"

He shrugged off his coat and ordered a drink from our waitress. "No, I'm actually flying to Virginia to spend it with family tomorrow afternoon."

He looked at me and winked.

While Catherine and he made small talk about holiday plans, I assessed Brian through her eyes. He was the all American GQ-type guy with sandy brown hair, baby face, and charismatic, whiskey-colored eyes. Standing over six feet tall, with a nice build and clean-cut looks, he definitely earned the attention he got from women.

"So tell me about the speed dating thing tonight. How did it go?" he questioned, earning him a kick under the table from me.

His laughing eyes flashed toward mine.

Luckily, Catherine took it in stride. I'd wondered if she would be sensitive to him knowing about it.

"You know, it went okay. Fourteen wanted my number and I narrowed the list down to a couple I may contact," Catherine provided. "I think I definitely had more fun than Sasha."

He gave me an amused look. "I think that you ladies need to get out of New York and come down South where men know how to treat a lady."

She grinned. "You could be onto something. Maybe that's part of my problem; I've been in this city too long."

"So how many men wanted your number, Sasha?" Brian asked.

"Uh, only a couple," I lied. "Not a huge surprise that I don't make a very good first impression."

He studied me for a moment and I fidgeted with the scrutiny. He could always tell when I wasn't telling the truth.

"RBF strikes again?" he teased finally.

"For your information I resisted it quite nicely."

"What is RBF?" Catherine queried.

Slightly embarrassed, I was about to answer, but he beat me to it.

"It's a disorder that affects one in ten women. Unfortunately, the majority of them aren't even aware that they suffer." He sounded like a damn infomercial.

I rolled my eyes and tried not to laugh. "It stands for Resting Bitch Face," I said to Catherine.

"Uh, what does that mean exactly?" she inquired.

"It means that when I'm sitting somewhere, minding my own business and not actively engaged in conversation, evidently I have a look about me that signifies I'm bitchy. Brian was brave enough to point it out to me a few years back."

Her eyes widened slightly, and she frowned at him disapprovingly. "That isn't very nice."

He blushed and glanced toward me. "I didn't say it to be mean. Sasha was asking for feedback regarding client impressions. And she didn't believe me at first."

"So what convinced you?" Catherine asked, looking between the two of us.

"He snapped a picture of me," I admitted with a sigh.

Brian chuckled.

Catherine shook her head. "Sorry, I don't buy it. I had a first impression with her. I thought she was poised and professional."

He glanced toward me and grinned. "Oh, I'm sure she was. But it isn't when she's on. It's when she isn't actively engaged. Thus the 'Resting' part. Show her, Sasha."

"I'm not showing anyone anything. Matter of fact, I think I'm cured," I quipped.

He pulled out his phone and started to scroll through. "There is no cure, only the ability to cope with the disorder. I wonder if they have support groups for this type of thing."

I lightly punched his shoulder and was curious why he'd taken out his phone. He was all about manners and wasn't normally one to have his device out at the table. "What are you doing?"

"Attempting to locate the picture in order to show Catherine. I thought I'd kept it—Hey—" he protested.

I snagged his phone out of his hand, horrified at the thought he might still have that photo. I'd never admit it to him, but I'd felt humiliated when he'd shown me that image. To see yourself through someone else's eyes critically wasn't easy to take. But when you built up a tough exterior, you had to be ready for criticism and teasing. "You'd better not still have that picture," I warned, looking at his screen.

He laughed, enjoying the fact that I was distressed. "No, I was only teasing. RBF is in remission. I believe you."

"If I find out that you kept that photo…"

He held up his hands in mock surrender. "I promise I don't have it."

His phone buzzed in my hand. Before I could help myself, I glanced down and read the incoming text message from someone named Jamie.

**"What time are you coming by tonight? Can't wait to see you, I've missed you, lover."**

I felt the blood drain from my face. The pang of jealousy that hit me was so profound that I could hardly breathe, let alone speak. I handed his device back to him like it was suddenly offensive.

Looking at me strangely, he scanned the screen, reading the words.

I busied myself with taking a large gulp of wine and gave a strained smile toward Catherine, who appeared to be studying us both.

"So, Catherine, who is your favorite of the five guys we narrowed down?" I inquired, needing to change the subject.

Graciously, she took the hint. "Uh, I don't remember what number he was, but he had dark hair, was tall, nice face."

I nodded. "Oh, yeah, red shirt. He seemed nice."

"Ladies, excuse me for a moment. I'm going to head to the restroom and will be right back," Brian announced, walking toward the back of the restaurant.

I wondered if he had left to respond to Jamie.

"So what was with the text message?" Catherine queried.

I looked at her, surprise registering on my face.

She shrugged. "I heard it buzz and saw you read something. You went white, and then he blushed when he read it."

I sighed. "It was something private that I had no business seeing on my boss's phone." Although I had no right to feel jealous, I couldn't shake the thought.

She raised a brow. "Sasha, the chemistry between you and Brian is off the charts. And although I can appreciate you lying to be a good friend at the speed dating thing tonight, I'd like it if you trusted me in some aspects of our friendship."

Smiling at being called out, I wasn't sure I could put something into words that I didn't understand myself. "It was a message from a woman obviously expecting him tonight. We've always been friends. I mean, we flirt and there's always been an attraction, but timing and God—I'm rambling." I rubbed my temples. My thoughts were all over the place. How could one text message have me completely reeling?

"So why haven't you pursued it with him?"

Settling for the most convenient excuse was less than brave, but I wasn't ready to verbalize the larger obstacles without delving into my history and subsequent baggage. "There are a number of reasons. The most obvious is that my career means a lot to me. What I've had to go through and the pressure, well I don't need to tell you. I'm the first woman to ever make vice president at Gamble Advertising. There's a big spotlight on my front and a target on my back. Sleeping with anyone could have professional ramifications. Now that he's my boss, it would ensure that everyone would question how I got promoted, not to mention devalue my current position. You know what I'm talking about, Catherine. You've seen it happen, and so have I." The thought of being judged like that in my career made me shiver with dread. My job was the only thing I could definitively say I'd ever been good at. And yet at the moment, it left me feeling empty.

"I get it, believe me. But considering how miserable you look right now, are you sure that's still a good enough reason?"

I shook my head. "I don't know. But even if I did, what if I'm too late? What if this Jamie person is someone significant in his life, and I missed my opportunity?"

Her eyes were sympathetic. "There's only one way to find out. You have to ask the question."

"I don't know if I'm ready for the answer, Catherine. I'm so confused." It was overwhelming to realize my feelings for Brian might be deeper than I'd ever acknowledged.

We both noticed him walking back to the table and slipped back into our earlier conversation.

My face managed a tight smile. Evidently my night of faking it wasn't over yet.

# CHAPTER TWO

*A*fter Brian returned to the table, he and Catherine resumed small talk for the next fifteen minutes and ordered another round of drinks. I was drawn in a time or two, but for the most part I merely listened as Catherine described her last trip to Paris. I wondered why he wasn't in a hurry to get to his booty call but instead acted like he had no other place to be.

"So, Sasha, you're flying home tomorrow morning?" Brian asked, turning the conversation to me.

"Uh, yes. Tomorrow morning." I didn't mean to be short, but I'd yet to recover from the thought of him with another woman.

Catherine apparently decided to allow us some time alone to figure it out by excusing herself to go to the ladies' room.

"Everything all right?" Brian inquired, turning fully toward me on his stool and brushing his leg up against mine in the process.

"Yeah. Why wouldn't it be?" I pretended to be nonchalant with my question. My mind might be spinning with that text message, but my pride wouldn't let him know it.

He studied me, and our eyes stayed locked longer than was appropriate for two people who weren't interested in being more than friends. "Because you've been awfully quiet since that text came in."

Oh, boy. I was much more comfortable with not actually acknowledging this elephant in the room than with addressing it head on. I wasn't naive enough to believe he led a celibate lifestyle, but knowing it and having it confirmed were obviously two separate things. "It's none of my business," I offered lamely, swallowing past the lump in my throat.

That statement lay there for the longest time until he spoke again. "Do you want to ask me something?" The tone in his voice was low and intimate.

I turned toward him, my eyes widening when he scooted closer and put his legs on either side of mine. "Aren't I keeping you from your other plans?"

"No, unless you want me to go?" he tested quietly, keeping his eyes trained on me.

Wasn't that the million-dollar question. The heat from his legs sent a delicious awareness over my entire body. "I didn't say that I did." I blew out a breath, realizing that, per usual, we were getting nowhere. I'd tried countless times over the years to visualize a scenario in which we could explore the *more-than-friends* concept, but I'd never been able to make the mental leap without getting cold feet.

Catherine approached, and I could see the indecision on her face since Brian and I were closely facing in toward one another. She was silently asking whether she should take a seat or make another excuse.

He looked from me to her, tossed out a smile, and turned back on his stool. But before he did so, he whispered, "This conversation isn't over, Sasha."

A shiver of anticipation coursed through me with his words. "Uh, do we want to do another drink?" I posed the question, trying to lighten the mood and met Catherine's eyes, silently imploring, *please stay*. I desperately needed the delay to get a handle on my emotions before any further conversation with Brian could take place.

"I'm in." He smiled, motioning for Catherine to take her seat.

"Okay, maybe one more, but then I must get home to pack," Catherine replied, sitting back down. "Does anyone feel like an appetizer?"

I nodded, having skipped dinner in favor of speed dating. I needed something to soak up the wine. Brian begged off, and I was suddenly curious. "What brought you up to New York? We talked yesterday, and I didn't know you were coming."

"I was up in New Haven with Josh. Mark and I were helping him to finalize some wedding plans," he explained.

The wedding in question was that of my friend, Haylee Holloway, to the owner of Gamble Advertising, Josh Singer. She'd been his assistant temporarily last year, which is how I'd met her, and they'd fallen in love. Brian, Mark and Josh had been friends for many years. With Josh currently living between New York and New Haven where Haylee was attending law school, it didn't surprise me to hear that Brian had been up visiting.

"What made you decide to travel down here tonight, then?" Oh yeah, I was well aware of the awkward spot I was putting him in. Even though I was pleased he wasn't in a hurry to leave to get to this woman's place, one of the things that confused me was why he'd called me to go out in the first place if she was expecting him.

He smirked before answering, indicating that he was on to my question. Then he turned on the charm. "We hadn't seen one another in weeks and I thought I'd ask if you were free." He glanced over toward Catherine. "We used to do dinner or happy hours at least twice a week when we worked together down in Charlotte."

Was it my imagination, or had his leg moved closer to mine,

touching slightly? I needed a change of subject. "Are you throwing a bachelor party for Josh?"

"No. There isn't a lot of time for one, not to mention the groom-to-be isn't a bachelor party kind of guy," he affirmed.

"I'm kind of surprised his younger brother, Colby, isn't insisting on one. According to the stories, that kind of party seems to be his specialty," Catherine laughed.

He grinned in response. "You're not wrong, but thankfully he's respectful of Haylee. Not to mention, he'd have to get his big brother to Vegas or out on the town and that's not going to happen."

The appetizer arrived and Brian went on to recall some stories about Colby's wild ways. We were all in the midst of laughing when a pretty blonde walked up and tapped him on the shoulder.

He turned, registering shock. "Uh Jamie, what are you—?"

She cut him off. "Oh, you said you were out with friends, and I had thought maybe it was Mark or Josh. And since this place is around the corner from my condo, I thought I'd stop by. Now I see you aren't with the boys, and I'm sorry if this is awkward." She glanced over at Catherine and me, smiling.

Brian fumbled completely. "Uh, right. Yeah, no, both Mark and Josh are in Connecticut. Um, so…" He looked from her to us and couldn't find any words.

Jamie raised a brow at him and then took matters into her own hands by addressing both of us. "I'm Jamie Morgan, a good friend of Brian's." Her eyes focused on me first.

Catherine tapped me with her foot under the table when I didn't respond right away. I must have been in shock.

"Hello, I'm Sasha Brooks," I somehow got out, actively working on appearing unaffected even though my heart was beating through my chest. She was beautiful and put together with her shoulder-length blonde hair and blue eyes. It was obvious this woman had too much knowledge of Brian's friends to be some random hook up.

"And I'm Catherine Davenport, nice to meet you as well."

Brian recovered slightly, but still looked uncomfortable as hell. "Sorry, I forgot my manners for a moment. Uh, take a seat Jamie, if that's okay with everyone?"

Catherine mercifully spoke for both of us. "Of course it is."

Since I was sitting next to Brian, I realized it made sense to give up my stool. It's what a normal work colleague who wasn't sick with jealousy would do when her coworker's girlfriend, or whatever she was, showed up uninvited. "Here, sit next to Brian. I'll move." It wasn't completely unselfish as taking the stool across allowed me a better vantage point to study them together.

"You don't have to," he started.

I was already up and moving. "No, I insist." Jamie had no issue with sliding right in. My leg instantly missed the heat of him when I sat on the cold stool across the table. Meeting his eyes briefly, I had to look away when I realized Jamie's were trained on me.

"I hope I haven't crashed anything?" she prodded, glancing at Brian who gave her a smile that didn't quite touch his eyes. He wasn't normally at a loss for words so I wasn't surprised that she appeared to notice something was off.

Catherine took the lead with a response. "Not at all. We were catching up, that's all. Do you live in the city, Jamie?"

She smiled and I noticed her gaze kept flicking back to me. I willed my face not to go into any type of *bitchy* place whether it was active, resting or whatever else it would do with the sick feeling I was experiencing. The stab of possessiveness was so sharp that it took a few minutes for me to realize I was biting the inside of my lip to keep from displaying any outward emotions. My nails dug into my thighs trying to get myself out of my own head with the twinge of pain, wishing I hadn't taken off my black elastic band. If I'd thought the text message was rough, this was so much worse.

"I've been living in New York City about ten years now," Jamie replied. "Moved here after college, which is where I met Brian, Josh and Mark. We've stayed really great friends through the years thankfully."

Again her eyes trained on me. It was as though I was in a fish bowl, and she was waiting to see how I'd react to everything she said. Maybe my paranoia was simply misplaced. "You guys have known each other awhile then?"

"We have, haven't we, Brian?" she murmured, running her hand down his thigh and causing him, if possible, to look even more awkward.

"Yes. Since college," he acknowledged with a stressed smile, purposefully avoiding eye contact with me.

It was irrational, but hearing that he and Jamie had been friends for that long sliced through me like a betrayal. I'd always thought my friendship with Brian was special. Now to find out that someone had known him longer was difficult to hear. I was about to escape to the restroom to get myself together when Jamie addressed me directly.

"So, Sasha, I swear I've heard your name a lot over the years. You work with Brian, right?" she inquired.

I forced a smile. "Yes, I do. But I'm in the New York office, and he's down in Charlotte."

"Yes, well lucky for me, he gets up here whenever he can." She turned toward him and rubbed his back, making it known that whenever he was here, they got together.

Gulping my wine down like it was my lifeline, I tried not to count the times he'd been up to the city over the last few months. Forget fleeing to the restroom, I needed to get the hell out of here. I was about to motion the waitress for the check when the bomb went off.

"Oh, I know where I've heard your name. This is Sasha as in

Sasha-B-Fierce, isn't it?" she questioned, looking toward Brian expectantly.

Taken off guard, I wasn't sure I'd heard her correctly. "Sorry, what was that?"

"Sasha-B-Fierce. Oh, my gosh, did you not know that was your nickname?" She swiveled toward Brian, swatting him playfully. "You never said it was a secret. You and Josh were discussing her with that term, and I figured it was a compliment..." She stopped and looked at me as if awaiting a reaction.

My eyes shot up to his face, watching as he turned red.

Immediately, I knew her game. I was the threat, and she was challenging me to take her on in front of Brian about the nickname. There was a brief second where I entertained the idea of going thermonuclear, but Catherine snapped me out of it with a nudge under the table. Sliding a glance her way, I caught her warning look.

"Given that you work with all men at your level, Sasha, I think the word fierce is definitely a compliment. Women don't get to the top without displaying that quality," Catherine defended.

Not to be out done, Jamie attempted to make this about her. "Oh, believe me I know. I'm a partner at my law firm. Talk about a lot of stress and responsibility."

Catherine, in uncharacteristic fashion, decided to take her down a notch. "Yes, well, as the fashion editor of Cosmopolitan Life Magazine, believe me, I know, too."

I was afforded a moment of satisfaction in watching Jamie blanch. *Uh, yeah, sweetie, Catherine is a big deal, and you could take a cue from her about being humble.*

Jamie attempted to recover. "I, wow, yes, I guess you would. I absolutely love fashion." She attempted to soften her approach, clearly impressed with Catherine's title.

Brian looked at me apologetically and took advantage of the other two women talking to each other. "It was never a bad thing,

Sasha. We were talking about you in a pitch and how you're fearless."

Giving him a tight smile, I endeavored to tamp down on the urge to storm out of the restaurant. Pride was a powerful thing, and I willed myself to stay where I was. "I'm not offended. I was merely taken off guard to hear about it from someone I don't know rather than from someone I'd thought I was close to."

The direct hit registered on his face, and he swallowed hard.

Our eyes were locked with a storm of emotions passing between us, and I didn't give a damn in that moment if his little girlfriend was part of the audience or not.

"What is everyone doing for the holidays?" Jamie asked, trying to change the subject.

Halfway listening while everyone chatted a bit about plans, I was beyond the point of being very good company. Brian's intense looks toward me weren't helping the situation and neither was Jamie's hand, which kept rubbing his thigh as if to remind him who he was going home with tonight.

The waitress thankfully came along to check on us, which provided the perfect opportunity to get the hell out of here.

"No more for me. Matter of fact, I need get home and get packed. Early morning flight tomorrow," I explained.

Catherine did the same. "I need to head out, too. Nice meeting you, Jamie. Will we see you at the wedding?"

Damn, I hadn't considered that possibility. Josh and Haylee were getting married down in Tortola on New Year's Eve. Catherine, Brian, and I were traveling down as guests. *Don't look alarmed, don't look annoyed and, whatever you do, don't look devastated at the thought of him bringing Jamie.*

"Oh, you must mean Josh's wedding. Talk about last minute and to a twenty-three-year-old. Makes you wonder, don't you think?" Jamie mused in a conspiratorial tone.

Before I could say anything, Brian lost his temper. "Actually, we all know and love Haylee, so we don't wonder at all. In fact, Josh is damn lucky."

Jamie appeared taken aback by his response. "I didn't mean anything by it. And in answer to your question, Catherine, that depends on if Brian invites me as his date. There's still time, you know." The last part was said with the first glimpse of vulnerability I'd seen from her all night.

Averting my eyes from her fingers curled around his bicep, I glanced at my watch.

"Oh, I thought you were a good friend who went way back with Josh. You weren't invited?" Catherine threw out casually.

I'd never witnessed a passive-aggressive comment leave my friend's lips before, and yet there had been two in the last ten minutes. I was shocked.

Brian must have felt the same, considering the amused look he shared with her across the table. I wondered if he realized that his *friend* had pushed the buttons of the nicest woman in this place.

Jamie managed a strained smile. "It's been a number of years. Anyhow, I hope you ladies have a good evening and a Merry Christmas."

I could've hugged the waitress when she delivered the check. "Yes, Merry Christmas. Take care." Getting up, I attempted to shrug into my coat.

Brian stood and, before I knew it, was assisting me with it from behind.

Always the gentleman, I thought, watching him hug Catherine first, kissing her on the cheek and then turn toward me again. To say it was awkward wasn't even scratching the surface.

His eyes searched mine, and I looked away, unwilling to address the situation in front of Jamie, who was observing us closely.

As I pulled out some cash from my purse, his hand touched my wrist, stopping my motion and making me flustered.

"This is on me, ladies," he insisted.

I didn't bother to argue as that meant I could get out faster. "Thanks, Bri." I was so frazzled in trying to leave that it took his slight intake of breath for me to realize I'd used a nickname that I hadn't called him in three years. If I thought for a moment that he hadn't noticed, the heat in his eyes refuted that possibility.

I practically tripped over myself to get out of the restaurant and into the night air.

CATHERINE JOINED me at the curb and didn't say anything until her car pulled up. "Come on, I'll drop you by your place."

I didn't protest. At thirty-two years old, I couldn't believe I was fighting tears over a guy.

"I take it that was the girl from the text message?" Catherine asked softly, bringing me out of my daze once we were in the backseat.

"Yeah, it sure was." I exhaled, staring straight forward. "I'm being stupid."

"If it helps, I think he was absolutely stunned she showed up. It was obvious that he didn't invite her."

"I figured as much. It's not his style, and we've sort of had this unspoken agreement that we don't bring people we're dating around one another."

"So you've known each other for almost eight years and neither one of you has ever brought a date around the other?"

Turning toward her, I shrugged. "I'm not really a relationship kind of girl, and he's never been serious about anyone that I'm aware of. But considering he's known Jamie since college, maybe he's been seeing her for years." The very thought made me want to throw up.

"I'm not criticizing your lack of long-term relationships. I'm only mentioning the fact that neither one of you wants the appearance of one. Or even a casual date. Almost like you're waiting for the other one to make a move. That kind of speaks volumes, don't you think?"

Sighing, I realized a good friend to confide in would be nice, and so I came clean. "We, uh, almost slept together three years ago down in Miami. But let's just say fate intervened, and it didn't end up happening. After I got promoted last year, I practically patted myself on the back for not crossing that professional line because he became my boss. But when I moved up here to New York, I missed him much more than I ever thought I would. All this time, and I didn't say anything. Now it's too late."

Catherine shook her head. "Who says? Remember you're fierce, which means nothing intimidates you. The only reason that twit brought it up was to try to undermine what you do have with Brian. She noticed something from the moment she sat down. It's one hundred percent certain she came tonight because she knew he was most likely blowing her off for you. Clearly, he's talked about you enough that she perceived you as a threat. She may have known him longer, but it's evident who knows him better."

I was grateful for her loyalty. "Thanks. I appreciate you taking her down a notch. I get enough shit about my natural tendency to be overly reactive, and you saved me from saying something I shouldn't have. It was impressive, Catherine." I cracked a smile at how smooth she'd been.

She laughed. "It was my pleasure. Believe me, you don't get to where I am without having to deal with plenty of catty women. And it was good that her little comment about Haylee irritated the crap out of Brian, so there's that."

The car pulled up in front of my building. "Thanks for being supportive and listening. I, uh—" I took a deep breath before I admitted, "I don't have a lot of female friends. Chalk it up to my RBF or the fact that I forget how nice it is for someone to have my back." Or maybe being fierce really meant I was too much of a bitch to sustain any real relationships. "Suffice it to say I'm glad we're friends Catherine."

She looked like she might tear up and squeezed my hand. "Me, too. Now go have a nice bath and a Merry Christmas with your family. I'll see you in a few days, and we'll spend a nice New Year's in paradise."

---

AFTER ENTERING MY APARTMENT, I poured a large glass of wine, took that relaxing bath, and checked my phone way too often. What was I hoping for? A message from Brian telling me that he wasn't going home with Jamie? God, what I needed was more liquor and my vibrator.

With two more glasses down and my suitcase packed, I was feeling slightly less anxious and ready for bed. Thinking back to that night in Miami three years ago, I sighed.

Brian and I had won a major campaign and our flow in the presentation had been amazing. We'd gone out for drinks later that night to celebrate in South Beach. Before we knew it, we were in the middle of a dance floor, hot and heavy. We shortened one another's names, as if we could be Sash and Bri for the night and thus shed any thoughts of our professional relationship. The sexual attraction over the prior four years had been building up to that moment. We'd gone back to the hotel in the cab with his hand inching up my thigh and had arrived impatient to get naked. He'd promised to meet me in my room in ten minutes and I remembered my eagerness to have him in my bed. And then the worst thing possible had happened. And I'd texted him that we couldn't.

My phone rang, interrupting my trip down memory lane. After looking at the caller ID, I tried not to appear anxious and let Brian's number ring twice. "Hello."

"Hey, do you mind telling me what the hell that was about?" his voice came through.

"Excuse me?" I could hear the sounds of the street on his end and had a sick feeling that he could be leaving Jamie's place now.

"The fact that you called me Bri for the first damn time since Miami."

My stomach clenched and I fought my irritation. "It wasn't intentional, and if we are seriously fighting about names, how about the fact that I had to find out from your girlfriend that you and Josh, my boss and the owner of the company, have a nickname for me behind my back?"

He sighed audibly into the phone. "That was not how it was meant. It was only ever a compliment and it wasn't done intentionally."

"You're telling me that she meant it as a compliment and let it slip unintentionally tonight?" Unbelievable.

"No, not Jamie."

The sound of her name on his lips made me cringe.

"I meant that Josh and I didn't purposely call you that in front of her. It slipped and was in reference to the Allied Airlines pitch four years ago where you were grilled by that jerk. Remember? We said that with one arch of your brow you had him regretting his tone. And for the record, she's not my girlfriend."

I tried not to analyze the relief that hit me with his last sentence. "So where are you that you're calling me right now?" I hoped my tone was non-accusatory.

"Getting into a cab."

"And leaving Jamie's place?" The words fell out of my mouth before I could stop them.

"Would it bother you, if I was?"

The wine was a hell of a truth serum. "I know I may regret saying this later, but yes."

He muttered a curse. "We've been down this road. You turned me down. Remember Miami?"

He was right, we had been. "I know. Look, I've practically inhaled an entire bottle of wine tonight which has me all out of sorts and I'm traveling home tomorrow for the holidays which always makes me feel weird. I'm sure by the morning I'll be back to my senses, and we can return to normal." The thought made me sad, but I was starting to overthink the situation and become anxious. Normal. I needed the normal routine without thinking about him with another woman.

Silence greeted that statement.

"Brian, are you there?"

"Call down and tell your doorman that I'm coming up. I'll be there in five minutes."

# CHAPTER THREE

*I* hung up the phone stunned. Brian hadn't left much room to argue. He was coming over. The thought of this being a potentially bad idea, given our working relationship, was replaced with overwhelming relief that he was on his way to see me instead of spending the night with Jamie. I quickly called down to the doorman.

Less than five minutes later, he was knocking on my door.

I opened it feeling my heart rate spike with the sight of him. "Hi," I breathed.

"Hi, yourself. Can I come in?"

"Oh, yeah. Sorry." I moved out of the way, not realizing I'd been standing there like a deer in headlights.

His eyes roamed over me from head to toe.

I was suddenly self-conscious in my cashmere tank set. "I didn't have a lot of time to change." I turned around and quickly fetched a silk robe from my room.

After I walked back out, tightening the belt, his head shook slowly with a smile tugging at his lips. "Your robe is almost as short," he pointed out huskily.

"If you wanted a long fuzzy robe and bunny slippers, you have the wrong girl." I crossed my arms, feeling defensive.

He quickly closed the gap between us. "I'd never picture you with the words fuzzy or bunny." He was standing so close that I could practically feel the chill of the outdoors rolling off his coat.

"So what happened with Jamie?" I sucked in a breath when his hand cupped my chin and he put his thumb on my bottom lip.

"Why don't we run through the scenarios, and you give me your honest reaction to them?" His eyes held an intensity that had my legs trembling. The pad of his thumb rubbed seductively over my lip before sliding to the side of my face.

"That's an advertising strategy, not one to use in this situation," I murmured.

He shook his head. "Oh, I think we both need to understand your motivation before we can gauge what will or won't happen next, Sash."

Heat flashed through me. He'd abbreviated name like in Miami. "Go on," I whispered.

"First scenario is that I went back to Jamie's place but afterward came here to ensure you're okay with us as we've always been."

His voice was hypnotic, and I was completely under the trance until his actual words sunk in. My temper flared. "Maybe you should let go of me if that's the case." I didn't want to picture that scene in the slightest.

He shook his head. "It isn't, and you know it." He moved his other hand up and positioned it at the nape of my neck. He was seducing me one touch at a time. "The second scenario is that I came here to you instead of going home with her."

His fingers started massaging the tender muscles in my neck, and I had to bite back the small moan threatening to escape. "I think I like that one better than the first."

He smiled, searching my eyes. "The most important question I have for you though is whether you're interested because you're being competitive with Jamie or whether it's because it's me that you truly want."

I tried to move back, offended that he would suggest that idea, but he wasn't having it. He tightened his grip and brought his hands on either side of my face, meanwhile stepping into me with the fabric of his slacks brushing against my bare legs.

"No you don't. It's a fair question."

Hesitating, I thought a moment. "The feeling hit me when I saw the text, not when I met her. I didn't like the idea of you with anyone. Her showing up only rubbed salt in the wound. If it had been about the competition, then I would have challenged her instead of leaving."

I knew that he appreciated my admission when his eyes softened. "I didn't invite her, but I did make the mistake of telling her where I was."

"But you had every intention of going there tonight after drinks?"

He let go of me, stepped back and ran a hand through his hair, looking frustrated. "I won't stand here and apologize for having plans. Did you think over the last few years I haven't been with anyone else? Or that I would think you haven't?"

"That's not what I meant. I'm being honest about my reaction, but I haven't figured it out any more than you have. All I know is that the thought of you leaving here to go to her makes me sick, but I don't know what to do with that." I was overthinking it, but with our history and the fact that we were in uncharted territory, I was paralyzed in place.

He stood there staring at me for the longest time. "What if I told you that I'd rather be here at this moment talking with you then doing anything with her? That I called you for dinner and met you out for drinks because you've always been the priority?"

I let out the breath I'd been holding. "Do you mean that? You two have a longer history than we do." I hated that fact probably the most.

31

"I'm trying very hard right now not to be turned on by your jealousy, Sasha." He moved close again. "I want us both to be certain, though, before we go down a road from which we can't return. If she hadn't shown up tonight, how would the conversation have gone after Catherine left?"

It was time to put up or shut up. "I'm hoping I would've been brave enough to ask you if you ever think about more."

His fingers stroked my cheek. "Every fucking day."

My lips were so close to his mouth that I could feel his breath with that admission. "Are you going to kiss me?"

His eyes darkened. "I want to so badly it hurts."

"Then what's stopping you?" Suddenly I didn't want to think about any repercussions.

"Things have changed since Miami. There are items we'd have to discuss before we could even consider sleeping together."

"I get it. You're my boss and—"

"There's that, but we'd need to come to some sort of agreement on things."

"Agreement, huh? What happened to just having sex?" I was both intrigued and amused with this serious side of him.

"Not that simple, gorgeous. Not with me. You'd have to agree to my rules, and we'd have to establish boundaries."

What in the hell was he talking about? This was fun-loving Brian, not some guy who had rules and limitations about sex. "I don't understand. Are you saying you'd turn me down tonight if I asked you to stay?"

"It might appear that way, but the last thing I want is a one-night stand with you. I need you to think about if you want to enter into a sexual relationship rather than simply react."

"I still don't understand what you're saying."

"I'm saying that it would be very easy for you to fall into bed tonight and then tomorrow have regrets. You think I don't know you well enough to understand all those doubts running through your mind with regard to your career and me being your boss, but I do. I know what your priorities are, Sasha, and I respect them, but I won't let you take the easy way out and chalk this up to a lapse in judgement."

It irritated me that he could read me so well, but it was also a relief. I wasn't always the best at expressing my emotions, and having him do it for in this case wasn't a bad thing. Unfortunately, my body wasn't getting the *sex-is-off-the-table* memo. I'd been aroused since his leg touched mine in the restaurant. "What are the rules?" I was suddenly very curious.

"If you make the conscious decision to move forward, we start with the question of whether or not you'd allow me to be in control in the bedroom. We can go over details and negotiate the rules, but you'd have to agree to that fundamental principle first."

"I think I may have hallucinated." I moved toward the kitchen and poured a large glass of water, needing to sober up. Meeting his eyes, I watched while he leaned against my countertop awaiting my next sentence. "Let me get this straight. By you saying you'd be in control, are you telling me you'd want to be dominant?"

He nodded, and I noted there was no amusement in his eyes. He wasn't joking.

"And by that admission, you'd want me to be submissive?" The very idea was laughable.

"Not the way you're thinking of it, but in a sense, yes, I would be in charge. But make no mistake. I'd do this for your pleasure more than mine."

His voice was doing funny things to me, so I gulped down more water. I couldn't believe we were standing in my kitchen having this conversation. "Maybe I like to call the shots with the men I date." Quite frankly, if they didn't like it, then too bad, I almost added.

"Yeah, and how has that worked out for you?"

His smug look made me want to wipe it off. "I'm not into long-lasting relationships, therefore it's worked out just fine," I retorted.

He chuckled softly and moved, boxing me in against the countertop. With his forearms on either side of me, he leaned in. His voice was low and gravelly as he murmured against my ear, "I was talking about the sex, honey. How was the sex?"

I wasn't sure I wanted to discuss my sexual history, let alone admit it lacking. Meanwhile, his nearness was wreaking havoc on my senses.

He pulled back and danced his fingers down my arm. "Actually, I could tell you how it's been for you."

I shivered at his nearness and sexy voice. "Do tell," I challenged on a whisper.

He smirked, knowing exactly the effect he was having on me. "It was *fine*. And the word *fine* is a throwaway word. It's what you respond with to the doorman when he asks how your evening was: "Fine, thanks." It's what you say to the client when they ask how your flight was: *"fine."* But it shouldn't be the way you describe your sex life. Hell, maybe the first time was okay and promising. The second time, perhaps a little bit better, but by the fifth time, you realize that's it. That was the main act with the encore. But it was *fine*, so you stick it out for a while. After all, it's nice to have a reason to wear something new and lacy with someone to notice. Nice to get dinner with someone. But then you find yourself bored and staying late at work even when you don't have to because, frankly, the alternative isn't as appealing, and that's not so *fine*."

"Okay, enough." I moved one of his arms and stepped out of reach to lean against the opposite counter. He'd touched a nerve, hitting too close to home on my sex life or at least the one that I could remember.

"I only tell you this because I've been there, and now it's time for something better than *fine*."

"Three years ago, was this—I mean were there rules?" I was looking at a man about whom I'd once thought I knew almost everything.

"No, not really, but three years is a long time. Now I know what I want."

"Okay. Are you going to tell me what these rules are?"

"Not tonight, but we can discuss them over the holidays if you decide this is something you want to pursue. We're not rushing into this, Sasha, and it's not going to be something we do because we've been drinking or you're jealous. You need to be sure." He moved closer, his hands framing my face. "I'd better go and let you get some sleep."

"Do you have to get a hotel room now that your plans have changed?"

"Is that your way of asking if I'm leaving here to go see Jamie?"

I smiled, not willing to give him the satisfaction that I'd been thinking of the possibility. "Either that, or looking for an excuse for you to stay here tonight." His expression was pure desire and I took the moment to put my hand on his cheek.

He closed his eyes like he was savoring my touch. "You have no idea how much I want to explore that scenario, but you have a lot to think about."

"About being submissive?"

He smirked. "I was thinking more about whether or not you wanted to pursue it at all given our working relationship. But if you did, then yes, you'd need to think about whether you'd be willing to let me be in control in the bedroom."

Right, my career. How the hell had I gone from panicking about the perception of sleeping with my boss to hyper-focusing on what Brian meant about rules? He'd completely thrown me for a loop with this new dynamic. "I'm having a hard time seeing you as dominant. And if I'm being honest, I'm not sure that sort of thing would turn me on."

His carnal gaze was possessive and as sexy as sin when he dipped his head and his lips crashed down on mine. My body instantly ignited when his tongue touched mine, and his hand wrapped in my hair. His kiss was all consuming. Then his hips shifted into mine, and I could feel his obvious desire against me. Jesus, this man could kiss. Then, as sudden as he'd started, he pulled away.

"Still think you wouldn't be turned on?" he asked, his breathing shallow.

At least he wasn't unaffected, I thought, feeling all out of sorts. "I, um, that was better than what I remember from Miami."

He grinned, leaning his forehead against mine so that we were eye to eye. "Yes it was. I'm staying in Josh's guest apartment tonight so you know."

Smiling, I was glad he'd told me.

He sucked on my lower lip one last time before heaving a regretful sigh and pulling away. Walking toward my front door, he gave me one more look over his shoulder before leaving.

Holy shit, the world as I knew it had been turned upside down in one evening.

# CHAPTER FOUR

hile waiting at the airport for my flight home the next morning, I kept replaying the previous night over in my mind. But instead of feeling panicked, I was disappointed that I'd been left with no more than a scorching kiss.

Taking out my phone, I quickly texted Brian a question I couldn't shake.

*"You and I both know I'd be terrible at being submissive. Why me?"*

After arriving at my parents' house and while sitting in the driveway, I read his response for the third time.

*"You're dominant in all things. Doesn't it get tiring? Don't you want to let go and have someone else take over and call the shots in one aspect of your life?"*

Curious, I had to ask, *"What kinds of things are we talking about? Furry cuffs and sex toys or like hardcore whips and chains? Details please."*

I was surprised when his reply came quickly.

*"No details until you agree. But in answer to your questions, I'm not into whips and chains. Furry cuffs are a bit cheesy. And YES to the other."*

Realizing what the *other* referred to, I blushed hotly. Jesus, he capitalized YES to sex toys. I was having a hard time picturing a man I'd known all these years, who I called a friend, colleague, and now boss, being into these types of things. You think you know someone. I'd always pictured he'd be sort of clumsy and goofy in bed. The type of sexual partner who'd make me laugh and be comfortable to be around but who wasn't going to make me burn with desire. And now I was aroused beyond belief merely over text messages. His next one came in before I could respond to the last.

*"How's the head? And how was the flight?"*

Normal conversation. Okay, I could do that. *"Head is all right, although I had to take some Tylenol to get it there. Flight was good. I'm about to go into the house, but I'll talk to you later. Safe travels to Virginia."*

---

I APPRECIATED the fact that I was able to spend the holidays with loved ones, but my home town of Beaufort, North Carolina was a reminder of the most traumatic event I'd ever experienced. I'd always felt like a piece of me was missing while growing up, but never understood why until the year I turned sixteen and discovered I was adopted. My life as I knew it changed drastically. It didn't help that since my father had been the Chief of Police for many years, I couldn't go one foot into town without running into someone who knew me and what had happened. Small towns. Gotta love them.

Breathing deep, I focused on the good memories. I loved the beauty of my childhood home with its historic tall ceilings and wooden floors built over a hundred years ago.

My younger sister and her family lived on the other side of town. This was probably a good thing at the moment because being under the same roof with four children would only emphasize my slight hangover.

It had been a few months since my last visit. My sister had delivered baby number four. As with the prior three, I'd made sure I went to the hospital, gave a lavish gift, and picked up a meal from the local restaurant for their first night home. I may not be very good with babies, cooking, or all the other domestic stuff, but I was a kick-ass big sister in ensuring I was home for the births of my nieces and nephews.

"Hi, Daddy." I embraced my big bear of a dad after walking in the front door. My father might not share my blood, but I was hard pressed ever to think of him as anything other than my dad. He'd retired from a career in law enforcement two years ago. I knew that most found his six-foot-four-inch stature and big barrel chest intimidating, but to me he'd always been a big teddy bear. He was a true Southern gentleman. Although he didn't typically have much to say, people listened when he did speak. His hair got a little grayer and thinner each time I came home, but to me he was perfect.

"Hi, sweetheart. How was your flight?" he asked.

"Oh, it was fi—, I mean, good, thanks." I smiled. Brian had turned me off of the word *fine*. "Hi, Momma."

My mother came into the foyer and hugged me too. She wore an apron over her sweater and pants, showing the evidence that she'd been hard at work in the kitchen. My mom might be sixty, but she could easily pass for ten years younger, with hardly a gray hair on her head or a wrinkle on her face. She might have gained a little weight in the last couple of years, but in true Norwegian heritage style, she wore the curves impeccably.

"Sweetie, look at you, you're wasting away." Leave it to my mom to always think I'd lost weight as an excuse to push butter-laden food on me for the next few days. I knew she loved me like I'd been her own from birth and that keeping me fed was her way of letting me know how much she missed taking care of me.

After making my way up the stairs to my childhood room, I put down my bags and took a moment to fight the disquiet over being in this space. Then I thought of Haylee who had lost her father a few years ago and her mother last year, and I felt appreciation for having a family to come home to over the holidays.

I went downstairs and hugged my mom again.

"Now, then, what's this?" she asked, turning and touching my chin. I was thirty-two years old, but she had a way of making me feel fourteen again.

"I love you, Mom," I responded thickly.

"I love you, too. Everything all right? Any new men in your life?"

I tried not to roll my eyes at the question. In my town, most people were interested in my love life or lack thereof. At church tonight I would have that question asked at least a half-dozen more times. "Everything is good, and nothing to talk about in the other department."

I nipped a piece of bacon that would go into some sort of side dish tomorrow and got ready to help with the preparations. Cooking wasn't my forte, but it wasn't that hard to chop or mix something, and I was certainly capable of washing dishes. Being in the kitchen, especially during the holidays, was a requirement for any Southern woman.

"Well, I know I don't say this enough, but you know I'm real proud of you, don't you, Sasha Jayne?" She had turned and was studying me, her eyes reflecting her words.

The tears pricked my eyes, and I swallowed hard. "Thanks, Mom. I appreciate it."

My parents hadn't judged, but I'd known it had hurt them that I'd been hell-bent to leave this town at eighteen and had never looked back except for the occasional visit. They'd lovingly raised me. But even they hadn't been prepared for the true circumstances of my adoption and birth to come out the way it had. My therapist called that revelation the traumatic trigger that had started my anxiety attacks. I called it the worst day of my life.

"Here, you can chop apples for the pie. Tell me about work. What's new there?"

I knew she didn't care much about the world of advertising, but I did share a couple of pieces. Then I switched to Haylee's upcoming wedding details as I knew this was a subject my mom enjoyed.

"You're leaving for the wedding from here?"

"Yes. I'm driving over to Charlotte the morning of the twenty-ninth and taking the plane down with some others." A buzz of anticipation hit me about seeing Brian again. He'd be taking the same plane.

"I'm thankful you'll be home for a few days at least. The kids will be happy to see you, too."

I gave my mom a smile, trying not to feel guilty over the fact that it would be the longest few days of my life. There was nothing she could do about the fact that I had anxiety while being home. It was a part of my past I'd learned to reconcile. "I know I don't say it enough, but I miss you and Dad."

"We miss you, too, but you know we're not here to make you feel bad about coming home. You've got your own life and we understand that."

I appreciated the fact that my parents had never put that kind of pressure on me.

"Now, then, after you finish chopping apples, why don't you go with your father into town? He's gonna pick up some pizza for tonight and lunch on the way home. I'll finish up in here. I only have the one more pie, and then I think we're set. We'll see your sister and family tonight at church, then they'll be over tomorrow afternoon, giving them time to be in their PJ's in the morning for Santa."

I finished up my task and made my break for it to accompany my father for the pizza pickup duty. It would give me a chance to go by the store and get some good bottles of wine. I loved my family, but alcohol wouldn't be their top priority for tomorrow's menu. I'd need a few glasses to get through the day with my sister.

---

AFTER LUNCH WITH MY FOLKS, I drove to a commercial business park on the outskirts of town and took a deep breath upon parking in front of the familiar office. Not even my family knew that I continued to see Dr. Marcia Evans when I was home.

Even though it had been months since my last visit, my therapist smiled warmly like we'd seen one another only days ago. The older woman had always reminded me of Blanche from the Golden Girls. She was sassy, Southern, and didn't mince words. I'd been seeing her since I was sixteen years old, so to say she knew me almost my whole life wasn't an exaggeration.

Her office hadn't changed much. Maybe some new furniture over the years, but the familiarity of things like her framed pictures on the walls and flower-printed curtains set me at ease. Being a clinical psychologist specializing in anxiety, you couldn't go about remodeling your office without throwing your patients into complete chaos, I imagined. The thought made me smile.

"Sasha, you look lovelier every time I see you. When did you get in?" she greeted.

"This morning. Thanks for agreeing to see me on Christmas Eve, Dr. Evans."

She looked at me thoughtfully. "You know I always have time for you. And although I'd miss seeing you, you do know that I wouldn't be offended if you were to find someone to talk to in New York."

It wouldn't be a session with Dr. Evans without her suggesting in a subtle way that she'd like me to see someone more often then maybe twice a year. "I know and appreciate it." I acknowledged her suggestion as I did every time.

"How was your anxiety level this time coming home for the holidays?"

Huh. It dawned on me that I'd been so preoccupied with Brian and what had transpired last night that I hadn't experienced the apprehension I normally did when traveling home. "I, uh, it was better this time."

Dr. Evans had the super power of knowing when I was holding something back and immediately arched a brow. She sat back with her interest obviously piqued. "What was different this year?"

I was hesitant to make Brian part of this session. She'd heard about him a little over the years as someone who I'd confided in about my social discomfort, but that was about it. "I went out of my comfort zone last night by accompanying a friend to a speed dating night. I can't say that I'd ever do it again or particularly enjoyed it, but it definitely tested my boundaries."

"That's good. But given that getting off the plane to drive home has always been a trigger point for your anxiety, I'd like to know what was on your mind instead of the usual in those moments."

There wasn't a non-awkward way of saying 'sex toys' to anyone. I felt my face heating just thinking about it.

She put down her pen and regarded me thoughtfully. "I'm not here to judge or criticize your choices. However, if something in your life is impacting your anxiety levels, either positively or negatively, then it's important that you tell me."

"Okay, here goes." I filled her in on some details about the prior night with Brian, including the text message, Jamie subsequently showing up, and finally him coming by my place.

"So did you two—?" she hedged.

I shook my head and smiled at her look of surprise. "To be honest, I would have, but he was adamant that it be a conscious decision instead of a reaction. Then he started talking about boundaries." I replayed some of our conversation with the exception of him wanting to be dominant. There were some things I'd rather keep personal.

I'd never seen her look quite so amused. She wore a barely contained smile. "Sounds like Brian knows you and wants to ensure that you're comfortable before starting something."

"He knows enough, I suppose." I didn't think it was a fair statement to say he really knew me when he was in the dark about my anxiety, my therapy, or the traumatic trigger for it all. "I know he's not purposefully messing with my head, but I'm all sorts of turned upside-down and can't make heads or tails of anything."

This time she didn't bother to hide the smile. "I don't think he's messing with your head, either. If anything, it would appear he wants to ensure you are both very clear where this would go and what would happen. Those are two things that hold true in how we've done our behavior therapy. You picture the scenario, you imagine yourself in it, and you prepare yourself mentally. If you had slept together last night, I believe you'd be anxious right now thinking about what it meant, and what was going to transpire as a result of doing so. It sounds like he values your priorities and wants you to be certain."

"He does and part of me has always wanted to, but then I overthink it and start worrying about what might happen."

As she often did to ensure I didn't get stuck, she changed subjects. "How is the anxiety at work? You mentioned the last time you were here that dealing directly with clients wasn't easy."

"It's coming along. There are a lot of happy hours and wining and dining which are all outside my normal comfort level, but I'm working through the challenges. Wine helps."

I had thought I was being funny but saw her eyes narrow. "Sasha, you pushing your limits is good. But I caution you not to bulldoze into things because you feel like you have to prove something to yourself or, worse, to anyone else. We've talked about this previously, and I've been very pleased with your progress. But remember to respect your disorder at all times. It's part of your life, and if you start believing that you no longer have it, then you risk having a panic attack when you least expect it. You need to be mindful of your triggers."

I took a deep breath. It had been at least a year since I'd had an attack, but one never forgot the feeling. And she wasn't wrong about my need to push myself. I was a glutton for punishment when it came to refusing to accept the control anxiety could have over me. As a result, though, I sometimes made things worse for myself by forcing issues before I was ready to deal with them.

"It's getting better, and I've learned to control it faster."

"I have no doubt you're controlling it faster. Look at your position and what you do for a living. But is your level of anxiety honestly getting better? Because I would venture as you've progressed in your career, it would naturally get higher."

"I think anyone in my situation would have high levels of anxiety about proving themselves."

She nodded and then changed the subject on me again. "I don't disagree. I like the fact that in thinking about Brian you were distracted enough not to have your usual discomfort in coming home. But talk to me about why you're hesitant to start something with him."

I went with the most obvious reason yet again. "My career is really important to me. I've worked my ass off the last seven years to become the first female vice president at Gamble Advertising. But with that, I'm under a microscope. It may be part of my anxiety, but I can feel people wanting me to fail."

"Oh, I'm sure it's true, for anyone in your position. People will be jealous or sexist or have whatever other reason for not wanting you to succeed. But do you feel like you deserved that promotion?"

Self-doubt was also a huge part of my disorder. "I do, most of the time. My biggest worry is that if someone were to find out about me sleeping with him, then they'd think that was why I got promoted. That it would invalidate all of my hard work."

"So take me through that scenario. Say Brian makes you happy and you two get serious, maybe fall in love. Would there ever be a point where you would feel comfortable with other people knowing?"

"I don't see that happening."

"Why not?"

Because Brian was attracted to a woman who was self-assured and put-together. Not one who had to snap a hair band to keep from freaking out in social situations. I expelled an unsteady breath. "He may know more about me than most, and I may feel comfortable with him, but if he were to truly get to know me, he'd be disappointed."

She put down her pen and studied me. "And there we come to the biggest fear you have, Sasha. I agree that your career is a valid concern. Anyone in your position would most likely feel the same, but the real reason for your hesitation is what you just stated. You don't feel like he'll accept you without the armor or that he could possibly love the real you. You've done a remarkable job in conquering your self-doubt with regard to your career, but you've hardly addressed it in your romantic life. I'd venture to say that you pick your career over love because there's security in knowing you've been successful in it."

"I hate it when you trick me," I muttered.

She grinned. "It's not as if you didn't realize that already. You simply didn't want to admit it. If you choose to embark on this relationship, I would strongly suggest you share more with him regarding your triggers and history Sasha. It would be helpful for the both of you, I think."

I wasn't so sure. "Do you think it's possible to have a successful relationship with an anxiety disorder?"

She smiled kindly. "Of course I do. I see it all of the time. I could call around and find someone in New York if you'd like to talk with someone more regularly. It may help."

"I'll let you know if I need that. Thanks for your time and Merry Christmas."

---

AFTER MY APPOINTMENT, I drove down to the beach only a few blocks from my parents' house, found my spot, and sat down to breathe in the smell of the salt water. The weather was chilly, in the forties, but the crisp, clean air felt good. Beaufort was a small coastal town, outside of the outer banks of North Carolina. Some people referred to it as the other Beaufort, since most people thought of South Carolina when they heard the city name. During the summer it had its share of tourists, either passing through or opting for a quiet beach vacation. But during the winter, it was all local residents. This was the time of year I liked the most as there was nothing like a deserted beach for soul-searching.

Pulling out my phone, I texted Brian. *"What are you doing?"*

*"Calling you,"* he replied.

I smiled when the phone rang immediately and answered, "Hey."

"Hey yourself. What are you doing?"

"Sitting on an empty beach. I have about an hour before I need to get back to the house and go to church with the family."

"I hope you're not sitting there regretting that kiss last night."

Considering it was quite the opposite, I eased his mind. "Oh, I'm thinking about the kiss, all right, but not with regret."

"It's all I've thought about the entire day."

His voice was doing that husky thing that made my stomach flutter. "Then why didn't you stay last night?"

"I told you, we need to set rules."

"Okay, how many are there?"

"There are a few, and you would have the option to choose your own so long as they don't directly conflict with mine, of course. We can make them up as we go, revise if needed."

"And no one outside of us would know about this, um, arrangement?"

"I think it would be best, both professionally and personally, that we keep it between the two of us. Neither of us need the extra pressure."

"So you wouldn't tell Josh?"

"No, as long as it didn't affect our professional relationship."

I let out a long breath.

"You're overthinking this, Sasha."

"Hi, have we met? Of course I am."

He chuckled. "Even more reason to have an aspect of your life where you don't."

"Hmm, maybe. You indicated this is more than one night. Okay, good, I don't do one-night stands either, but what kind of time frame are we talking?"

"Do we need to define one?"

"Neither one of us are exactly known for long-term relationships."

"Then putting a time frame around it isn't going to make a hell of a lot of difference, is it?"

"True. Okay, what are the rules?"

"I'm not trying to sound like a broken record, but I want you to be certain this is something you want first."

"Don't I have to know your terms before I can decide that?"

He was quiet and then answered. "Yes, I suppose."

"I'm not signing a document with the rules, right?"

"No. Not at all. We're both smart and capable adults, and we've known one another too long to start talking contracts."

"Okay. Tell me the first one."

"Rule number one is that if we are angry with each other, we fuck before we fight."

I couldn't help my intake of breath.

"Are you there?" he asked.

"I'm processing."

"You're scared."

"I'm not scared of anything." That wasn't true, but I definitely wasn't letting him know it. "For your information, the last thing a woman wants to do when she's pissed off with a man is to have sex with him."

"That's because you associate it with making love. A woman doesn't want to show love and affection when she's mad. This is angry sex, honey. Imagine putting all that irritation and frustration into a sexual act. I promise an orgasm will do more for your body than an argument ever could."

"You've had a lot of angry sex, I take it?"

"There's no other woman who pushes my buttons the way you do, so the answer would be no, but I'm kind of looking forward to it."

I swallowed hard. "Okay, what's next?" My voice betrayed that I was not yet recovered from rule number one.

"That's it for today. Why don't you think about it, and we'll talk again tomorrow."

"You're teasing me with only one? I want to know all of them."

"I think you need to learn some patience. We have plenty of time to talk about them over the next few days."

"You're kind of annoying me with the whole patience thing."

"Come on, you didn't honestly believe we'd go a day without irritating one another somehow, did you?"

"I foresee a lot of rule number one being evoked." I had the pleasure of hearing his intake of breath and saying good bye on that note.

# CHAPTER FIVE

*T*he next day on Christmas morning, I slept in which is something I rarely did anymore. The smell of cinnamon rolls baking came from downstairs. It was heavenly, but also convinced me to get up and go running. I loathed exercise, but I hated gaining weight more. I was naturally curvy with a larger butt and hips than I would have liked, but I'd made peace with my curves years ago and had learned to dress to flatter them. They might not be my favorite assets, but considering I'd been blessed with full lips and good skin—well, no one could have it all. I did a leisurely four-mile run and was greeted by my mother at the back door.

"Sasha Jayne, it's cold outside. Go on up and take a nice hot shower. I have cinnamon rolls. And Merry Christmas, darlin'."

I didn't bother to point out the rolls were the very reason I'd gone running but gave her a quick kiss on the cheek instead. "Merry Christmas, Mama. I'll be down in a bit." Somehow I doubted I'd ever outgrow my mother fussing over me.

Upstairs and logging into my laptop, I perused my work email quickly and was thankful that all of my clients were also enjoying the holidays. Taking some more time on the Internet, I started searching terms like "dominant sex" and "submissive roles." Slightly sick to my stomach, I ended my google search. The rules Brian had mentioned suddenly became a lot more important to learn more about. He'd said he didn't want to overwhelm me, which made me wonder what else he had in mind. Clearly, we needed to have to have a serious talk about what I would and would not do.

I dressed casually in jeans, a sweater, and my Ugg boots and made my way downstairs. "All right, Mama, what can I help with?"

She put me to work setting the table which was something that had been ingrained since I was young. If ever I needed to showcase a talent, setting a proper table would be mine.

---

I ENJOYED the peace and quiet, hanging with my parents until two o'clock when all hell broke loose in the form of three kids and one baby girl. The kids ran around while the baby was thrust on me like I had to hold my niece in order to prove my love for her. Babies made me nervous. I did much better with my older nieces and nephews who weren't so breakable. My sister, Addison, ignored any look of discomfort I exhibited and went about her business.

My little sister looked like my mother with her fair skin and blonde hair, but she had our father's striking blue eyes. She'd been the baby that my parents had always wanted and hadn't been able to conceive during the first eight years of their marriage. I'd long ago accepted after years of therapy that my parents loved me the same as they did their biological daughter.

"So tomorrow night, Sasha, we're heading to Ernie's Oyster Bar, and Eric Peterson said he might stop by. You know he and Tami got divorced a couple of years ago. And Leslie Hanson says he looks handsome, still has his hair and everything, which is saying a lot for a man your age," Addison announced out of the blue.

Ah, it wouldn't be a night at home without my baby sister rubbing in the fact that she was four years younger and also trying to set me up with someone while I was in town. Tonight's lucky winner was my former high school boyfriend. "Yes, having hair is definitely at the top of the list when it comes to qualities in a man."

Her husband, Ryan, chuckled at my sarcasm. He and Addison had met their freshman year of college and had been together ever since. It was the modern day cheerleader-meets-quarterback love story. He managed his father's profitable real estate business, and my sister was a stay-at-home mom with the four children. The thing I liked most about my brother-in-law was that he might love my sister, but he also didn't put up with her crap and would call her out when necessary.

"Eric also manages a car dealership in Raleigh, and he's only got the one son," Addison added.

"And therein lies the trifecta: hair, job, and only one kid. Look, Addison, I'm not interested."

"Excuse me if I only want to see you happy with someone."

Seriously? She thought being with someone automatically meant happiness. I sighed, gladly getting up to help my mom with the dishes and avoid any more talk of being set up.

We finished in the kitchen and set about opening gifts. I knew my parents would be hesitant about the one I'd gotten them, but considering they'd yet to visit me in New York, I was hoping to persuade them to accept it.

"Oh, Sasha, hotel and a show and airline tickets. It's too much," my mom admonished.

I shrugged. "I used points for the hotel and airfare, and I want you to see where I'm living. Pick a weekend, and I'll get the show tickets and tour you around."

My dad looked uncertain, and then Addison jumped in. "The

kids have a lot of sports and activities on the weekends. It's going to be tough for them to get away."

I swallowed hard and took another sip of my wine. "Even more reason to take a few days for themselves for a change, isn't it?" Yes, I was aware that my parents were heavily involved in my sister's life and spent a lot of time babysitting and attending their grandkids' events on a daily basis. But did I need to have kids in order for them to want to be a part of my life?

My mom chose to ignore our passive-aggressive sniping. "Well, we will look at dates and let you know. I've always wanted to see the Big Apple. Your father went years ago for some kind of training for work, but I've never been. And we want to see where you're living."

I smiled, appreciating the fact that they'd make the effort.

My sister's usual gift included this year's family picture of all of them dressed alike and looking perfect.

My five-year-old niece squealed at her princess dress-up set. I got some satisfaction as an aunt who'd selected the best gift when she insisted on putting on the dresses, shoes, and tiaras before continuing on with opening up her other presents.

"Did you not get the wish list of learning toys this year?" Addison inquired.

"I did. I simply chose not to be boring and instead get something I knew she'd want. Who'd like more wine?"

---

By the time I fell into bed, I was halfway buzzed and way too wound up to sleep. Grabbing my phone, I looked at the time. Only ten o'clock.

I texted Brian, suddenly anxious to hear his voice.

*"Hey."*

*"Hey yourself."*

*"Are you free to talk?"*

*"For you, anytime."*

My phone rang two seconds later, and I answered on the first ring. "Hi," I said, a little out of breath.

"Hi, back. How was your Christmas Day?"

I filled him in on the details, and he offered up some of his. Then there was an awkward silence.

"I'd like to know rule number two," I pressed.

"Are we agreed on the first one?"

"I think so, but I have questions."

"Ask me then, honey."

That term of endearment had my heart beating faster. "Are we monogamous?"

He chuckled, and I could hear him shifting the phone. "Very much so. I don't share, and I would hope you wouldn't want to, either."

I definitely wasn't into sharing, especially since the image of Jamie's hand on his thigh remained fresh in my mind. "Brian, we bicker all the time as it is. You're not worried this change in relationship will add more tension?"

"I think it may help with it and that brings us back to rule number one when we do fight."

"How many women have you done this with?"

"That brings us to rule two: you don't ask about my past, and I won't ask about yours."

"Considering my history isn't as colorful, that's hardly fair."

"All right, see this is where the negotiation is important. What if I give you five questions to ask?"

"I want unlimited questions."

"That's hardly a compromise."

"Compromise isn't something I do very well and neither is capping off my curious nature."

"There are some questions I won't answer, Sasha."

"Good, I feel the same." Not that he'd ever ask about my

anxiety, but it was a relief to know that we could both have some things in reserve.

"What do we do then?"

"Maybe we could preface if we're going to ask something sensitive. Almost like testing the waters. We'll say we have a question and allow the other person to decide if the subject is something they'll answer or not."

"So we'd have to agree to have the question asked?"

"Sure. We could even set a threshold. You get however many questions on a topic, and then I do. Whatever works, I guess."

"I'm okay with that, but all responses need to be truthful. I'd rather you not answer than to lie to me, Sasha."

"I would never be anything other than honest."

"Oh, you mean like you were honest about the number of guys who wanted your number for speed dating? What was the deal with that, anyhow?"

Of course he'd picked up on that. "I'd gotten the same number as Catherine, and for the life of me don't know why. I hated every minute of it and couldn't get out of there fast enough."

Brian laughed. "Speed dating not so much?"

"No, not so much."

"Are you comfortable so far with the rules?"

The first two sounded reasonable enough and he'd already compromised. "I think so. Did you have them with Jamie?" I had to ask.

"What happened to prepping me with asking if I'm willing to answer this question?"

"I haven't agreed to anything yet."

"Why is this thing with Jamie bothering you? I came over to your place instead of going home with a sure thing."

The way he phrased that instantly pissed me off. "Right, sorry to have ruined your evening, Brian."

"That's not what I meant. I'm only pointing out that you

shouldn't be jealous because I chose you, even knowing it would be much more complicated."

"Wow, you definitely know how to make a girl feel special. You know what? If you wanted easy, evidently you picked the wrong girl."

"This is coming out all wrong. Shit, I've gotta go. Colby is waiting on me. We're heading out."

"Out where? Everything is closed on Christmas Day."

"Uh, well, not everything."

It dawned on me. They were heading to a strip club. "Of course. Perhaps you'll find something less complicated there."

He muttered a curse. "I'm tempted to say, 'maybe I will' because you're seriously pissing me off to imply that I'd want to."

My stomach knotted with the thought. "Maybe I'm tempted to say that I'm interested when my sister sets me up with my ex-boyfriend tomorrow night."

"Good thing neither of us are *interested* in doing that sort of thing." His annoyance was obvious in his tone.

"Right. Good thing. Night, Brian."

"Night, Sasha."

And now I was back to feeling all out of sorts again, thinking about Brian heading out on the town with Josh's younger brother, who was known for his wild nights.

———

THE NEXT EVENING I decided to go to Ernie's Oyster Bar with my sister because I was bored, and Ernie's did have the best oysters in town. Plus there was the fact that I'd yet to hear from Brian today. My sister tended to get less bitchy when she had a cocktail in her hand and no baby at her boob, but unfortunately I found out shortly after arriving that she didn't mix the two.

"I'm breastfeeding, and although some women think it's

okay to pump and dump, I don't," she proclaimed self-righteously.

"Don't you worry, I'll drink for you," Ryan toasted.

My brother-in-law and I clinked glasses, which pissed her off even further. We continued to trade barbs until Eric came in the door.

Addison had been accurate; he did still have his hair, and he'd aged well. He came over with a smile.

Being accustomed to a man kissing me on the cheek; I was a little taken aback at being hugged like a rag doll.

"Hey, Sasha."

"Hey, Eric," I said, smiling.

He pulled up a seat. "You look great. So I know you're in New York, what do you do there?"

"I'm the vice president of the Gamble Advertising office."

"Wow that sounds important."

Addison interrupted before I could respond. "Sasha only thinks it is. I keep telling her there is more to life than a title and paycheck."

I rolled my eyes. "Don't mind her. She's extra cranky because she can't drink."

"I'm breastfeeding," she stated.

Eric was clearly uncomfortable with the turn of conversation. "Well I'd hoped to stay longer, but my plans changed tonight with my son coming over. So I'm getting dinner to go. He's fourteen and in the car playing his video game."

I was a little stunned to think of someone my age having a fourteen-year-old. But considering that having a kid at age eighteen wasn't unheard of, I shouldn't have been too surprised. "What's his name?"

"Devin."

"I'd love to say hi to him if that's all right."

His face brightened.

Meanwhile, I thought it ironic that I'd be willing to meet someone new in order to escape my sister for a few minutes.

"He's a flirt, and he'd love to say hey to a pretty girl. Come on, I'll introduce you."

After meeting Devin, I complimented Eric on having a teenager with good manners outside of the truck in a whisper so I didn't embarrass the kid. "Devin is very polite and definitely going to be a looker." He had dimples and blue eyes very much like his father.

"The manners I can't take credit for, that would be his mom. But the looks, well, maybe I can take half credit."

I gave him another hug and Devin a little wave. There might not be a spark with Eric, but there was something heartwarming about seeing the first boy I'd ever been with, all grown up into a man and father.

After heading back inside the restaurant, I went straight for the ladies' room. I was almost finished in the stall when the sound of my sister's voice stopped me cold.

"Why do I bother to make the effort? My sister thinks she's better than everyone in this town."

"I don't know why you try, either. And why did she go out there to meet his son as though she likes kids?" Leslie, her best friend, replied.

I held my breath, waiting for Addison to defend me to her friend. Explain to her that I had been here for the birth of every one of her four children. That the kids loved their Aunt Sasha. Point out that I was only being friendly to go out and meet Devin. Polite to meet the son of the man I'd dated sixteen years ago.

"Seriously she's like the worst aunt in the world. I had to practically shove the baby into her hands yesterday and I have to force the older kids to spend time with her. She hates coming home. It's like I'm the failure for finding love and being a stay-at-home mom with four children."

"Some people aren't cut out to be mothers. She can't even hold a man for any length of time. And by the way, I think she's gained some weight since summer. Her ass looks bigger in the pants she's wearing."

It took me a few minutes to realize it was now silent, and they'd walked out. Any scenario I had in my head of slamming the door open and telling them both where to go was now lost. I concentrated on my breathing and forced myself to relax. The thing about having anxiety is that I already had a complex that people were talking about me. To have that fact confirmed wasn't exactly conducive toward believing it was all in my head.

In pulling out my phone, I realized it was still early, only seven o'clock. Since I wasn't sure I could trust my voice, I texted Brian, figuring he would talk me down.

*"Overheard my sister tell her BFF that I'm the worst aunt in the world. In the bathroom stall, ready to embarrass her in front of everyone. Please tell me I'm being irrational and should go straight home!!"*

*"Leave no prisoners, SBF,"* he replied.

I smiled at the Sasha-B-Fierce acronym in spite of how upset I was. I needed a few minutes, and then I'd get it together.

*"Thanks for not talking me down, gotta go."*

*"Call me after."*

After making my way out of the stall, I reapplied my lip gloss, smoothed my hair, and headed back to the table.

"Where were you? Your food is getting cold," Addison commented, already shoveling down some oysters.

I took a moment to deal with her friend Leslie first. Considering the woman had at least thirty pounds on me, it was unbelievable that she would say something about the size of my ass. "Hey, Leslie, Addison didn't tell me. When are you due?"

Addison's eyes got big, and Ryan almost spit out his drink.

"I'm not pregnant," Leslie stuttered, instantly horrified.

"But I thought you were having a baby, or was I wrong?"

She appeared relieved, thinking I had the timing wrong. "That was last year. Chelsea is almost a year old now."

"I guess it's true what they say, then. Some women never lose that baby weight." I got some satisfaction watching her about choke on her food and faced my sister who was glaring at me.

"That was cruel. You have no idea how hard—" Addison started to say.

I cut her off. "You're right. I don't have any idea. After all, I'm clearly not cut out to be a mother. I think I'm better than everyone in this town, and I'm evidently the worst aunt in the world to your kids, too? You have to shove the baby on me." She paled considerably.

Ryan spoke up and looked between the two of us. "What's this about? Addy?"

At least my sister had the decency to look embarrassed.

"You know what? I'm probably going to skip the fried food. Evidently, I've gained a few pounds since summer and my ass looks kind of big in these pants. Right, Leslie? But it's okay; I'll be the cruel one."

She and my sister exchanged looks but neither knew what to do.

I wouldn't give them the opportunity to try to figure it out. "Ryan, it was nice to see you again. You tell my nieces and nephews we'll have to take a rain check on our movie day tomorrow. According to your wife, she has to force them into spending time with me, and I'd hate to do that to them."

My voice almost cracked on the last word, but I kept my composure and left a stunned Ryan, flushed Leslie, and pale Addison with the aftermath of Sasha-B-Fierce.

---

HOME WAS ONLY ten minutes away. My parents were in the living room watching television when I came through the door.

"Oh, you're back early. Everything all right?" my mother asked.

Plastering a smile on my face, I went over to give them both kisses on the cheek. "Yes, everything's fine, but I have to leave tonight. I was hoping to get through the week without a client crisis, but turns out I have to be in Charlotte in the morning. So I'm driving over now."

My mom looked disappointed and then inadvertently made me feel guilty. "I thought you were spending tomorrow with the kids. Kylie will be especially disappointed. She loves spending time with her Aunt Sasha."

"According to Addison, she doesn't. I don't want to get into it. I'm just going to get my stuff. I'll be back down." The very last thing I wanted to do was force my nieces and nephews to spend time with me. I was barely in their lives. To expect them to be excited about a seeing someone they hardly knew was selfish on my part and I didn't blame them for their lack of enthusiasm.

A few minutes later, I was ready to go, suitcase in hand.

"It's awfully late to be driving," my dad commented. The policeman in him was always worried about my safety.

I squeezed his hand. "I'll be in before midnight and send you guys a text when I arrive."

It was tempting to stay the night with them instead, but I knew my sister would be over with the kids in the morning, and I'd be trapped. No way would I make this easy on her.

My mom got up and moved toward the kitchen. "I wish you didn't have to work so much, but we understand. Let me pack up some pie and stuff to take with you."

It was futile to argue and, hell, maybe I would need some pumpkin pie for the road. I hadn't touched my dinner.

# CHAPTER SIX

The city of Charlotte was a five-and-a-half-hour drive west from coastal Carolina. I stopped twenty minutes out of Beaufort to fill up the rental car with gas and called Brian.

"Well, how did it go?" he immediately asked.

I relayed the details, then hopped back into the car and let the phone transfer to the Bluetooth while I continued driving.

"Wow, you didn't take any prisoners, did you? Your brother-in-law said nothing?"

"Oh, I don't doubt he had plenty to say later. I think he was stunned for the moment. Anyhow, I'm done and heading west as we speak."

"What do you mean heading west?"

"I'm driving to Charlotte, coming in a night early. I know if I'd stayed in town, Addison would have brought the kids over first thing in the morning, forcing them to spend time with me and trapping us all into an afternoon none of us would end up enjoying."

"Wait, you're heading to Charlotte now?"

I loved the way that I'd taken him completely off guard. "Yes, driving as we speak."

"Shit, I'm still in Virginia. Why didn't you tell me earlier?"

"I'd hardly expect you to drop everything. It'll be past midnight by the time I get there, and I'll get a hotel room. I might even go into the office to work tomorrow." I was full of adrenaline and wasn't sure what I wanted to do at the moment.

"Can I call you right back?"

"Sure."

It was ten minutes later when he did so.

"I'm sending you my address, so you can input it into your GPS when you're closer to Charlotte. My place is twenty minutes north of the city," he said.

"You're with your family for the holidays, Brian, and even if you weren't, I don't know that it's the best thing if I stayed at your place."

"I'm about to leave for Dulles airport. I should arrive before you do if I can catch this nine-thirty flight."

"You're joking." I had hardly expected him to drop everything.

"I'm not."

"It'll be late by the time I get there."

"I don't care if it's three o'clock in the morning. I want to see you."

Brian wanting to see me made me warm and tingly. "I should still be annoyed with you for calling me complicated last night."

"I should be ticked that you implied I should find someone else at the strip club and made that crack about your ex-boyfriend."

"But you're not?" I tested, smiling.

"The ex-boyfriend bit made me crazy jealous if I'm being honest."

"The Jamie comment set me off. No woman needs to hear that you have a sure thing any time you'd want it."

"I know and I'm sorry it came out that way. This is probably a good time to bring up rule number three, I think."

"Which is?"

"No dating or going out with anyone else."

"I thought we went over that, we would be monogamous. I get it." Considering I wasn't exactly doing a whole lot aside from working, it wasn't an issue for me. Besides this ensured he wouldn't be seeing Jamie, which was a relief.

"No, this is different. Our arrangement won't be known by a lot of people; however, we aren't dating others or taking anyone else to events in the meantime, either. Not even as a cover."

"Wait, but what if Catherine asks me to go speed dating with her or double?" Not that I sought to do either, but I also didn't want to abandon her if she needed me.

"That's exactly what I'm talking about. No."

I didn't mind not dating other people, considering I hadn't done it in quite some time; however I couldn't make my friend feel like she was now on her own. "I can't hurt Catherine's feelings, and more importantly, I don't want her going out alone with some stranger. Plus what would I tell her?"

"Tell her you have other plans, then come home and fuck me."

I sucked in my breath with that vision now firmly implanted in my mind. "I can agree in general, but not with Catherine. I need to be available to go out with her. I'm her wingman, or whatever you guys call it. She'd be hurt if I wasn't."

"Okay. I get it. Can we agree to discuss it ahead of time? Maybe I could meet you ladies out like the last time and assist with the mission."

I laughed thinking he'd probably make a much better wingman than I would. "All right, agreed. I'm assuming this doesn't apply to clients?"

"I would think it should. If there's a male coworker or client who wants to get into your pants, what's the difference from a date?"

"But it's not a problem if they're old or ugly?"

"If you send me a picture and I agree, then perhaps."

Imagining that scenario amused me. "Oh, yeah, I can see that. Uh, hold still. I need to take a picture of you and vet it according to rule number three with this guy I'm not yet sleeping with. Oh, good news. You're ugly enough that you pass. Congratulations, let's get dinner."

He laughed. "I'm sure we will have rectified the sleeping together situation by the time you're taking clients out."

"All kidding aside, I can't say no to clients for a drink or dinner. I'm sorry but it's not reasonable and it crosses the line from personal into professional."

He sighed heavily. "No, I guess you're right." He didn't sound happy about it, but at least he understood.

I decided now might be a good time to address some concerns. "So, I was on the Internet yesterday, and I have a few things to discuss about my limitations."

"Jesus, Sasha, you don't go and google shit like that. It's like typing in symptoms of a cold and the Internet tells you forty ways you could die. I haven't finished going over everything yet."

"I was curious, and wanted some ideas of what limitations I might need."

"Okay, hold on, I'm getting into the cab." The phone muffled, and he said something in the background.

"All right, I'm back. Let's hear them," he said, resigned.

"Okay, I don't want any sort of muzzle or gag in my mouth."

"That's definitely okay," he agreed quickly.

"No whips, canes, pain, or threesomes," I added, thinking of a list of things that came to mind.

"That isn't even remotely close to what I want."

"Okay. I'm assuming I don't need to tell you no animals."

"Christ, woman, you are starting to tick me off."

"Hmm, I believe that evokes rule number one."

"Now you're just fucking with me."

"Maybe a little. What if I want to negotiate some dominant time with you?"

"No."

"No?"

"No."

"Why not?"

"Because that is non-negotiable."

"Are you going to tell me why?"

"Not in the fucking cab I'm not."

His temper had me both smiling and turned on at the same time. "Did you want me to get a hotel room tonight, after all?"

"Of course not." His voice had immediately lost all irritation. "All right. Send me your address and have a safe flight."

"I will, and you drive carefully. I'll call you when I land, see how far out you are, okay?"

I agreed and concentrated on the long drive ahead of me.

---

IT WAS WELL past midnight by the time I arrived at Brian's house. After parking in his driveway, I sent a text to my parents letting them know I arrived safely, got out of the car and looked up, appreciating the enormous three-story town-house. Boy, did I miss the space I used to have in North Carolina.

"You having some size envy?" Brian quipped, standing outside the front door. He was wearing a pair of low slung plaid pajama bottoms and a Panthers T-shirt with leather slippers. He looked sexy as hell without even trying.

"I am. I've had hotel rooms bigger than my condo in New York."

"Here, I'll get your stuff. Come on in."

He grabbed my suitcase and led me inside. We entered a living area which was modern and spacious, running lengthwise back to a large gourmet kitchen. "You hungry?" he asked, ever the gracious host.

"Ah, no. My mom packed leftovers. Matter of fact, I have extra if you want some."

He patted his stomach and shook his head. "I'll pass for now. There are the stairs to the bedrooms. I'll give you an abbreviated tour tonight."

I followed him up to an impressive master suite. The center-piece was the king-sized bed against the wall, which had a massive wooden and steel bedframe. Everything else was also tasteful in rich woods, sort of like Pottery Barn meets Restoration Hardware.

"Master bathroom is that door over there. Laundry is in that large closet in the hall, guest room down the hall with another bathroom. In the basement is the theater room and my office. I tend to hang out down there mostly."

I nodded and realized we were both kind of awkward. "I can take the guest room."

"Actually my sister is already asleep in there. She found out I was on the way to the airport and decided to fly out with me. She wanted to be on our plane for the wedding. There's a pull-out sofa downstairs I'll sleep on since I'm going to watch TV for a while yet anyhow. I'd like it if you took my bed. If for no other reason, I can brag that you've been in it."

I smiled, and then his words hit me. "Wait, your sister is here?" I wanted to smack the amused grin off his face.

"Are you disappointed we won't be alone?"

I let out a breath as I realized that all along he'd known there wouldn't be a possibility of us sleeping together tonight. "You could've told me that in the car."

"I didn't know until I got to the airport and she decided to meet me there. And I wasn't going to risk you changing your mind."

"How was the strip club with Colby?" I decided to change the subject.

He held a finger to his lips and closed the door.

I held my breath when he came back and took my face between his hands.

His lips were at my ear, teasing me with their proximity. "It wasn't nearly as good as having you standing here in my bedroom." His hands roamed over my back, massaging gently.

"Mm, good answer," I murmured, leaning into him.

"How are you doing?"

"Fine." I practically moaned when his fingers kneaded my lower back.

He leaned back and his knowing smile made me catch my breath. "We'll have to work on the use of that word. I meant about your sister and what she said. Did she call you?"

Right, that's what he meant. "She did call. I didn't answer, and she didn't leave a voicemail."

"Are you okay?" His eyes searched mine, concern reflected in them.

Brian was aware that I didn't have the closest of relationships with my sister and that at one point I'd questioned whether it had to do with my being adopted. "I'll get over it." I shrugged to emphasize it wasn't a big deal.

He held my eyes with an uncanny ability to read me. "If you need to talk about it, you know that I'm a good listener."

I swallowed hard. "Thanks."

He pulled away and moved toward the door. "I'll be up a while. Help yourself to anything, take a bath if you want, get some sleep. I'll see you in the morning."

I nodded and stood there alone in the room for a moment before making my way into his bathroom.

It was a dream, with dual sinks, soaking tub and a large glass shower that included jets on the sides. I wasn't planning to wash my hair, but I couldn't pass up all of those streams of water.

After finishing with my amazing shower, I took my time getting ready for bed. I was too wired up to sleep, and the urge to touch myself was tempting. I should've felt relieved his sister was in the house to keep me from rushing into things, but instead I was disappointed. After throwing on my pajamas, I walked downstairs, wanting to discuss more about the rules. I was in the middle of the theater room in the darkness. When I listened there was no sound.

"Sasha."

"God, you scared me." I put my hand to my chest.

He flipped on the light and tossed me that boyish grin of his, and then his eyes ran down the length of me in my shorts and tank top PJ set. "Did you need something?"

"I wanted to talk more about the rules." I folded my arms over my breasts lest he see that my nipples were hard merely thinking about the subject.

He looked hesitant. "Hold on, let me shut the basement door."

I took a seat in the corner of a sectional sofa with my feet tucked up underneath of me. I liked the setup with the plushness of the sofa and the large screen television against the wall.

"What's on your mind?" he asked, sitting close and turning toward me.

"Explain what this would be. It wouldn't be a relationship, right? I mean you don't do relationships, and I certainly don't."

"I don't do girlfriends. It would be a sex between friends I guess."

"What about the whole boss thing?"

"I could have Mark draw up a nondisclosure agreement if that would make you feel more comfortable about keeping professional and personal totally separate. But I'd like to think that with our friendship we wouldn't need one. Unless you're afraid you can't keep them independent."

"Don't patronize me." I was instantly annoyed.

"My apologies. I didn't mean to." The amusement was back on his face.

"See, that right there. You're polite and charming, and everyone who meets you loves you. You're the perfect gentleman. That's why this other side of you is throwing me."

As if to prove a point, he leaned into me and cupped my chin, meeting my lips. They were soft; however his kiss was anything but. His hands moved to the back of my neck, holding me in place while he ravaged my mouth and inflamed my senses. His demanding tongue met mine, and I moved closer toward him. He slid his hands under my backside, moving me so that I straddled his lap.

In an effort to relieve the pulsing ache between my thighs, I ground my center against his hard length, whimpering at the friction.

"Fuck." He pulled his mouth away, looking as turned on as I was.

My hips rolled shamelessly into him, and I was rewarded with his groan.

His hands gripped my hips, pushing them back and pinning them in place. "Enough," he croaked out. His face looked pained, but I could tell by the look in his eyes he was serious.

I started to move off of his lap only to have him hold me in place.

"No, you don't. Don't get pissed off because I'm saying no."

It irritated the hell out of me that he knew what I was thinking before I did. "I'm not. You don't want to, and I get it—"

A second scorching kiss was the way he shut me up. His hands gripped my ass and rocked me into his erection, back and forth. "Does it feel like I don't want to?" he asked, tearing his lips away.

"But you need rules?" I clarified, breathing heavy.

He nodded and gently lifted me off of him and back into the

corner, swinging my legs over his lap so that I couldn't get up. "We both do, and even then, it won't be tonight."

My body rebelled at the thought, and I tried not to be petty. "I need to ask you something."

He exhaled, most likely knowing the direction this was heading. "Ask me, then."

"Did Jamie have these rules?"

His face told me the answer before his mouth did.

Unbelievable. I tried to get up, but he wouldn't let go of my legs.

"Sasha, wait—" He pulled me back down and leaned over me. "Look, I've known Jamie since college. I didn't have any rules with her because she wasn't someone I wanted to be monogamous with or who merited taking the time and effort to ensure we had everything agreed upon first. Also Jamie and I know a lot of the same people from school, and although it may not seem like it, I'd like to keep my personal shit, from being reunion gossip. Up until five months ago, she had a serious boyfriend. Before that, it had been six years since we, ah, were together. And although she may have implied I see her every trip to New York, the truth is that I didn't tell her every time I was in town."

"Why didn't you?"

"Because I didn't want anything serious with her. I could tell she had started to want more and was jealous of you."

I swallowed at his admission. "That's why she showed up at the bar?"

He nodded. "I think she believed she'd mark her territory, but instead, you know the outcome."

No, I didn't, and it was on the tip of my tongue to ask what was actually said to her to end things. But considering this was my first real affliction with possessiveness, and he'd made it clear we were monogamous; I decided not to push it. "Thanks for telling me that."

He regarded me for the longest time. "Come here, give me those lips."

Aroused by the command, I did a very un-Sasha like thing and leaned over without protest. I could tell from the flash of pleasure in his eyes that I'd pleased him by doing so.

He kissed me one last time and then sighed regrettably. "We'll talk more tomorrow. Did you want to go into the office or stay here?"

"Office." It was the one place where I was in control and could compartmentalize the holidays, my sister, and Brian into a nice neat box while I got some work done.

---

THE NEXT MORNING I showered and dressed quickly for work. The nice part about the Charlotte office was that I could dress more casually than I did in New York. There was also the fact that it was Christmas week, which meant hardly anyone would be in. The owner, Josh, had given the week off to all employees. He was a lot more generous with time off since he'd met his wife-to-be, that's for sure.

When I entered the kitchen, I spotted Brian's younger sister sitting at the small table eating cereal.

"Hey, McKenzie," I greeted, not knowing if she would remember me. It had probably been five years or more since I'd last seen her.

She looked shocked and then grinned. "Hey, Sasha. I didn't know you were here."

Getting up, she gave me a hug which I hadn't expected. Luckily, she didn't notice my awkwardness, but instead looked excited to have me here. She was tall like her brother and had turned into a natural beauty.

"I got in late last night. I was telling your brother only a few days ago that the last time I saw you, there were braces on your teeth. Now you're all grown up and beautiful." I meant the compliment sincerely.

She blushed prettily and resumed her seat. "I don't know about beautiful, but I am almost twenty-two."

Her self-deprecation reminded me of myself in my early twenties: in college, away from home, and feeling weird in my own skin.

"I didn't know you and my brother had gotten together. I think it's great, though. I always wondered if you would."

Oh, shit. I realized she was under the wrong impression. Or maybe the correct one, but considering nothing had happened yet, I amended her assumption. "Uh, we're only friends. I drove in last minute, and Brian slept downstairs."

As if on cue, he opened the basement door on the far side of the kitchen. He was adorable, all rumpled from sleep.

"Hey, Kenzie. Hey, Sasha. Help yourself to coffee. I'm going to grab a shower, and then we can go into work."

Kenzie's face fell with Brian's words.

Oh hell. I hadn't meant to leave his sister alone today by insisting on going into the office. "Brian, you don't need to come in with me. I'm probably only doing a half day, and you should hang out with Kenzie."

He looked between the two of us and stretched his arms up, affording me a glimpse of his abs. "How about we go in for a few hours, and then Kenzie can meet us for lunch? You wanted to go to the mall for a dress or something, right Kenzie?"

My eyes inadvertently remained glued to his stomach. By the time they journeyed back up to his face, he was smirking at me.

"Yeah, I'd like to get a dress for the wedding and maybe some shoes. I don't suppose I could convince you to come with me, Sasha, maybe after lunch?"

"Uh, sure." I didn't know how I could say no.

"Kenzie, she may not want to—"

I gave Brian a pointed look. "No, I do, really. I love fashion,

74

and I'd be happy to go with you." I might not know Kenzie very well, but I did love shopping. And it would be an opportunity to get to know her better.

She smiled. "Cool. Does that mean I get to drive your car today, big brother?"

He walked by and mussed her hair on his way to the stairs. "Sure. No problem."

I was thankful for the Keurig machine and made myself a cup of coffee. Meanwhile, I thought about how many guys would've freaked at the thought of their baby sister driving their brand new Lexus. But he hadn't batted an eye. He was laid-back that way. So how could he be dominant in the bedroom? Maybe he only thought he was. It could be that nice, easy-going Brian merely didn't say please or thank you during sex.

Kenzie's voice brought me out of my thoughts. "I suck at clothes big time. I brought a dress that I wore in high school, but it's kind of juvenile. I'd like something, I don't know, a little more grown-up."

I was still thinking about Brian's defined stomach. "Of course. It'll be fun."

# CHAPTER SEVEN

*A*fter spending the first couple hours in the office wading through emails and catching up on some correspondence, I felt back to normal. Work is where I found my equilibrium and sense of purpose. It's where I was in control and could feel confident, but by mid-morning I'd run out of things to do. Most of my clients were on vacation, and I was supposed to have spent the day in a Disney marathon with my nieces and nephews. I wondered if Brian was busy. Aside from a couple other people, we were the only ones in the office today.

I headed toward his side of the building where I heard the unmistakable voice of Juliette and the sounds of a toddler before I saw them outside of Brian's office. Smiling, I walked toward them. She'd had this week off, and I'd been afraid I would miss seeing her.

Juliette Walker had started in the Charlotte office over eight years ago as the receptionist, then began working for Brian directly. She was now officially the office manager, but she continued to perform multiple tasks specifically for Brian on a daily basis. She was the glue that held the corporate office together and had endless energy as well as sass. She was the type of person who talked enough for the both of us. In time, she'd eased me into a friendship whether I'd wanted it or not. You pretty much didn't have a choice but to like her. She'd wear you down otherwise.

I missed hearing her chat about everything from office gossip to what she'd seen on television on a daily basis.

"Hey, Sasha," she greeted, spotting me coming toward her and giving me a big hug.

"Hi. I thought you were off this week?"

Brian stood to the side, holding Tristan, her eighteen-month-old son, on his hip. The adorable little boy looked completely at home in his arms.

"I am," Juliette answered. "But Brian said you were in today, and I haven't seen you in months. Wow, you look skinnier. Turn around."

Ironic, considering my sister's friend had said the opposite about my weight. I turned, bracing myself for what she'd say next.

"Your ass looks fantastic in those black pants. Yep, you lost weight. Must be that New York living. No down-home cooking or real food."

Leave it to Juliette to both flatter and embarrass me with a compliment.

"Don't you think, Brian?" she teased, turning toward him. Only she could manage to make him uncomfortable and seemed to enjoy doing it as often as possible.

He blushed and then shook his head. "I'm not looking at any female's butt in this office, let alone that of Sasha-B-Fierce."

Juliette's eyes got large, and she quickly glanced at me to gauge my reaction. Ah, obviously she had known about the nickname, too. I shouldn't have been surprised; the woman knew most everything about everyone in this office.

I shrugged it off. "Good thing for both of you that I consider it a compliment."

Juliette grinned. "I missed you. Can you believe how big Tristan is now?"

I looked at the chubby little boy, and he reached toward me.

"Hi," he said, waving.

"Hi, handsome." I was unprepared for Brian to hand him over, but luckily Tristan was quite sturdy and completely enamored with my beaded necklace.

"Aw, Sasha, see, you're terrific with kids. And your sister, I hope you make her sweat it for being such a—" She covered Tristan's ears. "—bitch toward you." She uncovered his ears again and kissed his face.

My gaze slid toward Brian, and he winced.

Juliette jumped in before he could explain. "Don't be mad at him. I asked why you came up early. It was either he tell me the truth about your sister pissing you off with her awful comments, or I'd assume that you two were finally acting on your years of pent-up sexual frustration." She'd wiggled her brows to drive home her thoughts on the matter.

Terrific. Now both Brian and I were blushing.

"On that awkward note, thank you very much, Juliette. I'll leave you two ladies," he muttered, walking back into his office.

Her smirk let me know she'd achieved exactly what she'd wanted. "I was kind of hoping the separation might make you guys, I don't know; want to give it a try." She'd been convinced that we should be together since the very first year I'd started.

After accompanying me back to my temporary office, she placed Tristan on the floor with a cup of Cheerios. "That buys us fifteen minutes," she laughed.

"You know Brian and I are better off as friends," I said, revisiting her earlier comment. I did my best to sound convincing. All of a sudden, I was feeling unease about people finding out about us. "But it's kind of funny to watch him blush. Only you can manage that."

She tightened her blonde ponytail and grinned. "It's a gift.

And you know I'd never say something like that in front of anyone else, don't you?"

Juliette might be over the top sometimes, but for the most part, she did know the time and place for blurting out inappropriate comments. "I know. It's why I can laugh at your jokes instead of wanting to kill you for them."

"Ha. If looks could have killed me that first year, yours would have. But I knew I'd convince you eventually that we'd be great friends."

Our personalities could not have been any further apart on the spectrum, but that hadn't turned out to be a bad thing. "You definitely brought me out of my shell." I thought about how much more reserved I'd been only a few years ago. "How's Rob?" I inquired, wondering how things were with her husband.

Instantly, her eyes clouded. Juliette and Rob had been high school sweethearts. He was a police officer in a nearby suburb. She'd appeared happily in love until two years ago when he'd injured his back. Since then, he'd been moody and withdrawn according to her. Having a baby wasn't improving things.

"You know, all I'm going to say is that it's been tough. I want to work through things for Tristan's sake, though, so I'm doing everything I can."

I noted that she said 'everything she could' and bit down on wanting to give her my two cents. I'd never been in love, never been married, and I obviously wasn't a mother. I had no business giving unsolicited advice in those areas. "Please know that I'm here for you, okay?"

She looked relieved and let out a breath. "I was sure you'd have something more to say."

"Your friendship means a lot to me, and I only want to see you happy. Everyone has their own way of trying to do that in their lives." Maybe I was evolving and learning when it was appropriate to keep my judgement to myself. I'd come a long way in the last few years and now had some amazing women I could call friends. Considering my glass house, I was in no position to cast stones.

She let out a deep breath. "Thank you and I hope you know you and Brian are my best friends. Now if only my two besties could end up together, it would be a perfect world."

I rolled my eyes, feeling some guilt that her two best friends were definitely not telling her everything.

---

"Do you want the good or the bad news first?" Brian asked, filling the doorframe of my office. His body looked casual, but his eyes were intense.

My stomach fluttered with his presence. "Bad news."

He grinned and shut the door. "Eighty percent of people say good news first." He took a seat and regarded me.

"I'm a glass-half-empty kind of girl. So lay it on me."

"The bad news is that the new pitch I'm about to tell you about has an account representative known for being a tough sell. She's demanding and, according to Josh, will be difficult to deal with."

I blew out a breath. Difficult clients weren't anything new, but considering I was the point person in dealing with them now, they presented their own unique challenges. "Okay, what's the good news?"

"The good news is that we have four weeks to prepare for the pitch, and it's worth six million in phases. The client is Tryon pharmaceuticals. They have a number of drugs on the market but mostly specialize in diabetes."

"All right. I'm eager to get started." And, boy was I. The pitch was my sweet spot.

He shook his head. "We're traveling tomorrow. I'll give you the file to allow you to start brainstorming, but you aren't going to bother your staff over the holidays."

My temper flared. "Could you give me some credit?"

He looked at me like he often did when I was irritated. With patience and as if he had something to say. We both knew this interaction was a test of sorts. What was the professional land-scape going to be like now that we were thinking about moving into a sexual arrangement? "Of course I'll give you credit. However, we don't start working on it until the day we return. We have plenty of time."

I took stock of his answer and realized it was exactly what he would have said a week ago. For some reason, this was a tremen-dous relief to me. "Okay. Deal," I agreed.

He also looked relieved. Obviously, this was new territory for both of us. "What's the plan with my sister for this afternoon? You know you don't have to go shopping with her if you don't want to."

"No, it's okay. McKenzie is sweet."

He laughed. "Yeah, she is, until she gets fired up, and curses like a sailor. But considering she was around teenage boys from a young age, what can you expect?"

I could hear the affection in his voice and smiled at the image.

"Before I forget, here's my credit card," he said, digging into his wallet.

My brow arched as he handed it over. "This is on you?"

"Nice clothes, not New York-designer-nice. Reasonable, please."

I took the card, amused. "You're very generous with her."

"I don't get to chance to spoil her now that she's on the West Coast. How was your visit with Juliette by the way?"

"Good." I wasn't sure how to vocalize a worry about her figuring out we were starting a relationship without sounding like I was backpedaling.

He sat back in his chair, regarding me. "You do realize that her comments about us are nothing new. She's been doing it for years."

I bit my lip. "Right, but now that we're entertaining the idea —aren't you worried at all about what others will think?" A few years after I'd started working in Charlotte, Juliette had told me about a bet that some of the assholes in the office had made to see who I'd sleep with first. That information had served as a reminder that sometimes it didn't matter how well you did your job. There would always be people who would seek to bring you down.

He met my eyes and spoke calmly. "We don't work in the same office any longer. Juliette won't know anything. Neither will anyone else unless we choose to tell them."

I swallowed hard.

"And nothing has happened yet, so if you're having second thoughts, then we can go slower or not at all. The last thing you need is more pressure from me, either," he offered.

The thought of moving any slower or not at all left me unsettled. "Is Juliette as unhappy as I think she is?" I questioned, concerned for our mutual friend and desperately needing a change in subject.

Luckily, he shrugged, taking it in stride. "You know her. One minute she looks sad and the next she pulls it together and is her bubbly self again. I think she wants to make her marriage work."

"Well that makes one of them," I retorted.

"I don't disagree. Did you tell her that?"

"What do you think?" I was mildly offended.

"I think that sometimes your well-intended advice may be a little harsher than you realize."

I tried not to let his words sting. "Duly noted."

"I'll call McKenzie. You all right with heading out in an hour?"

"Sure. Send me that file on the pharmaceutical company, and

I should be." I was anxious to get some information about this potentially lucrative client.

He hesitated, knowing that once I got the file I'd want more time. "Okay, I'll tell her ninety minutes," he resigned, and left me to my work.

---

THE LATE LUNCH with Brian and McKenzie had been fun. They had an easy affection between them and made sure I was part of the conversation whether I wanted to be or not. Sometimes the people who put me most at ease were the ones not waiting on my cues but who instead charged forward with exuberance. McKenzie reminded me of Juliette in that way. Spending time with her was easy and found myself getting comfortable with her a lot more quickly than I normally would with someone new.

It was in the first dressing room, however, that McKenzie dropped a bombshell on me.

"I'm sorry, what did you say?" I inquired, thinking I must have misunderstood her.

"I asked if you could teach me how to seduce a man," she repeated.

Uh oh, it was what I'd thought. I hesitated, handing her the next dress to try on. After taking a seat on the stool in the corner of the large dressing room, I finally found my voice again. "I need a little background information first, McKenzie." Watching her sigh, I shook my head at the first dress she'd tried on. "Not that one. Try the pink and white one."

"I have a crush on someone and I'm tired of only being friends."

"Someone at school?" Before I gave advice, I needed to find out who she was trying to seduce. The last thing I needed was for Brian to discover I'd given his baby sister advice on how to blow her professor.

"No, someone from home. I've known him a long time, but he still sees me as a kid."

I arched a brow and looked at the flattering dress she was modelling. "Turn around let me see."

She was such a naturally pretty girl with her long, sandy blonde hair and puppy-dog eyes like her brother's. She wore no makeup, and yet her face was flawless. She only needed to learn to flatter her lean body better.

"I like this dress on you."

Kenzie looked in the mirror and frowned. "I want something a little more sexy."

Shaking my head, I reminded her, "You're attending a wedding shower on a boat filled with women. Who exactly do you want to be sexy for?"

She grinned sheepishly. "Good point. But I want the dress for the wedding to be a little more—you know."

Yeah, I did know. She was a young woman trying to pull it together and look like a grown up. I'd been there. "How much older is this guy you have a crush on?"

It wasn't a good sign when she paused. "Eight years, technically, but—"

"Eight years, Kenzie? Please tell me he isn't one of your teachers or someone you work for?"

"No. Our families have known each other for a long time, and eight years isn't all that much. Look at Josh and Haylee. She's only a year older than I am, and their gap is larger."

She had a point. "True, however that's not the norm."

"I know. But you should have seen them at the Christmas Eve party together. You could feel the love between them, you know. And with the exception of my awful sister-in-law, Rebecca, there wasn't one person there who thought about their age difference."

I wouldn't disagree. Haylee and Josh complemented one another fully. "Wait, back up. What did your sister-in-law say?"

She proceeded to try on a lavender dress which suited her coloring very nicely. "She's a bitch and trash talks her behind her back, saying Haylee is a gold digger and that she trapped Josh."

"I see. Is she coming to the wedding?"

"Unfortunately she is. Anyhow, she's jealous because she's miserable with my oldest brother. What do you think of this one?" She looked at herself in the mirror.

I walked over behind her and held up the back of her hair. We both looked in the mirror at the image. "Perfect for a beach wedding. It's subtle sexy, which is what you want."

"Will you give me some advice on what to do to get his attention, pretty please?"

Now I knew why Brian was hard pressed ever to say no to his sister. I might not be able to ever offer relationship advice, but over the years I had inadvertently mastered the technique of getting a man's attention.

"All right. Come on, then. We have some more shopping to do."

She hugged me exuberantly, practically squealing in delight.

———

AN HOUR LATER, McKenzie had new underwear, bras, and a couple cute outfits that she could wear both to school or out in the evening. And the most important thing: shoes. I talked her into two pair and told her to practice walking in them that night.

"Thank you for doing this. I know I kind of put you on the spot to take me shopping today," she said when we got to Sephora in search of makeup.

"I love shopping, and I'm having a good time, Kenzie." I was enjoying myself. It was like having a younger sister. One who wanted to spend time with me. A pang of regret hit me over the current tension with Addison. I checked my phone, but she'd stopped calling after several unanswered attempts.

"When do I get the actual seduction advice? I mean, all of these clothes are great, but if I flounder like an idiot, none of it is going to matter."

I swiped my card, opting to pay for her makeup myself as a gift instead of having Brian pick up that, too. Considering he'd already been generous with the clothes and shoes, I didn't want to push it. "I'll tell you on the car ride home."

She nodded, eager to leave with her bags in hand. "Thank you for the makeup. It was very generous. But, um, you'll teach me how to put this crap on my face, right?" She eyed the cosmetics dubiously.

"Yes, of course. And you're welcome." I smiled.

We got into the car, and I turned toward the younger woman. "Okay, you ready for the one thing you need to know about seduction?"

She nodded, enthusiastic to hear whatever I was about to say.

"It's simple. You need to stop trying." I'd learned this unintentionally due to my social anxiety. Ironically, my inability to be charming came across as playing hard to get. This made most men more interested than ever.

She frowned. "What?"

"You have to stop trying. Tell me the truth. Does he know he's your crush?"

"Probably. He used to tease me about it when I was younger. I'm sure he still knows I've got feelings." She sighed, obviously not liking that fact.

"That's the first obstacle. You've got him up on this pedestal, Kenzie, and I have news for you. If you keep him up there as your crush, he's not incentivized to get down and be part of the real world. Relationships aren't easy." From what little I knew about them. "What could be better for a man's ego than to have a woman adore him and not have to deal with any obligation?" I started the car and we exited the mall.

She thought about it for a while. "I get your point. Maybe I should sleep with someone else and try to make him jealous?"

Ugh. This was dangerous ground, I realized as I drove onto the highway toward Brian's house. "Absolutely not. First of all, it won't make you feel better, and secondly, it won't get the reaction you're looking for. However, you should go out on dates and with your friends. Let him see you looking great, feeling good, and not putting him as the center of your attention. Even if you have to go to Starbucks at nine o'clock on a Friday night to sit by yourself, make him think you're out. And let him know it's none of his business with whom." No one knew that I came home from the gym on Fridays and completely crashed on my couch while eating something indulgent. It was all about the image, and who was better at hiding behind it than I was?

"Okay. I can do that. What else? Part of me wants to try kissing him and see if there's a spark."

I smiled. "Then you need to figure out a plan to make that happen. However, you most likely will only get one shot, Kenzie. Don't take it on a whim because you've had too much to drink or because you're anxious. Once you put it out there, it's staying out there. If you make your move too soon, then it could be years before the timing may be right again, if at all." I knew that lesson all too well.

"It's kind of hard to be patient, but I get your point. What happens once I do go for it?"

I shrugged. "He either reacts with; 'whoa, that's not how I feel' or there's something there."

"But what if he rejects me?"

This was the tough part. The probability of getting hurt was high if he hadn't indicated to her over the years that he might feel more. "Then you put on your big girl panties and take it on the chin. But at least then you'll know for sure, and you can move on. I assume no guy in the meantime can hold a candle to your crush?"

She nodded. "I'm going to get hurt; I can feel it."

"If you tell your brother what I'm about to say, I'll kill you." If I was dishing out advice, I might as well go all the way.

She glanced over, curious, as we pulled into Brian's driveway. "I won't say a word. I promise."

"Okay. You get a big glass of wine, buy yourself a good vibrator, and you say to hell with him. If he can't realize that you're a catch, McKenzie, then it's his loss. You are too pretty, too smart, and way too special for you to allow any man to make you feel like shit." And there were the words of wisdom from my father when he'd spoken with his teenage girl back in the day. Minus the addition of the vibrator and wine, of course.

She grinned. "I knew you and I would be fast friends."

---

LATER THAT NIGHT, Brian and I flirted while watching television downstairs, but because his sister had hung out with us, the opportunity for anything else wasn't plausible. Our flight was early tomorrow, so we all turned in.

Now I lay in his bed, sexually frustrated. I needed to know what else I was getting into in order to make a decision. Reaching for my phone, I texted him.

*"I need to know the rest of the rules. All of them."*

I was surprised when my phone rang in response. "Are you seriously calling me from the basement?"

"You texted me from upstairs, and yes, it's easier to talk then to type. Plus I don't trust myself not to touch you if we have this conversation in person."

"I'm trying hard not to take offense at that statement." Part of me wanted to go down there naked and see what he'd do.

"It's the hardest thing I've ever done. But I'm in this for long-term gain, not short-term satisfaction."

"Your bed is sure comfortable," I teased, enjoying the sound of his groan.

"You're killing me, Sasha."

"You're the one with the rules. Are we doing this? Taking it to this next level?" It was surreal that I was entertaining the idea. Something about falling into bed with him after a few drinks sounded reasonable, but embarking on an arrangement in which there were rules felt a lot more official.

"You tell me? I know that Juliette kind of freaked you out today." His voice had a soft, sexy tone.

"Yeah, a little. I'm better now, but I'm still on the fence about the rest of the rules." I wished I could turn off the lingering doubts.

"And what would sway you to jump on over?"

"I need to know all of it."

"Okay, yes, the rules. Are we agreed on the first few?"

"Yes, I think so." Fuck before fighting, ask policy, and no dating other people. Sure, I could do that.

"Rule four is that we don't spend more than two weeks without having a night together."

"That's going to be tough considering our work schedules, clients, and your travel."

"I come to New York at least once per month. We both have airline mileage we can use every other weekend. And maybe we could take a vacation somewhere together in a few months."

The thought of a trip sounded wonderful, especially one that was with someone. "All right, every two weeks. We can both make the effort."

"I have a few more things we should go over, but in the meantime why don't you tell me yours?"

"I don't know my rules yet."

"Okay, how about you think about them?" His voice went an octave lower, making my heart beat faster. "I'll let you get some sleep. Sweet dreams."

"Goodnight, Brian." I lay there for a few seconds and then realized he still hadn't told me all of them. I cursed into my pillow. He was drawing this out way too long. I decided not to play fair and texted him.

*"Your bed smells like you which is NOT very conducive for sleep."*

*"Part of my seduction technique."*

*"It's working. Matter of fact I'm touching myself right now."*

I was pleased with my out of character bluntness and then jumped when my phone rang. When I answered it, he didn't give me the chance to speak.

"Another rule is no masturbating unless I'm involved," he ground out.

"Call me crazy, but isn't the whole point of *self*-pleasure to *not* have someone else a part of it?"

"Yes, but I want to participate in all of your pleasure, which includes that. We can do it over the phone, instant messaging, maybe FaceTime, or my favorite, in person while I watch."

All of a sudden I was hot and bothered. I wondered if perhaps I could get off with only my hand while he talked to me. "So why don't you come up here and watch, then?" I challenged, hardly believing I had done so. He was making me more adventurous for sure.

His breath hissed out. "You'd better not be touching yourself."

It wasn't in my nature to back down from a challenge. "What will you do if I am? I haven't agreed to anything yet, and considering I haven't had sex in over a year, I think I'm beyond being patient."

He inhaled audibly, and I realized what I'd revealed.

"Get down here and close the door when you do."

I heard a click. He'd issued an order and hung up the phone.

For the first time in my life, I didn't hesitate in obeying.

AFTER SHUTTING THE BASEMENT DOOR, I padded down the flight of steps fighting my nerves.

Once there, Brian stalked toward me, his eyes smoldering.

Anything I'd thought I'd say died instantly on my lips.

He reached for me and moved my body up against the back of the sofa, bracing my hips with both hands and putting his hard thigh between my legs. "I'm not going to fuck you tonight. Do you understand?"

My eyes met his, and I nodded, unable to speak. His declaration had muddled my mind completely.

He looked both agitated and aroused at the same time. "I need more time than tonight, and it will be planned."

"What exactly would you need that much time for?" My voice was a whisper.

His wicked grin made me crave his touch even more. "Because I want to eat your pussy for days, kiss every inch of your body, and then fuck you until you can barely walk."

I couldn't breathe. No man had ever turned me on with just his words. "I'm not sure I'll be able to sleep if you don't touch me now." My voice was raw. I couldn't believe I was on the verge of begging for sex.

"Has it really been over a year?" He aligned his hips to mine, rubbing his erection into my center.

"Oh, God." I couldn't process his question with that distraction.

"Tell me, and I'll take care of you." His voice was seductive and low and unlike anything I'd ever heard from him.

"Yes, it's been since I lived in Charlotte," I admitted.

He stopped and looked at me intensely. "No one in New York?"

I shook my head. "I've been busy with the job and—"

He held a finger to my lips. "Sash, you don't need to justify it. It turns me on even more that it's been that long. No wonder you're frustrated, honey."

He kissed me then with one of his hands gripping the back of my neck and the other one palming my sex over the outside of my pajama bottoms. "I can feel how wet you are through the fabric." He massaged me with both his erection and fingers.

The friction wasn't enough. I needed more. "Please, I need to feel you."

"If I touch you, I won't be able to stop. You're like water to a thirsty man. You don't know how much I want to taste you."

I had visions of him putting his face where his hand was and whimpered. I was close, and he wasn't even touching me skin on skin yet.

"That's it. I know you're almost there." He rolled his hips into me, rubbing harder.

Before I could respond, the wave hit me. My body tightened, and I arched into him.

He grabbed my ass and pushed his center flush with mine, absorbing my climax against his hard body.

"Bri—" Panting for air and limp against him, I was very aware of the hardness straining against his pants and nestled between my thighs.

He kissed my forehead. "Whenever you start to think this isn't what we should do, I want you to picture how much better that will be with our clothes off and after the fourth time."

His words sent a shudder through me. Jesus, had he just made me come without actually touching me directly?

Reluctantly, he pulled away, kissing me one last time before stepping back.

I shivered with the loss of his heat and was left gripping the couch in order to keep from falling on my face.

"Are you all right to go upstairs?" he smirked.

I nodded, unable to say anything else. It wasn't often that the best orgasm of your life came from being dry humped against the back of a basement sofa.

# CHAPTER EIGHT

*T*he flight down to Tortola the next day was on one of Josh's private jets. The plane was already carrying quite a few people from New York, most of whom I'd had the pleasure of meeting at Haylee's going-away party a few months ago. Only McKenzie, Brian, and myself boarded in Charlotte. Next stop, paradise. Evidently, there was a small airport on a neighboring island where we would land, while a bridge led to the resort on where we would all be staying. Not that we had to worry about logistics with the private plane, transportation, and accommodations already planned out for us.

"This is some style," Kenzie remarked upon boarding the luxurious jet.

I observed the younger woman's face as she got a first look at Will and smiled at her immediate interest. Will was a friend of Haylee's, someone she'd met last year on a model shoot. He was young, gorgeous—and from what I'd seen—nice and down-to-earth.

"Hi, I'm McKenzie, Brian's sister," she introduced herself, happy to take the seat beside him.

"Nice to meet you, McKenzie. I'm Will."

I had to bite my lip from laughing when Kenzie met my look with one of her own that clearly said, *Holy shit, he's Australian.*

Brian, being the over protective big brother, frowned, but I nudged him out of glaring at the younger man. He took a seat next to his friend Mark who hopefully would provide a nice distraction for Brian not to worry about his sister. Kenzie could do a lot worse than a guy like Will, and maybe it would be good for her confidence.

Nigel, Josh's long-time assistant, stood and took my hand in order to introduce me to his partner, David. Nigel had always been kind to me and had helped get me settled in New York when I'd moved up there. It was nice to see that David was looking healthy and feeling up for traveling. He'd battled colon cancer last year and was thankfully in remission. I had a feeling that everyone on this plane was looking for a few days of sunshine and celebration.

I went toward the back of the plane and took a seat next to Catherine. We caught up on our holidays, and then she leaned in and whispered, "Did he at least call and apologize for the other night and the nickname thing?"

Brian and I had agreed to keep our relationship on the down low; however I'd already confided my feelings about him to her so I didn't see the harm in revealing the latest. "Better. He came over that night."

"Holy shit balls," she blurted out, then looked around apologetically, clearly happy that it seemed no one had heard her over the sound of the plane taking off. "Sorry."

I laughed out loud. "Did you, Catherine Davenport, queen of all things classy and proper, just say, "shit balls"?

She giggled and turned slightly pink. "Not exactly an eloquent reaction, was it?"

"No, but it was hilarious." We were soon in a fit of giggles.

Finally, she leaned forward and spoke quietly, "So you two, ah—"

I shook my head, thankful I didn't have to lie about anything. "No, we're, uh, figuring it out. There's a lot at stake, and we're taking things slow." Much slower than I'd like, I thought wryly.

She smiled. "Did he tell you what he ended up telling Jamie?"

"No, we didn't get into that. Suffice it to say he wasn't happy with her for showing up, and he didn't go home with her."

Catherine sipped her water. "Maybe at the wedding, you guys…?"

I shrugged. "A lot of people we know will be there, and I'd like to keep it quiet. Chances are I'll screw it up before it starts. You're the only person I've told."

"You know you can trust me, but why would you say you'll mess it up?"

"There are a lot of reasons it could crash and burn." Matter of fact, I'd started to list them all in my head about five seconds ago.

"How about you focus on the ways in which it wouldn't? Obviously, he knows you, clearly you have chemistry, and you have history. Think positive."

If only she knew how those words were essentially a theme song for getting through most days. "I'll try. How about a cocktail?"

She glanced at her watch and laughed. "Why not? It's five o'clock somewhere."

"Good girl. I'm going to go see if I can mix up some mimosas. That way we can feel sophisticated about slugging back alcohol at ten o'clock in the morning."

I got up and helped myself to the bar in the back. Opening a bottle of champagne, I poured two glasses.

Brian's sexy voice came from behind me. "A drink, and it isn't even noon yet, huh?"

My lips curved into a smile, and I turned, meeting his warm

brown eyes with my own. "It contains orange juice, which makes it practically breakfast."

He smiled, glanced back toward our fellow passengers and then moved me toward the side of the bar, out of the line of sight of any of the others. Leaning in, he whispered, "I can still feel you from last night."

My breath left me, and I felt my cheeks flame in response. "Sounds like I should agree to everything, and we should get started."

"Then that's a yes?"

"If it is, then do we get started tonight?"

"What I have in mind means locking you in a room for at least forty-eight hours. No clothes and no interruptions."

Delicious anticipation flowed between us. "We'd have three nights down here in Tortola."

He seemed torn, and I had a moment of female empowerment.

"If you don't stop looking at me like that, I'm going to drag you to a place more private."

"Don't make promises you won't keep," I challenged.

He moved closer, his breath in my ear. "Is that what you want: everyone on this plane hearing you scream my name while I'm deep inside of you, taking you against the wall of the airplane lavatory?"

Holy crap.

He pulled back with a smug look of satisfaction in taking the power right back.

"I never thought I would have before this moment," I admitted, watching the disbelief flicker in his eyes.

"You surprise me." He touched his thumb to my bottom lip.

Before I could help it, my tongue darted out to taste the salty pad.

His eyes turned feral as he visibly fought for control. "I

swear to God, if my sister wasn't on this plane, we would test your theory of not caring whether everyone heard you."

"Oh, I think I'd care plenty afterwards." But only Brian could make me forget it for a little while.

He chuckled. "I'll let you get back to cocktails with Catherine. By the way, should I be worried about Will and my sister?"

I shook my head and grinned. "Oh, I think she'd do quite well with Will."

He rolled his eyes. "I wasn't talking about his looks."

I laughed. "Neither was I. After all, he's got that hot Australian accent going for him, too."

I was rewarded with a sour expression before he returned to his seat.

WE WERE MET with a limousine upon landing, and the champagne continued to flow. I was happy to see that not only was McKenzie enjoying Will's company but she also wasn't the novice at flirting that I'd assumed. Matter of fact, she was impressively cool and collected, holding her own and not making it obvious if she was into him. Of course, there was the possibility that she wasn't, but I'd be hard pressed to think of any crush better looking or nicer than Will.

Once we arrived at the resort and got checked in, there was a knock on my hotel door. I'd expected Brian on the other side, but was surprised to see McKenzie instead.

"Man, you didn't mention Will would be coming. He's gorgeous and super cool," she said the minute the door shut.

Smiling, I noted her cosmetics bag clutched in her hand. I might have been hoping for Brian, but considering how much I enjoyed his sister's company, I reasoned she could provide a nice distraction. "I'd actually forgotten about he and Haylee being such good friends. Did you want me to do your makeup?"

She instantly beamed. "I know I'm putting you on the spot again. Are you sure you don't mind?"

I shook my head and pulled out the desk chair to set it in front of the closet mirror. I'd often had hopes that this could be the sort of thing my sister Addison and I could have shared while growing up. But she'd never once asked me for help with clothes or makeup, always opting to go with her friends instead of spending time with me. Not that I could completely blame her as we'd never been terribly close. Then after I'd found out I'd been adopted at sixteen, I'd spent a lot more time keeping to myself. "Nope, I don't mind at all. Is there a spark between you two?"

She shrugged. "If I'm being honest, Will is great, but I feel like I can be completely myself with the other guy. He and I are friends first. I know it sounds corny, but I don't have to put on a pretense with him. I know he genuinely likes to spend time with me, laughs at my jokes, and gets where I'm coming from."

I knew exactly how she felt. Her brother was one of the few people who I'd let in over the years. It made me nervous, however, that even he hadn't seen the real me, the one I kept hidden from everyone.

Brian had questioned what was keeping me from saying yes. The answer I could never give him was fear. Fear of him seeing me vulnerable and finding out about my anxiety disorder. But he was only asking to see me every two weeks, which meant I'd still have my life, and he'd have his. If I thought about it that way, it was a lot less intimidating.

I went to work on Kenzie's make-up, and we chatted more about fashion and other things.

Hearing another knock, I smiled when I opened the door to reveal Brian. His hands automatically reached for my face and his lips were inches away from mine, when I suddenly pulled back remembering his sister.

"Are you here looking for Kenzie?" I asked, wishing he could have landed that kiss.

His raised brow conveyed his surprise. Then he glanced beyond me, and it dawned on him as to what I was talking about. He dropped his hands on a sigh. "Yes, um I was looking for you, Kenzie. To let you know that mom, your dad and Benjamin arrived."

I noted that they both displayed the same sour face. Was their family really that bad?

"I don't suppose Rebecca got the stomach flu and is puking her guts up back home instead of here polluting paradise with her toxicity?" Kenzie asked, looking hopeful.

They laughed, and Brian shook his head. "I wish, but unfortunately, she's here, too. Your makeup looks nice, sis."

Kenzie grinned. "Sasha is going to sex me up."

I winced at the sharp look coming from Brian, then shrugged. "She's a grown woman."

He let out a breath. "Do me a favor and don't make it too sexy. This is a wedding, not a frat party." He looked at both of us while he said it. "See you ladies downstairs in about twenty minutes."

When the door shut, McKenzie turned toward me. "Sorry. I was only joking."

"You're fine. Believe me, it wouldn't be the first time that I irritated your brother."

---

DINNER BROUGHT the first glimpse of the happy couple. I gave Haylee a big hug, delighted to see her.

Last year when Haylee had been working for Josh, she'd given me a huge break by incorporating my idea of a vintage jewelry angle into her fashion shoot for Cosmo Life magazine. She'd garnered the cover as the model and I'd made my client very happy during the pivotal first couple months in my new role as vice president. She was one of the few people I'd met who didn't have an agenda and simply did nice things for people.

Then she'd introduced me to Catherine. I'd gone from having Juliette as my only female friend to now having a circle of them, all who would do anything for each other. It was something I'd never thought to have, considering the first impression I made on most women was especially rough.

"I'm happy you could make it, Sasha. I love your dress. You always look so incredible," Haylee greeted.

I'd dressed in a print wrap dress which was chic and cool for the tropical air. "Thank you. You look amazing and happy."

She did, in a classic dress that most likely was a vintage design.

"Thank you," she replied and promised to talk later. She welcomed other guests while the groom-to-be came up and kissed me on the cheek.

"Nice to see you Sasha," Josh said.

"You, too. The resort and island are beautiful." Josh Singer might be the owner of the company and my boss's boss, but during this weekend I was going to think of him as my friend's fiancée.

"Good. I'm glad you like it. And I'm happy you could make it."

When I glanced over at Haylee and back at him, I nearly sighed at the way his eyes tracked her every move. I wondered what it would be like to have that type of peace and contentment in a relationship. It was a powerful thing to witness.

"Everything okay?" I asked when I noticed Josh's eyes narrow while watching a group arrive.

He hesitated but then met my eyes. "Can you do me a favor?"

I nodded. "Of course."

"Can I trust that if you hear about anyone saying anything that could be hurtful toward Haylee, you would let me know?"

His voice was low and the intent was clear as his eyes landed on Brian's brother and sister-in-law, Benjamin and Rebecca greeting Haylee across the way.

"Sure. They don't call me Sasha-B-Fierce for nothing." I sipped my drink and smiled at his look of surprise that I was aware of my nickname.

"I hope you know it's a compliment. Although my first choice was always Sasha Ice as you are the Ice Man of the advertising pitch. Nothing rattles you."

"Did you just Top Gun reference me?" It was amusing to see this side of him.

He chuckled and then winced. "I did. But on a completely different topic, let me apologize ahead of time for what's about to happen. Picture an exuberant Labrador retriever who hasn't learned any manners and isn't housebroken. He's harmless but still jumps up, pees on the carpet, and, unfortunately, has no sense of boundaries."

I looked at him like he'd lost his flipping mind until a handsome, younger version of Josh walked up with eyes only for me and dimples that should be illegal.

"Big brother, you've already got a beautiful, not to mention extremely patient, wife-to-be, so please introduce me to this vision you're talking to," he sweet-talked.

Ah, now the retriever comment made sense. I bit my lip to keep from laughing at the analogy.

"Sasha Brooks is a friend of Haylee's and is the senior vice president in the New York office of Gamble Advertising," Josh introduced. His tone made it clear to keep it professional. "Sasha, this is my younger brother, Colby Singer."

I extended my hand to his, thinking we were going to shake, but instead he brought it to his lips, kissing the back of it. Good Lord, he was laying it on thick.

"Nice to make your acquaintance," he said smoothly.

Josh offered me an apologetic smile.

"Uh, yours as well, Colby. Talk to you later, Josh. I should probably get to my seat," I excused, intending to break away.

"Wherever you're sitting, I'm taking the chair next to you. Lead the way," Colby insisted.

Turning, I arched a brow at his presumptuous self-invitation. This typically intimidated most men but not Colby, who only chuckled at the challenge.

"I'll be honest, my first impressions aren't always great," he admitted with a wink.

In spite of finding him slightly obnoxious, I smiled because I knew the feeling.

---

BRIAN HAD ACTED STRANGELY during the meal, giving me possessive looks and watching every move once Colby had taken the chair next to me. Josh's younger brother flirted mildly, but I'd mostly talked with Catherine, seated on the other side of me, about her upcoming trips.

I'd been anticipating the knock I heard on my hotel room door later that night, but when I opened it up, McKenzie was there.

"Hey, are you alone?" she questioned, looking unsure of herself.

"Yeah. Come on in. Why would you think I'd have company?" I wondered if she had clued in about Brian and I.

"Colby was into you tonight. I can't blame him because you're gorgeous, but you should know that he's a total player. He never commits. Besides, he's in LA working with all of those actresses and always has droves of women after him."

Holding up my hands, I clarified quickly, "Whoa, whoa, slow down. I'm not interested in Colby whatsoever."

The relief on her face spoke volumes.

"Oh, shit, he's your—" I didn't get a chance to finish when

another knock interrupted. "That's probably your brother looking for—" I opened it and—Ah crap, it was Colby.

His brow arched. "Uh, judging by your face, I'm guessing you don't want to take a stroll down on the beach?" Something told me he wasn't accustomed to a look of dread on a woman's face.

"Hey, is that my brother?" Kenzie asked, coming up behind me and sucking in a breath upon seeing her crush standing at my door.

Colby's face faltered. "Uh, I was—Shit."

While giving him an annoyed look at his pathetic attempt at a half-ass excuse, I heard Brian's voice come up from behind him.

"What's going on?" Brian's eyes flicked from Colby, standing outside my door, to me, facing him. His voice was casual, but his eyes were anything but.

"Well, I believe we were all heading down to the beach for a bit. You ready, Kenzie?"

Brian's expression changed immediately upon seeing his sister. "Uh, okay. Mind if I join, too?"

I grinned. "Of course not. Lead the way, Colby."

Colby was momentarily confused but went with the flow, falling into step next to an irritated McKenzie as we all made our way down to the beach.

"Okay, boys, do you mind grabbing us some beers," I suggested with a smile, wanting some time alone with Brian's sister.

The guys headed toward the bar while we girls meandered down toward the beach. We took a seat on a dock with our feet dangling over the water.

Knowing we only had a few minutes before they returned, I was blunt. "The crush is Colby, I take it?"

She didn't bother to deny it. "Is this the part where you tell me how screwed up that is?" Her eyes were focused on her feet.

I sighed. Who the hell was I to give advice about anything

romantic? So I went with my gut. "Crushes aren't about logic. It's simply how you feel. Of all people, I'm not in a position to judge that."

"He was coming to your room because you're the type of woman he wants. Sexy, confident, beautiful, polished—"

I shook my head and interrupted. "Stop, Kenzie. Do you want to know why Colby came to my room?"

She rolled her eyes. "Please don't tell me some story. I'm a big girl."

"I know that," I started, trying to mind her feelings. "And what I was going to say is that the reason why he came to my room is because of the challenge."

She looked at me curiously, and I continued.

"Men like Colby like the pursuit of a woman who isn't falling at their feet. You said it yourself. He's used to these droves of girls in LA throwing themselves at him. When one doesn't automatically do so, he's interested for the sake of the chase."

She blew out a breath of frustration. "And I've been the pathetic girl who doesn't pose a challenge at all."

I put my arm around her shoulders, hoping the gesture didn't come across as awkward since comforting others wasn't my forte. "There's nothing pathetic about you, McKenzie. He obviously has a relationship with you that he doesn't have with other women, which means he must show you another side of himself. And that makes you special to him."

"He does show me another side. But I always pitifully make him the priority. Maybe if I didn't, I'd be the chase."

I nodded. "Now you get it. This isn't a game per se but more of a strategy. Some men want what they can't have."

"Which is why you haven't slept with my brother?"

Oh, boy. "That's a bit more complicated."

"I've spilled my guts about a guy I've had a crush on since I was six years old."

I hesitated, thinking about how to put it. "Your brother is my best friend. And now he's my boss. Adding a third element gets tricky."

"You're his best friend, too. I hope you know that. He talks about you all the time. I mean, only to me, but I know that over the last year since you moved, he misses you a lot."

The thought warmed me. "I miss him, too."

"By the way, please don't tell Brian about Colby. I think he knew about it when I was younger, but I don't want him knowing about it now."

It meant a lot that Kenzie trusted me enough to confide in me. "I won't. We're here to have a good time, so the other piece of advice I have is that at the reception you should dance with Will as much as possible."

She giggled. "Oh, that won't be a hardship."

We accepted the beers gratefully when the boys found us a few minutes later.

"Everything all right?" Brian asked, looking at Kenzie and back toward me.

Colby appeared concerned, and I knew in that moment that at least he cared about Kenzie's feelings.

"Yeah, things are good. I'm doing one beer and then heading up," I said, slugging it back. I enjoyed the banter between the three of them as we sat dockside enjoying the warm evening and Caribbean breeze.

After finishing my drink, I stood up, ready for bed.

Brian got to his feet as well. "I'll walk you upstairs."

"Kenzie, you staying out?" Colby asked.

She shrugged. "Nah, I'm going to bed, too."

I noted Colby's surprised look and I was proud of her for not appearing eager to spend time with him.

---

BRIAN WALKED me up to my room, both of us quiet.

As soon as I put my key in, his body crowded mine through the door.

It hadn't even had a chance to close when Brian seized my hips with his hands and backed me into the room, kicking the door shut behind him. "Is it just me, or has this day dragged on?"

Smiling, I realized it had for me, as well. "It has seemed slow."

His hand stroked my face softly. "All I could think about was kissing you today." He dipped his head and tasted my lips, taking his time with the leisurely kiss.

Once my tongue met his, however, the kiss changed. Suddenly, I was pressed up against him and I took the opportunity to reach for the zipper on his shorts.

His hands moved quickly, though, closing over mine and preventing my intent. "Not like this. We still have to ensure we've agreed on everything."

"How about we hash out the details tomorrow? Tonight, maybe we could let it happen."

He closed his eyes and took a deep breath. "I can't."

"You'd turn down sex because these rules mean that much to you?"

His expression was pained and he nodded.

"Unbelievable. I'm practically throwing myself at you. This was a mistake. You don't want me, then, fine."

"Damn it, Sasha. Does it feel like I don't want you?" He placed my hand on his bulge where he was hard as steel.

Instead of moving my hand away, I slid it down the length of him and heard him hiss.

He threaded his fingers with mine and my mouth ravaged again. After backing me to the edge of the bed, he eased me down, following on top. His hips aligned with mine, grinding against my throbbing sex.

Intense heat spread throughout my body with the contact. I

moaned, cradling his hard length and arching toward him. He shifted me so that we were both on our sides and his leg scissored over mine, keeping me inches from him.

His fingers reached up under my dress, but, much to my frustration, stayed outside of my panties when he started massaging.

"You're right there," I gasped, frustrated.

"I'm going to make you come, but I'm saving the good stuff for when I have more—"

"Time," I bit out, finishing the statement for him. My voice was raw, and my body was desperate for release.

"Think of the last time you had foreplay. We're working up to the ultimate fantasy for both of us."

My body had started to respond to his fingers. I moved my hand toward his zipper again. "Okay, but I get to torture you, too." When he tensed, I argued, "We haven't started so you're not in control yet."

He hesitated but then let me proceed, sucking in a breath when I took hold of him through his boxers. "God—" He increased the pressure on me, rubbing harder and faster.

I did the same, wishing I could feel his actual skin. As it was, he was scorching hot through the cotton material.

My body tensed with the detonation of my orgasm. His cock pulsed, wetness seeping through the fabric onto my hand.

His lips left mine and he kissed my forehead, tucking my hair behind my ear. "Do you feel like you're back in high school?"

"Back then the boys would go all the way."

He grinned. "Teenage boys wouldn't have given you an orgasm."

"Ah, high school, where the boys didn't know what they were doing, and the girls didn't know enough to know better."

He chuckled.

We lay facing one another, and my heart beat faster at the intimacy of being eye to eye in the same bed together. "You have about ten minutes before I'm passing out. What else do we need to discuss?" I yawned.

"Are you willing to let me be in control in the bedroom?"

"Would it only be there? I'd resent you if it bled into any other aspect of our lives."

"Yes. Being dominant during sex doesn't mean I wouldn't respect and value your time or forget my manners."

"Would I have to call you sir?"

"Not my thing. I'd rather you say my name."

"What types of things are we talking? You're not into painful stuff, right?"

His slow smile made me shiver. "No, it's also not my thing, but I do intend to tie you up, and we'd use toys. Pleasurable things, not painful."

"But you won't allow me ever to be dominant with you sexually?"

"No. We already went over that."

"And what if that is a sticking point for me?" I had to ask.

"Then this isn't going to fucking work." He sat up suddenly, zipping up his shorts.

I propped myself up on my elbow, watching him. "Wow, bringing that up really pisses you off, doesn't it?" I had never seen this side of him.

He cursed softly and then asked, "Why do you want that?"

"Maybe I want to be spontaneous and take you in my mouth without permission some morning."

He muttered another curse, and his body tensed. "I can honestly say I have no problem with that. It isn't all about ruining the spontaneity. But I need you to respect the fact that I'm in charge in the bedroom."

"Okay."

He searched my eyes, most likely not knowing what I meant by that and kissed me one last time before leaving.

# CHAPTER NINE

$\mathcal{T}$he next day had been busy between the wedding shower and a planned shopping excursion for the women while the men spent most of their day golfing.

At dinner that evening, all the guests enjoyed a beach cookout and trivia. It was a lot of fun, especially with the cast of characters in attendance. A number of outgoing personalities in the crowd made it easy to be one of the quiet ones without anyone noticing.

After the parents retired, things got even more entertaining while the alcohol flowed. Brian was in his element with his friends, and it was easy to see the history between him, Mark, Josh, and Colby. We all heard lots of stories from college that made us laugh.

While most of the men had gone out toward the beach to smoke cigars, the women gathered around the seated bar area. I stepped up toward the bartender to order another round of red wine for myself and Catherine when unfortunately the dreaded sister-in-law, Rebecca, came up to my left side.

She turned her attention to me, narrowing her eyes. "You're Sasha, right?"

I braced myself, thankful I'd been forewarned about the type of person she was. "Yes, and I'm sorry. Your name?" I pretended not to know.

"I'm Rebecca. Benjamin's wife and Brian's sister-in-law."

"Ah, yes. Nice to meet you."

Haylee walked up and smiled toward the both of us.

"The shower today was nice," Rebecca complimented.

Haylee nodded. "It was a really great surprise. Josh's mom went all out with the boat."

I received the two glasses of red wine from the bar and was about to return to my table when I witnessed the next comment out of Rebecca's mouth.

"It's too bad we couldn't have combined the wedding and baby shower, but I guess you want to keep up the pretense that one isn't because of the other," Rebecca sneered.

Haylee's smile faltered. She looked at me, turning pink with embarrassment.

Haylee had confided in both Catherine and I last week that they were expecting. It hadn't been easy to share the private news as she'd been worried about perception. But Josh had spoken with Catherine and made it clear that although it wasn't planned, it was definitely welcome. The fact that Rebecca was implying that Haylee had trapped a man that so clearly loved her, brought out my protective side. Before I could stop myself, my entire glass of Pinot Noir was splashed on Rebecca's beige dress. "Oops."

She gasped. "You—you did that on purpose," she accused, looking at the damage.

"Why would I ever do something so mean-spirited on purpose?" I feigned innocence.

My eyes met Haylee's while I waited for permission to either let Rebecca have it or wait for Haylee to do so. I was delighted when she was more than happy to stand up for herself.

"You know, Rebecca, if you can't get that stain out in your

room, I'd be happy to talk to my fiancé about getting you an earlier flight home. But if you think you can possibly be more careful next time, maybe there's hope you can stay for the wedding, after all."

The message was clear, and when Rebecca huffed, stomping away toward her room, Haylee and I both burst into giggles.

Catherine joined us, looking toward the retreating woman. "What did I miss?"

Haylee looked between us both and grinned. "You missed a waste of a good glass of red wine." She filled her in, and then we all started laughing.

I'd never been so grateful for female friends who built one another up instead of cutting others down.

It was past midnight when the last of the partygoers headed back to their rooms. I'd barely made it in my own door when my desk phone started ringing.

"Hello," I answered.

"Hey, you sound out of breath." Brian's voice came from the other end of the line.

"I just got to my room." Taking a seat on the bed, I slipped off my shoes.

"Sorry. I'm impatient."

"Did you want to come over?" I was anxious to have him all to myself after a day of only being able to watch him.

"Uh. Probably not the best idea. We've both been drinking, and I don't trust myself around you at the moment."

I sighed heavily. "That's too bad."

"Tell me about it."

"I know we haven't officially started our arrangement, but I do want to ask some questions about your history." I slipped off my bra from under my dress and lay on the bed, now feeling more comfortable.

"All right. You can have six questions. But then remember I get the same number."

That sounded reasonable. "How many relationships have you had like this?"

I heard him sigh and realized talking about this wasn't something he was entirely comfortable doing.

"None like this, Sasha. But if you're talking about arrangements in which there were some type of rules, then I've done four others."

"Okay, and how long did they last?"

"Is this question two?"

Crap, my curiosity was eating at me. "Yes."

"The longest was five months. Most were, uh, month-to-month type things."

"How did you discover you, uh, like to be in control in the bedroom?"

"Question three?"

"Okay, yes, why not? Question three." To hell with it, I needed to know some things.

"I met a woman who wanted me to be, uh, dominant with her. At first I thought it was only to turn her on, but then I realized it came naturally to me and I enjoyed it."

"But you're not dominant outside of the bedroom." This was the part I was having a hard time fully understanding. Brian was the fun-loving, jokester who could always get along with everyone because he wasn't interested in pissing matches. What he was describing was the exact opposite of that type of personality, the laid-back easy-to-get-along-with guy.

"We've been through this, Sasha."

Yes, we had. "You go while I think of my final three."

"Okay, question one is how often do you masturbate?"

I definitely wasn't a prude by any stretch, but no one had posed this question before. "Uh, when necessary."

"Specifics and honesty," he reminded.

I blew out a breath. "Probably, once a month."

"With your hands or vibrator?"

I never thought I'd see the day where I'd be shocked at something Brian asked me. "Battery operated."

He chuckled, most likely because I was stuttering with my answers. "Do you come easily from it?"

"Are we doing phone sex?" Because all of a sudden I was feeling pretty hot and bothered.

"Honey, if you ever need to ask that question, then the answer is no. Now, do you orgasm with your battery-operated device?"

"Most of the time, yes."

"And are the orgasms better with the vibrator or the men you've been with?"

"Question four?"

"Yes. Are you going to answer?"

Considering my best orgasms had been with him, I didn't say anything specific. "Definitely a man over the device."

"What did he do?" His voice was low, and I was wishing I had brought said device with me.

"He, uh, used his hand." I wasn't ready to admit it was him, doing it over my clothing and against the couch in his basement. Then it would be obvious how pathetic my previous sex life had been.

"We'll have to work on your dirty talk, honey. What about when he went down on you?"

Jesus, now I'd need a cold shower. "No, he, uh—We didn't do oral."

"His loss. Please tell me it wasn't the ex-boyfriend from high school who you saw when you went home?"

"We went over this last night. High school boys don't give girls orgasms, let alone the best one of their lives."

He laughed. "Good point. Are you ready to say yes to me?"

"It's not like I want to say no. And even if I did say yes tonight, you still won't come up here. Either way you're making me wait."

"So you're delaying your response because I'm postponing when we'd start?" There was a slight edge to his voice.

"No, but if I'm being honest, I'm not sure it's in my personality to be submissive."

"I'm not asking you to be submissive as much as I'm asking for you to give up control sexually and give yourself over to me. There isn't anything I would do that you wouldn't enjoy."

Simply thinking about it had me aroused. "Okay, my final three questions. You mentioned tying me up in previous conversations. Tied up how?" I'd never been bound before, and it made me a little nervous.

"Hands together or feet to the bed."

Hm, that didn't sound too bad. "And no pain? I mean no whips or that kind of stuff?"

"No whips or pain. I'm not into it. You'll have to decide if you like the soft stuff like spanking."

"Okay, and the last question is: Would we use condoms or what?" There. I'd put it out there.

"Are you on the pill?"

"Yes, the shot. But, uh, are you clean?"

"Of course I am." He sounded irritated.

"Hey, don't get annoyed. You're the one having sex with women who are clearly a little more adventurous than I am."

"Fair enough, but I've never not worn a condom. I'd like to not use them with you. I'm clean."

"Seriously?"

"Seriously you're shocked I'm clean, or are you surprised you're the only woman I trust not to wear one with?"

"You know I meant about never having worn them before. Is it my inability to get kids to like me that enables you trust me?"

His tone turned serious. "We're friends and colleagues, Sash, and I know you're not trying to trap a man to take care of you."

I scoffed at the very notion.

He laughed. "See, the very idea doesn't compute. If you want to swap medical records, we can."

"I trust you more than anyone else I know. If you say you're good, I believe you."

"I trust you, too. I guess that's what makes this strange going into it. We aren't trying to get to know one another. We're more nervous about losing what we already have."

"You weren't worried before. You are now?"

"Please don't take this the wrong way, but you're not exactly flexible when it comes to forgiving people. I'd be lying if I told you that I didn't think at some point I would screw something up. I can only hope that we can give each other a learning curve."

I tried not to take it personally. He wasn't wrong. Exhibit A: I was still holding a grudge against my sister. Ironic, considering I wasn't the type of girl who made a good first impression, which meant I needed second chances myself. "You know that I'll most likely mess it up first."

"Doubtful. Do you think you can maybe learn to be a little more, uh, flexible?"

"Is that a double entendre?"

"Without even trying," he deadpanned. He laughed, and then I did too. "What you need to do is learn to be a little more relaxed. Take off the pencil skirt and let your hair down, so to speak."

"Considering I'm at a wedding for my boss's boss with my supervisor and other people I respect, it's sorta hard to do that." Yes, I was kind of reserved. So what?

"Mm hm. Nice excuse. We could be anywhere, with strangers, friends, wherever, and you'd never do anything out of your safe zone."

"I went speed dating with Catherine. That was way outside the perimeter of my comfort zone."

"I can only imagine, but I'm talking about doing something

on a whim. Like getting up and singing karaoke or skinny-dipping. I bet you've never done either of those activities."

"You're right. I haven't," I conceded. With my history, the very thought of putting myself out there on purpose for people to judge petrified me.

"Promise me if you ever decide to do something crazy, that I'll be around for it. It would be a sight to behold to watch you let your hair down."

Somehow, I was suddenly inspired, with the wine and vodka fueling my adrenaline and overriding the conservative part of my brain that was protesting. "It's your lucky night, then, because I'm about to do one of those things. And here's a hint: it isn't singing."

---

BY THE TIME I made it down to the shoreline and looked around, I'd completely chickened out. Someone could see me, there could be sharks, I'd have to shower afterwards, and last, but not least, my excuse was something along the lines of how ridiculous it was to do something like this without anyone else daring you. Wasn't that the whole point of doing stupid things? Good grief. Then I turned and saw Brian standing there smirking.

"You talked yourself out of it, didn't you?" he teased.

I took a deep breath and, before I could lose my nerve, kicked off my sandals and pulled my knit dress over my head. It was amazing what a little competitiveness and challenge could do to trump my feelings of anxiety. As my therapist had pointed out, I liked to bulldoze through some obstacles to prove I could.

I heard his muttered curse and tossed him a triumphant smile. "I figured it wouldn't count unless someone could see proof." I hadn't bothered to put my bra back on, and observed his eyes go wide at the vision of me topless. Stepping out of my thong, I heard his breath hiss. I laughed, running into the water so that that he wasn't afforded too much of a view.

Thankfully, the water was warm and the bottom was sandy. I waded in to my waist and crouched down to my shoulders, enjoying the fact that I'd actually done it.

When I glanced up toward the shore, I saw Brian whipping off his shorts and shirt and, finally, his boxers. I wished I was closer to get a better look. Rolling my eyes internally, I reminded myself that in fact I was an adult woman who had seen a penis before, not some adolescent girl hoping to catch a peek.

He splashed in and stopped a foot away from of me. "How does it feel to be a rebel?"

"If you ever tell anyone about this, I will find a way to—"

He held up his hands in mock surrender. "I solemnly swear that what happens on this beach stays on this beach."

I giggled.

He raised a brow. "Did you, Sasha-B-Fierce, just giggle?"

I was in a fit of them and nodded, enjoying his playful grin in return. When he moved closer, it felt natural and comfortable. That lasted five seconds because when his mouth met mine, my entire body ignited with desire.

His hands roamed my nude body, sliding over my breasts and down to my hips. His tongue explored my mouth expertly. He pulled away reluctantly. "This wasn't a good idea. Especially now that I've had a glimpse of that Brazilian wax you're sporting."

I wasn't listening. My body ached for his touch and craved release. With him naked and touching me I couldn't help but wrap my legs around him.

"Christ," he muttered, gripping my ass and grinding against me. His mouth took mine again. We were both desperate for the skin on skin contact we'd been denying ourselves over the last few days.

I rocked my hips into him and gasped when his fingers

worked their way inside of me. Our eyes locked, and I lifted myself up slightly, setting down on the head of his erection.

"I—" he started to protest.

I didn't let him finish, instead kissing him with everything I had. All of the pent-up frustration, desire, and attraction from the past few days poured into it.

He shifted me slightly and then drove home. "Sash—"

I arched back, stretching with his full length, loving the sound of my name on his lips. We were frantic with our hands and mouths. There was something about taking Brian out of his control zone that fueled me.

He withdrew a fraction, but then slammed back into me, holding my hips in place while he thrust, setting a frenzied rhythm. His lips traveled down the curve of my neck, and my nails raked over his back. When his hand slipped between us and rubbed my clit, he sent me completely over the edge within minutes. His pace increased, and, on one last thrust, I could feel his scorching hot release deep into my core.

As we fought to get our breathing regulated, I sensed the moment Brian withdrew, both literally and figuratively. He set me down on my feet abruptly and waded up toward the beach, leaving me stunned and a little unsure what to make of it. Was he angry?

He dressed quickly on the shoreline and looked surprised I didn't follow. He picked up my clothes, shook them free of sand, and waited.

After walking up out of the water, I snagged my dress from his outstretched hands and put it on quickly without my panties. I slipped on my sandals, and regarded him with his tense jaw and gritted teeth. "Do you want to tell me what's going on with you?"

He ran a hand through his hair. "You had to—what? Prove that you could take control?"

I was stunned. First, I'd never seen Brian this angry. Second, if anyone were to freak out after the first time we'd had sex, my money would have been on me. But instead I was the calm one? "You can't be serious. I didn't take control. We both lost it."

"That wasn't the plan. We were supposed to agree, and then we'd have time to do things properly."

"Do you think I prearranged this? You practically dared me to do something spontaneous, and all of a sudden I'm the bad guy. Why does it matter? We were leading up to this either way."

"It matters because I didn't want this to get screwed up like it is right now."

"The only thing screwed up right now is your reaction to what just happened."

"I told you how I wanted this to be. This wasn't it. This was you pushing it."

"Maybe I did push it, but it wasn't because I was against the agreement. It's because up until three nights ago, I didn't know what it was like to crave sex with anyone. You asked me who my best orgasm had ever been with, and you know what? It was you, up against your damn basement couch. So you'll have to excuse the fact that when you waded in naked after me and then touched me, I lost my mind."

He stood there staring at me for the longest time, apparently absorbing what I'd revealed.

"You know, for someone who didn't want a one-night stand, you're doing a hell of a job heading in that direction. Good-night." I turned on my heel and started walking.

"Wait," he called after me. He finally caught up as I was about to enter the lobby.

We both froze when we saw Brian's mom making a beeline for us.

"Ah, shit," he cursed, clearly bracing himself.

Giving her a tight smile, I was about to excuse myself from whatever she wanted with Brian when she pointed at me.

"Oh, no, you don't. You're the one I want to talk to. Did you spill wine on Rebecca tonight and then threaten that she'd be sent home?" his mother questioned.

Fan-fucking-tastic timing. I'd just had sex with her son minutes ago and now was being confronted while holding my panties in my hand.

Judging from the look on her son's face, he was completely clueless. I squared my shoulders and gave her my best unaffected look. She might be Brian's mother, but I'd hit my absolute max when it came to dealing with people today.

"I did," I said without further explanation.

She narrowed her eyes. "Why are you both wet?" That fact apparently just dawning on her.

Brian answered, "We were swimming. Now what's this about?"

"It's about your brother's wife in tears, saying that Sasha here spilled wine on her and then threatened her," his mother accused.

Actually, it was Haylee who had issued the threat, but I didn't bother to point that out. "I'd suggest, that you inform Rebecca that if she can't say anything nice, then not to say anything at all."

Brian's mom looked furious. "I don't know who you think you are, but I've been friends and neighbors with the Singers for almost forty years, and if you think—"

"I'm going to stop you there. Josh and his family would do absolutely anything for Haylee. They adore her. Do you think they'd like hearing what Rebecca said to her or, better yet, the fact that you're defending her? Now goodnight to you both." It was tempting to reiterate for Brian's sake what was actually said, but I realized it didn't matter. It was my word against hers and there was no way I was allowing either one of them to approach Haylee the night before her wedding for confirmation.

I held my head high and walked away with as much dignity as a woman with panties balled up in her fist could.

# CHAPTER TEN

*T*he moment I entered my room, the phone started ringing. I chose to ignore it. My adrenaline had run its course, the alcohol had left my system, and I was left reeling at everything that had transpired during the last hour.

After taking a hot shower, I came back into the room in my towel and scowled at the sound of a knock on the door. Exhaustion had set in and I refused to answer. I especially didn't need shit from Brian about my soft skills regarding his sister-in-law or mother. I was too raw from what had happened at the beach and the aftermath of him being angry about it.

Lying down on the bed, I tried to shut my mind off. I wasn't panicking, which was an encouraging sign. Sometimes it was the little victories when it came to coping with anxiety. The sound of my hotel door opening made me sit up. Brian's profile was illuminated by the hall light before he shut the door behind him.

"You're breaking and entering now?" I muttered, watching him from the bed.

"I had to. You wouldn't pick up the phone or answer the door."

"Do I even want to know how you got the key?"

"Probably not. Look, before we get into what happened between us, I'd like to talk about what transpired with Rebecca." He flipped on the reading light on the nightstand.

I watched him sit on the bed and met his eyes. "I'm not apologizing—"

He didn't let me finish. "I'm embarrassed to be related to someone who would say anything negative about someone like Haylee, and I'm glad you were there for her tonight. I'm sorry that my mom would confront you like that."

I was stunned. I'd assumed he would tell me I'd been too harsh or, worse, make excuses for their behavior. "You're not going to lecture me on how I could have handled it better?"

He shook his head. "If anything, I admire the fact that you stayed calm. And I need to—"

I launched myself at him with a kiss, not allowing him to continue.

His surprise turned to reciprocation quickly with his hands weaving into my hair. He pulled back, searching my eyes. "What was that for?"

"For believing me," I said simply.

He stroked my face. "I know I've criticized your first impressions and the ways you communicate, but that was from a work perspective to help with clients. I understand you well enough to know you're not spilling wine on someone unless it's warranted, Sasha."

I couldn't begin to tell him how much his words meant. Almost always, people assumed I was the one being the bitch. "Thank you."

He placed his thumb on my bottom lip as was his habit. "The other person handling things terribly this evening was me."

"Agreed. Why were you angry?"

He took a minute to respond. "I'm used to being in control, and when I lost it, I took it out on you."

"Okay, I think I get that part. But what I don't understand is why our first time was so important to you."

His look was vulnerable. "I've had this fantasy of how I wanted it to go if ever given a second chance with you. I didn't want to take any risks ruining it or blowing it like in Miami. And I screwed it up anyhow, but I won't be able to stand another three years waiting."

Oh, Jesus, he thought it was his fault in Miami. "Brian, you didn't blow it that night in Miami. It was—" I didn't get the opportunity to finish.

"I know you say that, but one minute I'm supposed to meet you in your room and the next you were sending me a text message not to come. Obviously, I pushed it too far, too fast."

Shaking my head, I murmured, "You didn't. It wasn't that."

He got up from the bed to pace. "I saw you leave the hotel. You sent me that message about not coming up, and then twenty minutes later I saw you walk through the lobby to get into a cab curbside. I never knew if there was another guy or what, but you left."

Oh, God. I put my hands over my face and breathed deeply. "I have a confession to make about Miami."

He stopped his pacing and stared at me intently. "I don't think I want to hear this if it was another man, even three years later."

I shook my head. "It wasn't another man. But this isn't easy. I've never told anyone before. Could you please sit?"

He must've sensed my unease because he was on the bed in a second, holding my hands. "I should have left it alone. It was three years ago, and I don't need to know the details."

"Yes, you do because you've had the wrong impression all this time. When I went up to my room that night, I had every intention of sleeping with you." My stomach tensed with the memory and tried to keep the emotion out of my voice. "But my cell phone had died earlier, and when I charged it after getting to my room, I had several voice messages. They were all about my mother from the police and hospital."

He looked shocked and then confused. "Something happened to your mom?"

"My birth mother," I clarified. "She'd been beaten up and left for dead three days earlier outside of Raleigh, completely strung out on heroin. Evidently someone dug up my information."

"That must've been a shock for you."

Nodding, I recalled the full-blown panic attack into which the situation had sent me. "It was. Anyhow, long story short, they wanted to put her into a treatment facility. Rehab, if you will. They'd been trying to track me down for days, and I was told that if they didn't get the money wired to them that night for her to enter this facility, then they'd have to release her back onto the street. The director of the center made it clear that she'd already been clean for three days. Time was of the essence to get her into that place."

"That's why you left, to wire the money?"

I nodded. "I had no clue that you might be in the lobby or how it might have appeared to you." I was tempted to tell him about the anxiety attack, but admitting I'd been birthed by a junkie mother was enough vulnerability to expose for now.

He looked a little hurt, but being the type of guy he was, he put my feelings first. "Did you see her? I didn't think you'd ever met her before."

And now was the hard part. "I'd met her once a long time ago. It didn't go well." That was quite an understatement, but I didn't have the emotional energy to air all of my baggage at the moment. "The facility doesn't allow visitors until week four, but by the time I flew to Raleigh, she'd checked herself out. Ten thousand dollars for nothing, and she hadn't bothered to stick around to see me." My voice was small, and I rolled my neck. Recalling the mistake of being sucked into her life three years ago made me tense.

"Why didn't you tell me, Sasha? You could have confided in me. You had three damn years and plenty of opportunity. Maybe it's selfish to ask, but if that was the only reason you turned me down, why didn't you make another attempt?" His eyes searched mine.

"I did try again, two weeks later."

He shook his head. "I would have known had you attempted."

"We were at Claudia from accounting's wedding. Remember she invited the entire Charlotte office down in the Outer Banks at that hotel? I was supposed to have driven to my parents' house that night. But after the reception, I went upstairs and knocked on your hotel room door instead."

Confusion clouded his expression, and then it dawned on him. "Shit."

I blew out a breath. "Yeah, the cute little blonde singer for the band opened the door. I pretended that I had the wrong room."

"I had no clue." He pinched the bridge of his nose, looking pained at the fact that I'd met his one-night stand.

"I know, and I told myself it was my fault for screwing up Miami and not telling you the truth."

"Okay. But what about later on? It's been three years."

I realized I had a bevy of excuses that, when told separately, didn't justify why I hadn't. "I don't know. Pick your reason: I got cold feet, fear of rejection, thoughts of you with the blonde two weeks later. I was ashamed of the fact that my real mom was a druggie and that I'd been duped into losing ten grand. Or maybe it's the fact that you got promoted a couple months later." I stopped and looked at him. "I know all of those excuses by themselves sound trite, but when I added them all together, I convinced myself that it wasn't meant to be. That we were better off friends. Matter of fact, I thought you were kind of unaffected by the whole thing." He'd moved on quickly to another woman and had appeared to slide right back into our friendship much easier than I'd managed to do.

"Of course, I didn't seem to let it affect me. I had some pride. Rejection stung, but I knew we still had to work together."

"I know. I had pride, too. I'm sorry that I didn't tell you the truth that night or later on."

"I'm sorry, too, that I assumed something instead of asking." He leaned in and captured my lips softly in a kiss.

Pausing, a smile teased his lips. "Timing hasn't been very good to us, has it?"

"No, it hasn't." I reached up and cupped his face. "I agree to the rules, and although I was upset at the way you reacted tonight, I don't regret what happened."

He let out a breath. "Remember the part about being flexible because I was bound to mess something up at some point?"

"I do." I smiled, once again thinking it ironic that he'd done so first.

"I'm really sorry. Do you think I could get a second chance?"

"Yes, but are you going to make us wait for it?"

He grinned wickedly. "Not with the way timing has fucked us before. Not a chance. But first I need to take a quick shower to get the ocean off of me."

"You could use mine, and maybe I could join you," I suggested.

He shook his head, turning off the bedside lamp. "Oh, I think we've had enough water sports for this evening." He breathed in my ear, low and slow, "I want you to lose the towel, honey, lie in the middle of the bed with your knees apart and your pretty pussy on display for me. Put pillows under your head and relax because when I come out, I plan on spending a lot of time down there."

Holy shit balls, as Catherine would say. I think it took me a full minute after he'd closed the bathroom door to realize I hadn't moved.

I DIDN'T HAVE long to wait before Brian came out of the shower with simply a towel around his waist. The only illumination was the light coming through the bathroom door. My gaze tracked his movements as he crossed over toward the bed. I swallowed hard at being naked and on display for him.

His eyes took their time soaking in my body from head to toe. "You're unbelievably sexy, Sasha. More beautiful than I could have ever imagined."

I shivered with anticipation and expelled the breath I'd been holding. There was no panic, only an overwhelming eagerness for what was about to happen.

Brian proceeded to drop his towel, and my mouth went dry at the sight of him. I had known he was built in the arms and chest since he worked out regularly, but the size of his erection—Jesus, had I really had that inside of me?

"My face is up here," he teased.

My eyes rose to his, and I flushed. "Sorry, I was momentarily distracted." I wasn't the least bit sorry.

"Keep your hands above your head. Hold them together or in your hair, but do not under any circumstances touch me or yourself. Do you understand?"

I nodded and then complied without question, curious about this side of him.

His body crawled up the length of mine until he braced himself on his forearms with his knee between my legs. Then he captured my mouth like a starving man. Pulling back momentarily, he traced my lips with his thumb. "God, these lips are by far my favorite thing: sexy, full, sinful." He punctuated each compliment with a kiss.

Lost in his words, I about bucked off the bed when his finger dipped down into my center.

"You're positively drenched for me."

A whimper fell from my lips in response.

"I've dreamed about tasting you for too long." And just like that, he shifted down and buried his face in my cleft. His tongue was diabolical and relentless. His fingers worked my slick entrance like magic as I tried to remember to keep my hands above my head. He devoured me with ferocity, like he couldn't get enough. I'd never had a man go down on me like this in my life, but when I was about to come, he eased back.

"Brian—" I couldn't believe that was my voice practically begging for release.

"Tell me what you want."

Was it not obvious? "You know what I want," I exhaled. Arching toward him, I was on fire from his kisses teasing the inside of my thighs.

"Ask me, Sasha. Ask me, and I'll do it."

Talking dirty was not something with which I had a lot of experience. But my body was desperate for release, and his torture was almost too much for me to handle. "Please, make me come."

"Do you know how much it turns me on to hear you talk like that? To ask me for what you want?"

He settled between my legs, parting the lips of my sex. His tongue delved inside of me while his thumb pad rubbed circles around my sensitive clit.

My hands moved of their own volition, grasping at his hair while he administered such unbelievable pleasure.

He froze.

It took me a moment to realize why. My hands weren't where I'd promised.

His eyes locked with mine. Amusement danced in the depths of his. "Hands, honey," he reminded me.

I quickly obeyed and had expected him to go back to the task at hand. But Brian had left the main highway and was now on the scenic route down my thighs. I growled in frustration over being so close. "You're tormenting me."

He chuckled. "Mm, I am. Are you going to keep your hands where I told you this time?" His lips made a path up my inner thigh, and it was all I could do not to grab his head and direct it where I needed him. His display of control gave me chills over my body.

"Yes, yes, my hands are in place." My voice cracked when his face dove back in, eager to get back to business. Between his fingers and tongue, it took about three seconds before my eyes rolled back in my head, and my climax consumed me. I'd never experienced anything as powerful in my life.

"That's it, honey. Let it go."

I did, but he wasn't letting up. I'd never experienced consecutive orgasms and wondered if it was possible to pass out from pleasure.

"Another one. Come in my mouth again, gorgeous."

"I can't—"

"Yes, you can. You will." He was unyielding with his assault, commanding I come again.

After the second orgasm, my body felt like it had been put through an entire workout. My lungs burned from breathing hard, and my arms ached from holding my hands tightly together above my head.

"I want you inside of me," my voice hoarsely pleaded as I watched him work his way up my stomach to my breasts.

"Patience, Sasha. I won't be denied worshipping your delicious body. I've waited too damn long. You're better than the fantasy." He sucked on one nipple and then teased the other, rolling it between his fingers. "Have you ever had someone fuck these gorgeous breasts of yours?"

I shook my head and closed my eyes, picturing him doing just that.

He tsked. "More for me, and I'm greedy. You should know that. I won't ever get enough of you."

The thrill of that statement shot through me. I was fascinated when he hovered over me, bringing my hands down next to my body.

"Wrap your legs around me."

As I complied, he slid another pillow under my hips before thrusting into me, filling me to the hilt in one motion. We both groaned in pleasure at the swift intrusion. His eyes met mine. All I could do was watch him watch me while he drove deeply with long, deliberate strokes.

"I—Oh, God—" My body, which I was convinced was out for the count, started to respond again.

He was unrelenting, pounding deep over and over, causing pure electricity to course through my body. His fingers entwined in my hair, and my hands ran over his back, feeling his taut muscles. He shifted his weight and pinned my hips down to the bed.

I was thankful now for the pillows that allowed some leverage for me to meet his thrusts. The rhythm of his heavy balls slapping the curve of my ass was driving me mad. With a flick of his fingers reaching between us to my engorged nub, I was done for. I careened over the edge, relishing the primal growl ripped from his throat in satisfaction. With one final plunge, he collapsed on top of me.

We both lay like that for a while before he eased out. He maneuvered to the side and pulled me on top of his chest.

"You all right?" he whispered.

I nodded dumbly.

"Tell me what you're thinking."

"Hmm, I'm not sure what to say." Did I want to admit that it had been life changing? How was I ever supposed to have sex with another man again? That thought left a crumb of fear that I didn't want to examine.

"For starters, was that better than *fine* and better than the vibrator?"

I pushed up on his chest and looked him in the eyes. "It was a lot better than *fine*, although the vibrator does have some advantages."

He arched a brow. "Such as?"

"For one, it could be ready for another round right now." I squealed when I was unceremoniously flipped onto my back, and he impaled me on one thrust. He obviously hadn't yet softened fully.

"Jesus, I was only kidding." I shifted my hips to accommodate his ever-growing size.

He nipped at my ear, thrusting again. "What were you saying?"

"I was saying how you're part machine and superior to the vibrator." I reached up, stroking down his shoulders and then his biceps.

"Look at me while you touch me. Don't close your eyes."

His demanding tone fueled my arousal. I gripped his muscular backside. We moved with eyes locked on one another for several strokes. Then he stilled.

"Turn over. Up on your knees." He pulled out, and moved the pillows in front of me. "Rest your elbows on the pillows and grab the slats of the headboard."

I moved as instructed, and he pulled my ass further into the air. Pushing back into me, he went deeper in this position than the previous one. I could already feel myself ready to climax yet again.

"Your ass is definitely my second favorite thing." His hands caressed, squeezed, and then gripped, holding me in position while he pumped hard and fast. Then his fingers reached around to ensure the orgasm came exactly when he wanted it to.

# CHAPTER ELEVEN

*T*he wedding ceremony was exquisite, and Haylee could not have been a more stunning bride. I never would have thought myself the type of girl who teared up at a wedding, but I could feel my eyes getting misty while watching the emotion between the happy couple. Brian sat beside me, and I found myself wishing he could touch me. He must've felt the same because his leg scooted closer to mine, connecting by the slightest fraction.

After Josh's speech about his beautiful bride at the reception, followed by his surprise, pulling her into his first public dance ever, there wasn't a dry eye in the crowd. When their dance ended, other couples started out onto the floor, and a warm hand tapped my shoulder.

"Dance with me?" Brian asked.

Smiling as he took me out onto the floor, I noticed he was careful to keep the touching appropriate for two friends.

"I didn't know you could dance," I remarked lightly, noticing he moved smoothly.

"I'm a man of many talents."

"Mm, I do look forward to exploring them all."

He missed a step, his eyes meeting mine. The heat evident in them made my breath hitch.

"I underestimated your ability to talk dirty. Your approach is subtle, yet I'm on the dance floor with a hard-on now." His voice was low and seductive.

A shiver lanced through my body. I hardly noticed I'd leaned against him until he exhaled heavily and reluctantly pulled back. How quickly my world had changed that the thought of having this particular effect on a man had me turned on.

We moved in silence until the end of the song. I could sense his hesitation in breaking the contact. I'd experienced the same feeling when he'd reluctantly left my room at three o'clock this morning.

"The drawback of a New Year's Eve wedding is that people will expect us to stay until midnight, won't they?"

The resignation in his voice made me laugh. "Afraid so, but I can kiss you without anyone thinking anything of it."

"Kissing you at midnight in front of people is not a good idea, but by twelve-thirty I expect to have you naked, wet, and beneath me."

My face heated. My thoughts were focused solely on that picture he'd painted in my mind when Colby came up to request a dance.

Brian's tight smile and his possessive gaze let me know how he felt about it. But it wasn't like dancing with another man at a wedding was against the rules we'd negotiated. I rolled my eyes internally. Since when was I a girl who was worried about obeying rules, anyhow?

"Why do I get the impression that I interrupted something?" Colby queried before leading me into the middle of the floor and showing off some dance moves of his own.

"I don't know what you're talking about." I hoped I wasn't blushing.

"In that case…" He turned me with ease and then dipped me dramatically.

I giggled when he brought me back up. Colby Singer might not be the kind of man I could ever date, but his boyish charm was irresistible. "Are you ready to become an uncle?" I asked, attempting to steer the conversation onto safer ground.

Colby's features softened. "Yes, definitely, and we found out the baby is a girl. Haylee told Josh on the dance floor."

I smiled. "That's really great."

"Can I say one thing about Brian, and then I'll leave it alone?"

Obviously, he wasn't waiting for my consent.

"He's like another older brother to me. Maybe it's the wedding or the whiskey making me sentimental, but I love him like one. Do me a favor and be good to him, all right?"

Huh. Maybe I'd underestimated Colby's depth. "Okay." I didn't acknowledge whether I knew what he was talking about or not.

"Was Kenzie upset about the other night?"

I decided to play dumb for her sake. "Uh, no. Why?"

He shrugged. "She's had this crush on me for years and seeing me at your door—Let's just say I try to be respectful when it comes to, uh, interest in other women around her."

"I think it's nice that you're sensitive to that, but she didn't mention anything to me." I wasn't going to reveal something that might embarrass her or overstep my bounds. I'd already done that enough during this trip by 'accidently' pouring wine all over Rebecca.

"Oh."

If I wasn't mistaken, he appeared disappointed by my response.

"Thanks for the dance, Colby." When the music ended, I made my way back to my chair. I was happy to take a seat and get off my feet. Gorgeous heels didn't always afford a lot of comfort, especially while dancing. I smiled at the fact that Colby was now leading McKenzie out onto the floor.

"It makes me crazy jealous to watch you dance with Colby," Brian's low voice whispered in my ear. He'd taken a seat beside me at the table.

I turned toward him and laughed. "You think I'd be interested in Colby?"

"Even if I wasn't in the picture, I'd hope the answer would be no."

I couldn't resist the urge to mess with him. "Because if we are taking stock of the room, I think Will would have the best chance." I tipped my head toward the handsome Aussie standing by the bar.

His expressive brown eyes immediately showed his temper. "Seriously?"

"You know I'm completely messing with you, right?"

"Jealousy isn't something I deal well with, and you doing it on purpose pisses me off. Why do you think I specifically said no dating other people?"

This alpha side of him was doing strange things to my libido, but the independent-woman-of-thirty-two years balked at the concept. "We're at a wedding where even the bride is dancing with other men. It's what you do."

He sighed. "I know, but that doesn't mean I have to like seeing another man's hands on you. It may be irrational, but now that I've been inside of you, I'm possessive as hell."

I sucked in my breath. How was it that this man could make me feel hot all over and infuriate me at the same time? I took a big gulp of my wine, knowing it was going to be a long night.

---

AN AMAZING DISPLAY of fireworks rang in the New Year and capped off the amazing wedding reception. It was late by the time we arrived via limo back at the resort. I had a hard time keeping my eyes off of Brian during the ride.

After entering in my room, I undressed, showered, and slipped nude between the cool sheets, where I waited for the knock on my door. My eyes were heavy, and with one last glimpse at the clock, I fell asleep.

I woke to a hot body sliding in behind me and hands skimming my side. "To find you naked like this is like Christmas morning," Brian murmured into the crook of my neck.

"What time is it?" I stretched, feeling his erection behind me and his hands now on my breasts.

"It's after two o'clock. Lots of family drama and no way of calling you without making it obvious."

"Please tell me I wasn't the cause this time."

He chuckled, moving his hands down to my stomach and breathing in my scent. "Nope, not you. But it was Rebecca, and if a man could hit a woman, she'd be out cold."

"Must have been bad. I can't imagine you wanting to hit anyone."

"Not me. Colby got into it with her over something she said. Then Benjamin got involved, then my mother. But I don't want to talk about that anymore." His fingers found me wet and wanting.

My body started to respond when he found my clit, but if I'd thought this would be a slow and sleepy lovemaking session, I was quickly proven wrong. Suddenly, the sheet was lifted and he stood up, sliding me to the edge of the bed by my ankles. Kneeling on the floor, he put my legs over his shoulders and dove straight into my trembling sex.

"Ahhh." I was fully awake now. But suddenly my legs were dropped and he'd stood up. "Bri—where are you going? Oh—"

He'd gone into the bathroom and flipped on the light, casting the bed in soft light and shadows.

"I need to see you." His voice was gruff as he assumed the same position.

I gasped in pleasure. Gone was the slow seduction and in its place a scorching hot urgency. His tongue separated my silken folds while a finger slipped inside of me. He sucked my hardened nub between his teeth, teasing it until I was practically clawing at the bed. His fingers moved in and out of my slick entrance while his talented mouth traveled south. I inhaled when his tongue speared into me while his thumb rubbed my clit with diabolical precision. "Come for me now."

The gentle command was all it took. My body went taut and then melted from the scorching wave of heat that rolled through me from head to toe. I came with an explosive cry.

He stood and thrust into me, prolonging my orgasm. My core muscles clenched, making me impossibly tight around him.

He paused for a moment, and when I met his gaze, the restraint was evident in his expression. "You okay?"

I nodded, and he pushed in further. I moaned with unfiltered pleasure.

"You feel incredible." The angle with my feet up by his head made this the deepest he'd ever been inside of me. His pace quickened as I accommodated his size.

My body started to respond to the spot he was hitting with focused intent. I'd always believed a purely intercourse-induced orgasm was a myth, so it took me completely off guard when the climax ripped through me. His groan echoed in the room before he stilled inside of me.

Kissing the inside of my right calf, he rubbed some circulation back into it before taking it off his shoulder and then did the same for the other. "I wish we didn't have to catch a flight in a few hours." He climbed into the bed, enveloping me into his warm body.

I buried my face in his neck and inhaled the masculine scent of him. "Me, either. And here I thought you we were going to do a sleepy making love thing."

"Are you disappointed?" He bit my shoulder lightly.

"Not at all. It was merely unexpected."

He kissed behind my ear, and I sighed with the delicious tingle it provided.

"I don't make love." He leaned back to meet my eyes.

"Ever?"

He chuckled. "Sure, when I was seventeen and sucked at it."

"As previously established, I think we all did."

"Does it offend you that I'd rather fuck you than make love?" His hands gripped my ass, and he pressed himself against me. He was already hard again.

"I think it turns me on more." I whimpered when he threw one of my legs over his and brought our hips in line with one another.

"It's more honest."

"Why's that?"

"Making love sort of implies that you're in love. I've always had a tough time understanding how you make love with a stranger or how you make love when you don't love that person."

"Mm." That made sense, but I was having a hard time concentrating when he rubbed against me.

"I don't want to make you too sore," he whispered, taking himself in his hand and stroking the tip of his cock against my tender cleft.

"I'll have two weeks to recover."

His smile made it obvious that I wouldn't get any sleep the rest of the night.

———

THE TRIP HOME was quite a bit less energetic than the flight down since most of the guests were hungover or had enjoyed little to no sleep. Myself included. The soreness between my legs reminded me why.

It was a different cast of characters this time around. For one, Kenzie had gone back to California on another plane. Meanwhile, instead of Charlotte, we were stopping in Virginia, where Brian would depart with the rest of his family. The final stop was New York.

Catherine and I chatted for a few minutes but then both lay our heads back for a nap until the first stop. I knew that I wouldn't get much of a chance to speak with Brian before he deplaned with his family. I wasn't prepared for the longing I already felt over his impending departure.

"Is Brian coming to New York?" Catherine inquired.

I could feel the plane start to descend. "No, he'll fly out from here back to his place in Charlotte." I tried to hide my disappointment.

She stood up smiling. "I'm going to go talk to Will. I have another fashion shoot I'd like to discuss with him."

"Mm," I replied, distracted and not realizing until Brian came back to sit down that Catherine had given him the opportunity to do so.

"Hi." He smiled.

I was unable to help the grin on my face. "Hi, yourself."

"Are you wishing I was heading up to New York with you?" His voice was husky.

I shrugged. "Maybe I'm looking forward to a good night's sleep."

He chuckled. "You've always been a terrible liar, Sasha."

I swallowed hard when his hand brushed against my leg. "I, uh, what are your plans for this weekend?" We'd only have two work days left in the week.

Amusement showed in his eyes. "Laundry, gym, probably

clean the house—although I'm keeping the sheets as is because they smell like you."

"Now you get to be tortured like I was."

"It'll add to the anticipation for seeing you the next weekend."

Right. Our two-week agreement. At the time we'd agreed to it, I'd thought it might be too much, and now I was lamenting time apart. "What's the plan for that?"

"We can discuss it in the next few days if that's okay? How are you feeling, by the way?" His tone was back to low and intimate.

"I'm reminded of you every time I cross my legs. You could say I'm a little sore."

Air hissed between his teeth, and his eyes dilated with desire. He opened his mouth to speak but then closed it again. Finally, after taking a breath, he whispered, "I meant if you were tired or hung over. Once again, you've caught me off guard." He shifted in his seat uncomfortably.

Oh, shit. I'd made him hard without even trying. Maybe I could do this dirty talk thing, after all, I thought, feeling my face heat. "Ah, sorry. I had the other on my mind and answered accordingly."

He shook his head. "Not helping. Change of subject, please."

"What would you recommend?" I grinned.

"Let's talk about the team you're going to put on the new pharmaceutical account. I'm kind of surprised you didn't bring it up the entire time we were in Tortola."

Huh, I couldn't believe it, either. I'd never been able to shut off work for more than a few hours at a time. And yet it hadn't crossed my mind in days.

# CHAPTER TWELVE

*T*he next day in the office was productive. I went through emails and got more information on Tryon Pharmaceuticals, the prospective client on which we'd start to focus in earnest next week. I planned on spending my weekend studying the board members and performing my research on everything from the company's website to its social media presence. Having the proper background information about a client could mean the difference between landing or failing to land the account.

It was unbelievable that I'd shut it off the way I had during the days I'd spent in Tortola. Brian had told me to wait, not that there was much I could have done while on vacation, but normally I would've been stressing about it.

I'd obviously been distracted by Mr. Keep-your-hands-above-your-head. Damn, I'd never before had sex on the brain like this. I sat back in my office chair and took a deep breath, resolving to put it out of my head. Maybe I needed this two week break to ensure I could keep it in perspective and still concentrate on my job. This was friends with benefits, not a relationship that should threaten to consume my every thought.

Since my assistant, Nancy, was out on vacation like most of the others until Monday, I answered my own phone today, even during work hours. When I saw Brian's number come up, I smiled. So much for putting the distraction aside.

"Sasha Brooks' office."

"Either Nancy is still on vacation, or you were so anxious to speak with me you picked up your own phone during the day," he teased.

"Nancy is still on vacation."

"If ever my ego needs a check, all I need to do is pick up the phone and call you."

"You asked." I grinned.

We chatted some about work, and then I recognized the sound of the announcements in the background. "Are you at the airport?"

"Sure am. My flight is boarding soon."

Why did I hope he'd tell me he was coming to New York? "Where are you off to?"

"I'm flying to Hong Kong."

"Oh, wow. For how long?"

"What if I told you I'll be traveling for the next two weeks and that it would be three before I saw you again?"

I hoped he was messing with me. "I'd say you're in violation of the rules and then ask if there's a punishment for that sort of thing."

I was rewarded with his intake of breath. "You're convinced to get me hard every time I get on a damn plane, aren't you?"

I laughed and then got a little nervous. "Uh, I wasn't serious. About the punishment thing. You said you weren't into that, right?"

Now it was his turn to laugh. "You dish it out and then start to get worried about it being taken literally?"

I was glad he couldn't see my face. So I was a lot of false

bravado followed up by a quick over analysis of everything. "You know I hate when you avoid the question. It makes me overthink it even more."

"I know. And the answer is that my idea of punishment involves tortured pleasure, not pain. I already told you I'm not into that sort of thing."

I was relieved to have the confirmation again. "When are you truly coming back?"

"I'll be back next Friday evening. I could either fly into Charlotte and meet you there or come back through New York and spend the weekend."

It wouldn't be fair to ask him to come to New York straight off a week-long trip overseas. "I'll meet you down there. But you'll be jet lagged. Are you certain you'll want to get together that weekend?"

"Two weeks is the max. With the time difference, I may not get a chance to speak with you a lot over the next few days, but I'll be thinking of you."

Smiling, I returned the sentiment. "Same here. Let me know your flight information, and I'll try to make mine come in at the same time."

"Okay, and Sasha?"

"Mm."

"Don't bother to pack a lot of clothes for the weekend."

And with that parting shot, he destined me to be sidetracked for the entire week.

---

THROWING myself into work during the next few days made it easier to avoid thinking of Brian or our upcoming weekend plans. I assembled my team on the Tryon Pharmaceuticals account and started the strategy meetings. We'd have a mock done and ready to present to Brian by the end of the following week.

By Thursday night the boards were done, and I felt confident enough to take off tomorrow after work for my flight down to Charlotte. I was busy packing my suitcase in my bedroom when my phone rang.

"Hello," I answered.

"Hello back. How are you?" Brian's sexy voice asked.

"Good. How is Hong Kong?"

"It's all right, but I'd rather be there."

"It's been less than two weeks." I was defensive, and couldn't help it. The thought of missing one another wasn't one with which I was entirely comfortable with, especially when we used to be content to go for days without talking.

"It feels like longer. What are you wearing?"

I couldn't help it; I burst out laughing.

"Honey, you're kind of deflating the ego here," he said dryly.

I realized he was probably serious. "I can't help it. The way you asked was like an infomercial for phone sex."

"That's a no to it, then?"

"I need to ask you something first." I couldn't help my curiosity.

"Go ahead."

"Have you ever done it before?"

He chuckled. "No, I've never done phone sex before. Have you?"

"Given my inability to purposefully talk dirty, what do you think?" I enjoyed the sound of his laughter on the other side.

"It's a perfect time to work on that. Matter of fact, I'm willing to do most of the talking."

I was already turned on, simply thinking about it. "Uh, how does this work?"

"I want you to strip down naked and get into bed. Put your phone on speaker."

I could hear him sipping something. "Talk to me while I undress. What are you drinking?"

"Orange juice with breakfast. I'm packed and waiting on the car to take me to the airport. In the meantime, I'm staring out the window, looking out at the city and anxious to get on the plane so I can bury myself deep inside of you all weekend long. Now tell me what you're doing?"

"I'm stepping out of my thong and climbing into my bed, thinking about seeing you in less than twenty-four hours."

"Twenty-three hours, thirty-six minutes and fifteen seconds, but who's counting?"

That certainly made me smile. "I'm all packed. Leaving from the office tomorrow afternoon."

"Good. Do you have your vibrator in the drawer next to your bed?"

"How do you know that's where I keep it?"

"It's a reasonable place."

"Mm hm." I brought it out and turned it on for the sound effect.

"I'm jealous of that thing. Turn it off for a minute. I want to get you ready for it first."

I complied, anxious for his next instruction.

"Now I want you to move your hand down and touch yourself. Are you wet for me?"

"Drenched."

He sucked in a breath. "Christ, I thought you said you weren't good at this."

"I didn't say I wasn't good at it. I just said I hadn't done it before. Plus if I can't turn you on while I do it, what's the point?"

"I'm so hard it hurts."

"Maybe I need you in your bed when we do this. I have to admit the thought of you touching yourself while I do the same is a big turn-on."

Silence.

"Are you there?" I asked.

"Yeah, I'm here, taking off my clothes, getting back in my bed. We only have twenty minutes before my car arrives, though."

"Ooh, I like this a lot."

"I need you to touch yourself. Tell me how you feel."

I lay back on my pillows, dipping my hand down and closing my eyes.

"Say something." He definitely had the voice for phone sex.

I licked my lips and let myself relax. "I'm thinking of you."

"And what am I doing?"

"You're licking me, down there." I blushed when he chuckled at my lack of description.

"All right. How about I'm burying my face into your sweet, delectable pussy? Then what?"

I swallowed hard. "And I'm wet, really wet, and I can feel your thumb rubbing my clit."

"Tell me more."

The desire in his voice spurred me on past my comfort zone and into new territory. I wanted to hear him groan my name in pleasure. "Your fingers are inside of me, and I'm clenching them."

"Any chance I can talk you into FaceTime?"

"Baby steps." I wasn't confident I'd ever get there, but then again, I'd never imagined doing this, either.

"Fair enough. What am I doing now?"

"You're rubbing and sucking, and I can feel your hot breath on me."

"You'd feel my beard stubble from the day past tickling up against your sensitive thighs and then my tongue licking your slit. You'd be so turned on that you'd push my head further into your pussy, fisting my hair and grinding your hips against my mouth."

146

I wouldn't need the vibrator. My fingers rubbed; I was frantic to reach my orgasm. "I'm going to come—"

"Me, too Sash," he groaned.

I was inflamed with the knowledge that I had done that to him. I let myself go, climaxing for the very first time with my own hand.

After a couple minutes of listening to one another breathe over the line, I broke the silence. "Are you there?"

"Uh huh. I'm not sure what I expected, but I didn't think it would be quite that fast." He sounded slightly self-conscious.

"It's a good thing it was because I'm completely exhausted now. And although you haven't asked, that's the first time I've been able to do that without, uh, battery-operated assistance."

"Great. I'm hard again."

I laughed. "At least you're not getting on the plane with it this time."

---

UPON LANDING in Charlotte on Friday evening, I was anxious to see Brian, but in a good way. It felt strange to associate the word *good* with *anxious*, but here I was, excited to spend the weekend with him. Turning on my phone as I deplaned, I read the message from him.

*"Call me when you get in. I'm stuck in DC."*

I dialed his number, and he picked up on the first ring.

"Hey. My connecting flight is delayed. They're saying we'll leave in another thirty minutes, but if it's much longer than that, I may rent a car and drive it." He sounded tired.

"How long of a drive is that?"

"Like six hours. Hopefully, we'll be boarding soon, though. I have a key to my house hidden in the back yard. The gate is open, and it's in the flower pot to the right, in one of those fake rocks. I can call a car service to take you."

"No, no, it's not necessary. I'll either rent a car or take a taxi."

"I'm sorry about this," he apologized miserably.

"It's not your fault. And it'll give me time to rummage through your drawers and see what kind of secrets you have in your house." Although I never would do so, I did wonder if he had a secret stash of sex toys.

"You'll be disappointed, I assure you, but at least the cleaning lady should've come. I'll let you know once I'm on my way from the airport."

"Do you want me to pick you up?"

"No, I prefer you naked in my bed, waiting for me."

---

AFTER ARRIVING at Brian's house, I parked the rental car and tromped around to the back yard to retrieve the key. He'd texted he was boarding a few minutes ago, which meant that he should arrive in less than two hours.

Unlocking the door, I let myself in and hauled my suitcase up to the master bedroom. I took a shower and headed down to his kitchen. I wasn't surprised that it was bare bones in the food department. Since the holidays, he'd hardly had a chance to spend any time here. I helped myself to a bottle of water and the apple from my purse and then walked down to the basement. It took a few minutes to figure out the remote, but finally I was able to flip the massive television on.

I must have dozed off, losing all track of time. When I opened my eyes, I was shocked to see that more than two hours had passed. Turning off the television quickly, I hit the top step at the same time I heard the front door open. I walked down the hall to greet him, but I didn't even have a chance to say hello before he was on me, and my clothes were being dragged off.

His lips were demanding, and his tongue worked mine with an aggressiveness that ignited my arousal.

"Have a good flight?" I asked, smiling.

"No, it didn't go by fast enough. God, I need to be inside of you." He frantically fumbled with my leggings while I rid him of his belt. He backed me into the living room, making it only as far as the sofa before he thrust inside of me.

I gulped at his primal groan of pleasure, feeling the same.

He stopped for a moment and grasped my face between his hands. "Hi." He grinned.

I giggled, moving my hips and enjoying the sweetness of his thumb tracing my bottom lip. "Hi, yourself. Glad to be home?" He drove into me and I arched my head back in pleasure.

"I've been hard for the last two hours, forty minutes and thirty seconds, so yes."

My nails raked his back. "Turns out you've come to the right place."

I had barely gotten the last word out before he started to pump in earnest, gripping my backside and pinning me to him. He tilted my pelvis up, and suddenly my orgasm exploded through me. I trembled from the power of it, and then moaned in satisfaction, when his climax followed a minute later.

---

"I LIKE YOU IN MY BED," Brian murmured, running his hands lazily over my backside while we lay curled up together in the wee hours of the morning.

"I'd dozed off downstairs but meant to be up here waiting."

He kissed me and, as was his habit, nibbled on my lower lip. "I don't think it would've mattered, I was going to jump on you either way. I'm normally a bit more in control, but you have me all out of sorts."

"I like having you out of sorts."

He cocked his head and studied me. "Why's that?"

I shrugged. "Because you've had me out of sorts since the night you kissed me after our drinks when you said that we needed *rules*." I did air quotes and watched him smile.

# CHAPTER THIRTEEN

*I* woke up alone in bed. Alone and sore. Not a bad sore, just a very thorough reminder of the fact that Brian had woken me in the middle of the night for another round. After taking a quick shower, I stepped into the bedroom and smiled at the silk robe laid out for me on the end of the bed. After donning it and some light makeup, I went downstairs where I could smell breakfast cooking.

"Hungry?" Brian grinned.

"I could eat. You cook?" I was surprised.

He came toward me in low-slung flannel bottoms and nothing else. "I do, indeed. How do you like your eggs?"

"Over hard."

He quirked a brow, and we both laughed. "Here's coffee. One sugar and some milk for you." He put a big steaming mug in front of me at the breakfast table and went back to the stove.

Of course he would know how I take my coffee. "How do you remember these things?" I liked watching him move comfortably about his kitchen. This domestic side of him was sexy.

He shrugged. "I don't know. I remember little details for clients, and it makes them feel special."

"Girls, too," I muttered.

He came over to where I was sitting and smirked. "I've never remembered what girls want. Only you. Well, and Juliette, but that doesn't technically count. She's been my assistant for over eight years, and after she had the baby and was up nights, you'd best believe I had her coffee ready for her in the morning. She's not a morning person, FYI."

Laughing, I pictured it all too well. I inhaled the lovely scent of my coffee and murmured, "God, how I love you." I opened my eyes, and it took me a moment to realize he was staring at me, stunned. "I meant the coffee. Sorry."

A wry smile played upon his lips and he went back into the kitchen.

I let out a breath. I truly had meant the coffee, but now that we were sleeping together, it was clear that the L word was off limits, even casually. "Isn't this the point where you tell me the next rule is not to fall in love or mention an actual relationship?"

He regarded me thoughtfully from the stove and shook his head. "Maybe with other women, but with you, I don't think I need to worry about that."

I tried not to let that statement bother me. So what if I'd never been in love? I'm sure plenty of women my age hadn't. Yeah, right.

"And do I need to worry about you?" I tested, sipping my coffee calmly.

He considered my words and then gave me the typical nothing-bothers-me, Brian smug look. "What do you think?"

I shrugged, wondering if this was his general viewpoint on relationships or just regarding ours in particular. "I'm not sure. Two weeks ago I would have said that there was no way you were going to give me the best fucking orgasm of my life. Maybe I don't know you at all."

"Don't say *fuck* again unless you want me to put you up on this counter and demonstrate it thoroughly while your eggs get cold. And you do know me. You simply weren't aware of this side of me."

"Can I ask you something?"

He nodded.

"Have you ever been in love?"

He contemplated before answering. "Honestly, maybe once, but I don't know for sure, which probably means no. With love, you should be certain, right?"

"You're probably asking the wrong person." I'd never spoken the words romantically nor had I heard them in return.

"Which means you haven't, not even in high school or college?"

Normally I broke things off before they got serious. I'd had one boyfriend tell me he felt like I never relaxed with him. He hadn't been wrong. "No, I never wanted the pressure. A relationship is a lot of effort, and when I'm putting so much into my job, I guess I didn't need the extra stress." Trying to hide my anxiety disorder while being in a committed relationship would have been impossible. No, thank you.

"I completely get that." He dished up my eggs, along with bacon, and placed them in front of me. Then he took the seat across from me at the table.

"So who was the maybe?" I wasn't sure I wanted to know, but I couldn't hide the curiosity.

He looked at me funny and finished chewing. "A girl here in Charlotte a long time ago. She moved away, and I never told her how I felt. End of story."

Why was I jealous to hear that? "You didn't keep in touch?"

"Come on. I can't manage a local relationship, let alone one that's long distance."

At least that was a relief. "I think long distance might be easier. You wouldn't get into the rut of everyday stuff. Even if I did believe there was such a thing as a happily ever after, the 'what's for dinner, how was your day, did the DVR record our shows' is definitely not appealing." I made a face, horrified at the thought.

He grinned. "You don't believe in the fairy tale ending?"

"Uh, no. And I think I'd fucking shoot myself before getting into the mundane everyday stuff where I'm arguing about who left the toilet seat up." I took another bite and saw his eyes narrow. Oh, shit, I'd said the F-word again.

"Up onto the countertop you go." He was lifting me onto the cold black granite before I could protest. Not that there would have been much of one.

---

"I'M RUNNING to the grocery store as I have no food in the house. Do you want to come with?" Brian asked, framing the door of the master bath. He wore blue jeans and a gray pullover, making him look younger than his thirty-three years. I realized I didn't often see him dressed casually. After we'd finished our countertop adventure and a cold breakfast, we'd topped it off with a nice, long, steamy shower together. The smirk on his face told me he was still thinking about it.

I was in the middle of doing my make-up. "Sure. Give me ten minutes, and I'll be right down."

He winked and turned around, offering up a nice view of his backside framed in jeans. His ass looked spectacular encased in denim. Of course, having seen it in the shower twenty minutes ago could be making me hyper aware of it at the moment. It was as though someone had taken the plastic film off of my eyes, and I could see him in a totally different light now.

After I walked downstairs, I found him in the front entryway.

He was looking outside at my rental car in the driveway. "How about we swing by the airport, and you can turn in the car?

I can drop you off tomorrow myself. It's only a fifteen-minute drive."

"Uh—" I know his plan sounded logical, but I had some trepidation about being car-less.

He must have sensed it because he took my hand and pulled me into an embrace. "Too practical for you?" He pinned me against the foyer wall and tilted his head down for a quick kiss.

"No, but I wondered if we'd end up wanting to kill one another, and I would overstay my visit, if I'm being perfectly honest." It wasn't like I wanted to fight with Brian, but during the last year it seemed all we did was push one another's buttons. On the other hand, maybe he'd been onto something about relieving the tension with sex because we hadn't done as much arguing lately.

"Hmm. One, you wouldn't overstay. I like having you here. And two, I don't think we've ever gotten along as well."

"All right, but I need to do something before we take care of the car." I got the satisfaction of his confused expression when I dropped to my knees and unfastened his jeans in a hurry, freeing him. Quickly, I took him between my lips.

"Christ, I—"

Taking his hardening length to the back of my throat, I swirled my tongue around his velvety softness. He was rock hard in all of four seconds. My fingers curled around his base and I licked along the seam, loving the sound of his groan. Why we hadn't gotten around to this earlier, I didn't know, but I was determined to make this the best blow job he'd ever received. I worked his impressive erection with my hand, pumping it in a rhythm, then went lower to take each of his balls in my mouth, paying attention to them one at a time.

"Take off your clothes; we can do this together," he protested, trying to pull me up.

I shook my head, gripping his ass and taking him deeper. Hollowing out my cheeks, I sucked harder, increasing the pace.

Looking up at him through my lashes, I enjoyed the sheer pleasure reflected on his face. The fact that he had his hands entwined in my hair, almost as if trying to restrain himself from pushing my head into him, made me even crazier for him. One of my hands moved to cradle his balls while the other one pumped his shaft in cadence with my wet mouth.

"Stop now, or I'm going to come."

I took him further into my throat, almost to the point of gagging, but I was suddenly frantic to make him go over the edge like he'd taken me so many times. I needed to taste him. His body shuddered, and the thick liquid hit the back of my throat. I greedily swallowed all of it, then licked the tip for the last drop.

"Get on the couch," he demanded shakily.

I shook my head. "No can do. I have a rental car to return. I'm Hertz, by the way. Take a few minutes and then meet me there." I grabbed my purse, walked out the door, and could hear his irritated shout after me. I had in fact warned him I wasn't going to be very good at being told what to do.

---

RETURNING the car was fast and painless. Afterward, I stood on the curb, checking email on my phone while waiting for Brian.

When he pulled up, I slid into the passenger seat. I could tell immediately that he was angry by the set of his jaw and the fact that he would only look straight ahead.

"Are you actually mad because I gave you a blow job in the hallway?" I turned toward him, watching his features while he concentrated on the road.

"You know that's not why I'm angry," he finally said.

"You said spontaneity was an option. Plus I told you I wasn't always going to be all right with taking orders. So if this kind of thing pisses you off, maybe you should take me back to the airport." I hadn't left anything I absolutely needed at Brian's place and could be back on a plane within an hour.

That certainly got his attention. He turned and glared. "We're going back to the house."

"I thought we were heading to the grocery store."

"We have unfinished business. And I'm pissed off, which invokes rule number one."

"Tell me why you're angry. Any other man would have been happy to receive a blow job in the hallway."

"And I'm certain many a man has done that with you, Sasha, but I'm not that guy."

His insult immediately ignited my temper. "And is that what is making you angry? To know that you're not the first guy I've given a blow job to?"

His jaw ticked and my stomach tightened when we pulled into his driveway. He got out of the car, not bothering to wait for me.

Fine, let *him* wait. I sat in the passenger seat, watching him open the front door and then look back, obviously furious that I wasn't following.

I'd gotten a glimpse of *Angry Brian* on the beach, but it was such an anomaly to witness full-blown pissed-off-Brian that I could only sit there, stunned. When he stalked back to the car and opened my door, I found myself shamelessly turned on by it.

"Get out of the damn car." He took my arm firmly and escorted me inside the house.

I was aware that if I'd wanted to, I could've pulled out of his grasp. But I was far too curious to see where this was heading to draw away. Even with this rare side of him on display, I'd known Brian long enough that I didn't feel one ounce of distress that he'd ever get too angry.

After the front door closed, I did pull my arm out of his grasp. "You're being ridiculous—"

"Stop talking. Just stop. First we fuck, then we'll fight."

Swallowing hard, I instantly became wet at his suggestion. "Fine," I fired back, purposefully using that word. Defiantly, I pulled off my sweater while kicking off my boots.

He watched for a moment and then quickly took off his shoes and yanked down his jeans.

I did the same. His eyes went dark when I took off my bra and slowly dropped my panties.

"You're so unbelievably beautiful," he whispered, catching me off guard with the compliment. Then he kicked off his boxers and took my hand to lead me upstairs to his bedroom.

"Lie in the middle of the bed," he ordered and then disappeared into his walk-in closet.

I trembled with anticipation.

When he walked back toward the bed, he narrowed his eyes. "Are you cold?"

"No."

He knelt on the mattress straddling me and pulled my hands up to the headboard, tying them there securely with a silken tie. Next, he wove longer scarves to the footboard and secured my ankles. Finally, he put a strip of silk over my eyes.

"I'm not sure I want a blindfold when we're doing angry sex."

He exhaled heavily, and then his body covered mine, hard and strong. His lips sealed over mine. They weren't gentle but neither were they punishing. It was as if he was trying to pour out his feelings in that kiss, and then he was down, down. Holy wow, his mouth was completely devouring my center.

"I'll never get enough of your sweet cunt."

I'd never heard that word in the bedroom before, but the way he said it had been hot instead of crude. "You said we'd—Oh—"

His tongue flicked over my clit while his fingers kept me open for his assault. My hips moved of their own volition, arching up into his mouth. His hands held me still, not allowing my movement. While he gripped my ass, holding me up at an angle, his tongue plunged into me. My hypersensitive nub was tortured by his thumb drawing circles. My body strained against the ties as my release hit me hard and fast. I screamed his name with the pleasure that overwhelmed me.

"And now we'll fuck, but first I needed to level the playing field."

Ah, I was starting to understand. But before I could verbalize anything, my arms and legs were untied. I was unceremoniously being turned over and put onto my knees with my ass up into the air.

"Your ass is perfect." His hands rubbed and squeezed the cheeks.

I wiggled, trying to find his body by moving back.

"Not yet," he teased.

His weight departed, and I listened for him to come back. It didn't take long before his heat returned behind me, but this time his hands were massaging some kind of oil over my backside. Before I could ask him what it was, he thrust deep inside of me.

He held himself to the hilt, and his fingers massaged my each cheek as well as my lower back. My skin, where touched, started to heat up with a slight tingle. Those same magic fingers reached around, rubbing over my sensitized clit. I moved my hips back, practically pleading for him to move.

"I need—" I didn't know what I needed.

"Patience, honey," he purred. His finger gently grazed my previously forbidden entrance.

"Brian, I—"

He leaned over me and kissed my lower back. "Don't worry, not yet. But I will have your ass. We'll work you into it. Just think of being filled both ways."

It was too much. I tried to push back into him to end the sweet torture.

He grabbed my hips and started to move. His thrusts were measured, delivering pleasure with each stroke. His finger circled my pucker and when it slid slowly inside, I came harder than I ever had before. He grunted and buried himself on one final push, spilling into me.

He removed the blindfold and pulled out. I winced at the loss of contact, but he quickly tucked me into his chest. I enjoyed the warmth of his nude body pressed against mine.

"Here," he offered, grabbing one of the blankets and pulling it up over us.

"Thanks," I mumbled, feeling sleepy.

His breathing evened out, the rise and fall of his chest slowing. "I didn't like your refusal to let me pleasure you after you sucked me off in the hall."

Not only was I not used to this way of talking, I wasn't accustomed to a man who got more pleasure from giving than receiving. "Considering we're at, like, a two-to-one ratio for orgasms, I don't know why. You get pleasure from pleasing me, I get it, but the same goes. I simply wanted to surprise and indulge you, too."

He chuckled and rubbed my back. "You did surprise me, and you definitely pleased me. Those lips of yours are the most erotic fantasy ever."

"Are they still your favorite thing, with my ass being second?"

"They are. Although I'm also a big fan of your tight pussy."

My cheeks flamed with heat.

He pulled away to look down at my face. "I love that I can make you blush."

"Hmm, let's get back to what pissed you off. I think you'll need to deal with sometimes taking pleasure without giving it."

"Meaning?"

"Meaning I might want to do that again sometime. Maybe in your car while you're driving or something." Had I really said that? Give Ms. Never-do-anything-spontaneous a feel for great sex, and suddenly I was thinking up all sorts of adventurous things.

"The thought of your mouth on me while I drive ..." He shivered. "That's definitely going up there on the bucket list."

Huh, evidently I needed a bucket list now, too. "Bri, the point is that I'm not keeping a tally of orgasms. I don't think you should see it as me owing or you owing."

"Okay, upon occasion I can handle it, but only when I know I can devour your sweet pu—"

I held a finger to his lips and shook my head. "I get it."

He chuckled. "You don't like it when I talk dirty?"

I shrugged. "If I'm being honest, it turns me on when you do it, but I'm not sure words like that will ever come out of my mouth."

"I like that. You're adorable when you turn pink. And I think I get why ex-boyfriend Eric wanted to meet up with you if you were giving blow jobs like that in high school."

"Is that a way of trying to ask me if I do that with every guy?"

"I keep telling myself that I don't want to know."

"Normally I'm not a fan of swallowing, let alone having a man come in my mouth."

"Why did you with me?"

"You make me feel like you'd do anything to please me sexually. Plus you didn't expect it. I liked that you obviously didn't think I would."

"You don't have to swallow again if you didn't like it."

I propped up and looked him in the eyes. "I was so crazy for the taste of you that I couldn't get enough. I enjoyed it, but I did brush my teeth when I turned in the car."

He laughed and kissed me on the nose. "We need to go to the store, but maybe we could go out for a late lunch first."

"Are you okay with going out in public? I thought about it on my way to the rental car return. What if someone we know sees us?"

He shrugged, getting out of the bed and leading me by the hand into the bathroom. "We used to meet up for dinner all the time and I don't care enough about someone seeing us. We could refrain from kissing and touching in public if you want, though."

"Are you able to?" I challenged.

He turned on the shower, letting the water get hot and then pulled me in, shutting the door. "I'm already having an issue with it. Let's take a quick shower before we end up spending the whole day here and starving to death."

I giggled at the image. Death by sex.

By the time we actually got out of the house, it was late. We drove straight to the restaurant for a lunch. I was smiling, and we were playful getting out of the car. Then it hit me: Brian's first rule had in fact resolved the issue a hell of a lot faster than arguing about it.

His wink made me realize I didn't have to admit it. It was as though he already knew what I'd been thinking.

# CHAPTER FOURTEEN

*A*fter getting lunch on Saturday and stocking up on food, we didn't leave the house again for the remainder of the weekend. Matter of fact, we hadn't bothered with much in the way of clothing, either. Now on Sunday afternoon, it felt strange to have Brian drop me off at the airport.

Curbside, he leaned across the car, cupped the back of my head, and kissed me like he already missed me. His thumb rubbed my bottom lip while his forehead rested against mine. "Safe flight, okay?" His voice was gruff, and there was longing reflected in his eyes.

"I'll see you again in two weeks?"

"What if I told you it would be sooner?"

My heart beat faster since I knew I'd have had a hard time waiting another two weeks before seeing him again. "How soon?"

"We both need to meet with Josh on Thursday before your mock pitch on Friday. I figured I'd do that in person rather than via video."

"And you're only mentioning this now? Does this meeting have the potential to change the pitch?"

He shook his head. "I told him last week who was on your team. There won't be any changes to that, and the mock remains set for Friday. The meeting with Josh is to discuss other details, maybe go over the presentation itself. This is a big account, and he wants us all on the same page."

"Same page how?" I was caught off guard, and that put me on edge.

"Ensuring that every detail is thought of."

He was being vague and I didn't like it. "To include my involvement?"

His eyes softened. "Of course not. You're the lead, Sasha. No one does a pitch better than you do."

I was placated with his compliment. "Okay. I guess I'll see you later this week, then."

He kissed me one last time. "Will you text me when you get in?"

"Sure." I was a grown woman who traveled frequently and independently, yet the thought of having someone ask for a check-in, like my father always requested, sent a warm feeling through me.

---

It was Thursday afternoon and my meeting with Josh was set for two o'clock. I sat at my desk pouring over the pitch deck one last time. Of course I'd already emailed a copy to Josh yesterday as a pre-read, but that didn't keep me from searching for ways to improve it. I'd half expected Brian to come by last night, but he hadn't. I reasoned it was just as well. It might be easier if we kept things separate considering our appointment later today.

It would be our first professional meeting since starting our sexual arrangement, and I was trying to quell my anxieties. I didn't want to walk into Josh's office, look at Brian, and blush. The thought of making our relationship obvious in front of the owner of the company was unnerving at best. It didn't help that, aside from texting him on Sunday night when I arrived home, I hadn't spoken with him this week. We'd emailed a couple work-related items, but hadn't held a conversation.

Of course I could have called him just as easily as he could have called me. My stomach growled reminding me it was lunch time. It was tempting to order something in, but I knew the fresh air would do me good. I spent enough time at my desk as it was. I was about to step out when my assistant, Nancy, buzzed in.

"Sasha, Brian Carpenter is here for you."

"Uh, send him in. Thank you, Nancy." My pulse raced.

"Good luck to your son with his basketball tournament this weekend, Nancy," Brian chatted with her while coming through my door.

I narrowed my eyes when the door shut. How the hell did he know these things? "You make me look bad when you remember shit like that," I mumbled.

He laughed, taking a seat across from my desk. "What can I say? It's a gift. How's the mock coming along?"

I was relieved that there wasn't the awkwardness I'd been expecting. Matter of fact, we were starting out much like we had previous to the change in our relationship. "It's good."

"Great."

My relief had come too soon. Dead space and awkwardness.

Finally, I broke the ice. "How was your week? We didn't talk, so…"

He arched a brow. "The phone works both ways, and I knew you'd be busy this week preparing."

He was right. I had been working late nights. "When did you fly in?"

He raised a brow. "This morning. Why? Would you rather I'd come in last night?"

"If I said it didn't matter, would you believe me?"

He leaned forward. "I wouldn't. But I figured today might be uncomfortable enough without the thought of me having been inside of you first thing this morning on your mind."

My cheeks heated. "Well, thanks for not making it uncomfortable, Bri."

His eyes lit up with amusement. "Do you want to get some lunch and then head over to Josh's office?"

I stood up, grabbing my coat and laptop. "Lunch would be good."

Sharing a meal with Brian before a meeting was typical. It was what we'd done a thousand times before. So why was I worked up and wanting to rip off his clothes because of the simple touch of his hand on the small of my back? Swallowing hard, I squared my shoulders and smiled toward Nancy while letting her know where we'd be.

---

Lunch had proven that Brian was able to remain on good behavior and keep the two worlds separate, at least for a couple of hours. I'd worried about how I'd be able to balance the personal and professional when we were working, especially when we were alone. But over lunch we chatted about the mock pitch, Juliette, and other office things, allowing me finally to relax.

Upon arriving at Josh's office across town, the headquarters for Gamble Enterprises, we took his private elevator to the penthouse and were shown right into his spacious office. As I mused that the last time I'd seen Josh was at his wedding, I realized that I was surrounded by personal and professional worlds colliding on multiple levels.

"Sasha, nice to see you. Brian, how was the flight up?" Josh welcomed.

We made small talk and then got down to business. I'd emailed Josh the mock pitch deck ahead of time and was prepared to take notes. Taking out my laptop, I assumed he'd have some changes.

"I read through your presentation and have to say it's solid. I don't have any changes at this point," Josh commented.

I was somewhat surprised. "Okay. Thank you."

If he didn't have any changes to my pitch deck, then what did he want to talk about? My confusion turned to trepidation quickly when he and Brian shared a look. Sighing, I decided to state the obvious. "I'm assuming by the glance you two just shared that there's something you're reluctant to discuss with me?"

Josh nodded, amusement flashing in his eyes. "Yes, specifically I want to talk to you about Vanessa, the client contact for Tryon. I'm assuming Brian provided you a brief overview?"

"He mentioned she's difficult," I returned.

"That's putting it mildly. One of my colleagues worked with her at a previous job. He gave me a little background or, for lack of a better term, a 'warning' about her."

Terrific. Because I was such a people person as it was. "Okay, what do I need to know?"

"I'm told you have Charlie and Logan on the team presenting with you?"

"Yes, it's the three of us on the pitch. I plan on bringing Carly in to observe as well."

Josh threw another look toward Brian.

"It would be better if you left Carly out of this one," Brian suggested.

I narrowed my eyes. "It would be helpful to know why. It's common practice to bring a junior person to carry the boards and get a feel for what a pitch is like."

Both men appeared uncomfortable. Finally, Josh put it out there. "Vanessa is threatened by women. Especially younger women. I don't know what Carly looks like, but if she's like most younger ladies in the advertising industry, then she's attractive, and that could be an issue for her."

What. The. Hell? They weren't seriously discriminating who could be in this pitch based on looks. It wasn't in my nature to make this easy on them. "I take it that I'm not a threat with either my looks or my age, then?"

As predicted, neither man knew how to answer that question without insulting me. I'd be lying if I said I didn't enjoy their discomfort.

Brian finally decided to try his hand. "Look, Sasha. Like I said, you have this pitch. This is your client, and we both know that you're going to do a terrific job. But we need to give it the best chance we can, which may mean dictating who attends and what is worn."

I'd always understood that business came first. Hell, if they didn't want Carly there because Vanessa got her nose out of joint with a younger woman, fine. Advertising 101 dictated that the pitch was about the client, not about us. But I didn't like the direction this was heading. "Is this the point where you tell me how I should dress?"

Brian cleared his voice. "Actually, we hired a company to do that for us."

Josh handed us each a document. "This is an uncomfortable conversation, but I know that you're a professional, and our goal is the same, which is to win the business." His voice didn't leave any room for argument.

As much as it absolutely pained me to do so, I had to ask, "If you're that concerned about it and think that we may lose the account because I'm a woman, then why not pull me from it?"

Josh shook his head. "Because you're the best pitch person, hands down, and there's a board of directors who needs to be impressed, too. We hired a company that specializes in profiling and does the analysis regarding the best things to wear. It's all there on that paper. You aren't the only one, either. There are specifics on both Charlie and Logan, too. And the company confirmed it would be a good mix to have the all-male board more focused on you while Vanessa gets attention from Brian and the two other men on the team."

I skimmed the document that had everything from tie color to the type of clothes I should wear. My pride was stuck in my throat, but I'd learn to swallow it. This was business. "I'll look this over and ensure that Logan and Charlie have the specifics as well."

"Good. I know Charlie. He'll be good in the pitch. How's Logan?" Josh queried.

Looking up from the document, I was candid. "He's young, eager, and very attractive. He should do quite well with Vanessa." I glanced at both men and was rewarded with the flash of irritation in Brian's eyes before I turned my attention back to Josh.

"Will you be attending the mock pitch tomorrow?" I asked him.

"Yes, but via video conference as I'm heading up to Connecticut first thing in the morning. Haylee's last test will be over, and we're baby shopping this weekend." Josh's entire face lit up at the mention of his wife.

I wasn't as smooth with slipping from business to personal, especially since I was currently irritated with the document I was holding, but I was happy for them. "Uh, tell her hello."

"I will. I won't take up any more of your time. I'll see you tomorrow via video."

I nodded and rose to leave, surprised when Brian got up, too.

"I'll see you out. Be back up, Josh," he indicated and then walked quietly beside me to the elevator.

Once behind the closed elevator doors, he started the placating. "It's only business, Sasha, and this is a large account."

His tone reminded me of a kindergarten teacher who had endless patience and needed to explain that children couldn't always get their own way. But instead of having a calming effect, it irritated the hell out of me. "I get it, and I'll get over it."

"I have dinner plans with Josh this evening, but afterwards I can come by."

"I'm going to be working late on the mock." I started digging in my purse.

His jaw clenched. "Am I to assume that's a way of saying you don't want my company tonight?"

Finally finding what I was after, I pulled out my keys and peeled one off the ring. "That's not what I'm saying. Here, you can let yourself in." I handed him the key and witnessed the priceless look of shock on his face.

"You're giving me a key?" His tone was a mix of apprehension and astonishment.

"Don't get weird about it. It'll be late by the time I get there."

We hit the ground floor, and the elevator doors opened.

He swallowed. "I had thought maybe—You know what? Never mind."

He'd obviously assumed I'd be pissed off enough about the clothing specifications that I wouldn't want to see him later. Maybe having terrific sex was softening me. "Hmm. Yeah, well, sometimes I even surprise myself. See you later."

The sound of his chuckle followed me out the elevator doors.

---

I FINALLY STEPPED into my eighth-floor condo after ten o'clock that night. I'd sent my team home two hours before but had wanted to put the finishing touches on the presentation myself before calling it a night. Yes, it was only the dry-run tomorrow, but it didn't matter. I would still be one hundred percent prepared. It was hard to explain to most people, but anything else stressed me out. Therefore, there was no point in settling. I'd learned a long time ago that I could lie in bed sleepless, obsessing about outstanding tasks, or I could stay at work until I was satisfied.

The sound of the television came from my bedroom. I hadn't bothered to put one in my living room when I'd moved in because I only watched it on the weekends. My New York home was a one bedroom, one and one half bath that was all of eleven hundred square feet. The kitchen and living room were all one space. The bedroom and master bath were straight back.

I slipped off my heels and drew in a deep breath, taking stock of my feelings. Knowing that Brian was in my space as no other man had ever been and that he was waiting on me made me restless, but not in a bad way. When I walked into the bedroom, I saw him propped up against my queen-sized bed's headboard.

He smiled at me, pausing the television. "How was your day, honey?"

I laughed, knowing he was teasing, which was a nice way to avoid any weirdness. Obviously, this was new for both of us. "Productive. When did you get in?"

"About an hour ago. I pretty much had to babysit Josh to ensure he didn't hop on a plane and go up to Connecticut tonight. Haylee requested a night to herself in order to study for a final tomorrow while he's at his max time away from her. It's funny to see him so—I don't know—smitten."

I shrugged out of my suit jacket and crossed to my walk-in-closet. Having such a large one had been the selling point of this condo. "I bet. Does that mean he's planning to do less travel?" I unzipped my skirt and hung everything up.

"Yes. You noticed tomorrow is via video instead of in person. And he's tasked me with Hong Kong for the most part. I don't think he's building any more hotels anytime soon. He's nesting."

We both laughed, and I enjoyed the small talk.

I walked out in my bra and panties and observed his eyes rake over me from head to toe. "I'm going to take a quick shower, and then I'll be back out."

"Really quick, please." The huskiness in his voice let me know he was impatient to have me in the bed with him.

That made two of us.

After placing my hair in a shower cap, I'd barely gotten under the hot stream of water when Brian opened the glass shower door and stepped in behind me.

"Nice look," he chuckled, touching the plastic.

"I hadn't intended on you seeing me in it," I murmured, a little embarrassed.

"You're adorable." He turned me around and kissed me passionately. Pulling back, he sighed. "I couldn't wait any longer to touch you."

"Mm. Let me wash quickly. Then I can take off this ridiculous cap."

"I'll help." He proceeded to fill his hands with my shower gel. Inhaling the scent, he closed his eyes. "It smells like you. What is it?"

"Gardenia." My breath caught when his hands started down the sides of my neck and then down both arms.

"I'd always wondered." He reached around, soaping up my back and then proceeded up to my shoulders, massaging the entire way. His attention shifted to my breasts and then down to my stomach and hips. Down one leg and up the other. With another handful of soap, he massaged my sex.

He was an expert with his ministrations, and I sucked in a breath when his other hand slipped around to the back side and slid between my cheeks. I was quickly climbing toward orgasm and decided to return the favor by taking his hard length into my hands. I was rewarded with a low groan.

"Oh, no, you don't. I have plans. Let's get you rinsed." He moved out of the way and then out of the shower, waiting for me with my towel.

After rinsing quickly, I turned off the water, removed my shower cap, and stepped out.

He smirked, wrapping me up in my fluffy towel. "What if I wanted you to keep that on?"

"Not happening." I was unprepared for him to pick me up and take me into my bedroom where he set me down gently on the bed.

"On your knees, gorgeous."

Over my shoulder, I watched him take something out of his suitcase.

"We're going to play." His strong hands massaged my lower back and then focused on my backside. "This will feel strange at first, but it'll soon feel good, I promise."

I heard the sound of lubricant and then something hard slid into my back entrance, then stopped.

"This is an anal plug. You'll get used to it, honey."

The feeling was strange but not unpleasant. His fingers rubbed between my lips and then slid into my heat, finding the slick evidence of my desire.

"You're so aroused. I knew I'd find your vibrator in your drawer next to the bed, and since we didn't get to it the other night, we're going to use it now."

Oh, God, I couldn't believe he had it in his hand. The tip teased my wet entrance and then slid home. A flick of his fingers turned it on and the vibration started. I was in sensation overload.

"Scoot up. I want you to grab the top of the headboard," he instructed.

I was kneeling at an angle; my hands clutching the bedframe with my knees back a foot. Suddenly I realized his tongue was on my clit. He'd slid between my legs with his face literally between my thighs and his hands on my ass pressing me into him.

"Brian, I—" I didn't have the ability to form complete sentences.

"Ride my mouth, honey," he demanded, rocking me harder,

grinding me into his face.

The unbelievable sensation created by his mouth was overwhelming, especially considering the other two items in play. While one hand worked the vibrator in and out, his tongue and lips were unyielding. My entire body shuddered, and then I was exploding like I never had before. But it wasn't enough. He pushed me further, never satisfied with only one. My thighs trembled from the pleasure, my nails dug into the wood of the headboard. I screamed his name and lost all control, climaxing spectacularly against his face for a second time. He dragged it out, leisurely licking me in deliberate strokes and flicking my sensitive clit. My lower extremities were completely numb, and my body hummed with raw sensation, pulsating at my core.

Luckily Brian moved before I collapsed. Otherwise, I fear I would've smothered him without the ability to move. Deft fingers came from behind me and removed the vibrator, causing me to wince with the inadvertent stimulation of nerves.

When he rolled me onto my back, I bestowed a silly, just-been-thoroughly-satisfied grin. He was rock hard, but when I reached for him, he shook his head.

"Don't make me tie your hands," he threatened.

I quirked a brow and rose to my knees. It was tempting, and he could see the challenge in my eyes.

He smirked, and I leaned in and kissed him passionately. He pulled back abruptly and studied my face. "It turns you on to taste yourself on my lips?" he asked hoarsely.

I nodded and moved in to kiss him again.

"Jesus, woman—" His hand fisted in my hair, and his mouth crushed mine. "Get on your knees. I want you hard and deep."

His voice was shaky. It appeared his control was being stretched to the brink. I obeyed, and he thrust in fully. He was deep in this position and was holding nothing back while he gripped my hips. The plug remained in place and moved deeper with every drive, setting up yet another orgasm.

I recall hearing his long, drawn-out growl when he met his climax deep inside of me, but I think I may have blacked out after that. Brian clearly must have taken over as I felt him remove the plug and then fold my boneless body into him.

"How did that feel?" he asked

"Just when I think I've had my best orgasm, you take it to another level."

"Did you like the toys?"

I knew I was blushing. "Uh, they were fine." I shrieked in surprise when he pinned me beneath him.

"Did you use the word *fine?*"

Uh oh. A thrill moved through me. I giggled and quickly modified. "I didn't mean it that way. I have a hard time talking about it, though."

He studied my face and then kissed me softly. "But if there's something that doesn't turn you on or you don't like, you have to be able to tell me."

"I would, I promise. Everything has felt incredible, but verbalizing it is tougher. It's all new to me. Then I think about how it's not new to you, and I start overthinking it."

Rolling to his side, he gathered me close. "Tell me," he demanded softly.

I shrugged. I didn't know how to put it into words. All these things he'd done with me that blew my mind with amazing orgasms, he'd also done with other women. "I don't know how to explain it. This is the part I kind of suck at, or haven't you noticed?"

He tipped my chin up, meeting my eyes. "I won't say that I haven't already done some of the things we've done or will do. But with you it's so drastically different, that I can't recall my history. There's no room for it because my mind is filled with thinking of new ways to please you. I want all of you, everything you'll give me. I meant it when I said that I'm greedy, and I won't ever get enough."

The weight of the insecurity inside of me that I hadn't wanted to admit suddenly felt lighter. "You always know the right thing to say." I kissed him softly appreciating that he'd make the effort.

"I want to ask you something. Something I keep telling myself I don't want to know, but then come back to."

"I don't think you'll like the answer to that question, but you're welcome to ask if you're prepared to answer the same."

"Okay. How many men have you had sex with?"

"I'm assuming that we're not judging one another for something we can't change?"

"Of course not, and if you're uncomfortable, then you don't have to answer."

"Oh, I'll answer. Five."

He simply stared at me. "Five guys ever?"

"Six, including you."

"I—Explain that to me. Men practically break their necks looking at you when you walk by."

I rolled my eyes. "Even if that were true, do you think I'd hop on them as a thank you?"

He chuckled. "No, that came out wrong."

"I had one boyfriend in high school, slept with one in college, three since then, and you. And since most of the time my vibrator was better than the men I'd had sex with, you get the picture."

"Haven't you ever had a one-night stand?"

"No. You know more than anyone I have a hard time feeling comfortable with new people. I take it you have?"

"Uh—Wait, back up. Why did you tell me that I wouldn't like the answer to the question? Five makes me quite happy."

"I figured it might, but what you aren't going to like is telling me your number now."

He flushed. "Ah, yes, my number. Uh, in light of yours, mine isn't quite as, um—exact."

"Meaning you don't know how many women you've been with?"

"You're right, I don't like your answer because it makes mine not so great." His face turned beet red.

"Why, Brian Carpenter, have I made you blush?"

He gave me an apologetic smile. "Okay, there were quite a few in college. A lot less in recent years. I'm not exactly proud of it, but it's not something I can change, either."

"I'm not judging." I caressed his face and watched him relax.

"It's late. You need to get some sleep. Big presentation tomorrow for your awesome boss. Oh and my boss too, but we both know who you want to impress the most."

I shook my head and yawned on cue. "The first half hour will feature a fashion show so that I can be told what to wear. It will introduce the most fashionable muumuu choices the world over, so we can ensure I don't take any attention away from an insecure and difficult female client contact."

"Cute. And even in the ugliest muumuu, you'd manage to look sexy."

I scoffed.

He rolled me toward him, suddenly hard and back inside of me, holding my face. "You'll handle that meeting like the professional that you are."

He moved deeper, and I moaned, flexing around him. "Are you talking about work while you're inside of me?"

"Not anymore I'm not. Christ, when you flex like that, I feel like I'm eighteen and unable to control myself."

Huh. I rather liked that idea. I squeezed again and then rocked my hips up.

"Ah, Sash, do you really think you can take charge?"

It was evident I'd had a false sense of being able to do so when he held himself completely still. I squirmed, craving more. But he had other ideas. His head dipped down, taking one nipple in his mouth and then the other.

177

"Oh." I reared up trying to get him to move, but he wouldn't budge. The only evidence of his acknowledgement was the growing girth of his cock buried deep inside of me. "You're in charge," I whispered roughly.

His eyes snapped to mine, and I knew I'd given him what he wanted.

"Hold your legs up by the knees and hang on." His hips moved in perfect rhythm, but instead of waiting on my orgasm like he normally did, he reached his first. I wasn't sure what to think until he pulled out, and his mouth descended into my cleft.

"Jesus, Bri, we just had sex—" The protest died on my lips when he brought me quickly to my own release with his tireless tongue. His lips lazily traveled up my stomach and then his head lay there.

"Do you think there's anything that wouldn't turn me on when it comes to you?" he murmured in the darkness.

My fingers stroked his hair, and I sighed, barely able to keep my eyes open. "I hope that's not a challenge?"

He lifted his head and grinned. "Mm. Sleep, beautiful. Not everything needs to be."

# CHAPTER FIFTEEN

*T*he mock pitch had gone as expected in that the content had been on point, but we needed to work on the transitions between Logan and Charlie. Charlie was one of my senior managers and had been in the advertising business for seven years. He was a family man who stayed calm under pressure and was easy to work with. Logan, on the other hand, was young and trying to make a name for himself. Although I admired a go-getter attitude, it had to be controlled, which is what I'd coached him about earlier in the week. This wasn't a one-man show. If we weren't all on the same team boosting one another, then there was no place for him. He'd taken the criticism in stride, and I was pleased with his progress.

Brian came into my office after the mock to share his thoughts and those of Josh in a recap session. As always, he picked up on the details and nuances that would make the pitch much better. Since he was part of this high-profile presentation, executing the introductions, he and I needed to ensure we were on the same page, too. I made my notes and knew we'd perfect it in the upcoming two weeks. "We'll start working on the changes come Monday."

"I'm glad that you're not insisting on doing it today."

Being in charge sometimes meant I needed to take a step back and reward my staff instead of piling on more work. "They did a good job today and should have the weekend off before I crack the whip again." Next week would mean long nights.

Sitting back in my visitor's chair, he regarded me. "Logan appears anxious to please you."

I shrugged, wondering what he was getting at. "That's what anyone who wants to be successful strives to do: make their boss happy."

"But not everyone wants to please you quite the way I think Logan does."

I shot him a warning look, not liking his tone or what he was implying. "You aren't being serious right now, are you?"

"I'm only making an observation. That's all."

The hard look in his eyes told me different. "Okay, because it sounded like you were implying something inappropriate was going on."

"You told Josh that he was very attractive."

My temper started to rise. "Josh posed the question, and I answered. And yes, he is attractive. It's advertising, Brian. Everyone is good-looking, or if they're not, then they're put together and have great personalities. We sell ourselves in order to sell our services. That's why you don't want me parading young, pretty associates in the pitch in front of what's-her-face. And why I have to be very careful to dress conservatively. Because looks matter in this business."

The truth was that Logan was hot, but I didn't personally find him attractive. Matter of fact, I'd never been into any of my good-looking colleagues, with the exception of the one sitting in front of me.

"I agree with you, but he wants to fuck you, and that's simply fact."

My face heated. "Are you kidding me? He does not. Where

is this coming from?" I was exasperated and wondering how the hell we'd started down this road.

He shook his head. "I have a secret for you, Sasha. Men rank a woman in their head on a scale of one to ten regarding how badly they'd like to sleep with her. Especially the young, single guys."

"I don't need this shit here. He may or may not want to sleep with me, but guess what? I only have control over my thoughts. Not his and not yours. And if you're going to sit there and tell me that I need to act differently or that I'm somehow encouraging it, you can walk your ass out of here. I'm not even all that nice to him most of the time." The more I thought about it, the more fired up I was getting.

He smirked. "Being tough on him only makes him want to fuck you more."

"I can't believe we're having this conversation. You do realize that you're acting irrational, right?"

His jaw clenched. This side of him was so out in left field. "It's very rational that Logan, along with any other man who sees you, would want to sleep with you. The only difference I'm pointing out is that he's hoping it will happen on a daily basis. Reasonable thought goes out the window when I have to watch a man trying to accomplish that goal in front of me."

"Is this the point where I'm supposed to reassure you that isn't ever going to happen?"

His laugh was void of humor. "Only you would take a shot at my ego instead of boosting it at this point."

"If you need your ego stroked over your misplaced jealousy, then you made an arrangement with the wrong girl. Now, I have work to do."

I could tell he wanted to say something else on the subject by the barely restrained anger reflecting in his eyes.

"Fine, I'll let you get back to work. I'm meeting with Mark for dinner, and then I'll see you back at your place later. I want you to wear those red, fuck-me shoes you have on and nothing else. I'll text you when I'm on my way so you can wait for me on your knees in the middle of your bed."

I sucked in my breath and narrowed my eyes. "We're not doing this here." I didn't know how I could verbalize how that command in my office made me feel, but his words incited my indignation.

"Do what, exactly?"

"You're dominant in the bedroom because, frankly, I let you, and I like it. But you can't come in my office where I'm in charge and say something like that to me. I can't mix the lines like that. It pisses me off and makes me feel weird about being given a sexual demand where I work. I—"

He got up, clenched his jaw, and let out a breath. Moving closer toward me, he raked a hand over his face. "You're right. I'm sorry. I didn't think about it. Obviously I didn't think about the entire conversation."

I simply looked at him. His eyes were full of regret, and all of my frustration evaporated instantly. "Okay."

"You were preparing for a fight?" he questioned, studying me.

"Yes. Maybe. I wasn't sure if you'd get it."

"I do, and I was way out of line. Do you still want me to come over tonight?" He looked wary.

"Yes. You have the key if I'm not there by the time you are. I have a spare if I arrive before you."

He glanced at me one last time and then left my office.

---

WHEN I GOT HOME, I was thankful Brian hadn't arrived yet. It gave me some time to get my thoughts together. I'd felt off after what had transpired earlier and couldn't figure out why. I'd made my point, he'd apologized, so why was I feeling uneasy? My phone rang with his number, and I picked up, expecting him to tell me he was on his way.

"Hey," I answered.

"Hi," he responded, without saying anything else.

"Where are you?"

"I'm, uh, heading up to Connecticut with Mark. I had planned to go in the morning and thought maybe I'd go tonight instead."

"Okay." I swallowed hard, trying not to get emotional.

"I crossed a line today," he said quietly.

"It was bound to happen at some point with either of us."

"Yeah, I guess. I think it would be good for me to take the two weeks before we see each other again. And maybe next time we have meetings or something big scheduled, not to spend the night together beforehand. It obviously put me in a weird place today, and I'm sorry."

"You already apologized, Brian." I rubbed my temples and realized that this newfound arrangement was not as easy as we'd hoped.

"I'll, um, call you later this week, okay?"

"All right. Have a good weekend."

Hanging up, I fought the tears. I had no regrets when it came to establishing the boundaries, especially in my office. However, it was clear I wasn't the type of woman he typically involved himself with. With other girls, he could truly be dominant all of the time, whereas with me, he couldn't. He'd most likely realized, or soon would, that it wasn't worth the effort. That I wasn't able to give him what he wanted. Sighing, I realized PMS was making me overly emotional, and maybe this weekend alone might not be a bad thing.

---

I ENDED up relieved that Brian had decided to spend the weekend with Mark because I started my period on Saturday afternoon and was somewhat moody and bloated. I used the majority of the day to plot out what I'd do with my parents next month when they visited. The fact that they were making the effort meant the world to me, and I wanted to show them a great time while they were in New York City. Once their itinerary was finalized, my agenda for the night included a pint of Ben & Jerry's Boom Chocolatta and an episode of Game of Thrones. Something about chocolate and grisly death scenes were especially appealing at the moment.

Halfway through the show, a knock sounded at my front door. I paused the TV and put the lid back on my pint of ice cream, sticking it in the freezer before checking the peephole. Shocked, I opened the door.

Brian's smile faded. "Um, I take it you aren't big on surprises."

Considering I was hormonal at the moment and he'd basically told me he needed a break, yeah, I wasn't big on the surprise. "I thought that you were spending the night with Mark, and you didn't want to see me for two more weeks." I was defensive, but damn if he hadn't put me through a gauntlet of emotions over the last twenty-four hours.

"Uh, right. Goodnight." He turned to go.

I winced. "Wait. Look, you're catching me off guard."

"I should have called."

"It's okay. The timing is kind of awkward, though."

"Why's it awkward?"

I exhaled. "Because it's that time for me."

He looked completely confused.

"My period," I clarified, watching him pale. "Yeah, not something we non-relationship types have had to discuss before. Um, anyhow, I was—"

He held up his hands. "No, I get it. I'll call you, uh, later."

I nodded, trying not to let it hurt my feelings that he couldn't get away fast enough. Then again, I hadn't exactly invited him in. After I shut the door, the tears started, and I cursed. Stupid hormones.

---

THERE WAS another knock less than twenty minutes later. When I opened the door this time, Brian was standing there with a bag in hand.

"Can I come in for a few minutes?" he implored.

Nodding, I was curious why he'd come back and what was in the bag.

"I owe you an apology," he started, taking my chin in his hand and kissing me softly. "I shouldn't have bailed on Friday, and then I blew it again by leaving tonight."

"I didn't exactly make you feel welcome," I conceded.

He sighed. "With good cause.

"What's in the bag?"

He smiled and set it down on my kitchen counter. "First of all, I have Haagen Dazs ice cream."

He pulled out the container, and I had to bite my lip to keep from laughing.

"Secondly, I have a bag of salty chips. Next, I have Motrin and water pills, which are supposed to help with the cramps and bloat. And finally, I have bubble bath. I'm told that a soak will help you sleep better."

"Who told you to get these things?"

He looked instantly uncomfortable.

"This is very sweet Bri, but you ran out of here like a deer in headlights at the mere mention of the word *period,* and now you're back like you've read a *how to deal with a woman on her period* handbook."

"Okay, but don't get angry because I didn't mention any

names. I only said that I blew it with someone I'd been seeing, and you know he's my best friend, plus he's married—"

Heat flooded my face. "Brian, please tell me you did not call Josh, the owner of the company we work for, not to mention my boss's boss, to ask him what to do with a woman on her period. Did you?" Josh may not know about our arrangement, but to have this type of intimate question asked of him mortified me just the same.

He shifted his feet. "No, I didn't call him."

I breathed a sigh of relief.

"Technically, I texted him."

"Oh. My. God." I put my hands over my face, beyond embarrassed.

"Please don't be mad. I needed advice after screwing up. And I'm not here for sex. If you'd like me to stay, maybe we could hang out, and I can run you a bath. But if you want me to go and be alone, I'm cool with that, too."

I had to process for a moment. How the hell could I stay irritated with a man who would text another man to ask for advice, especially on this subject? "I'm not mad. But I am taken aback that you went to all this trouble, Bri." I was quietly trying to get a handle on my emotions over such a gesture.

"We were friends first, Sash, and the amazing sex aside, I do enjoy being with you. I've never been in a steady relationship, so I was dumbly ignorant of, you know."

"My period." I giggled at his wince.

"Sorry, it's something foreign to me, that's all."

I took his hand, grabbed the ice cream and two spoons, and then dragged him into my bedroom. "Come on. I'm catching up on Game of Thrones."

He grinned. "I'll try not to ruin it for you then. How far back are you?"

"You watch it?"

"Big fan. Matter of fact, I have you to thank for getting me hooked last year when you mentioned how you liked it. McKenzie is into it now, too."

He kicked off his shoes, shed his clothes, and climbed into bed in his boxers. We settled down to watch television like a normal couple.

---

By the time the last recorded episode finished, it was near midnight. We were a pint of Haagen Dazs down, and I'd taken two of the Motrin to help with my muscle aches.

"You want me to draw a bath for you?" he offered.

"Sure. Will you join me?"

He looked surprised but then pleased. "Of course. You, um, go get ready, and I'll get the bath prepared."

I was grateful for my half bath that I could use out in the hall. When I stepped into the master bath, I could hear him humming under his breath. I observed his fluid movements from the doorway while he poured the bubble bath, with a glass of wine and candles already set up.

"Pretty romantic," I said, hating that it sounded like an accusation. Why couldn't I be a normal girl who didn't overanalyze everything?

Luckily, he didn't notice and was focused on turning off the water. "Why don't you climb in? I'll be right back."

I stepped in and closed my eyes. The water felt good on my muscles, and the fragrant scent of the bubble bath was soothing.

"Scoot up, honey. I'll get behind you," he suggested.

His strong legs rested on either side of mine with my back tucked into his chest. Breathing deeply, I enjoyed the feel of him around me. Although we hadn't brought it up all evening, I couldn't help but do so now. "The last time we spoke on the phone, you said it would be a good idea not to see me for another two weeks."

He hugged me tight from the back. "Clearly I didn't mean it when I couldn't last twenty-four hours."

"I started to think maybe you..." I couldn't quite finish the thought without getting emotional.

"Maybe I—what?"

I took a deep breath. Something about being in the tub, facing away from him, made me braver. "Maybe I wouldn't hear from you at all. I'm not the sort of girl who's ever going to let you be dominant in all things, and I think that's what you've had before. And perhaps you were rethinking the entire thing."

"That's the last thing I—Shit—I was afraid if I came over last night, you'd tell me it might not be working for you because of my earlier behavior. I thought a break might remind you that I'm not normally like that. The truth is..." He hesitated. "Although the thought of being in control in the bedroom turns me on, I feel the same when you challenge me. And there's no doubt that you should've challenged me in the office, but I've never dealt with the two combined."

"And the thing about Logan?"

"I'm not jealous in the way you're thinking. I don't know why I brought it up except for the fact that I'm envious he gets to spend every day talking with you, working late nights, and seeing you all the time. That used to be us in Charlotte."

I missed that, too. "It was, but we weren't doing this, so maybe the move was a good thing. By the way, were you serious about all men rating women in their heads?"

He chuckled. "Yeah, I'm afraid so. But it's probably guy code, so don't go spreading it around."

"It's unnerving to have a glimpse into the male psyche and the fact that men are such pigs."

"If you could look inside our minds, maybe we are, but we clean up nice for presentation purposes."

"Hmm. Fair enough. By the way, I asked Logan. He assured me he doesn't want to sleep with me."

"WHAT?"

I burst out laughing. "I couldn't resist. Like I'd ever ask him that question."

"Your laughter is worth the heart attack you almost gave me."

I giggled again and enjoyed the feel of his hands washing my arms and back.

"Can I ask you something?" His voice was low and intimate.

"Mm." I couldn't manage a yes with his hands on my breasts.

"Do you regret starting this?"

I turned to face him and put my hand on his jaw. "No, do you?"

It was an emotional, intimate moment. When he opened his eyes, looking at me with unfiltered passion, I knew that he didn't have any doubts.

"Not even for a second. Turn back around and relax into me. I want to wash your beautiful body."

I lay back, gasping when his soapy fingers reached down and found my clit. "Bri—"

"Shh, I'll only touch you here. Open your legs."

I let my knees fall open to the sides of the tub.

"That's it."

Giving myself over to the sensation, my toes curled with each stroke of his fingers.

His lips trailed kisses down my neck, and then his breath was near my ear. "Come for me, sweetness."

My muscles tensed and the roar of blood rushed in my ears. Suddenly, I climaxed with a breathless whimper already wanting more.

"I wish I could have you inside of me," I panted, feeling him hard behind me.

"I don't mind, Sasha. I mean only if you want to."

"I do, but—"

I didn't have a chance to finish voicing the insecurity before his hand roughly pushed between my legs and pulled the string out in one fluid motion. I was shocked by how aroused I became with that motion. Then he, no-nonsense, simply leaned over, grabbed the trash can, and deposited it in there. Before I could process feeling self-conscious, he lifted me up, and aligned his hardened length to my slick entrance.

"I can't believe that turned me on so much," I muttered. I felt his chuckle at my ear and gasped in pleasure when he filled me completely.

His hands grasped my hips, setting the rhythm. "Me too, gorgeous." He groaned with pleasure, increasing the tempo. "Your breasts are heavier, and you're tighter around me. You're more sensitive, aren't you?"

His hands were everywhere at once, it seemed, and my body was on overload. "Oh, God, yes," I moaned.

He reached around to my swollen nub, circling it expertly.

My body clenched, and I threw my head back onto his shoulder. His growl of ecstasy fueled me. Neither of us cared about the water sloshing all over the floor. His teeth nipped at my neck, and we went over the edge together.

After a few minutes, our breathing steadied, and he sighed. "Are you all right?"

"Mm-hmm." I was unable to form any coherent words at this point.

"I'm sorry. This was not what I intended when I came back tonight. I was only going to rub your back in the tub and maybe cop a feel, but, no, I'm like a damned animal when it comes to you."

"I'm the one who said I wanted you inside of me. I guess I didn't think you'd actually do it though." I was too embarrassed to vocalize it in detail.

"It's probably good we're in the tub," he said wryly.

I winced at the tenderness when I got up and stepped out of the tub. I made sure to go straight into the shower.

He drained the water and then joined me. "Are you positive you're okay? I didn't hurt you, did I?"

I turned, smiling. "No you didn't hurt me. Um, it wasn't too bad for you, was it?" My cheeks burned. What was I asking, exactly?

He grabbed my chin and held my face. "No, but I feel terrible because I came back here to prove that it wasn't only about the sex."

I soaped up and ran my hands over his chest. "I know it's not." We locked eyes and a myriad of emotions passed between us. "Um, I need a few minutes to wash."

He kissed me deeply. "Let me rinse, and I'll give you some privacy, okay?"

I nodded, grateful that he understood.

After my shower, I dressed for bed and climbed in, enjoying the feel of his arms coming around me. Then his hands were massaging my lower back, and it felt divine.

"Bri—"

"Mmm."

"I'm glad you're here."

"I can't think of anywhere I'd rather be, Sash."

I smiled in the dark.

# CHAPTER SIXTEEN

*I*t was like every other pitch day. I arrived early at the client site, excused myself to go to the restroom, and there pulled my hair back quickly while upchucking breakfast into the toilet in front of me. Thankfully, I was alone in the women's bathroom. But even if I hadn't been, I'd long ago perfected the art of keeping quiet. Putting a few seat covers over the top of the water helped muffle the sound and minimized the splashing. The last thing I needed was to have anything land on my Jimmy Choo shoes or conservative, "consultant approved," black Chanel suit. I'd learned over the years to eat something starchy and drink a lot of water. It hurt my throat less that way and came up a lot easier. As an added bonus, I wouldn't have the calories later.

Great, now I was thinking like a bulimic teenage girl. If only it was that easily controlled, I thought and then winced. Oh, sure, judge someone else's disorder while I battled my own on a daily basis. Nice one, Sasha.

I steadied my breathing and visualized the pitch deck I was about to give the clients. I didn't think of Vanessa being insecure around women. I didn't think about the dress code or Brian.

Instead, I cleared my mind and proceeded into the zone like I always did.

But first always came this. After flushing, I came out of the stall, pulled the toothbrush from my purse for a quick brush, touched up my makeup, and put in my earbuds. My song choice for today was a personal favorite: "Titanium" by David Guetta. I let the words wash over me for the duration of the three minute song and took a final look at myself. I was the vice president for Gamble Advertising out of the New York office for a reason. I was successful, confident, and I would kill this presentation. I visualized it, rolled my shoulders, and put on my game face.

Coming out of the ladies' room, I smoothed down my long skirt and then walked the short distance back to the reception area. There I smiled at Charlie and Logan, who were waiting, and reassured them that everyone would do great.

Brian joined us in the lobby a couple minutes later. I'd been relieved that he hadn't come in last night as I was neurotic when it came to pitch day and didn't want the distraction. I'd always heard about NFL players having quirky traditions or throwing up before the big day. Well, this was my playoffs, and I was the quarterback. The pitch was my sweet spot, and we'd been preparing for weeks. I was damn good at it, and now that I'd put my anxiety into a box, the adrenaline was kicking in. I was ready.

We all filed into the conference room. It was show time. Introductions were made, and I officially met Vanessa. She was upper-thirties, petite in stature, with dark brown hair pulled back in a severe bun. She wore a low-cut blouse paired with a designer jacket, skirt, and leopard print pumps. Yeah, leopard. Clearly no one had ever done a survey dictating that she wear something conservative.

The board in attendance was made up of five gentlemen, all white-haired and dressed in black or navy suits. The man in charge was named Michael Dobson. He'd served as CEO of

Tryon Pharmaceuticals for the last ten years and only recently retired to become the chairman of the board. I knew about each of these men, their biographies, their work history, and anything else I could dig up.

My advertising pitch deck followed a well-known formula of five stages or steps. The first step was where Brian did most of the talking. Since he was the senior person, he took care of the introductions and talked about the credentials of Gamble Advertising as a whole. His voice was melodic, and he was straight and to the point. The second step was to throw the ball over to me for our focus on strategy. This was where we sold the idea that this was a niche of the market in which we'd proven ourselves. It was a stretch, however, considering we'd only worked with one pharmaceutical company, and it was quite a bit smaller than Tryon. It wasn't normal practice to field questions during this part of the presentation, however it happened often enough. I'd prepared, considering Vanessa was the type of woman who'd want to make her presence known early on.

"You only have the one other pharmaceutical company?" she inquired, tapping her pen.

I smiled. "Yes, only one, however we have two home health care accounts. And, instead of having to split creativity amongst several identical pharmaceutical companies, all of the ingenuity would be focused on yours."

She looked like she was about to speak again but was interrupted by the chairman, Mr. Dobson. "Very good answer, Ms. Brooks. Please continue."

Good to know she didn't have control over the board. But considering these gentlemen wouldn't be present for most client meetings and discussions, it wasn't going to do much good later. Moving on to stage three, we provided the meat of the presentation, the creative pitch. Logan presented the magazine ad concepts, and Charlie moved into the television campaign proposal. Then it was back to me to discuss the miscellaneous ad space, which included stadiums and airports. We expected questions and comments during this section. I noticed Vanessa only addressed her questions to the men on the team.

Once she was finished, Mr. Dobson, the chairman, took his turn while thumbing through the presentation packet in front of him. "Tell me, Ms. Brooks, why did you target the Dallas Cowboys' stadium specifically for an ad?"

My smile came easily. "Mr. Dobson, the Dallas Cowboys are the most televised team in America, giving you the best camera time for your ad. It's also a newer stadium and the largest, which means that the film crew is panning around to show the home-viewing audience a glimpse of it more often than in an older stadium. And, last but not least, considering you have season tickets, where better to see evidence of your company's ad dollars than where you can do business with potential investors?"

His wide grin let me know my homework had not been in vain. "Very nice, Ms. Brooks. Now tell me how you think the Cowboys will do this year?"

I paused, pretending to think about it. "I believe losing Demarco Murray will be a large hole, and the jury is out on whether or not McFadden and Randle can replace that gap. Between the two of them, my money is on McFadden to be the starter, but the real question is if they can keep their offensive line healthy. Without that, you'll have an injured quarterback with a domino effect. Of course, defense is where it's going to make a difference if they can have the same sort of year as the last one with takeovers. If you ask me, Tyron Crawford is under-rated and this could be his breakout year." And thank you, Daddy, not only for my love of the game, but also for teaching me the best strategy for dealing with most men: football. He'd always said that you could fundamentally be at odds with a man politically or religiously, but if you could talk football, all the other stuff wouldn't matter.

"It takes a lot to surprise me, Ms. Brooks. We may need to fly you out for a game." Smiling, he looked toward his fellow board members, of which I knew two of the three also held Dallas Cowboys season tickets.

"That would be a dream, Mr. Dobson," I replied graciously.

Turning back to my team, I noticed that Logan's gaze was akin to hero worship. Charlie looked impressed, and Brian's eyes showed unfiltered amusement.

Vanessa, however, had a sour expression on her face.

The fourth stage was my least favorite: the budget. Clients didn't typically like to spend money, but since the six-million-dollar figure on the table had been offered up before we'd prepared the pitch, the board didn't bat a lash at our estimates. Finally, after no further questions, we proceeded to the summary or the final step of the presentation. Charlie and Logan hit their cues flawlessly, and we killed it.

The only personal hitch to the entire thing had been watching Vanessa eye fuck Brian. She was an attractive woman who was not hurting for confidence, hanging on his every word and lingering with *innocent* touches as we made our goodbyes.

We would find out in the next couple of weeks if we'd made the cut to the next round. There was always the chance we wouldn't win the business, but I was confident that we'd left it all on the field. And the football metaphors stayed on the brain.

---

AFTER ARRIVING BACK in my office, I felt the adrenaline start to evaporate from the high of the pitch, and I was left exhausted. It mentally and physically drained me every time. Coffee was the only thing keeping me awake at this point. Thankfully, Brian had gone without me to meet Josh for lunch, and I'd let Charlie and Logan go home early with high praise for their efforts. My intention was to head out soon, too. I didn't know what time Brian would come over, but I was hoping for an hour to take a nap or, at the very least, grab another caffeinated beverage to catch my second wind.

I let Nancy know I'd be leaving soon and was about to grab my things when she buzzed me.

"Ms. Brooks, there is a Ms. Jamie Morgan in reception, asking to see you."

I was stunned. What in the hell would Brian's one-time girl-friend be doing here? "Uh, please tell the receptionist that I'm finishing a meeting and then retrieve Ms. Morgan in ten minutes." I might not have the energy deal with her, but I'd be damned if I'd let her have the gratification of intimidating me on my own turf.

"Not a problem, Ms. Brooks," Nancy replied.

I immediately dialed Brian's cell phone and was relieved when he picked up.

"Hey, you, good timing. We just finished up lunch," he greeted.

"Hi. Uh, is there a reason that you can think of that Jamie Morgan would be here to see me right now?" I didn't have time to beat around the bush.

He cursed a string. "What does she want?"

"I'm not sure yet, but I'll find out in in a few minutes. Any idea why she'd be here?"

He exhaled audibly. "We had dinner last night, but she didn't mention anything. Who the hell knows?"

The stab of jealousy hit me hard. "How could you have had dinner last night with Jamie if you flew in this morning?"

"I came in last night but knew you wouldn't want to see me with the pitch today. Jamie wanted to clear the air and apologize. Maybe that's what she's doing there. I'll call her after we get off the phone."

Were men really this naïve about the agenda of a woman? "First of all, you'll do no such thing. I swear to you, Brian, if you so much as text her at this point, I'll never speak to you again. I don't need that woman thinking I can't fight my own battles. Secondly, what happened to not dating other people, or were the rules only applicable to me?"

"It wasn't a date. It was dinner with—"

"An old girlfriend," I supplied dryly.

"Sasha…"

"I don't have time to argue about this right now. But I want you to think about a scenario in which my ex-boyfriend shows up to see you in your office in Charlotte. You call me and find out that I not only came into town the prior night without telling you, but that I'd also had dinner with that same ex. Let me know how that would make you feel. I've gotta go." I hung up the phone before he could respond and slipped the hair band around my wrist, giving it a snap for good measure. Something told me I was going to need it.

---

NANCY SHOWED Jamie into my office while I was composing an email. I glanced up and finished typing to give the appearance of being interrupted. "Thank you, Nancy," I said and noticed the protective look she gave me the minute Jamie stepped in my office. Well, good to know I had an ally in my assistant.

I greeted Jamie warmly. Okay, lukewarm. After all, I was only human. But I'd have no reason not to act warmly unless I was in fact jealous, and I wouldn't give her the satisfaction. "Hi, Jamie. Nice to see you again. What can I do for you?"

She smiled, taking a seat in her designer pantsuit and four-inch heels. "Oh, I won't take up too much of your time. I had dinner with Brian last night to apologize for the last time we were out. I evidently spoke out of turn revealing the Sasha-B-Fierce nickname, and he suggested there may be some hard feelings." Her tone held absolutely no sincerity.

"No hard feelings on my part. In fact, I've embraced it like the compliment it was intended to be." My voice was luckily steadier than my emotions.

"Good, and I guess congratulations are in order?"

"I'm afraid you've lost me. Are you congratulating me?"

"Yes, it appears that you and Brian are quite happy together."

I arched my brow. "I don't know what you're talking about." There was no way that he'd told her.

She uncrossed her legs and leaned forward. "Come on, Sasha. Woman to woman, I came here to apologize. The least you could do is be truthful."

"That's a curious thing, Jamie, considering I've yet to hear an actual apology from you."

Her eyes narrowed. "You know, I didn't give you enough credit, even knowing your nickname. You're tough, and if you want to play it this way, then obviously that's your prerogative."

"If that's it, Jamie, I do have some clients to get back to."

She stood and turned to leave. "One last question." She faced me.

I braced myself, knowing without a doubt her parting shot wouldn't be a pleasant one.

"I'm curious how much Brian won in the bet now that you two are sleeping together. I heard the pot was quite large down in the Charlotte office on whom you'd sleep with."

It took every minute of therapy I'd attended and self-visualization techniques I'd learned to pretend I didn't know what she was talking about. "It's an interesting approach you have Jamie. You'd like to be in a relationship with Brian, and yet you seek to cut down those in his life whose opinion he values. I'm not sure how that'll work for you, but good luck."

Her clenching jaw was enough for me to know I'd scored a direct hit. She left through my door without a backward glance.

It had barely closed before I dialed Brian again.

"Hey, has she left?" he answered.

"Yes. Were you part of the bet?" My voice was barely audible while my breathing started to slide out of control.

"What are you talking about?"

"Don't play dumb. Were you part of the bet my first year in Charlotte about who I'd sleep with first?"

"Sasha, it's not what you think."

"Yes or fucking no?" My voice cracked, and I could feel the panic welling up.

"Yes, but—"

I didn't let him finish, instead slamming down the phone. The betrayal lanced through me with physical pain. Suddenly I was at school, sixteen again, having a strange woman with eyes like mine show up during lunch and ask me for money. I'd found out the people I trusted most in this world had kept the biggest secret of my life from me. Shaking the painful memory from my head, I reached for my waste basket just in time to throw up my coffee.

# CHAPTER SEVENTEEN

*B*rian found me ten minutes later still hovering over the trash can.

"God, are you okay?" He obviously didn't bother to knock or have Nancy buzz me before coming into my office.

I nodded, thankful there wasn't much more than coffee to come up, and my breathing had almost returned to normal. I had to remind myself to stop clutching my chest. "Fine." I grabbed a bottle of water from my desk drawer and took shallow sips.

He knelt beside me, looking concerned. "Are you not feeling well?"

"I'm good. Please go," I managed.

"Not going to happen." He dialed my assistant. "Nancy, please have a car meet us downstairs in front of the building."

I wanted to argue, but all of my concentration was centered on getting my heart rate and breathing back to normal and hoping that he wouldn't suspect my panic attack. I couldn't even properly tell him to go to hell. The only silver lining was that I'd gotten a handle on things about a minute before he'd come barging in.

By the time Nancy knocked and peeked in to let us know the car had arrived, I was feeling marginally better.

Packing up my things, I walked unsteadily out the door. "Thank you, Nancy."

She patted my shoulder awkwardly. "Anytime, Sasha. Feel better."

I was quiet until Brian and I reached the car waiting curbside. Turning toward him, I held up my hand. "I can take it from here."

"I don't think so. We can have this discussion on the street in front of the office or back at your place. Your choice, but you'll hear me out."

Some choice. I got into the back of the car and stared out my window, refusing to look at him. We were silent the entire ride and until we stepped inside my door.

"Why were you sick?" he queried softly.

Under no circumstance would my pride allow for him to know that his ex-girlfriend had put me into a panic attack. I wouldn't give either of them that knowledge. "You wanted me to hear you out, so say your piece and then go."

He hesitated and then walked into my kitchen. Grabbing a glass, he filled it with water and handed it to me. "That stupid bet seven years ago was made shortly after you started. I suppose Juliette told you that ten of the guys in the office bet on who you'd sleep with first. I wanted no part of it, but one evening when we were all out and you'd left early, they started razzing me about it, trying to get me to lay my money down. I bet that you wouldn't ever sleep with anyone, including me. And I never, ever put money on it. It was, at least in my mind, a way I could get them off my back by showing that I respected you way too much to make a bet like that. You can ask Juliette if you don't believe me."

"How did Jamie find out about it?" I needed all of the pieces before I could process it all.

At the mention of her name, Brian's eyes immediately reflected his anger. "We were chatting months ago, and you came up in the conversation. She was talking about how hard it was being a woman in an office with men commenting on who she'd sleep with instead of her work ethic. I brought your situation up, meaning it as a compliment in saying that these assholes had made a bet when you'd started, and you hadn't given any of them the time of day. She wondered if I was part of it. I told her my bet was always that you wouldn't sleep with anyone. Telling her that seemed harmless at the time. Is that why she came by, to bring this shit up out of the blue?"

I sat down on my sofa and rubbed my eyes. Absolute fatigue was seeping into my body now that my panic attack had fully subsided. It had been a roller coaster day, and I was about to crash. "She came with the pretense of wanting to apologize about the nickname comment, moved on to congratulating me for our relationship, and then ended with the finale of asking how much money you'd won on the bet because you'd slept with me."

"I'm so sorry. I didn't tell her we were together, but it wasn't because I didn't want to. It was because of her connection to Josh. I didn't think you'd like it."

"What did you tell her?" I had to ask.

He looked uncomfortable. "That it wasn't going to happen with us. She'd thought if she apologized for that night at Evan's that we could move past it. She brought you up, and I told her we were good friends. But I think she's always known I had a thing for you."

I wasn't completely over it, but I didn't have the energy to stay mad either. "I need a shower, then to go lie down."

"Tell me what I can do, and please don't say to leave."

I inhaled deeply, trying to decide. His face look pained, and he was eager to do something. "Maybe you can order in something for dinner in a couple of hours. I'm feeling better, and I never got around to eating lunch." I didn't mention that breakfast had come up earlier.

Moving toward my bedroom, I was thankful that for now, my secret stayed my own. How ironic that on the day I'd been at my best, by the end of it I'd go to my worst.

Later that evening after my short nap, we dined quietly, eating pasta on the couch in my living room by candlelight. My stomach started to recover after getting some food into it. When I couldn't eat another bite, Brian took my hand and led me into my bedroom.

"Let me blow out the candles and clean up dinner. I'll be in shortly."

I nodded and got ready for bed. After climbing in nude between my cool sheets, I closed my eyes briefly. A short time later, I felt him slide in beside me.

He didn't move toward me but instead lay on his back and stared at the ceiling. "You were right about how I'd feel if the positions were reversed today. I would have flipped out if an ex of yours showed up, and you'd been in town without calling. I'm an idiot, and I'm sorry."

"Were you ever planning to tell me that you'd met up with her?"

"I'd like to think that eventually I would have. She'd been calling and apologizing for weeks. I have issues with things that are unresolved. I thought I owed her at least some sort of closure."

"I get it. You're always the good guy trying to smooth things over, but we had an agreement over rules that you set. You should've told me ahead of time, or, better yet, you could have talked with her over the phone."

"I know. It pisses me off that she purposefully went in to upset you, especially when you killed the pitch earlier today. This should've been a night of celebration, and instead I ruined that. What did you end up saying to her?"

I filled him in on my parting shot, and he whistled.

"You're impressive with things like that. No flinch, no prisoners. I've always admired that about you."

Rather than take it like the compliment he intended, it was a little depressing that Brian admired traits that didn't describe the real me. He, like everyone else, believed I had a natural ability to deal with situations like that. If he knew the truth, he'd be sorely disappointed.

"Do you forgive me?"

I didn't hesitate, knowing him well enough to believe his intentions were exactly as he'd explained. "Yes, but don't lie to me again, Brian. Omission is the same thing, especially to me." I didn't want to go into how not knowing I was adopted had affected me, but it was a definite trigger for when someone hid the truth about something involving me. I had a twinge of guilt that hiding my anxiety disorder was not being entirely honest but reasoned that it was a private matter that was nobody's business. It certainly wasn't something we'd put on the table to agree upon like in this situation.

"I won't do it again."

It was ironic that I was once again on the receiving end of an apology. It was also somewhat of a relief. His mistakes made me feel less intimidated and that I wouldn't be the only one to screw things up.

We both heard the sound of his cell phone coming from his pants pocket. He picked it up, frowned at the caller ID, and then silenced it.

"How many times has she called?" I asked.

"Too many. I'll need to talk to her sooner or later, though, or she'll keep calling."

"Jamie is going to be an issue for me. I know you're friends, and I'm trying hard not to give an ultimatum, but—"

"You don't have to. Regardless of our relationship, I don't want someone like that a part of my life. She's obviously changed, or—I don't know—maybe she was always like that, and I never noticed. I'll send her an email tomorrow. What she said to you was inexcusable and I don't care what her story is."

My mind was marginally pacified by his lack of hesitation. "Wait. What story?"

He shrugged. "I don't know yet, but I'm sure she'll have something. It doesn't matter, though."

Once again, his complete faith that what I'd told him had actually happened humbled me.

"Were you sick because you were upset?"

I knew this question would come up again, and tried to play it off. "I was about to go home early and had just told Nancy I was about to leave because my stomach wasn't feeling great when she buzzed in. Bad timing all the way around."

He reached for me and sucked in his breath upon finding me naked. "Can I rub your back or hold you?"

It was significant that he wasn't playing his usual role in the bedroom and was asking me what I wanted rather than dominating. "I'd rather have you inside of me."

He inhaled sharply. "Are you sure? You've had a hell of a day."

"I know. But the only time my mind truly turns off is when you take over." And this was my fundamental realization. Brian's dominance in the bedroom allowed me a freedom that I'd never experienced before. One that I craved at the moment more than anything: escape from my own mind and thinking about my panic attack or past.

He quickly slipped off his boxers. "What about your stomach?"

His hesitancy made me want him even more. "I'm feeling better." Reaching for him, I found him hard already. His velvety softness and the bead of wetness at his tip made me want to taste him. I moved down, only to have his hand fist in my hair and stop me.

"I don't think so," his low voice warned. The absurdity of denying me the ability to pleasure him was a testament to how much he'd rather have the control instead. "Sit up against your headboard with your knees apart."

I moved, trembling already with need. Before I'd had a chance to settle into position, his mouth found my center. But instead of moving fast and furious, he went slowly. His languid tongue trailed along my cleft, and I whimpered, yearning for more.

"You like it when I take control in the bedroom?" His eyes locked on mine, illuminated only by the moonlight coming in through the bedroom window.

"Yes," I whispered and felt a shudder run through him.

When his lips descended onto my clit, my fists gripped the sheets as the electric current coursed through my body. His finger pushed deep into my slick flesh, causing me to moan with the delicious torture he was inflicting. He looked up and grinned. "Remember when I told you to keep your hands on your head the first time I did this?"

I nodded, awaiting the same request.

"This time I want them on my head, showing me how much you want me down here."

Now it was my turn to shiver. My hands threaded through his soft hair and pushed him back to the task at hand. He went to work like a man possessed, and I hit my climax swiftly. When I glanced down, I realized how hard I'd been shoving his face into me and let go. "Sorry about that."

"Don't ever apologize for showing me how much you want me." He seized my hips and lifted. "I want you to straddle me." He moved onto his back and assisted my movements.

I swung my legs over him, spanning his hard length. It was the first time we'd been in this position, and I rubbed Brian's chest, loving the feel of his muscles. Easing down onto his erection, I closed my eyes when the pleasure literally and figuratively filled me. But if I thought being on top meant I'd be controlling things, he quelled that notion quickly. One of his hands dug into my hip and held me in place while the other one grasped one of my breasts.

"Don't move and give me that mouth."

My body rebelled, wanting to feel the friction of motion, but I leaned down, meeting his lips in a searing kiss. The erotic way his tongue stroked mine made me want to grind myself into him, but he wouldn't allow it. "Touch yourself," he ordered in a raspy voice.

Moving back, I watched, fascinated, when he took one of my hands and sucked on two of my fingers, coating them in his saliva. I placed them onto my swollen knot and rubbed tiny circles while he guided my hips into a rhythm.

"Look at me," his raspy voice commanded.

My eyes met his while I took in the fact that his hands had shifted to my breasts, and he was now letting me dictate the cadence. Wrong again. I tried to increase the pace, but his hands shifted back down, holding me in place.

"Make yourself come." His voice was pure sin, and I breathed deep. This wasn't something with which I was particularly experienced, however having him deeply sheathed inside of me definitely increased the odds in my favor. I rubbed harder, and he shifted his body, putting us into a sitting position.

His head dipped and took one of my nipples into his mouth. Scorching heat tore through me. I'd never been one of those girls who enjoyed having her breasts played with during sex, but damn if I couldn't feel myself on the edge of an climax now that his hot mouth was fixated on one while his hand toyed with the other.

As the orgasm washed over me, he moved my hips while arching his, prolonging the explosion ripping through me.

"Ahh," I moaned shamelessly, throwing my head back in unbridled ecstasy and taking him to his brink, too. His hips thrust up two more times before his satisfied groan filled the room. I collapsed against him and felt his strong arms come around me.

"You're damn sexy, Sash," he murmured into my hair.

"You're not so bad yourself."

---

As WE LAY THERE SHORTLY after sex, my mind relaxed for the first time in a week. Brian's hand stroked lazily down my side while we lay facing one another, heads on our pillows in the bed.

"You were the one who helped Juliette win Fantasy Football three years ago when she played with all of the guys in the office, weren't you?" he alleged, humor in his eyes.

Of all of the things he could have brought up at this moment —I had to giggle. "What makes you say that?"

He pulled me closer and nuzzled my neck. "I love that sound from you. It was your little speech to the chairman today about Dallas. Holy shit. I think every man in that room got a hard-on for you in that moment."

"Not the goal I'd hoped to achieve." I enjoyed the sound of his chuckle.

"Seriously, though, it was probably one of the sweetest moments I've ever seen. I told Josh, and he looked at me and said one word."

"What?"

"Epic."

I grinned. "It did feel good. Although it didn't seem like Vanessa enjoyed it quite as much."

He shrugged. "Where did it come from?"

"Sports Center mainly." I yawned. My eyes were getting heavy.

"No, silly. Your clandestine love for football?"

This was one secret I didn't mind sharing with him. "My dad. Football is like a religion to him, and we used to watch together on Sundays. It gave us something to talk about, and it still does. Bottom line, though, is that the Cowboys don't have a chance this year. They had an easy schedule last season, and losing their star running back will decimate their ground strategy."

"I knew it. And admit it. You helped Juliette dominate our league that year she played in the office, didn't you?"

I laughed. "Guilty, but then she didn't want to play the following year because she said too many of the guys would attempt to talk to her about her draft choices and matchups. She didn't know what to say without confessing."

"So what will you do if Michael Dobson invites you down to Dallas for a game?"

"Uh, go to the game, of course. And hopefully see their new ad, courtesy of Gamble Advertising, from his luxury club level box seats."

"If his reaction to your little rundown on his team was any indication, then I think both those things look promising."

---

THE NEXT MORNING I stretched and realized Brian was asleep beside me. I knew he had to fly out today for a meeting down in Miami, but the clock showed it was early enough for what I had in mind.

For the first time in my life, I knew what it meant to take more pleasure from giving than from receiving when Brian awoke to the feel of my mouth around his quickly forming erection. The way his body quivered when he came awake sent a shudder of desire through me.

He propped a pillow under his head, watching me with hooded eyes. "Holy shit. Good morning to you, too."

"Mm," was my only response as I swirled my tongue around the head of his cock and enjoyed the way his breath sucked in. Grasping him with one hand at the base and the other stroking his balls, I took his impressive form all the way to the back of my throat.

"Fuuuck…." he hissed.

Knowing it was a matter of minutes before he insisted on taking over meant I had limited time. I made good use of it, sucking harder and bobbing with a precise tempo and purpose.

His hand fisted in the sheet and then stopped before reaching my head. Mr. Dominant, for some reason, was hesitant to push things, so I took matters into my own hands. Literally, I took his hand into mine and placed it on top of my head, encouraging him to do as he'd requested of me last night.

"No, I don't want to make you gag or throw up again." His voice sounded pained, and his fingers barely skimmed my hair.

Frustrated that he'd witnessed me getting sick yesterday, I scraped my teeth along his ridge. "I need you to show me that you want it, too, Bri—"

That was all the encouragement he needed. His fingers tangled in my hair. He pushed my head down and arched his hips, thrusting up into my mouth.

My eyes watered with the first couple strokes, but then I relaxed and took him in fully, enjoying the glimpse of power over him I had in that moment.

"Sash—stop—Jesus, stop…"

I paused, giving him enough of a window to extract himself. "Why did you want me to quit?"

"Because I was going to come. Get up on your knees." He was behind me in an instant with his hand running along the length of my slit. "Honey, you're soaked. Did you get this way sucking on me?"

"Yes, and it would've been better if you would've let me finish you."

He guided himself into me one inch at a time. "What kind of man would I be if I had you swallow the day after getting sick? You're exquisitely tight."

I should've been comforted by his consideration, but there was a larger part of me that wanted to affect him the way he did me. I enjoyed being dominated in the bedroom, but for once I wanted to concentrate on how I was pleasing him.

But his perfect thrusts made a good case for why this wouldn't be that day. His hands were everywhere, caressing and enticing. Soon he settled on that sensitive nub, and I was done for. His last thrust and the tremor of his muscles gave evidence that he'd reached his climax as well.

———

"WE NEED A VACATION, a place where, for an entire week, we can soak up the sun and then I can be inside of you every day," Brian said, soaping up my breasts in the shower a short time later.

"We had a vacation a few weeks ago." Had it been only that short a time? My hands ran down his strong arms and onto his chest, reciprocating the exploration with enthusiasm.

"That wasn't a vacation. That was attending a wedding while not actively in bed with you. I want a full week together."

That thought sent a thrill through me followed by a stab of fear. "Won't we get sick of one another?"

"Yeah, right. Wouldn't it be nice to do this every morning for a week, and then go get a massage or lie by the pool?"

That did sound like heaven. "We're waiting on Tryon Pharmaceuticals to come back with a decision, and things are busy at the moment."

"I didn't mean next week. How does the third week of March work for you? We'll go somewhere warm and tropical." He was serious.

"I've got to ask my boss for the time off."

He chuckled. "Approved."

My eyes met his, and I sighed with happiness when he took

my lips in a kiss. It would be nice to look forward to a real vacation for the first time in years.

"Leave the plans to me, and I'll let you know the details."

"Okay, but do not pick up the tab for this. I will pay my part. Tell me where to book the airfare, and we can meet down there."

I could tell he wanted to argue with me, but then his face broke out into a smile. "I can't wait to see you in a bikini."

I shook my head with a smile. "Uh, I'm naked right now in the shower with you, and you're looking forward to a bikini?"

He nodded and then nibbled on my ear lobe. "It's such a guy thing, I know, but a woman in a bikini, poolside, is one of the sexiest things there is."

Huh, that gave me an idea or two.

# CHAPTER EIGHTEEN

*I* couldn't believe we had finally escaped to paradise. Ever since booking this vacation, I'd felt the weeks drag while waiting for it.

My parents had come up for their weekend in New York, which had been a lot of fun. Unfortunately, the weather had been brutally cold, so most of our activities had been indoors. Ironically, after my speed dating disaster that had included the man who wanted to be a flying monkey in Wicked, we'd gone to see that very Broadway musical.

The best news came during the week before my vacation when my team got called in for a final pitch with Tryon Pharmaceuticals. In my opinion, it had gone great, but we awaited their final decision. This trip was near perfect timing since there was nothing to do but wait anyhow.

Brian and I scheduled our flights to arrive twenty minutes apart. Once we met up, we made our way to a beautiful resort in Aruba in the back seat of a sedan. The sun felt good after a particularly long, cold winter in New York. The calendar might say spring, but the city had yet to recognize the fact that in a week we'd be heading into April.

"What did you want to do first?" Brian asked, massaging a finger over my knuckles while holding my hand.

"Hmm, the pool looked amazing online, or we could check out one of the four restaurants, or..." I purposefully played coy, enjoying the flirting.

"I vote for *or*...." he replied playfully.

I laughed. Brian and I had been consistent in seeing one another every two weeks, but those had been short meet ups. The thought of a full week together left me feeling anxious. I'd never spent this amount of time with a man and wondered if we'd run out of things to talk about or would end up on one another's nerves. Although a full week of having sex could be interesting, as three months in our appetite for one another only seemed stronger.

He was of like mind, leaning in to whisper, "Oh, do I have plans for us this week."

His promise gave me goose bumps, and I found myself buzzing with anticipation to get up to the room. Maybe I really could put work away for a few days, and we'd be able to decompress and relax.

Once we arrived, we were whisked to the front desk, given a couple fruity cocktails, all-inclusive bracelets, and then shown to our suite. The moment the door closed, he was on me.

"These last two weeks have felt like two months," he muttered, unbuttoning my blouse.

My hands skimmed up his chest; I was anxious to feel his skin. "I'm guessing you don't want to go to the pool first?"

He smiled. "You are as smart as you are beautiful. Now wrap your legs around me."

---

WE SHOWERED after our quickie and then took time to explore the room, which was a spacious one-bedroom suite. There was a beautiful view of the ocean and a balcony on which I couldn't wait to have coffee in the morning. The large tub held promise for how we could spend an evening or two as well.

"Are you sure you don't want me to wait for you?" Brian hesitated after grabbing his sunglasses and tablet, ready to go to the pool.

I had a surprise for him and figured the best way to pull it off would be for him to go down before me.

"No, no, go on. I'm finishing up an email to my sister about my parents' anniversary party in a few weeks. I need to send her money for my half. Then I'll meet you out there. Get a good spot and a margarita for me." I fired up my laptop to prove my intention.

He gave me a quick kiss and stopped at the door. "See you down there."

The minute the door closed, I sent my reply to Addison and used PayPal for my half of the party to be held at her husband's country club. It was going to be pricey, but I wouldn't expect anything else from my sister.

After that was finished, I jumped up and pulled the barely-there bikini from my suitcase. I couldn't wait to see Brian's reaction to this number. It was a bright coral with gold rings between the cups of the bikini top and on the sides of the scraps that made up the front and back. I looked one last time in the mirror, thinking my ass looked exceptionally good in the low-cut back. Throwing on a white mesh cover-up, matching wedged sandals, and sunglasses, I pulled it all together.

Arriving poolside, I grinned when I saw him across the way. He was under a beach umbrella with his back to me. He was so handsome, I thought, approaching him from the side and looking at his body in only his swim shorts. His chest and arms looked exceptionally good. I walked over and slipped into the seat beside him.

"That was quick," he said, barely looking over while fiddling with his tablet, most likely trying to get the Wi-Fi to work.

I got settled in my chair. "Yes, easier than talking to her. Thanks for ordering my drink." I sipped the margarita that was waiting on the small table between us. "Did you want to do a snack, too?" I glanced over the little laminated menu.

He shrugged. "Sure. I made dinner reservations for seven o'clock this evening. A snack in the meantime would be good. Do you want me to go over to the grill and get it?"

"Nah, I'll do it. Be right back." I stood up, angled behind his line of sight, and tugged off my cover-up.

Smiling, I bent down briefly and kissed him on the cheek. I then sashayed over to the grill across the pool. I hoped by now he'd noticed. If I wasn't mistaken, he wasn't the only one. Swallowing down the unease of having the attention, I reminded myself this was for him. I placed my order and was told they would bring it to our chairs soon.

Making my way back, I kept my eyes on Brian, who clearly was no longer reading his device but was watching me intently, his face completely unreadable. Well, that was disappointing. But as I got closer, I could see his eyes, and those told me all I needed to know. Taking my seat beside him, I saw lust, appreciation, and a heavy dose of irritation.

"What the hell kind of bikini is that?" he ground out.

I slipped my sunglasses down and eyed him. "Excuse me, this is a designer suit. You don't like it?"

He sighed heavily. "It makes me want to throw you over my shoulder and carry you caveman style to the room and not come back out the whole damn week."

My brow arched. "I'll be sure to post that in my online review of the suit. We could've stayed indoors at your house for a week if that's all you wanted to do. This is a vacation: pool, drinks, dinners, and your favorite: bikinis." I heard him practically growl and smiled in response.

"Right. Vacation, where every other man gets to stare at your ass in that poor excuse for a bikini."

I turned toward him. "I don't give a shit about the other men. I bought this to look good for you because you said you were looking forward to seeing me in one. The best part about this week is that we don't have to pretend that we're not together in public, which means that you can lean over here, kiss me, and put your hand on my ass, letting everyone know just who gets to take it off of me later."

His eyes darkened, and then he was taking my mouth in a scorching way, skimming his hands over my backside and squeezing possessively.

My cheeks flamed in embarrassment at the indecent display of public affection, but it also sent a thrill through me to feel this wanted.

He pulled away slowly and smoothed his thumb along my lower lip. "That makes me even hotter for you. Did you truly wear it for me?"

Nodding, I thought the satisfied grin he shared was well worth it.

"I'm a lucky man, then. Food is here," he said, sitting back and accepting the tray full of nachos from the server.

"This is pretty amazing," I remarked, snacking on nachos and sipping on my drink a few minutes later.

"It is, isn't it? Have you ever done this kind of thing before?"

"Are you asking me something?"

"Yes, I guess I am. Have you ever vacationed with another man?"

"No, not really. I did an overnight thing for a wedding once, but that was definitely not a vacation. How about you? Any dom time in paradise?"

He rolled his eyes, evidently not enjoying my joke. "First of all, you have no idea what a real dominant would be like.

Secondly, in answer to your question, no, I've never taken a woman, aside from my sister, on vacation with me."

The fact that we were in new territory together, pleased me. But then I keyed in on his first statement.

"What do you mean I have no idea what a real dominant would be like?"

He smirked. "You read about it on the Internet. I like to be in control in the bedroom in a dominant way, but we definitely aren't in a dom-sub relationship, Sasha. Not even close."

I had read about it, and he wasn't wrong. He might be bossy and take over with sex, but he definitely didn't treat me like I was submissive. Which made me wonder about the other girls he'd been with.

"I'm glad I'm here with you," he murmured, kissing my hand.

"Right back at you."

---

WE WALKED hand in hand on our way to dinner. Wearing a little black dress that showed off my legs, I enjoyed the way that Brian looked in his linen pants and a light blue, button-down shirt. Thus far, I'd answered some emails late this afternoon but then had been able to turn work back off. As he had during our time in the islands for the wedding, Brian seemed to distract me from my normal obsession with my job. The result was I felt more relaxed than—well—ever. We took our seats at dinner. Although I would put the number of meals we'd shared throughout the years in triple digits, I could practically feel the air sizzle when he took my hand over the table and kissed the inside of my wrist.

"You look very sexy this evening," he commented in that low tone that made me quiver in expectation.

"You look very good yourself. I like that color of blue on you."

He found my compliment amusing. "Does this feel like a date?"

"Considering I'm comfortable and enjoying myself, uh, no."

He threw his head back and laughed, then leaned over. "I wonder. Do you put out on the first date?"

I shrugged. "Keep the margaritas coming, and I might."

After an amazing dinner, I sat back, stuffed, and contemplated a burning question. "I want to ask you something about the other women you've been with in these types of arrangements."

He wavered and then took both of my hands. "Okay, ask me."

"Were they more submissive? I mean, were you a lot more dominant with them?"

He looked at me for the longest time and then swallowed. "Yes."

His answer bothered me more than I thought it would. His eyes hadn't left mine, and I knew he waited for whatever I was about to say in response.

"Why haven't you done it with me, then?"

He looked surprised and then shook his head. "Because for you, giving up any amount of control is a big step. I don't want to do something you won't enjoy."

"But there's more you could do?" I hedged, watching his eyes flash with interest before they hid it again.

"Sasha, one of the things that's most attractive about you is that you do, in fact, challenge me. None of those other women did, in or out of the bedroom. It's tough to explain, but the fact that you can test me intellectually and look at me with defiance even when I'm demanding is a bigger turn-on than ever having you be completely submissive. Plus I told you I'm not into pain or punishment. Pleasurable torture maybe, but not the other stuff."

I swallowed hard. "What does pleasurable torture involve?"

Heat radiated from his eyes. "Do you honestly want to know?"

I nodded, taking another gulp of my drink. Something told me I was going to need it.

The waitress came over to clear our plates and ask if there was anything else we needed. Brian grinned. "Two shots of Patron, please."

After our shots arrived and we went bottoms up, he sat back. "I'd like for you to make your way to the ladies' room and take off your panties. Bring them to me."

I sucked in my breath at his request and felt myself flush. For a brief moment, I contemplated denying him. But it didn't make sense for me to do so. My consent to his requests merely heightened the sexual tension, and we both benefited from that. And I had, in fact, wanted the challenge. I knew it turned him on to see me accept it. "Excuse me a moment." I slid my chair back and then made my way to the restroom.

Resuming my seat at the table, I passed him my thong underneath. Then I watched him ball it up in his hand and bring it up to his nose, inhaling. Jesus, this man made me feel on fire. Next he tucked it away in his pocket like nothing had happened. His chair moved closer to mine, and I held my breath in expectation of his hands on me, but they didn't come.

"Did you want to check out the dance club?" he queried.

I quirked a brow. "You want to go dancing at a club?" I couldn't see it.

"Mm-hmm."

Given our earlier conversation, I was disappointed we weren't heading back up to the room, but I tried to hide it.

He took my hand, and we made our way to the nightclub on the other side of the resort. Their version of a club turned out to be a bar with a dance floor. We found a dark corner booth easily as there was hardly anyone here yet.

He slid in next to me, and I sucked in my breath when his

hand found my thigh. I wasn't sure what you could see, if anything, under the table, but Brian didn't seem to care.

"Did you mean what you said earlier about wanting to know what pleasurable torture was?" he asked gruffly.

Desire coursed through me, but so did trepidation. I nodded, keeping my eyes trained on him.

"Open," he commanded.

I swallowed hard, slightly spreading my legs for him.

"Further. No one can see under the table."

As soon as I did so, his hand glided along my inner thigh and then right up into the heat.

"You're burning up here. And drenched already, aren't you?" His fingertips skimmed my slit, teasing.

I found myself pushing toward him while trying to remember that we were currently in public. Sucking in my breath when his finger probed deeper, I squirmed to try to find relief without it being obvious to anyone who may be witnessing us.

"Can I get you two something to drink?" the waitress asked, snapping both my thoughts and legs shut.

"Honey, what would you like?" Brian questioned casually, as if his hand wasn't currently crushed between my thighs.

"I'd love a margarita, no salt, please," I choked out.

"Same, thank you." He turned toward me, and I flushed at his gaze. "Open."

"Brian, we're in public," I protested weakly, and then my knees fell open; I was unable to resist him.

His fingers reclaimed my pulsing sex. "That means you need to get better at putting on a poker face because after that waitress sets down our drinks, I have plans for this sweet pussy of yours."

I shivered in response to his crude language.

"Thanks darlin'," he said once the drinks were dropped off. He took a sip with his free hand.

I almost downed mine in one gulp.

"Easy now, or she'll be coming back to get you another drink sooner than I'd like," he whispered. "I want you to relax."

I tried to do as he requested, but when his finger pressed deep into me, I gripped the table. "Bri—" My entire body was on the brink, and he knew it.

His expression looked pained. "Fuck it, we'll explore pleasurable torture some other time. Let's go." He downed the rest of his drink. I didn't get a chance to finish mine before he was pulling me out of the club.

Once we reached the elevator, Brian cornered me, kissing me soundly. "The look on your face is about to do me in."

I could feel his erection pressed up against me and bit my lip at the fact that I was practically dripping with anticipation.

When we arrived on our floor, I was unceremoniously scooped up and put over his shoulder. Once we got to the room, Brian wasted no time in tossing me onto the bed with his face following between my legs.

I screamed when the orgasm came crashing down over me. Breathing hard, I looked at him when he stood up, a frown marring his handsome face. "What's wrong?" I asked, noting the frustration in his features.

"Nothing," he muttered.

I narrowed my eyes. "Lie to me again and see what happens."

Evidently we could read one another accurately in that department. His hands captured my face, and he sealed his lips over mine. He slipped his tongue greedily into my mouth, and then he pulled back, putting his forehead on mine. "The truth is: I'm not dominant with you like with other girls because you make me lose control. Like in the club five minutes ago, our first time in the ocean, and too many other times to count. Pleasurable torture is supposed to be an exercise, not only in pleasuring you, but in my control. Instead, I completely lost my damned mind not even five minutes in."

His admission didn't come easy, I could sense. "Do you hate that?"

He hesitated, vulnerability evident in his eyes. "Only if you do."

I smiled and touched my lips to his. "You make me lose my mind, too."

We proceeded to lose it together.

---

THE NEXT DAY we slept in past breakfast, and I was absolutely starving by the time we made it down for lunch. We both piled our plates with the fresh seafood, and I indulged in the pasta bar.

Brian quirked a brow, taking in the fact that my plate was larger than his.

I shrugged. "I need it to keep up with you," I muttered.

He smiled, surprising me by taking my hand over the table. "I'm glad we're doing this."

"The sex or the trip?"

"Definitely both, but this vacation feels good with you here."

I had to agree it felt good for him to be here, too. It was almost like we were in a real relationship.

"Hey, do you two want to sign up for the trivia hour at the pool in an hour?" the bubbly guest relations girl came up to ask us. "It's like a traditional pub quiz."

Brian looked toward me, and I shrugged. Trivia sounded pretty tame. So long as it wasn't something like chugging beer or playing volleyball in a team of strangers, I was game.

"Sounds good. We'll see you there," he answered.

---

WE WALKED up to the bar an hour later, and it looked to be overrun with other couples who were chatting it up at different tables in groups. When the activities girl came over and told us to pick a table with two people because we'd be playing in teams of four, I lost all desire to play.

Sensing my immediate discomfort at the idea of sitting with strangers, Brian grabbed my hand and kissed my wrist.

"Who would you like to be?" he asked with an amused look on his face.

"Excuse me?" What on earth was he talking about?

"I'd like to be Austin. I've always thought that was a cool kid's name."

"You want to pretend to be different people?" I clarified, completely dumbfounded.

He laughed and took both my hands. "I know meeting new people is uncomfortable for you. How about you relax and become someone else for an hour?" His voice had turned into an overly dramatic drawl.

Oh, the irony of that question, considering I always pretended to be someone I wasn't. "I'm not sure how. This feels more nerve-wracking than walking over to the other bar and keeping to ourselves." I eyed the other couples, noting that they looked extremely friendly and excited. Those two words instilled fear in me immediately.

"We'll grab a cocktail to relax you. All you have to do is follow my lead. Think of it as something light and fun, plus we'll never see these people again."

I knew he wanted to do it. I could see the competitive gleam in his eyes. He was a people person. He would naturally do great in any sort of social setting and most likely craved some other conversation beside mine. "What if I mess it up?" I voiced my insecurity.

He shrugged. "Who cares? We fess up and say we're role-playing for a sexcapade or something."

As if that would be less embarrassing. But he made it sound so easy, and I wanted to be a fun girl for him on vacation. "Okay, if you're Austin from the South, I need a similar name." I paused. "I'll be Mary Beth. Any true Southern girl would have two names."

His mouth twitched in amusement. Taking my hand, he led me over to one of the few tables remaining with only one couple already seated.

"Hi, guys. I'm Tami Sue, and this is Lester. Where are you guys from?" the friendly woman spoke up first.

They appeared to be in their upper thirties and, judging by their accents and names, were definitely from the South. Tami Sue looked like the nice soccer mom who was on vacation for the first time in years. She and Lester appeared to be the typical all-American suburban couple, right down to their fanny packs.

"We're from Dallas originally. This is Mary Beth, and I'm Austin," Brian introduced in a heavy twang. We all shook hands. "Where y'all from?"

"Raleigh, North Carolina," Tami provided, clearly the more assertive one of the couple.

"I hear North Carolina is real nice," Brian commented while we proceeded to start the game.

Turned out the boys were good at all sorts of random trivia. Tami was able to contribute some, but the only thing I'd been able to answer was a football question about how many Super Bowls the Patriots had been to in the last fifteen years.

During the hour we hadn't had much time in-between questions to discuss a whole lot of personal things. I'd been relieved, but evidently it had only been a temporary reprieve.

"Are y'all on your honeymoon?" Tami inquired after the resort people gathered our sheets to score the teams.

"Technically, we're on hers. See, Mary Beth's wedding was on Friday, but you know the part where they ask anyone to say something or forever hold your peace?" Brian had them hanging on his every word.

Tami nodded, her eyes big.

I had the sensation like watching a car accident about to happen and not being able to look away.

"Well, it was my duty to speak up and tell everyone I objected," Brian finished on a shrug, like this was everyday conversation.

I was at a complete loss for words. Improv was not my thing. Hell, socializing wasn't my thing. Suddenly I felt like one of those small goats that go paralyzed when spooked.

He stroked my arms. "Sorry. Mary Beth is a little embarrassed that I told y'all. But it's all right, darlin', they aren't going to judge. Are you?"

Both Tami and Lester shook their heads while I sat there trying to figure out what to say.

"What did your fiancé do?" Tami questioned, riveted.

I took a deep breath, happy when Brian rescued me with the next part of his story.

"He was an unfaithful bastard is what he was. I accused him of cheating right there in that church in front of God and his mama, and he didn't bother to deny it. It's one thing to watch the woman you love marry another man, but to know that man is out and about cheating on her—I had to do it."

They both sat in awe, and so did I.

"Uh, did you love Austin all along, then?" Tami asked, addressing me.

I finally got up the courage to try my hand at this. "Uh, I did. We were high school sweethearts, but then he left to pursue his music career, and I moved on with Clayton." I got a wink of approval from Brian, who was clearly enjoying this. I needed more to drink and ordered a shot, which merely made him chuckle.

"What happened at the church, then? Did people freak out?" Lester questioned.

I could tell he too was being sucked into the story. Before Brian could answer, I got up some more courage. "They were shocked that he'd been cheating on me with my sister. I think everyone was speechless. And she started crying because turns out she's pregnant."

Brian choked on his drink.

"Baby, you okay?" I soothed, patting him on the back and watching him try to recover.

"Oh, yeah, dumpling, I'm great," he cooed.

I had to bite the inside of my cheek to keep from laughing.

Tami clucked her tongue. "That sounds like an episode of Jerry Springer. You poor thing. But you two—I can't imagine you not together. I have this thing about me, Lester will tell you. I have what I call the love meter. And the one for you guys is off the charts. Seriously, we saw you guys by the pool yesterday. Not to sound like a stalker, but when you two kissed poolside— Wowsers, I knew that was love."

My cheeks heated, and I could hardly swallow past the lump in my throat.

Brian squeezed my leg, and I was thankful when he finally broke the awkwardness. "You know how it goes with high school sweethearts. It was good for me to be on the road awhile getting some experience, if you know what I mean. Because this hellcat, she's not easy to keep up with." This little adlib earned him a kick from me under the table.

He winked at Lester, and it was all I could do not to spit out my drink this time. He was upping the stakes so that when I looked over at the karaoke machine, I couldn't help myself.

"Sugar pie, you should go show them how you sing. Hand to God, it's better than a deep-fried Oreo at the Texas state fair," I drawled and watched his eyes get big.

It was his turn to keep from laughing. "They aren't doing karaoke right now, and you know me, I'd hate to show off," he deflected, pretending to be modest.

"Oh, I bet they'll make an exception, maybe after they score these cards and decide the winner. We'd love to hear you sing,"

Tami encouraged, getting out of her chair and making a beeline for the activities director.

She came back squealing with joy. "They said after dinner tonight they're having karaoke. What song will you sing?"

Brian was momentarily speechless, then finally recovered. "Uh, I'm not sure."

I enjoyed the moment, but it was short-lived.

Brian came back with a doozy. "What was the name of that song playing the night I met you? Do you remember, cupcake? You were on the pole, and we swore it would be our song."

Oh, no, he didn't. Now I was a stripper? I reached over, my nails digging into his shoulder, and I heard his grunt from the pain.

"I thought you guys met in high school," Tami remarked, confused.

Oh, sure, in an effort to try to one-up me, he had now cast doubt on the entire thing. Luckily, I was always good in a pinch. "He met me doing one of those strip exercise classes with my sister, who was the one who suggested it. Should have known about her, right? Anyways, him and his buddies were working out at the gym and came to watch." I swatted him on the shoulder. "I can't believe you had them thinking I was a stripper in high school."

He looked amused by my recovery. "See? Hellcat. Taking strip aerobics in high school. How the heck was a boy to keep up?"

How, indeed? "I believe it was "Pour Some Sugar On Me." God, I love me some Def Leppard." Checkmate.

But of course he wasn't backing down. "You know, I'd rather sing a ballad for the woman I love. How about I let it be a surprise?"

I tried not to let that fake term of endearment affect me, but my stomach fluttered with his declaration. "I look forward to it, pooky bear."

Tami suddenly had an idea. "We absolutely have to do dinner tonight. We have a reservation for the Italian place, and you could join us. It would be fun to go as a foursome."

She wasn't leaving us much choice, but that was good because I realized having dinner together would ensure that Brian had to sing.

"Well, now that's right kind of y'all. We'd love to join you, don't you think, baby?" I responded before Brian had the chance.

"Great, tell the front desk that you will be with the reservation at seven o'clock for Gordon," Tami squealed, clearly excited.

Oh, boy, it should be an entertaining evening.

# CHAPTER NINETEEN

$\mathcal{W}$e spent the afternoon snorkeling and swimming and then took a long luxurious bath together before arriving for our dinner reservations. Brian hadn't once tried to back out of the plans for the evening or the singing. Could've been male competitive pride, but more likely he'd figured out how he was going to embarrass me via the microphone. I could only guess what crazy song he was planning to pick.

At dinner that evening, they seated all four of us, Tami, Lester, Brian, and me, at a corner table of the restaurant.

"We're celebrating our fifteen-year anniversary. The three kids are with the grandparents," Tami revealed when a champagne bottle arrived.

"Congratulations," Brian said, toasting them.

I instantly felt terrible. "Are you certain you want us joining you this evening? We don't want to impose." To make fifteen years was something not many couples did anymore. Suddenly I worried, both about intruding and the faking it thing. The game was quickly losing its appeal.

Tami smiled. "We've had only each other all week long. This

231

is exciting for a change, especially on our last night. You guys are so much fun."

And there it was. Even amongst my closest friends, I'd never be considered a lot of fun or the type ever to let loose. But Mary Beth had possibilities. The idea was thrilling. I let my hand wander to Brian's thigh, happy that the tablecloth and darkness would help conceal what I was about to do.

"What are you doing, muffin?" he whispered.

I smiled at that absurd term of endearment. "What does it feel like, lamb chop?" I got the satisfaction of his intake of breath when I rubbed him through his slacks.

"I thought you weren't into public displays," he ground out, tensing when my fingers unbuttoned his top button.

"Oh, I'm not, but Mary Beth is. She's quite assertive when it comes to her man."

"Remember turnabout is fair play."

I shivered in anticipation of what that might mean for later tonight. Then I looked up to see Tami studying us across the table. I removed my hand, too embarrassed to continue with an audience. Damn, Sasha was back and overriding Mary Beth's minute of brazen confidence.

"Sorry to stare, but you two have this amazing chemistry. I guess since we've been together fifteen years, Lester and I seem dull to y'all," Tami sighed.

I wasn't sure how Lester would've felt being called dull on his anniversary, but luckily he'd made his way to the men's room.

"All you need is one night to rekindle the magic. You have to keep it fresh, Tami. Buy some toys if you have to," Brian commented.

I swatted him, horrified that he would suggest something that private. "We just met them. Stop." He merely laughed it off. Yeah, I definitely wasn't letting loose like Mary Beth would.

"I'm sorry if I offended you. But I could have a little talk with Lester," Brian hinted.

Tami's eyes got wide. I was about to swat him again when she practically lit up like a Christmas tree. "Oh, my goodness, that would be wonderful. I love my husband, but we've got to spice things up. And you two—Man alive, you both are so hot for one another." She blushed and then looked at Brian. "Was it love at first sight with her, and you never stopped loving her all those years you were apart?"

I sipped my champagne, not knowing what he would to say to that.

He contemplated the question and then smiled. "I reckon I have a hard time remembering when I didn't love her."

ARRIVING AT THE BAR, I could see them setting up for karaoke and decided it was time to give him an out. His earlier words had put me off my game and suddenly I wasn't sure I wanted to hear another fake love declaration. It made things weird. Plus Brian was much too relaxed not to have something up his sleeve—and with a microphone. Lord help us.

"We could say you strained a vocal cord or that singing is a painful reminder of a career gone wrong," I offered.

He only smirked. "Afraid I'll embarrass you in front of the entire bar, Mary Beth?"

I rubbed my hands on his chest. "Keep in mind we're here for five more days. If you choose to humiliate me, I may not want to face anyone here the remainder of the time."

He kissed me playfully. "There's always the thought of holing up in our room."

Now I knew he was definitely up to something. "I'd allow you to bow out gracefully."

"Not a chance, snuggle bunny. I'm in it to win it."

I rolled my eyes. Brian would never say something silly like that.

"Did you get signed up, Austin?" Tami inquired, coming up with her husband and clearly enthusiastic about the whole thing.

Brian nodded. "Yes, ma'am, I did. Lester, you want to go get some drinks with me while we wait for them to set up?"

I watched the men walk away and wondered what advice he was giving an unsuspecting Lester.

"I hope he can talk to my husband. For once, I'd like to be swept off my feet. Have him make the first move for a change," Tami confided.

"You always have to make the first move?" I pried, curious.

She nodded. "For the most part, yes. It's like he thinks I'm fragile. After all these years, you'd think he'd realize sometimes a woman needs to be tied down and ravaged. Oh, my Lord, I can't believe I shared that. I'm sorry, I've had a lot to drink."

I only laughed. "Don't worry. Lester is definitely talking to the right guy."

---

THEY CALLED AUSTIN'S NAME, and in slow motion, I observed Brian get up on stage. My heart was in my throat. Not only was he sexy with his stubble and tan, but he only had eyes for me.

"The way he looks at you. It's sigh worthy," Tami exclaimed.

I took another long drink of my margarita. Something told me I was going to need it.

"I'd like to dedicate this song to my beautiful girlfriend. Baby, you are the firefly to my summer night," he crooned.

I grinned like an idiot at the declaration while Tami clapped, thinking it was the most romantic thing she'd ever heard. I prepared myself. My entire body was stiff with anticipation as to what form of embarrassment this would take. Then the music started, and it wasn't anything kitschy or obnoxious. It was

Johnny Cash's "Ring of Fire". Oh, no. If you were going to do a parody or sing something poorly, you did not do it with Johnny Cash.

He winked at me. Then his baritone voice started, and I froze. It was good. Like, really good, and I was completely transfixed. Holy shit, Brian could actually sing.

"Oh, wow, he's fantastic. And look, he's singing it to you, Mary Beth," Tami squealed.

I nodded dumbly and merely sat there, soaking in the words. I was completely intrigued with this man up on stage of whom I had very intimate knowledge, while having no clue about his hidden talent.

He finished the song to a standing ovation, me included, and made his way over. Dipping me down in dramatic fashion, he kissed me fully to another round of applause.

I could only stare at him, completely stunned.

Once karaoke was over, we said our goodbyes to Lester and Tami and returned to the room, both happily buzzed. When the door shut, I took him completely off guard by launching myself at him.

"Damn," he cursed.

My hands worked his pants, and I had my dress over my head before he could even help me.

"Someone is a fan of Johnny Cash," he quipped.

I unbuttoned his shirt. "That was seriously hot, Austin," I drawled, smiling.

He took my hands and tried to take over the kiss.

I pulled away. "No way. I'm Mary Beth, you're Austin, and tonight I get to call the shots."

He froze.

I stepped closer to him, caressing his face. "Please, Bri. I want to explore you the way you have me. Give me one night."

"Sash—"

"One night," I repeated, watching him wrestle internally.

235

"If I say yes, then you agree to anything I want to do for the remainder of the week."

I shivered, thinking about what that could entail, but I wanted him too badly not to take the deal. "Would you let me tie you up?"

He hesitated. "It's probably better that you do. Otherwise I can't promise I wouldn't try to take over."

Smiling, I crossed to the closet and came back with my silk robe tie.

He took my wrists. "Do we have an agreement on the rest of the week?"

Swallowing hard at the implication, I nodded. I'd take it. "Yes."

His wicked grin made me wonder if I'd made a deal with the devil himself.

"Tie them tight, baby, because once you release me, I won't be responsible for my actions," he vowed, watching me thread the silk ties around his hands.

I made short work of tying his wrists together and then maneuvered him on his back in the middle of the bed. I shed him of his boxers and took a moment to appreciate how very sexy he was. Normally he was so busy giving me pleasure that I didn't have a chance simply to study him.

His eyes were fixated on me. "Christ, I love the way you look at me."

I smiled a slow smile. "And how am I looking at you?"

"Like you want to eat me alive. Like what you see, do you?"

Taking off the rest of my clothing, I moved up the length of his body. His chest was strong and tan, and at the moment, I had all access.

"Talk to me. Tell me if you're turned on." His voice was hoarse.

Straddling his thigh, I rubbed my wet sex up the length of it watching him hiss out a breath. "Oh, I'm turned on, all right. I love your chest." Caressing it, I bent down to capture his nipple between my teeth, enjoying the air he held in response. "I think it's my second favorite thing about you."

"And what's the first thing you like?"

"Oh, that would be your smile, especially when it's only for me. It makes me feel things."

"Like what?"

I flicked my tongue down his abs and enjoyed the way he was practically panting for air. "It can mean a lot of things, but it makes me want you. Every. Damn. Time." I punctuated the words with a flutter of my tongue on the tip of him.

"You're enjoying this torture, aren't you?" He attempted to lean up to watch me.

I took pity and propped his head up with a pillow. "Mm, is this what you'd call pleasurable torture?"

He chuckled. "It's pleasurable, but no. That will have to wait for another time unless you want to give up control right now."

"Not a chance." I smiled, licking his impressive length from root to tip and causing him to test the knots in the ties.

He gave me a pained smile. "I'm dying here. I want to touch you so badly that I'm ready to start in on the ties with my teeth."

Sweat was beading on his forehead, and I knew I was on borrowed time. Swallowing him whole, I enjoyed the fact that he practically convulsed from the pleasure. I worked him with my tongue and moved lower. My eyes met his, and I saw such naked desire that I shuddered with ecstasy. I could feel him getting close. His thighs trembled, and his cock swelled. When he exploded in my mouth, I swallowed down the thick, hot evidence of his orgasm with enthusiasm knowing how much it turned him on to watch me do so.

"Untie me," he begged.

I shook my head. "You said all night, and I'm not done." I was enjoying this way too much to stop now.

He groaned when I pressed my wet center into him, pressing our heat together. I could feel him start to harden again already.

"Sasha, honey, I need to touch you."

I smiled sweetly. "Not yet."

Stroking him between the sensitive lips of my sex, I enjoyed the aroused expression on his face. I rose up and fed him into me slowly, savoring every inch as I sheathed him deep inside of me.

"You feel amazing. I want to touch your clit and make you come," he pleaded.

My hands found his chest and rubbed down his hard abs. "What if you watch me do it?"

His eyes closed and a tremor ran through him. "Yes."

I dipped my finger into my slick entrance, locking my eyes with his. The heat reflected in his depths sliced through me like a knife.

"Let me taste you," he whispered.

Offering up my index finger, wet with my desire, I watched as he leaned up and took it into his mouth. I was transfixed while he worked it with his tongue thoroughly. Taking it back, I placed it on my swollen clit and rubbed.

Shifting my hips, I started to move. The string of muttered curses let me know that he was getting close.

"Slow it down, honey, or I'm going to come again." His voice sounded strained.

It only served to fuel my pace from fast to furious. Rubbing harder and faster, I joined him over the edge and collapsed on his chest. After lying there a minute, I missed his hands stroking my back. Rising up, I leaned over him and untied him slowly.

I was unceremoniously flipped onto my back, the moment he was free with his face diving at my center with a vengeance.

"I can't believe that turns you on after."

His fingers worked our combined wetness. "Knowing this is you and me together is incredibly hot." He kissed, sucked, and rubbed until I was crying his name and lay there boneless.

How could I possibly argue with the man?

———

WAKING UP THE NEXT MORNING, I attempted to stretch, only to find my hands and legs bound. What the hell? A momentary flash of panic hit me, but Brian's voice came from behind me.

"You were sound asleep, so I couldn't resist." He came into view and stood beside the bed.

I twisted my head to see him. "What is it you plan on doing with me?" The possibilities were starting to turn me on.

"Feed you."

Did I hear him correctly? "You tied me up to feed me?"

He chuckled, leaving for the door when a knock sounded. He returned with a tray in his hands. "You sound disappointed."

I offered him a wry smile. "Actually, I'm hungry, too."

"Good. Here, let me put a couple pillows under your head." He stood back and popped open a bottle of champagne. After pouring it into a flute and mixing in some orange juice, he sat down next to me on the bed. "Want a taste of mimosa?"

I nodded, and he brought the glass to my lips. I sipped slowly, letting the cool bubbly slide down my throat. Next he held up a strawberry. I took a bite, hardly believing how intimate it was to have him feed me. He repeated the pattern one last time. After eating the last strawberry, his fingers danced over my stomach. Then lower, palming my sex. I closed my eyes at the exquisite way his touch could make me feel.

"Do you know how incredibly sexy you look, tied up and at my mercy?" He set the glass down on the table.

I shivered with the thought. "Should I be nervous?"

He flashed me a wicked grin. "I did warn you that you'd be mine the rest of the week after last night. By the way, our champagne is courtesy of Tami and Lester. I have a feeling Tami had quite the evening last night."

"Well, happy anniversary to them." I inhaled sharply when his thumb went to work on my clit, massaging expertly precise circles.

He grabbed the champagne bottle and splashed some over my stomach and chest, following with his hot mouth. I moaned in delight at the sensation of him lapping the cool liquid off of me. He sucked and teased my nipples to hardened peaks, bringing me to climax with his skilled fingers. When my eyes finally flickered open, I saw him observing me intently.

"I love watching you come." He took bacon from the plate and waved it in front of my mouth.

I nipped it away from him, making him laugh. "As much as I love bacon, please don't rub that over me."

His lips twitched. "That does have possibilities, but I'd rather just serve it to you." He spent the next hour feeding me breakfast morsels, alternating with eating his own meal off of me.

I never would have associated being fed with the word erotic, but I certainly did now.

Later, we lay in bed, slugging the afternoon away after an entire morning devoted to sex and food. "I have something I'd like to ask you for." I held his hand and traced the lines.

He looked like he was bracing himself. "What's that?"

"That in another few months, maybe I can have another evening like last night."

His face was unreadable. "Why?"

"Because sometimes I'm so caught up in what you're doing to me that I don't get to pay attention to you. And now that I have those little groans and growls as a soundtrack in my head, I want more. And I feel like you haven't trusted another woman like that before."

His arms went around me. "In the spirit of being vulnerable, I will tell you that I haven't done that before. And I do trust you, but it's hard for me to give up complete control like that.

However, for you and only every few months, I will do it if it makes you happy."

I smiled enthusiastically and kissed him for agreeing. It wasn't lost on me that we'd made the assumption that there would be another few months together.

When Brian's phone rang, he got up and answered it in his 'office voice' and then took it out onto the balcony. I couldn't make out the words, and when he came back in the room, it was hard to read his expression.

"Everything okay?" I asked.

He sighed. "Do you want the good or the bad news first?"

"Bad news," I answered without hesitation.

He rolled his eyes and took a seat next to me on the bed. "Tough. You're getting the good news first. It flows better that way."

I would have preferred to hear the bad first and get it over with, but he was probably still figuring out how to spin it as was his nature.

"The good news is that was Vanessa from Tryon Pharmaceuticals. We got the account."

"But—" I hedged, bracing myself for the negative. Was I off the account? Were they changing the team?

He leaned in to kiss me. "But we'll have to fly out tonight and meet with them tomorrow. I tried to get it delayed until Monday, but she said the only day she and the chairman can do is tomorrow."

Oh, our trip was being cut short by a few days. It was disappointing but not as terrible as I'd been expecting. "That's unfortunate, but other than that, everything else is okay?"

He narrowed his eyes, and I could tell immediately that I'd said something wrong. "Sure, other than having this time together cut short, everything else is fine."

He was definitely pissed if he used the word *fine*. "Brian, wait—"

But he was already changing quickly into his swim trunks. "I'm going to do some laps at the pool. If you don't mind calling our travel agent to book flights home tonight, I'll be back in an hour or so."

Our perfect bubble had popped with one phone call. I was proud we'd won the business with Tryon Pharmaceuticals, but something told me tomorrow would be a reality check of epic proportions.

# CHAPTER TWENTY

*T*he meeting with Tryon Pharmaceuticals was set for this morning. Brian thankfully had been back to his old self by the time he'd returned from the pool at the hotel yesterday and we'd packed up, taking an evening flight back to New York. But now I didn't know what to expect. Getting ready with him back in my condo was throwing me off my game. It was getting harder to draw professional lines when we'd spent the last few days being intimate, carefree, and a couple. Then this morning we woke up, showered, and ate breakfast together ready to go to work.

"What's wrong?" Brian asked on the cab ride over to Tryon's offices.

"Nothing," I murmured, smoothing down my long black skirt. Once again, I was covered from head to toe courtesy of the profile sheet, this time in the skirt with a blue long-sleeve blouse. The look was crisp and professional, but I'd mixed it up a bit with my black four-inch heels. A girl had to preserve some personal style.

"Lie to me again and see what happens." He'd repeated the words I'd said to him in Aruba.

When I met his eyes, I saw amusement and something else I couldn't put my finger on. "Okay, for a pitch I can prepare, rehearse, and definitively know that I'm ready. For straight-up meetings, it's more difficult to know what to expect." I was careful not to say anything about my confidence level or insecurity. He wouldn't expect that from me, and I wasn't going to share it.

His eyes softened, and he took my hand. "There's never been a time where I haven't seen you handle your own. Keep in mind this is business, and that means swallowing your pride. You may have to defer to the client even when you don't want to. Vanessa is the alpha, but it'll help to have the chairman, Michael, there today. Considering he practically lit up during the second presentation when you walked in, it's clear the old man is a fan. You'll do great."

As usual, he could make me feel better by laying out the facts in a way that eased my mind. I smiled tightly and took a breath. Unfortunately, though he might have a gift for smoothing things over, he couldn't predict the future.

---

WE MET in the same conference room at Tryon Pharmaceutical's offices that we had the previous two times for the pitches. Michael Dobson greeted me warmly. Maybe this meeting wouldn't be too bad, after all.

Vanessa kissed Brian's cheek, and I had to carefully mask my expression at her enthusiastic greeting. Clearly, she was happy to see him, but her glance toward me was downright frosty.

"Brian, you look tanned. Did you get back from vacation? Actually, Sasha, you look like you got some sun, too," Vanessa commented with a brow raised.

Before I could register what she was implying, Brian covered smoothly. "One of the perks of working for Gamble Advertising would be the Gamble Properties' hotels and the fact that we have retreats in Vegas and other sunny locales. All of the vice presidents came back last week."

Brian could do improv full time; he was so exceptionally good at it.

Vanessa smiled, and Michael got down to business.

"We wanted to go over some specifics and, of course, sign on the dotted line today," Michael started out. "Vanessa will be your point of contact, and she'll keep the board up to date. I'm assuming, Sasha, you'll be our client care representative at Gamble Advertising?"

I smiled. "Yes. I'll be the account manager." My eyes met Vanessa's and saw the challenge.

"You know, I spend quite a bit of time out of our North Carolina plant these days. Might be easier if Brian was the lead on the account since he's located in the Charlotte office," she reasoned.

Oh, she'd like that. "It's not a problem. I'm down in the Charlotte office often and will ensure that I make arrangements to be there whenever we need to meet." I tried to keep my voice friendly.

Her smile didn't reach her eyes. "Fine. I'll get the best of both worlds with the two of you."

Brian didn't miss a beat. "I assure you, you're in the very best hands with Sasha. However, it would be my pleasure to attend meetings when possible."

I tried not to let it make me feel jealous. This was business, and I'd seen Brian charm women young and old. Vanessa was not the exception, and yet her smile toward him made it clear she thought she was.

Michael launched into a few specific details, and forty minutes later we had the signed contract in hand. He turned and looked toward me. "Are you counting the days toward preseason yet, Sasha?"

I nodded, but before I could answer, Vanessa interrupted.

"Michael, I would think it would be obvious that Sasha read you were a Cowboys fan and came prepared to flatter you with regurgitated details of your favorite team. I highly doubt she's truly a fan of football."

Michael blushed slightly, and Brian nudged me under the table. He undoubtedly knew which direction this was heading.

I smiled tightly. "In the interest of full disclosure, Mr. Dobson, I did know you were a Cowboys fan. However, I could recite the same type of information on any team in the league or on any Super Bowl dating back the last thirty years. I'm unequivocally a diehard football fan."

He brightened and then looked thoughtful. "Super Bowl thirty-four," he challenged, sitting back in his chair.

I grinned. "The Rams beat the Titans that year. It was quite the game when the Titans came back to tie it after being down sixteen points. McNair was the quarterback for the Titans, but it was Curt Warner for the Rams who would complete his Cinderella story and earn the MVP for the game. Personally, it was one of my favorite Super Bowls in recent history."

He slapped the table. "I tell you something, Sasha. If your boss wasn't sitting right here next to you and it wouldn't be considered highly inappropriate, I'd either try to hire you on the spot or try to set you up with my grandson. But because I'm old, my filter fails me from time to time, so I'll say it even knowing I can't act on it." He looked toward Brian. "I hope you don't allow her into your fantasy football league, else she'd most likely clean up."

Brian's smile was strained, and I realized in looking at Vanessa why he'd nudged me. Her eyes were narrowed. Shit, I'd won a challenge I hadn't meant to participate in.

"That's good advice, Michael," Brian said. "Sasha will call today to get the ad placed in the Cowboys' stadium. Monday we can meet wherever your preference, Vanessa, for the magazine spots for phase one."

"Why don't we meet in New York after all on Monday as I'm spending the weekend in the city. I look forward to it." Vanessa barely flicked her eyes back in my direction.

Michael stood up ready to go. "I know this is in good hands between the three of you. Vanessa will keep me updated. I'll be in touch about those Dallas tickets, Sasha." And with that, the chairman left us.

Vanessa went over a few more logistics but essentially treated me like a third wheel for the remainder of any conversation.

———

ONCE WE GOT into a taxi heading back to my office, I let out a sigh, knowing I was about to get a lecture. The thing was that Brian's lectures weren't all that bad if I was being honest. He never got angry and always tried to keep things positive and fair. But I wasn't in the mood even for that.

"You didn't actually expect that I'd sit there and listen to her tell him that I'd simply studied the Cowboys for no other reason than to regurgitate details for him?" I broke the silence.

He exhaled heavily. "Did I expect it? No. Did I hope that perhaps you could have smiled and said that you're a football fan of all teams without showing off? Yeah, I did have a sliver of optimism." He sounded weary in his response.

"It would be easier sometimes if you got angry instead of this *I'm disappointed* tone."

He shook his head. "And sometimes it would be easier if you listened to me and to Josh when we tell you that Vanessa needs to be treated with kid gloves, not shown up. This is business, Sasha, not personal, which means that we suck it up and defer to the client."

I fought my temper. It wasn't that he was wrong. Once again, my pride had gotten involved and I'd opened my big mouth. "Michael is our client, too," I defended.

He gave me a pointed look. "You proved that he absolutely loves you and would like to either hire you or set you up on a date—which only went further to piss off Vanessa."

"He's her boss, so that can't be all bad. Plus it's obvious she wants me off this campaign when she made the comment about hoping to move things to Charlotte. We both know the majority of her business with the board is up here. She only did that to see if it would be a way of getting me off the account." The taxi pulled up in front of the building, and we walked through the lobby, putting the conversation on pause until back in my office.

"And you did nothing to try to convince her that you belonged on the account, except to say it wasn't a problem for you to travel down there when necessary. Come Monday, you need to put the same research skills you used to charm Michael into making an effort with her, at the very least. I'm not going to sit in meetings and play mediator between the two of you."

"I don't remember asking you to." Funny how this was the first time in months that we were sniping like we used to do quite often.

"I think it's clear she would like me there for a reason."

"Yeah, no kidding." I took a seat my desk and didn't bother to hide the sarcasm.

He leaned forward, sitting in the visitor's chair across from me. "You're going to have to stow the pride or any jealousy. You can be pissed at me, but I'm speaking to you as your boss in this moment. This account is huge, and you put a lot of effort into ensuring we beat out five other agencies. You need to refocus that energy on keeping the client happy."

I swallowed hard, knowing he was right and, although I'd never admit it, being turned on that he never backed down from telling me the truth even if I did get pissed off at him. "I will do better come Monday," I vowed, knowing it wouldn't be easy. "I'm working late tonight, but I should be able to show you something by tomorrow for Monday's presentation."

He nodded. "If you need anything, call me. Send me the draft once you have it ready. I'll be available this weekend."

I tried to hide the disappointment that he was leaving tonight. But hadn't I said I'd be working late? The part that bothered me the most was that he hadn't said anything about coming in Sunday and seeing me, either. His trip back to New York on Monday was obviously going to be all business, and he was making that clear. I should've been relieved but instead confusion peppered my thoughts. "Yeah, okay."

With one last look he said, "I'll let you get to it, then and see you Monday."

---

I worked until almost midnight in the office. Before leaving, I emailed Brian the first draft of the presentation. Once again, work was my salvation to turn off everything else. When I got home, I saw that he had already reviewed the draft and only had a few minor changes. Obviously, he was up, too. It was tempting to call him but I decided I wouldn't be the first to do so. Instead, I made the changes, and emailed them back at two o-clock in the morning. Once my head hit the pillow, I basically passed out.

The next morning I saw that he'd responded with a generic 'thank you' at two-thirty, and that had been it. I wondered if he'd also been thinking we could still be in Aruba enjoying our last couple of days. Most likely he remained pissed off for what had transpired during our meeting. Shit. That was the number one item on my agenda today. Research on one Ms. Leopard-print-fuck-me-heels Vanessa Warner. And the first order of business was to stop referring to her as that in my head if I was to make a sincere effort.

By four o'clock that afternoon, I felt better about a couple of different ways I could attempt to relate to Vanessa. She was born and raised in North Carolina, not far from where I'd grown up. She'd gone to Duke, which was my rival school having gone to UNC, and she was a class A bitch. Damn, two steps forward and one giant one back.

I needed advice on how to make nice, and for that, I called Catherine. Considering I had no other plans for a Saturday night, I was pleased when she suggested dinner and drinks.

I met her at a busy restaurant near her condo on the Upper West Side. I hadn't seen her in a few weeks and looked forward to a quality girls' night.

"Sasha, you look lovely. You're growing out your hair. I like it." She kissed me on the cheek, and we took our seats at the table.

I smiled, taking in her impeccable taste in fashion with her stunning black-and-white checked dress and four-inch heels. "Thank you. You look amazing, Catherine. I love the dress and have you lost weight?" Not that she needed to, but she looked slimmer than the last time I'd seen her.

"Thank you. The irony of a divorce and then having him remarry quickly is that you may feel like shit, but you tend to look good because you aren't eating or going out as much. Of course, the minute you're happily in a relationship you gain those few pounds back."

I grinned at the thought. I fluctuated a couple of pounds every time I spent a weekend with Brian. "Have you gone out on any dates since the speed dating night?"

"Nope. It's been a virtual desert of dating activity. But how about you? How are things with Brian?"

I shrugged. "A few days ago we were in paradise, and I would've told you things were great. But then we had to cut it short for a work meeting, and I got lectured from my boss." I sighed. "It's difficult to balance the two, but I know he has the same issue. And it wasn't like I didn't deserve it, which only made it harder to hear."

"Why did he lecture you?" she questioned.

I relayed the details of Vanessa and our encounters. We ordered our drinks and salads, and I saw her consider my words.

"Women like that piss me off, but unfortunately, it's more the norm than not. Like it isn't hard enough in a predominantly male workplace, we women have to go and cut one another down."

I nodded. I might not be the friendliest woman in the world, but I definitely didn't bring other women down unless they duly deserved it. I knew how it felt and loathed that kind of pettiness. "It pains me to say it, but Brian is right about it being business and needing to put the personal shit away. The thing that sucks is I hate that part. I'm great in leading a pitch and doing all of the research, but the client relations—Ugh. I could use some advice."

She looked surprised, and then her eyes were sympathetic. "My best advice would be to go into every meeting knowing that she'll make passive-aggressive comments and ignore them. Almost like you don't catch on or didn't hear them. If you raise a brow, stare her down, or flinch, she'll know she's gotten to you and consider it a challenge. If you ignore them, either she'll think it's not worth the effort because you aren't rising to the bait, or she's going to get more aggressive."

I sipped on my martini. "What if she does get more aggressive?" I already knew Vanessa would most likely be the type.

She contemplated. "Hopefully by then she's making herself look unprofessional, but watch when you're alone with her. A woman like that may take only small shots at you in front of Brian or anyone else, but she'll save the big guns for when you're alone, expecting that you'll then reveal your reaction in front of others. In that case, you're going to look like the hostile one. It's almost like two toddlers. It's not the first one who hits that gets caught, it's the one who retaliates."

"Sounds like good advice even if it does compare us to toddlers."

She chuckled. "So, uh, do you have plans for later tonight?"

I shook my head. "Nope, I sure don't. Why, did you have something in mind?"

"Well, you know I'm trying to get myself out there. I need to move on from my divorce and start dating again. The thing is that until I can get my confidence up and feel good about myself again, I have no desire to date. But I also hate the thought of being alone. Although my ex-husband turned out to be a complete asshole, I miss being married. I want a relationship again."

"How do you propose to do that?" I honestly didn't have a clue and knew I'd fail miserably if she requested advice in that arena.

She shifted in her seat, looking uncomfortable. "Can I tell you something that you swear you'll never tell another soul?"

"Of course you can, Catherine."

"I've never been that sexually confident. I struggle with— Oh, this is humiliating." She paused, swigging back the rest of her martini and signaling the waitress for another.

I waited her out, concentrating on my food, knowing she needed a minute. And evidently some more liquid courage, based on her slugging back half of her new glass.

"I struggle with feeling desirable and confident in the bedroom. My ex basically told me he was tired of having to do all the work. That my insecurities were his breaking point."

Regarding her thoughtfully, I pictured Brian and the way he made me feel desirable merely by looking at me. "Catherine, your ex obviously didn't understand what it is that a woman needs. He should've made you feel wanted and sexy. Some of that confidence can come naturally. But the bedroom should be the one place where you can let go of your insecurities instead of piling them on, especially with someone you love."

"I know he was a selfish prick. But because he was also the last person I've been with sexually, it isn't exactly inspiring me to get out there."

"We need to figure out a plan. Let me think of someone I could possibly set you up with, or I could ask—"

"Actually, I have an idea already. I either need you to talk me out of it or go with me."

"All right, let's hear it." I was intrigued and apprehensive all at once.

"I wouldn't ask you except that I figure you're pretty open when it comes to sexuality and won't judge."

I had definitely become more open since being with Brian. "I won't judge, Catherine," I whispered, looking around to ensure our privacy. Catherine had a high enough profile in her profession that I didn't want to take any chances.

She picked up on it, too. "I'll tell you in the car ride over. If you decide you don't want to go with me, I'll drop you by your place instead."

We requested the check and finished our drinks.

---

HOLY SHIT, we were on our way to a sex club. I had barely paid attention to anything else after Catherine had dropped that initial bomb shell once we got into the car.

She was still talking nervously. "They are supposed to be discreet, giving clients wigs and masks. They have these classes for women who only want to get their confidence up."

I was speechless.

"Say something, please. I'm scared shitless, but if I can't learn to give myself an orgasm and only have my ex as my last memory, I'll go crazy."

I spoke carefully, knowing how fragile her self-confidence was. "Okay, first off, I think you're beyond brave. I'm in awe at how much courage it takes to want to do this, let alone trusting me with it."

She swallowed hard and regarded me for a moment. "But…"

"There's no *but* to it. I think getting out of your comfort zone and doing something like this may be what you need." I could never imagine myself doing what she proposed, and for that reason alone, I applauded her bravery.

Her smile could have lit up a room.

I hesitated but had to say it. "The small 'but,' however, is to ask if you have thoroughly researched this place. How can you guarantee your anonymity and safety?"

She breathed a sigh of relief. "Thank you for not criticizing. I knew that I could confide in you. This place was recommended to me by a woman I met in Paris. She's recently divorced, and when I asked what her secret was for being confident, she told me about this club. She recommended someone there specifically. At first I was appalled, not that I let her know that. But then she stressed that it wasn't sex; it was about building sexual confidence."

Clearly, I was behind the curve when it came to what to expect in a sex club. "Uh, so you're not having sex?"

She shook her head. "It's an option, but not with the guy she recommended or the package I signed up for."

I could only nod, thinking about the various "packages" they had available. "If I'm accompanying you, what does that mean exactly?"

"Oh, no worries. There's a bar where you can sit, and you can wear a mask, too. I was thinking maybe you could wait for me. And then if you hear me scream, you could, like, call the police or something."

My eyes got big even though I knew she was kidding.

"Sorry, bad joke. I think it'll be fine, but I don't know what to expect. Evidently, I have a meeting with the woman who runs the place first to discuss my options and what I'm looking for.

And if you're uncomfortable because of your relationship, I get it. You don't have to go with me."

Brian and our rules. Shit. "I don't want you going alone." I meant that. "But I think we need to tell someone where we are. Sorry, my dad was a cop for many years. I'm only thinking of safety. Is there anyone we could trust with this?"

She shook her head. "Not that I could confide in. Any chance you could trust Brian?"

Oh, boy. He was going to have a coronary. But I wouldn't hide it from him, either, like he'd done with Jamie. And I'd warned him that we'd have to revisit the rules with regards to me accompanying Catherine. "Okay, I'm texting him to let him know that I'm going with you to the address." She flashed her phone over with the destination while I typed. "The name is vague enough; Travesty could be any bar in New York City."

*"Hey, I know you're mad at me, but I'm out with Catherine and we're going to a new place across town at the address I'll forward you. Do you mind if I check in with you in a couple hours so that someone knows where we are?"*

His reply came quickly. *"WTF kind of place is it that you're worried about being safe?"*

I forwarded the name and address and thought about my options in answering the question. I could play dumb and say I didn't know exactly what it was. I could be honest, or I could say I'd talk to him tomorrow. Option three sounded good, but I didn't get a chance to respond because once I forwarded the name and address, I got the following text.

*"Absolutely not. Call me NOW!"*

Wait, did his response mean he knew what this place was? "Catherine, if I type in Travesty online what does it say it is?"

She blushed. "It says it's an exclusive member's only club and gives a number. I couldn't see anything online linking it to the activity. Also, I was told that we have to sign something when we get there saying we can't post anything doing so, either. They are very discreet with their clientele."

That was a relief and made sense, but how did Brian know of it? I texted him back. *"No can do. About to go inside. We can talk later."*

*"Do you have any idea what kind of club that is?"*

I quirked a brow while reading his words and replied, *"Do you?"*

*"YES, which is why you are not going inside. We have an agreement."*

*"I'll be sitting at the bar. I don't want her going alone. And this needs to remain in extreme confidence!!"*

Catherine looked nervous when the car pulled up in an alley. "To be on the safe side, someone will come out and give us masks to put on before we go through the door. You're doing a lot of typing over there. Everything okay?"

"It's fine." Then I read his next message.

*"You are NOT going in there."*

"Last chance, Sasha, are you in or out?" Catherine asked as the car came to a stop.

# CHAPTER TWENTY-ONE

*I* was *in*, all right; *in-sane*, that is. But at least I was being supportive with my insanity. Yeah, at least there was that. And a good friend didn't allow someone to get murdered or sexually assaulted without offering to sit in a bar and wait to give the police report. Ugh.

*Sure, officer, my friend said she wanted to go to a sex club and learn to be more confident, so I went to have a drink and tried not to wonder what was happening behind those massive closed doors to the left.*

Oh, geez, they looked soundproof.

I replied to Brian. ***"Too late. Bar is safe, mask is on. How do you know about this place?"***

***"Text me in fifteen minutes,"*** was his terse response. He hadn't answered my question but at least he was being a little more reasonable.

***"Will do."***

Ordering a diet soda, I tried not to make eye contact with anyone else in the bar area. Although I had a mask on, I still felt exposed and certainly didn't want to call any attention to myself. If I'd thought speed dating was out of my comfort zone, this was to-the-freaking-moon awkward. But at least I didn't have to participate in conversation. All I had to do was sit incognito at the bar and wait. Catherine had prepped me that she'd signed up for an hour-long session. She'd also confided that she might be out a whole lot sooner if it didn't go well.

The bartender was nice and, of course, hot. After all, that was their business. After fifteen minutes, I texted Brian and frowned when he didn't reply. About twenty minutes in, the bartender came over to check on me.

"Waiting on a friend?" he inquired, having probably seen this scenario play out on any number of evenings.

"Yeah. Tell me something, Eddie," I said, looking at his nametag. "Are the walls soundproof? Because I'm thinking I may not be able to hear the screams of my friend if she needs me." I was only half teasing.

He chuckled. "Your friend is plenty safe, I assure you."

I wasn't so confident, and even through the mask, my eyes must have conveyed that.

He shrugged. "Considering you're here with her, I'm assuming this is a first-time thing and she's nervous, which means she signed up for the beginner's package."

I had to ask. "And what exactly is the beginner's package?"

His eyes lit up in amusement. "You want a menu, beautiful?"

I rolled my eyes and was about to respond when a familiar voice over my shoulder did it for me.

"No, she does not."

Holy shit. Brian was here.

---

I COULD TELL he was beyond pissed off with the clipped tone and hard stare he was giving me.

"What are you doing here?" My voice cracked at least three times in those five little words.

The bartender raised a brow and made himself scarce, wanting no part of whatever was coming.

"Oh, I think you can guess. Come with me."

I took out some cash and laid it on the bar for my soda, only to have Eddie wave me off.

"On the house, love. You two have fun."

Uh, what the hell did he mean by that?

Brian's hand took mine in a death grip, and he practically dragged me down a hallway.

"Where are we going?" I squeaked, looking at the line of closed doors down the corridor.

Suddenly, we stopped in front of room number twelve. He produced a key, unlocking and opening the door.

The lights were low in the small space when we entered. It reminded me of a massage room with the dark, soothing colors on the walls and the table in the middle that was draped with some sort of satin-looking sheet. There was a large wingback chair in the corner, and my shoes sank down into the plush rug. I turned toward Brian, figuring he'd somehow gotten this room for us to talk privately. "Look, I know you're pissed off and—"

He held up his hand and glanced over at the table. "Don't. We're not fighting about this now."

I blew out a breath of frustration. "You can't be serious. You come down here—which, by the way, why are you still in New York, and how the hell did you know about this place? And now you won't discuss it?"

That earned me a tick of his jaw. It was both fascinating and intimidating. In all these years of knowing one another, I'd never seen him like this. His eyes raked over my body from head to toe, which appeared to further piss him off when he took in my short red dress.

"We can fight after," he muttered, turning on his heel and moving toward the table.

"After what?" My heart rate shot up.

"Rule number one."

A shot of desire coursed through me as I thought about what truly angry sex would be like with Brian. Then it clicked what we were doing in this room. When our eyes locked, a chill covered my body. "This room is for that?"

"It is. Lose the clothes and get on the table," he demanded, taking off his shoes.

I stood in place, making no move to do as requested. "Catherine will be waiting—"

"If she is, she can do so at the bar or go home. They will tell her that I'm here for you, and we've gone into a couples' room. Now we can do this the easy or the hard way, Sasha, but either way, I'm going to fuck you right now."

How could I be impossibly aroused and pissed off by his arrogant words at the same time? "Oh, I think I'll try the hard way, please," I challenged, liking the way that his eyes darkened.

He strode toward me like a man with a purpose, lifted me off my feet without a word, and practically dumped me on the table. He raised my arms up and tugged off my dress, securing my hands with two of the restraints up at the top of the surface. Next, his deft fingers unclasped my bra and then yanked my panties down, leaving me completely naked.

"You want it the hard way, do you?" His voice was husky, and I could tell that his control was frayed. He secured my ankles to the end of the table. These restraints allowed enough room to bring my knees up, while my hands weren't going anywhere.

I nodded, my libido spiking up again. I watched, curious, as he opened a drawer beneath where I lay.

He quirked a brow and ran his hand down my thigh. "Very well, you want to play games, we will." He replaced my mask with a blindfold. His fingers glided up, finding me drenched already. Then a digit plunged into me. "This turns you on, doesn't it?"

I nodded, enjoying the pleasurable way his fingers moved. He removed his hand suddenly and I could hear his clothes rustling. His weight was hovering over me, and I gasped in surprise when he entered me fully on one stroke. His thrusts were long and slow, and my body tried to catch up with the sensation. Then, abruptly, he was out. "Bri—" I didn't like the fact I couldn't see.

Suddenly, my hands were being released and a pillow was slid under my neck. "Squeeze your tits together and suck it. I want you to taste yourself," he whispered, using the wetness from me as lubrication between the valley of my breasts. The tip of him was at my lips. I opened my mouth and he shifted forward affording me more of his hard length.

He thrust his hips while I squeezed his cock with my breasts, providing friction. He thickened, which gave me a slight warning before the hot liquid hit the back of my throat. I swallowed instinctively and when he stayed in my mouth, licked every drop, enjoying the sound of his satisfied groan.

He crawled down the length of me, flicking his tongue and teeth along the way.

"Do you know how sexy your pussy is? It's positively glistening and all from you sucking me off."

I shivered with his words.

"You have no idea how much I wanted to punish you for being here tonight. Were you tempted by the menu?" he asked, with his fingers teasing me in my most sensitive spot.

"No, I was only waiting in the bar," I insisted, my voice thick with lust.

"You weren't curious?" His finger dipped back inside of me.

"No, I only wanted you."

His hands reached back over me, securing my wrists back into the restraints. "Brace yourself," he warned, spearing me in one thrust.

"Ah, yes."

He pushed in and out in a frenzy and then, much to my dismay, stopped and pulled out again.

I could hear his ragged breath and fought my annoyance. I arched my hips, trying to feel him again, only to get air.

My thought of wanting him to fill me again was completely forgotten when his mouth descended to my clit. He slid my ankles up on the table so that my knees were now bent. I gasped when his tongue trailed lower, then started circling that taboo place. "Oh, God, you—" I was unprepared for the shock of his tongue flicking at my pucker. His fingers worked my clit at the same time. "Please—" My voice didn't sound like my own. I was at the brink when he paused again. "Dammit," I muttered.

He repeated the action three more times until I was ready to scream in frustration. "No more. You've proven your point."

"Not even close. You wanted to know what tortured pleasure is? This is it, but I didn't figure you'd be this quick to give up."

I clenched my teeth, hating the fact that he was challenging me. "Fine," I hissed.

"Wrong word to use, honey."

I gasped when he slid something hard and long into my slick channel, only to slide it back out and then slowly into my backside. The fact that he'd used my slick heat as lubricant was wildly erotic. My breaths came slowly as the foreign object slid home.

"I'm going to thrust inside your pussy, and you're not allowed to come. Do you hear me? This is for me."

He moved quickly, filling me completely and pounding into me like a man possessed.

Jesus, I wasn't sure how I'd keep myself from coming or why it turned me on to know he didn't want me to. The dual penetration made it impossible to keep from climaxing. "I can't. I'm going to—"

He froze completely. I had the slight satisfaction this was taking its toll on him as well when I felt his harsh puffs of air on my face. He pulled out, and I could feel his weight leave the table.

I lay there in anticipation, unable to see anything but hearing him open some sort of packaging. "Please tell me these toys are new things and not part of the room." Could I help the fact that hygiene came to mind when left alone for a few moments? My mind was an overthinking machine.

"They're new, and you can take them home after," came his terse response.

Was he really that pissed off? My body tensed when soft earphones came over my ears, and I could hear music. "I'm not sure I—" I moaned when his mouth fixated on my breast. He knew gagging me was against one of my rules, but I couldn't touch, see, or hear him now. While his tongue circled around one nipple, there was a pinch on the other one of pain. "Ah—" then his mouth was circling and soothing it. I could only guess these were nipple clamps. Pleasured torture indeed as he repeated the action with the other nipple. I couldn't hear my breathing, but I imagined I was loud as crap right now, panting in anticipation, all random thoughts replaced with raw sensation.

A vibration at my clit had me nearly rearing off the table. I dug my fingernails into the sheet and tried to take deep breaths. My hips arched, but just as I got close, he'd take the vibration away. He did this four times. Christ, I didn't think I could take anymore. The tears involuntarily leaked out of my eyes, and I only hoped the sob was quieter in my head than it had been out loud.

Ripping off my earphones and then the blindfold, I saw his intense brown eyes staring into mine. He looked like he wanted to ask me something but decided against words, and instead he buried his face in my cleft with his lips enclosing my clit and sucking. He glanced up and twisted one of my nipples with his fingers, causing a twinge to shoot through me with the clamp in place. "Come now, Sasha."

My climax was so consuming and so unbelievably powerful that I wouldn't have been able to recall my own name by the time my eyes regained their focus. But he wouldn't stop, insisting that he bring me to orgasm again, unrelenting in his ministrations. As I came down from my second scream-filled orgasm, he moved between my legs, aligned with my slick entrance, and pushed slowly back inside of me. He stayed rooted deep without moving and then leaned over me, capturing my lips in the most erotic kiss I'd ever received from him.

Reaching up, he freed my hands, and then his eyes locked on my face. "Say you're mine."

He pulled out, thrusting deeply, and I arched, running my hands down his powerful arms and gripping his hips.

"Yes, yours," I whispered, watching a look of pure possession float over his features.

He stopped on the precipice of my third orgasm and removed the dildo from my back entrance. He then hovered back over me, locking on my eyes. "I want you there."

His tone left no mistake that he wasn't asking. Yet knowing the man that he was, I knew if I said no, he wouldn't proceed.

I nodded and was met with another searing kiss.

"Get on your knees."

Complying, I felt a vibration then something large was inserted into my wet entrance. Oh, my, he was going to fill me both ways.

"Relax and let me in." His tip was probing and the distinct sound of lubrication came from behind me.

I steadied my breathing as much as I could but the anticipation was killing me.

He held my hips and the first inch of him stretched me. A delicious burn reminded me where he was, and his erratic breathing told me just how turned on he was at the prospect.

He moved slowly, letting me adjust when he was finally past muscle. I could hear his ragged breaths, and when his fingers reached around to my clit, I was in pleasure overload. I rocked back into him and heard his hiss.

"Fuck. Go easy, I don't want to hurt you."

I pushed back again, enjoying the rare moment where I got to take him off guard. I rose up on my knees slowly until my back was flush with his chest. His hands gripped my hips and with a final drive he was all the way in.

His hands shifted to my breasts while he moved with shallow thrusts. "Do you like it with me here in your ass?"

His dirty talk would be the death of me. "Yes," I whispered, shamelessly moving back into him on a deeper thrust.

He muttered a string of curse words, driving me to do it again. His fingers strummed my clit and suddenly I was out of my mind with lust. I about blacked out from the building pressure and, in spectacular fashion, my core muscles tightened and I exploded. I don't know how long my orgasm lasted, but I vaguely registered his groan and then the wetness on the small of my back.

I collapsed down onto my stomach, feeling him next to me.

Removing the vibrator, he wiped my back with a towel, and got off the table. He released my ankles from the ties first. Then reaching over, he expeditiously turned me over gently, removing the little clamps from my nipples and throwing them into a bag along with what I guessed were the other items used. He crossed the room, opening a door in the back. A few minutes later, his footsteps came in my direction again. My heavy eyes watched him pull on his clothes.

"There's a bathroom in the back where you can wash up or take a shower. I called up front. Catherine is finished and waiting for you in the bar."

I pushed up and noticed he was barely making eye contact. I couldn't read his mood. "Okay."

"Text me when you get home. I want to know you arrived

safe." He managed one last glance and then disappeared out the door through which we'd entered.

———

AFTER TAKING a few minutes to pull myself together, I cleaned up and dressed quickly before making my way to the bar to fetch Catherine. We didn't speak until we were in the car, both of us seemed to be whirling with what had transpired over the last hour.

Finally unable to stand it any longer, I stole a look at my friend. "So …" I prompted.

She turned crimson. "It was good, but I think I'm still processing. We talked the whole time."

Shit, this was the part where I was a sucky friend because I didn't know whether to leave her alone or push. I decided for a compromise. "Would you go back?"

"Maybe," she sighed. "Probably. We, uh, mostly spoke about what the lessons could or would entail. Part of me feels like a complete loser that I would need to stoop to this." Her eyes looked teary.

I squeezed her hand. "Catherine, you're not a loser. Get that out of your head right now. What you are is a woman who is brave, smart, beautiful, and kind. Your husband turned out to be a real jerk, and this may be your opportunity to get back out there and put him out of your mind once and for all. What you need to think about is how you felt in there, not what someone else thinks about it. I'm one hundred percent supportive as long as you're happy and comfortable. Okay?"

She smiled. "You're a good friend, Sasha. Thank you. So, uh, how did things go with you?"

It was my turn to blush three shades. "He's ticked off, and I learned they rent rooms to couples. Beyond that, I couldn't tell you much more."

"I'm sorry that I put you guys in that kind of position." Her eyes widened, and then she shook her head. "No pun intended. Sorry."

I couldn't help it; I burst out in giggles, and suddenly she did the same. By the time we made it to my place, we were both wiping tears from our eyes.

"If you can't laugh at moments like these with your girl-friends, then you truly haven't known friendship," Catherine finally said.

I couldn't have put it any better. "I'm lucky to call you friend. And for the record, Brian was plenty pissed off before we even went this evening." The car came to a stop in front of my place. I hugged her, and she pulled back, motioning out the car window with her hand.

"Oh, I'd argue that he can't be that pissed off because isn't that him?"

Looking at the entrance of my building, I saw that, sure enough, there he was in the lobby waiting on me.

# CHAPTER TWENTY-TWO

*W*ith the way Brian had left me, I was astonished to see him here at my building. But damn if my pulse didn't race at the sight of him. We rode the elevator in silence to my floor. I unlocked my front door, and he quietly followed me in.

Slipping off my shoes, I faced him. "I didn't expect you to be here tonight."

He shed his coat. "I owe you an apology—"

I hadn't expected that. "Okay, I'm listening."

He pulled me into his arms, and led me gently onto his lap on the sofa. "I'm sorry for getting mad." He kissed my neck.

I took a deep breath and realized those words held a lot of power. Especially being someone who didn't say them often enough myself. "I'm sorry we didn't discuss it ahead of time, but it was sprung on me last minute. I hope you understand why I had to go."

"I didn't at first, but then I realized I'd do anything for my friends and you were doing the same for yours. Plus you were up front with me with where you were. If anything, at the end I was angrier with myself than with you. I shouldn't have treated you the way I did."

I couldn't help but smile. "I think it could be argued that kind of tortured pleasure wasn't so bad."

He let out a sigh of relief. "You liked it?"

I felt my face heat, but was honest. "I did, but maybe next time we could do it without invoking rule number one."

He smiled and held me a few minutes. "Definitely. We're both tired, and I'd like nothing more than to take a nice hot shower and slip into bed with you. Can we do that?"

I nodded and was led into my bathroom. He warmed up the water and we both stepped in under the spray. We took turns silently washing one another, and I finally couldn't stand it any longer. "I need to ask you something ..."

He tensed and then sighed. "I knew about that place because I'd been there with someone a couple of years ago. The woman I was with was into some pretty hard-core things, and she wanted me to learn how to be more dominant, incorporating the pain aspect. She had me watch another couple with her. I hated it. Call me crazy, but whipping or caning a woman isn't something I can stomach. She wanted it. I didn't. End of story and our arrangement. And maybe my history had something to do with my initial reaction to you being there."

I stood there a full minute processing, unable to respond.

"You wanted to know," he muttered defensively, waiting for my reaction.

"Uh, no. I didn't. I wanted to ask you if you enjoyed it tonight. I don't have a frame of reference for that type of sex."

Now it was his turn to look stunned; then his arms went around me. He let out a shaky breath. "Remind me to never answer a question that you haven't actually asked."

I smiled, thinking I would've gotten around to it eventually. "I'm still glad you told me."

"As for the other: I have no words for how amazing it was,

and I love that I was your first like that. Especially since it was my first time, too."

Holding my breath, I let it out slowly as his words soaked in. "What?"

He gave me a goofy smile and kissed me softly. "I've used, uh, other things, but I've never wanted to until you."

I met his eyes and pleasure overwhelmed me. "Why didn't you tell me?"

He looked a little embarrassed. "Because you trusted me to take care of you, and I worried if I told you it was my first time, then you might not be into it. Male pride, I guess."

Hugging him close, I felt sleepy under the warm water.

"Let's get washed up and get some sleep," he murmured in my hair.

---

I'D ALWAYS HEARD the throes of passion could get you to say things you might either regret or, in my case, overthink later, but I'd never pictured actually doing it. I thought about what Brian had meant about being *his* earlier tonight. I was a grown woman, financially secure, professionally successful, and the natural inclination was to balk completely at being *owned by anyone.* But it had been carnal and so alpha in that moment that I'd also been extremely turned on by it.

We lay there in my bed, both unwilling to start the day and break the intimacy.

I leaned back, my fingertips brushing the planes of his face.

"I need to ask you something," Brian whispered.

"Okay, go ahead." I braced myself, as he seemed serious.

"Could you promise me that you won't go back there? Hell Catherine shouldn't need to go there either."

"I can't promise that. I think it could be a good thing for her confidence. Not everyone has been Brianed and can say they've experienced great sex."

"Did you turn my name into a verb?" His face looked a mix between amused and horrified.

I grinned. "Every woman needs to have sexual confidence in the bedroom."

"Agreed, and I'm not judging Catherine for that. I just don't like the thought of you two ladies in that place without some sort of protection. Like I said earlier, I completely respect that you didn't want her to go by herself. You're a loyal friend. I guess if you need to go back with her, I could go with you. It'll be safer and everyone will know you have a boyfriend. We could even go back into a room, if you wanted."

The thought of going back to the club with him made my skin tingle. Then I realized what he'd said. I propped up on my elbow and looked at him. "Wait, did you call yourself my boyfriend?"

I expected him to retract or get embarrassed like he hadn't meant to, but instead he loomed over me, pushing me back into the bed. He pinned my hands down in a show of dominance that made me instantly hot for him.

He grinned. "Damn right I did. I sang you "Ring of Fire" by Johnny Cash." His fingers stroked, finding me wet for him. "And you said you were mine. Did you not mean that last night?"

His voice was that husky, gravel tone that did things to a girl. I arched my hips, not believing that he could make me ache for his touch so quickly.

He removed his fingers and hovered at my entrance, taking my lips in a deep kiss. "Are you my girlfriend, muffin?" He pressed ahead one delicious inch.

I smiled, wanting more. "Only if you promise never to call me that again."

WITH THE ART of sexual distraction, Brian made it very easy to get outside of my head when it came to the possibility of overthinking the *boyfriend* thing or the fact that I'd once again confirmed that I was *his*. Our sex-charged morning turned into eating Chinese food in bed and then enjoying an intimate bath together.

"Where's your stuff?" I asked, realizing that, aside from the bag he took from the room last night full of our new toys, he was sans extra clothing. And he hadn't in fact answered the question about why he was in town.

"Josh's guest apartment. I'll spend the night over there this evening, give you some space before tomorrow's meeting." His dirty clothes were in his hand. "You doing a load of laundry?"

I nodded, watching him, while only wearing a towel, shove his clothes into my washing machine located in the closet next to the bedroom. He then climbed back in my bed and flicked on the television.

"You never told me why you stayed in town over the weekend." I threw in a few of my things to make a load out of it and started the machine. Something about washing our clothing together and having him casually turn on the TV started to freak me out.

"If you stop overthinking the laundry and come over here, I'll tell you."

I was annoyed at the fact that he could pick up on my facial expressions. "I'm not overanalyzing the damn laundry," I mumbled, crossing over to the bed, only to be snagged by the wrist and pulled down into him. "Like we haven't had enough time in this bed today?" My breath caught at feeling him hard already pressed against me.

He nuzzled my neck, choosing to ignore my protest completely. "I warned you it would never be enough." He kissed down my throat and over my collarbone, and pulled back, grinning, when I sighed in pleasure. "I stayed because I was pissed off Friday and didn't want to leave it that way for Monday. I kind of hoped you'd call me Saturday, and we could get together. Then I got your text, and the rest is history."

"I spent Saturday studying up on Vanessa and trying to find ways to start over. Then I called Catherine, and we met out so I could get some advice."

He looked surprised. "Huh."

I narrowed my eyes. "What do you mean by *huh*?"

He shrugged and brushed his fingers down my back, settling on my backside. "Are you sore from last night?"

Talk about a change of subject. My face heated, and I tried to pull away, only to have him keep me caged. "I'm fi—good. And stop trying to change the subject."

He chuckled. "Nice save with the word. The *huh* was me being impressed that you're trying with Vanessa."

"You mean *shocked,* don't you?"

He shook his head. "No. Impressed that you haven't let your pride get in the way of what needs to be done. I know that isn't easy for you, but I do appreciate the effort."

"You had a point on Friday. I didn't like it, but per usual your lectures aren't off-base."

His face looked stunned.

"Close your mouth, Brian, and stop looking so astonished. Although I don't say it often enough, you're a good boss, and you're great at what you do."

His expression was priceless with my compliment, which instantly made me feel like the biggest bitch in the world.

"I know I'm not the easiest person to deal with …" I took a deep breath.

He cupped my chin and kissed me deeply. "Sasha, you do your work, and you do it well—"

I shook him off. "Stop trying to make me feel better and let me finish." It was just like him to try to soothe me and only made me feel worse about the number of times I'd never bothered to give him positive feedback.

His mouth twitched in amusement. "Okay, please continue."

"What I wanted to say is that I'm sorry for Friday. My pride got in the way, and although I could say it won't happen again, I think we both know the best I can do is to say that I'll try."

He threw his head back and laughed. "Apology accepted, and don't worry. You're not as difficult to manage as you think you are."

The unsettling thought hit me later that he might not mean that entirely in a professional capacity.

# CHAPTER TWENTY-THREE

*B*rian left following a quiet dinner on Sunday night. While I appreciated the separation in order to mentally prepare for tomorrow's meeting, I missed his company immediately. And that was the problem with spending so much time together lately. Maybe it would be good to get back into our two-week routine.

I puttered around my condo, getting my laundry done and prepping my *approved* outfit for the next day. The routine reminded me of high school. Setting out my clothes the night before and talking myself into why I needed to go the next day.

I suppose I should be grateful there hadn't been social media back then; otherwise, I could've counted on a YouTube video or Facebook status to complete my humiliation on that terrible day my junior year in high school. It had been bad enough that the majority of my class had witnessed it in person.

My living nightmare, the one that had started my everyday battle with an anxiety disorder, started on a beautiful spring day, one like any other in April. Most of my class was eating lunch outside. A homeless-looking woman approached the table. My heart beat faster when I realized that beneath the filth, her eyes looked like mine. She knew my name. When I asked what she wanted, she demanded money. I whispered I didn't have any, and she lost it. She began screaming at me that I was her daughter and that my adoptive parents hadn't given her the money she deserved.

I completely shut down in the form of my first official panic attack. My father arrived with the paramedics to find me on the ground gasping for breath. When he'd taken me to the hospital, it was the first and only time I'd ever seen him cry.

At sixteen years old, I'd found out my entire life up until that point had been a lie. By not telling me the truth, my adopted parents had allowed a drug addicted stranger to destroy the world I'd always known. Betrayed by the people I'd trusted the most, my relationship with my adoptive parents had taken a while to repair. As I'd gotten older, I'd learned to forgive and finally accept that they'd believed they'd been protecting me. But the bitter lesson of what a lie of omission could do would never leave me. After that first panic attack, striving to remain unaffected while those around me whispered and worried had become a coping mechanism to get through each day. People mistook my introverted personality for snobbery, but finally, I'd gotten to an age where I cared less about that. Addison may have accused me of thinking I was too good for my small town, but the truth was that I'd always felt lacking.

Thinking of home reminded me I needed to call my sister. She'd left a voicemail on Friday regarding my parents' upcoming anniversary party. Evidently my return email hadn't been good enough for her because she kept calling. Rolling my neck to ease the tension, I figured now was as good a time as any.

The phone rang three times, and I started to get my hopes up for voicemail. Ironic to call someone and hope not to speak to them, but it was typically a relief for me to hear a recording rather than to reach a live person. Voicemails could be easily controlled, but conversations were dynamic and subject to go to shit in a second. Sighing when her chipper voice said hello, I bit my lip and prayed for patience.

"Hi, Addison. It's Sasha."

"About damn time. I've left you, like, five messages," her response came.

It was all I could do not to point out it had only been two and that it was interesting how she had no problem leaving a message when it came to something she wanted, but had difficulty when it came to leaving an apology about Christmas. Yeah, maybe I still harbored a small grudge months later. "I was out of town. What did you need that an email wouldn't have answered?"

"I wanted to talk to you in person. You know the party's the weekend after next. I realize you paid your half, but it would be nice if you took an actual interest, too."

Dammit, why did I feel guilty, and how the hell had the date snuck up on me? "It's not that I'm not interested, it's that I know you have all of the details covered." Of course there was the fact that one could only deal with so much passive aggressiveness in one day.

"Something tells me you're still angry with me about what happened over Christmas." Her voice sounded vulnerable, which was out of character.

I breathed deeply, not wanting to get into that now. It still hurt too much, and frankly, it would go a long way if she could have started out that sentence with *I'm sorry* instead of implying I was angry for no reason. "Is there anything I can do to help on Friday or Saturday?" Emotionally, this was all I could offer at the moment.

"Could you to pick up the cake that Saturday morning? I'll send you the woman's address. I don't know why Dad insists on getting it from her, but Mom says it's the only cake he'll eat. Anyways, it needs to be there one hour before the party starts."

I wanted to ask why it had to be an hour exactly, but kept my mouth shut. "Okay, got it. See you in two weeks."

"See you then. Remember, one hour before."

I clicked off the phone and poured a large glass of wine. It was as close as I could get to relaxing.

---

ARRIVING at work early the next morning, I fully intended to make the most of the extra time before my meeting with Vanessa. On this occasion, she was coming to our office location. I'd recruited Logan and Charlie for the assist. Not only would she enjoy the male attention, but I could use the reinforcements. I was dressed in a crisp blank pantsuit with conservative heels and a white shirt. Conservative, professional, and boring, as instructed. I was about to head into the conference room to ensure everything was set up, when Nancy's voice cut through on the intercom.

"Ms. Brooks, there's an attorney on the line who says he needs to speak with you. His name is Michael Frank."

"I don't recognize that name, Nancy. Can you get his number and ask him what it's regarding? I'll call him back." The last thing I needed was to be tied up before an important meeting with a solicitation call.

"Certainly."

She came in a short time later with the note while I was gathering all of my presentation materials.

My eyes glanced at her face, and I was immediately on guard. Nancy never looked nervous. Two years away from retiring, she was a battle-ax from the days of smoking and perforated printer paper in the office place. She'd softened toward me some after the throwing-up incident in the office but always held herself cool and reserved.

Looking at the message, my face drained of color. In her perfect handwriting was:

*"Michael Frank, attorney for your mother. Need to talk ASAP about rehab center."*

"Sasha, I hope you know I keep everything in confidence."

I swallowed hard. "Thank you, Nancy." And because I didn't want to appear a horrible human being when Michael Frank rang back, since I had no intention of returning his call, I decided to be blunt with my assistant. "She's my birth mother. I've only seen her once in my life, and it didn't go well. They're looking for money again, I'm sure."

She nodded. "Then I'll be certain to screen all of your calls carefully and won't pass on any more messages from Mr. Frank."

"I appreciate that, Nancy." After she left, I crumpled up the note and threw it away. Maybe I'd jinxed this invitation back into my life when I'd been thinking about her yesterday. Or perhaps the timing served as a reminder that the only reason my biological mother ever looked me up was when she needed money. I'd already made that mistake once. I wouldn't repeat it. With Vanessa coming into my office any moment, I couldn't afford the distraction.

---

I NEEDED a moment before heading into the conference room to put the call out of my head and prep. Time to slip in my earbuds. Thankfully, meetings didn't make me throw up, but I still needed the calm of a motivating song to get me into the right frame of mind. Today's choice was Kelly Clarkson's "Invincible". I closed my eyes, let the song end, and breathed deeply. I could do this.

After walking into the conference room, I ensured everything was ready, including the projector and handouts. Logan and Charlie came in ready for the meeting.

Brian strolled in a couple minutes later, greeting both men. He then turned toward me. "Sasha, nice to see you. Do you have a minute before Vanessa arrives?"

"Uh, okay," I murmured, wondering what he had on his mind.

We turned the corner toward my office, and I could feel his eyes on me.

"Everything okay?" Brian asked.

I bit my lip. Now wasn't the time to tell him about the phone call. "I'll, um, tell you later."

He nodded, and we went inside my office, only to have Nancy buzz right away announcing Vanessa's early arrival.

Turning toward Brian, I asked, "Do you mind bringing her back to the conference room? I know she feels most comfortable with you."

He looked surprised. "No. I don't mind. We can talk afterwards."

Look at me, a poster child for a fucking work in progress, trying to defer to what the client would want instead of attempting to mark my territory. I was determined to make today successful and not above asking for help to ensure it happened. Whatever he'd wanted to talk about could wait.

I returned to the conference room in time to greet Vanessa warmly when Brian showed her in.

She was dressed in a red-colored top that stretched across her chest, putting impressive implants on display. I had to keep myself from looking further down to her skirt or shoes. The client could dress in hooker boots and a thong, and I needed to pretend like it was normal. Her smile didn't touch her eyes, but I wouldn't let it faze me.

"You remember Logan and Charlie from the initial presentation?" I said.

"Yes, nice to see you gentlemen. Sasha, whatever do you do with yourself, surrounded by such nice-looking men?"

It was tempting to say something outrageously snarky and inappropriate, but instead I merely smiled. "The world of advertising does have its perks."

"I'm definitely in the wrong business, then." She took a seat, and Nancy graciously offered her a beverage.

She glanced toward my assistant. "Tea with milk. Skim, if you have it, with two sugars—but only if it's real sugar. I don't want the fake stuff. If you don't have skim, then don't bother. You can get me water instead, but only if it's purified."

Nancy smiled tightly. I was relieved that I wasn't the only one rubbed the wrong way by Vanessa. Evidently, she had a talent for pissing off any female within a ten-foot radius. "Now, then, I think you'll be very pleased with our phase one approach," I started out.

She raised her brow. "I think that remains to be seen."

Taking a page from Catherine, I ignored the poisonous dart and flipped on the projector. Logan got the lights while giving me a *she's a piece of work* look.

Thirty minutes later, Vanessa had oohed and aahed over everything Brian, Logan, and Charlie had presented but gave me the third degree over my ideas regarding radio advertising. It was ironic as almost all of the ideas introduced had been mine; only those presented by me had set her off.

"I'm not convinced that radio would be the wisest use of our money," she contemplated, tapping her pencil and then sipping her tea.

I bit my cheek, praying for patience. "Certainly, it's your decision, and you can think it over. But our research shows that a Sunday countdown show would do great with your targeted demographic. The cost is exceptionally low compared to the television spots."

Brian backed me all the way. "I think it's worth a couple of them, Vanessa, but like Sasha said, it's your call."

"Who am I to argue with your logic, Brian?" Vanessa stood up, looking at her watch. "I've got a flight to catch. But thanks again for the drink last night and safe travels this week. I've never been to Dubai. Hopefully, you'll get some time to explore."

Thankfully, my face was hidden from view as I'd gotten up to get the lights. I took several shallow breaths, wishing I could give the band a snap without anyone noticing. So he'd left my place to have a drink with Vanessa, and this is how I found out he was traveling to Dubai this week. I'd asked him not to hide shit like this from me, and yet he'd chosen to ignore that request.

Tamping down my temper, I turned toward Vanessa. I didn't catch his reply to her but needed to get my niceties out of the way.

"Safe travels. I'll be in touch later this week to give you details on the photo shoots." I smiled, hoping it was convincing. I didn't dare glance toward Brian.

"Sounds good. Logan, Charlie, thanks for your time on this. Good work," she complimented.

Oh, sure, the boys got the credit.

Brian walked her out, and I let out the breath I'd been holding, careful not to vent or show any of my emotions in front of my staff.

"Did it dawn on anyone else that she has an issue with women?" Logan said the minute the door closed.

Charlie nodded and then looked toward me. "Definitely."

I didn't have the luxury of commiserating with my staff. "It would appear so, but it doesn't matter. The client is always right even when she's not. Thanks for your work today, gentlemen. Charlie, I trust you can book the studio and get the photographer lined up. Logan, I'd like for you to bring me competitive samples over the last year. We need to ensure we aren't doing something that's already been done."

They both nodded and got back to their tasks while Nancy came in. She started cleaning up the conference room and asked, "How did it go?"

"Okay, all things considered. Thanks for getting Vanessa her tea and setting this up, Nancy." I needed to retreat to my office to regroup after hearing Brian had met her for drinks and also regarding the earlier call.

"Sasha, you know I have your back, right?" the older woman said, surprising me.

I looked at her a moment and saw loyalty. Something that I'd never thought I'd rate in her book. "That means a lot, Nancy. Thank you." It was nice to hear that someone did.

She nodded curtly and proceeded to go on with her chore.

AFTER RETURNING TO MY OFFICE, I sank into my chair and wasn't surprised when Brian came through my door a couple minutes later.

"What did you think about the presentation and her reaction?" I preempted anything else he might have wanted to say with a business-only tactic. It was the safe zone and one I intended to stay in until I could calm my heart rate.

He took a seat and regarded me cautiously, obviously not expecting that I'd start off with this question. "I think it went better than expected. Good call bringing Logan and Charlie in."

"Yes, well, it appears she is much more open to my ideas when presented by them as opposed to by me."

"It's nothing to take personally. Maybe she truly didn't like the radio idea."

"Maybe next time you two have drinks you can pick her brain about why."

He muttered a curse. "That's what I wanted to discuss with you before the meeting. Look, she called about eight o'clock last night, saying she had something to discuss. She asked that I meet her for a drink."

"Let me guess. It was geographically convenient to meet her at her hotel."

"Are you pissed off professionally or personally?"

"It's nice that you can draw the lines when it's convenient for you. Let's go with the professional line first, shall we? How do you think any one of your vice presidents would feel to know that you got a call from the client on their account and had a drink with said client without them being in attendance or being informed of such a meeting? Do you think that they might be the slightest bit peeved and feel like, oh, I don't know, you left them out?"

A muscle in his cheek throbbed, clearly showing he was getting annoyed. "I would think that most of the other VP's would understand that I'm here to make the client happy, and that we're on the same team. I'm good at my job for a reason, which includes holding the client's hand or helping you out when it comes to customer relations. And I'd hope none of them would make it personal."

"You mean the way you might take it personally if I were to have dinner with Logan?"

"You're the one that pointed out we couldn't have rules when it came to clients or co-workers and I agreed it was an unreasonable expectation. If you needed to have dinner with Logan for a professional reason, I may not like it, but I'd trust you."

I didn't like that he had a point. "But I would at least tell you about it."

He ran a hand over his face. "I'm telling you now. And it was only drinks to discuss the client budget and the fact that they may be looking at raising it."

"Vanessa doesn't have that kind of authorization, which only proves it was an excuse to see you. Bottom line is that you left my place last night to go have drinks with another woman who'd like to sleep with you. Who also happens to be my very difficult client who'd like nothing more than to cut me out completely from being her contact."

"Ask yourself this question: if she'd called Josh and he'd met her for drinks in order to put the client first, would you be as upset?"

I hated the fact that my answer was no. Shit, maybe my personal feelings were clouding my professional judgement. "You didn't mention you were traveling to Dubai next week."

He sighed. "I had a meeting with Josh this morning, which is where the travel got brought up. That's why I was too late to tell you this morning."

"I warned you after the Jamie thing that I don't like having things kept from me." Under my desk, my fingernails bit into the palms of my hands, trying to keep me calm. The fact that I'd received the call about my birth mother this morning wasn't helping my mental state regarding this conversation. I'd been so convinced I was in the right, that his reasonable explanations were throwing me.

"I didn't mean to keep things from you, Sasha. It was business and I made a decision."

"So you think I'm overreacting?"

He took a moment before responding. "I think if the positions were reversed and I'd heard about a similar situation in the conference room like you did, I would've been pissed off too. I'm sorry it came out that way. I did have every intention of telling you. And any of the VPs would be irritated to find out that their client called me and not them. But I would hope they and you understand why I had to go." His voice was quiet but sincere.

I looked at the time and realized I had a conference call in twenty minutes for which I needed to prepare. "I appreciate your apology and I do believe you were going to tell me. I'll need to get over it." Then something dawned on me. "Wait, if it's true that you found out you're traveling this morning from Josh, then how did Vanessa know about it?"

"Of course, it's true," he said, exasperated that I was questioning his honesty. "The reason she knew is because when we walked into the meeting together this morning, she wanted to know if I was heading back to Charlotte afterwards. I told her I was traveling internationally instead."

"Oh, sorry." My day was packed, and I couldn't afford to let this eat at me any longer especially since I wasn't thinking rationally. "When are you going?"

"I'm leaving in the next thirty minutes for the airport to get back to Charlotte. I didn't want to get lumped into a flight with Vanessa. That's why I told her I was flying directly to Dubai."

I stood quiet appreciating that he'd done so.

He continued. "I won't be back until the middle of next week. Look, I'm not trying cut you out. The only thing Vanessa and I discussed was the budget and phase two, with the television campaign. I was with her a half hour because I thought it was an excuse to get together and hope for something personal. I had texted Josh ahead of time to call and interrupt just in case."

I hated hearing this and had to reach down deep to move on from it and trust him. The fact that he'd preempted the meeting with a rescue call gave me some satisfaction. "Okay. I'll keep you updated on the shoot next week."

He looked relieved for the change in conversation. "Good. Are you coming down to Charlotte the weekend after next?"

I shook my head. "My parents' fortieth anniversary party is that Saturday. I'll be home in Beaufort, but I could come down the following weekend."

"We have a two-week rule." His voice was quiet.

"You're out of town this weekend, and I'm out of town the

following one. You need to be more flexible." Great, now my agitation was back.

"You could invite me to the party."

Whoa. I was stunned. We didn't do family things together. "You want to go to the party with me?"

He shrugged. "Why not?"

I could think of a lot of reasons, one of which was that I need more than five minutes to get over him meeting Vanessa last night. "What would we tell everyone?"

"We could simply say that I'm your date for the party. If they ask, we met at work and are friends. We wouldn't be lying."

"I didn't RSVP to bring someone." I knew the moment it left my mouth it was the lamest excuse in the book.

He arched a brow. "If you're going to come up with a bogus reason, you should try harder for a good one. I'll leave you to your conference call. Keep me updated on the campaign." The intensity in his look let me know he was annoyed.

Well, I was, too. "All right. Safe travels."

He stood up and crossed over toward me and then stopped.

I waited for him to come closer for a kiss or something, but when he didn't, vast disappointment hit me. Considering I'd practically jumped down his throat the last time we'd crossed a personal boundary in this office, I knew I couldn't have it both ways.

"You know I'll miss you." His face softened, but his clenched fists appeared to signify that he wanted to reach out but wouldn't.

"I, um—I'm certain we'll talk." Damn my awkwardness. I would miss him too, even if I couldn't bring myself to verbalize that yet.

He looked wounded for a moment, then was back to *nothing bothers me* Brian. "Sure, I'll call you, or you can call me. Bye." With one last look, he left out my door.

I let out the breath I'd been holding and thought about the

idea of bringing a man home to meet my family. It was something I hadn't done since high school, and it intimidated the shit
out of me. Then again, the thought of having someone there on
my side was appealing.

Shaking myself mentally, I brought up my calendar. My work
day was absolutely packed, and I didn't have the luxury of
dealing with the personal aspect of my life. Some might call it
avoidance; I called it my only way of coping when emotions
threatened to overwhelm me.

# CHAPTER TWENTY-FOUR

*A*fter leaving the office early on Friday, I flew down to my home town for my parents' anniversary party, scheduled for the next day.

I'd talked to Brian a couple of times over the last ten days, while he'd been in Dubai and then London, but the majority of our conversations had been work related. He hadn't brought up coming into town this weekend for the party, and I assumed he must've changed his mind. Of course, he could've been waiting for me actually to invite him, but I'd chickened out every time I'd thought about it.

He most likely thought my silence on the subject had something to do with residual anger over the Vanessa situation, but the truth was that home represented a place where I felt vulnerable. I wasn't sure if I was ready to have the two worlds collide and chance he might find out about my traumatic past. Of course, as far as my family or anyone else knew, my first panic attack had been a one-time reaction brought on my shocking confrontation with my birth mother. At least, that's what I hoped they still thought. I was proud of myself for not asking Nancy if the attorney who'd left the message about my birth mother had called again. I didn't need that shit clouding my mind. The past needed to stay there.

Pulling into the driveway of my parents' house, I sighed at the sight of my sister's mini-van with the stick figure family on the back window. It was a comical reminder: I wasn't in Manhattan any longer.

Lugging my suitcase inside, I was surprised to see Addison sitting at the counter in the kitchen on a stool—without the kids. I smiled and hugged my mom while she prepped dinner across from Addison.

"Hi, Sasha Jayne, how was your flight?"

"Good, Mom, thanks. Hi, Addison."

My sister looked up from her notebook and offered me a little wave of acknowledgement. It was the first time we'd seen one another since our Christmas incident. "We have fifty-four people coming tomorrow and I didn't get your RSVP. I guess you assumed I'd know it was only you?"

Instead of bothering with a response to her bitchy greeting, I rolled my eyes and walked into the living room, satisfied to hear my mom giving her a lecture behind me. I leaned in and gave my father a hug in his La-Z-Boy recliner.

"Hi, Daddy."

"Hi, darlin'. Nice to see you. How was the flight?"

"Good thanks. I'm heading up to put my stuff in my room, then I'll be down to visit."

"All right, baby girl," he said, going back to his paper.

After closing the door to my room, I immediately dialed Brian's number. I wondered if it was too late to invite him for tomorrow's party. Or if he'd still want to even come.

"Hi, stranger," he greeted, picking up on the first ring.

"Hi, yourself. Are you back home?"

"No. How about you? Are you at your parents' place in Beaufort?"

I tried to hide my disappointment that he was traveling. What did I expect when I hadn't extended an invitation to come here? "Yeah, just got in."

A knock startled me.

"Hold on." I said, opening the door.

Addison stood there. "Hey, Sasha, I didn't mean—" she began, only to see me on the phone and stop. "Oh, sorry, I didn't realize. I'll, um, talk to you later maybe." She turned suddenly and was back down the stairs before I could even respond.

"Okay…" I shook my head, wondering if my mom had sent her up here to give an apology. I shut the door again and took a seat on the bed. "Sorry about that. Um, we didn't get around to talking about this weekend." I wished more than anything I could see him.

"I didn't get the impression you'd want me there the last we spoke."

"You're right. And it's unreasonable to bring it up on the day before."

"Let me ask you something. If it was possible, would you want me there now?"

I didn't hesitate. "Yes, but if you're out of town, it's last minute …"

"I'm at the Harbor Inn in town."

"Wait. What? In this town?"

He chuckled. "It's been almost two weeks, and I wanted to see you. If you don't want me to come to the party, I'll understand. But I didn't like the way we left things."

Raw need coursed through me. "Do you, um, want me to come by tonight?" Get a grip. Why was I asking so nervously? Clearly, the man was here to see me.

"Of course, but I know you're with your family."

I was halfway tempted to ask him to come over for dinner tonight, but I didn't think I should see him for the first time in two weeks with my mom and dad watching. Self-preservation. I didn't want to jump on him in front of my family. "My parents go to bed early. I could be by about nine o'clock?"

I could practically feel his smile through the phone. "I'm in room two fifteen."

---

LUCKILY, Addison was gone by the time I came back downstairs. I contemplated calling her to add my plus one but preferred to piss her off by bringing him to the party tomorrow without a RSVP. It was passive-aggressive, but what the hell. She brought it out in me.

I ate dinner with my parents and practically had to shove my mom out of the kitchen in order to wash the dishes. She was one of those women who didn't know what to do with herself if she wasn't taking care of others. I smiled, peeking into the living room to see her kissing my father's cheek. Now there was a love story, and tomorrow would mark forty years of it.

As they were about to retire for the evening, I let them know that I'd be out late and not to wait up. If they thought it odd, they didn't comment. After all I was thirty-two years old. What were they going to do, impose a curfew?

Wired by the time I drove the few blocks over to the hotel, I fought my nerves while knocking on Brian's hotel room door.

He opened it, and my mouth went dry. He stood there in nothing but a pair of pajama bottoms slung low on his hips. Had I forgotten how unbelievably hot he was?

He chuckled. "Is my body all you want me for?"

"Mm, you do have a pretty face, too." I met his eyes and let the door close.

The moment it clicked, we were all over one another with hot, hard, and relentless kisses. Pushing my back against the wall, he pinned my hips with his own.

Pulling away reluctantly, he gave me a slow, lazy smile,

running his fingers down the side of my breasts. I shivered with his touch. "You have too many clothes on," he murmured, unbuttoning my blouse and then sliding my jeans down. "There, now, that's better."

I was on fire everywhere. His hands held my face, and the desire reflected in his eyes matched what I was feeling.

He nibbled my bottom lip while unclasping my bra, letting it fall to the floor. Between the kisses down my neck, he stopped at the sweet spot behind my ear. "I take it you're no longer angry with me about the Vanessa business?"

I let out a little sigh. "No, I get it. I don't like it but you're right. If she'd called Josh, we'd both be irritated, but it's the client's right to do so. And I do trust you. But I can't stand to have things kept from me. I'd rather be pissed because of something you tell me rather than learn about it from someone else."

"I'll try better next time." He kissed me deeply and then pulled back, naked desire evident on his face. "But right now I'm going to have you against this wall." His hands worked down my panties with his mouth diving straight for my throbbing sex.

This was the side of Brian I'd come to know. The one in charge in the bedroom who would take me any way he wanted without apology. The moment he touched me, we were back on familiar territory with all previous irritation forgotten.

"Open your legs, gorgeous. I'll be down here awhile."

Absolute need hit me when his slight stubble grazed my inner thigh. I clenched with expectation, leaning my full weight against the wall lest my legs give out on me completely.

His hot breath was against my cleft and I weaved my fingers in his hair, pressing him into me further. I shivered when he inhaled deeply.

"I love your pussy, especially your scent. It's like a drug for me, and your body is my addiction."

He buried his face in my center with a vengeance, his hands gripping my hips and pulling me into him. I moaned, unprepared for the full assault when his fingers delved deep inside of me and worked me in tandem with his mouth.

I climaxed before I could even fully comprehend all of the sensations he was inflicting on me. I was lost and completely at his mercy.

His tongue lapped up the evidence of my need, feeding on it as though it was the best thing he'd ever tasted. The image had me completely undone. In that moment, I realized I had no reservations with this man. He could do whatever he wanted to with my body. I trusted him that much.

As I came down from my climax, he rose, kissing me with the taste of my arousal fresh on his lips. It was beyond erotic. He shed his pants quickly, then his hands gripped my backside, lifting me up, enabling me to wrap my legs around his waist. He thrust hard into me with delicious precision. The angle against the hard surface afforded him the ability to bring me quickly to another orgasm as he hit a spot that only he'd ever discovered. Plunging one last time, he threw his head back, groaning with his own release while pinning me completely against the wall with his weight.

We stayed there while we caught our breath. He then carried me over to the bed, not breaking contact before starting again.

Evidently, we wouldn't be getting much sleep tonight.

---

THE NEXT AFTERNOON, I dressed in a beautiful coral-colored, cotton eyelet spring dress with a sweetheart neckline and long, flowing skirt. A nude belt cinched my waist and I complemented it with the same color wedges. It was a soft look for me and a complete Coastal North Carolina type dress. I wondered what Brian would think. Considering I was lucky to have the ability to walk today after last night, he'd probably think it a miracle to see me upright.

After picking up the cake, I drove over to the country club to deliver it precisely one hour before the party, as instructed. I tried to help my sister set up, but after an hour of listening to her sniping and with people starting to arrive, I was relieved to go pick up my date.

I parked in front of Brian's hotel and walked into the lobby. He was there waiting, and I took a moment to appreciate how very handsome he was. He glanced in my direction and then did a double take. His slow smile and head-to-toe assessment made me flush with delight.

"I'm sorry, I'm expecting Sasha-B-Fierce who wears pencil skirts and four-inch killer heels. Have you seen her?"

I swatted at his arm, pleased when he kissed my cheek.

"You look beautiful," he whispered in my ear. Then he took my hand, holding it on the way out to the car.

"Thank you. And stop looking so surprised at the way I'm dressed. It's my parents' anniversary party at a country club in front of a lot of people I went to church with growing up. I couldn't very well wear fishnet stockings and stilettos."

His brows shot up with that visual. When we got into the car, his hand skimmed up my thigh. "Great, now I'm having a church girl gone naughty fantasy in my head."

I chuckled. "You clean up nicely, too, Bri." He was dressed in a classic gray suit with a crisp white shirt that made me want to wear it and nothing else some morning.

His fingers danced up my thigh, and I smiled.

"Ask me something," I requested, watching his grin and then enjoying the intake of his breath the moment he realized I was going commando.

"Why, Sasha Jayne Brooks, are you not wearing any panties?"

The way he said it in his drawl made me giggle.

"Why, I declare, you're full of surprises. I think I'll be scoping out a coat closet when we get there," he threatened.

I shook my head. "No way. What part of *country club* and *people I went to church with* don't you understand?"

His hand crept up under my dress again with his fingers finding my bare center.

I gasped in pleasure. You'd think after last night I would have calmed the ache. Instead, his mere touch inflamed me.

"Let me get this straight. You can go without panties, but I have to behave? Interesting."

I tossed him a wicked smile. "Maybe I want you thinking about it during the party."

He smirked. "Oh, believe me, I will. And I'll behave but only because I've got plans for you later. Now ask me something."

"Are you nervous to meet my family?" I found myself slightly disappointed when his fingers retreated back into his lap.

"Not at all. You know I don't get uneasy meeting anyone. I'm a people person."

That was true. I don't know why I would think it would be any different in a personal situation. Obviously, I was making this a bigger deal then it needed to be. "That's true, and they'll probably love you." He chuckled and then glided his fingers over my thigh again, teasing me with little circles, but not going any higher. "I would hope so. I'm a lovable kind of guy."

He wasn't exaggerating. Everyone who met Brian adored him. I drove the short distance to the country club and parked the car. Turning off the ignition, I inhaled sharply when his fingers slid up into my slick heat. Gripping the steering wheel, I'd practically asked for this when I went pantyless. Luckily, I'd opted for the far corner of the lot, away from any other cars. Closing my eyes, I thought an orgasm might relax me before spending the next couple of hours amongst family and old family friends.

"Time to go."

My eyes snapped open when I realized his fingers had retreated.

He winked, clearly enjoying the advantage.

Snagging his hand, I captured the finger he'd used on me, sucking it between my lips seductively. I relished the flash of desire in his eyes and the hiss of his breath. Now I wouldn't be the only one sexually unsatisfied for the next couple of hours. After releasing his hand, I touched up my lipstick in the rearview mirror and got out of the car nonchalantly.

When Brian didn't move, I went around to his side and opened his door, cocking my head to the side.

"I'm not meeting your family with a hard-on," he muttered.

I burst out laughing. Sometimes it was nice to take Mr. Control completely off guard.

We walked into the country club five minutes later, and it dawned on me that we hadn't covered what our status was. "Uh, what will we tell people?" A lot of guests were already here.

He turned me toward him and smiled. "Relax, we'll tell them that we are friends who met at work and let them assume whatever the hell they want to. All right?"

I let out the breath I'd been holding and met his smile. He made it sound so simple. "Okay. Ready?"

Upon entering the private room reserved for the party in the elegant country club, we immediately ran into my parents' neighbors. I introduced Brian, and by the time we made it to my mom and dad, three couples later, I realized he was completely at home, charming everyone.

My parents were gracious, but I could tell my mother was surprised. My father had gotten straight to the point by asking Brian which football team he favored. With the answer of the Carolina Panthers, he had definitely passed the test.

But most astonished of all was my sister, who looked from me to Brian and back again before forming words. "Uh, who is this?" He held out his hand. "Brian Carpenter. You must be Sasha's sister, Addison."

She took his hand warily and then looked at me. "You didn't RSVP to bring a date."

I was glad we were out of earshot of my parents. "You're right, I didn't. But considering I cut a check for half the cost, I think I can bring a plus one without a problem."

"That's what you're good at, cutting the check while I do all of the actual planning."

I regretted that Brian had to witness the petty sniping with my sister and was shocked when he interrupted smoothly.

"It's a lovely party, Addison. Sasha mentioned you've worked extremely hard to put this all together. Your parents must be pleased to have this many people who love them in one place."

She studied him for a moment, gaging his words, and must have believed his sincerity. "Thank you, and I didn't mean to complain. It's not that big of a deal to have one more. Um, I'd love for you to meet my husband. He's over here at the table."

I found it both amusing and exasperating that Brian could charm my sister so easily when I could barely get along with her. Maybe the problem was more me than I'd like to admit. After walking over, I hugged my brother-in law, Ryan and made the introductions.

"I'll get you a drink, Sasha. Addison, Ryan, would you like anything?" Brian offered.

They both declined, and I tracked him across the room toward the bar while bracing myself for my sister's questions.

"Are you guys together?" she zeroed in.

"We're friends." I enjoyed the annoyance on her pretty face probably more than I should have.

"Uh huh. How do you know him?"

"We used to work together in Charlotte."

"And he's here in Beaufort for you and for the party, but you're only friends?"

"Addison, give her a break, babe," Ryan, interjected.

I cast him a look to convey my appreciation. Brian returned with the drinks just in time.

I was sorely in need of one. "Are you hungry?"

He offered me a lazy smile that let me know he was thinking of something entirely different than what I'd meant. "I'm all right. We can visit and then eat in a bit if you'd like." He was sitting close to me but not so close as to imply that we were a couple.

"I was asking Sasha how you two knew each other," Addison started while Ryan rolled his eyes at his wife's tenacity.

Brian didn't even sweat it. "We worked together in the Charlotte office for a number of years." He took a pull on his beer and glanced at the label.

"You like the hops? It's a local brewery," Ryan provided. And with that, the men bonded instantly over IPAs, entering into an entirely different conversation until Addison could wheedle her way back in.

"So, Brian, what, uh, brings you to town?" she finally got in.

He handled her like a seasoned pro. "You're looking at her." He put his hand on my back and rubbed gently.

Her eyes widened. "You guys are a couple, then?"

I was confident Ryan just kicked her under the table. God bless him.

Brian's eyes flashed toward me, amused, and then focused on my sister. "I think the proper classification would be friends, but I was happy to be her date tonight, meet the family, and see her hometown."

Addison scoffed. "Considering she can hardly stand this place and avoids coming home whenever possible, I'm surprised she'd invite anyone to see it."

His hand squeezed my thigh, and before I could say anything, he jumped in. "Huh, that's surprising, considering how fondly she's spoken of y'all."

She was stunned momentarily and then rolled her eyes. "Oh, sure she has."

My temper was bubbling up and was about to let her have it when he quietly did it for me.

"I have to say, Addison, I'm surprised at your animosity toward your sister with all the kind things she's told me about you."

She arched a brow. "Really?"

He leaned back and went directly for the sweet spot. "Don't believe me? Okay, how's this: you and Ryan were college sweethearts. And you have four children: Kyle, Kayla, Kevin, and the baby. Ah, Kassandra, right?"

She nodded dumbly, and he went on.

"She's commented many times what a great mom you are and how your children are lovely. She flew in for each of their births, and although she doesn't live locally any longer, I'm pretty sure she doesn't miss a birthday for any of her nieces or nephews. Matter of fact, wasn't it that Star Wars Lego set that I helped you pick out for Kyle's birthday?"

I nodded and had to bite the side of my cheek to keep from laughing. Brian remembered details about everyone in and out of the corporate world.

My sister was more than impressed. "I had no idea."

I couldn't help my shock when I observed her tearing up. "Addison—"

She held up a hand and sniffed, looking in her purse for a tissue. "I'm such a bitch. Brian is right. You have been there. I always thought you didn't tell anyone about us, like we didn't exist in your world. And me being a stay-at-home mom made you dismiss me. I had no idea you thought I was a good mom. And then I never apologized for what happened over Christmas. What I said about the kids—it was horrible and untrue. I'm so sorry." The last part was said on a near sob.

I gave both men a look that begged them for help and was grateful when Ryan scooted close and put his arm around her.

"Babe."

Brian nudged me under the table.

Ah, crap, I needed to say something. "Uh, it's okay, Addison. I haven't exactly been overly pleasant to you over the last couple years, either. I don't know where this animosity has come from, but it would be nice to put it behind us."

"And be real sisters?" There were tears in her eyes.

Uh, did that mean she hadn't considered me one before? Like I didn't have enough of a complex about being adopted, she had to go and say that now. I sighed, trying not to read more into the comment than she'd intended.

Brian rubbed my hand supportively.

"Absolutely," I choked out.

She practically knocked me out of my chair with a hug.

---

I WAS SPRAWLED NAKED on top of Brian after an exuberant hour-long sex session. We were going to kill one another, I was convinced. All of that foreplay in the car ride back here with no panties had worked us up to the point that we practically started in the hotel elevator.

"Whatcha thinking?" His lips peppered my shoulder with butterfly kisses.

"I owe you a big thanks for defusing the sibling rivalry at the party. You knocked Addison's socks off with the fact that you could recite all of her kids' names. Her face was priceless."

"I only know them because you've talked about them. She's, uh, very different from you."

"Well, I'm adopted, so I guess that's a given. But she's a good mom. Maybe I needed to tell her that more often."

"I don't think the adoption thing is it. Take me and my brother Benjamin. Same parents and complete opposites. Kenzie and I share a mother and didn't grow up together, but we're closer than a lot of siblings. And only my opinion, but maybe if

Addison wasn't busy taking shots at you, you'd be more inclined to tell her she's a good mom."

I hugged him tightly. Once again, he was on my side without being asked. The fact hit me that this day could have turned out much differently if he hadn't decided to show up. "I'm sorry that I flaked on you when you first brought up coming with me. I was taken off guard and—"

He interrupted. "It wasn't very good timing on my part to bring it up, given I'd just pissed you off. You have a nice family, Sasha. Your dad is intense, but I like that he's still protective over you."

I smiled. "Can I ask you about your father?"

"What do you want to know?"

"What was he like?"

"He died when I was young," he murmured.

"How old were you?"

"Seven."

I kissed his chest. "Tell me about a memory of him, something happy."

"He worked a lot," he started, and then took a deep breath. "He, uh, one time came home on a Friday early and told my brother and me that he had tickets to a baseball game. It was only minor league, but you would have thought we were going to see Babe Ruth play. We never got time alone with him, so it was pretty special. He took us to the ballpark and got us hotdogs, cotton candy, and soda. He made us promise not to tell our mom."

"I bet he would've been really proud of you."

He exhaled heavily and pulled me closer. "I feel guilty that I don't miss him more, but it's been long enough that I don't remember all that often. My mom changed a lot after he died. Anyhow, I'd love a change of subject about now."

"How about you made today a lot better than it would've been without you. I'm glad you were there with me."

He rubbed my back. "I'm glad I could be, too. Plus now you owe me."

I propped myself up on his chest to see his amused grin. "Owe you how, exactly?"

"You can return the favor by coming with me to my sister's graduation party next month in Virginia."

"Your mother and sister-in-law hate me. And wouldn't Josh be there also?"

He smiled. "Kenzie would be over the moon to have you there. And Josh will be on baby watch, so I doubt he or Haylee can come, but even if they can, you should go anyhow. And you know I don't care about what my mother or Rebecca think."

"Where's the party? I thought your sister went to school in California?"

"The actual ceremony is the weekend before in LA, but my mom wants a party back home."

That made sense. "Okay. In order to set the expectation if I do come, I have to warn you. I'm probably not going to bridge any sibling rivalry, enhance any relationships, or inspire any tender moments. So you may be getting the shit end of this deal in other words."

He laughed. "You could assist me by agreeing to a coat closet if I need to blow off any steam from dealing with my family."

I rolled my eyes. "Yeah, because having my panties in my hand after sex while your mother confronted me for pouring wine on Rebecca wasn't humiliating enough. Like I need a second bad impression."

"Ah, good times. I think I'd worry more if my mother did like you."

"Can I ask you something?"

He tensed. "If it's about my mom, I don't want to talk about it."

"Okay," I sighed, tabling my question. I'd wanted to ask why he continued to go home if she was that miserable to be around. I could guess it was for Kenzie, but considering she was out of the house, too, it begged the question why either of them still chose to do so.

He snuggled me to his side, bringing my face within inches of his. "Is that an annoyed *okay* or an understanding one?"

"Understanding. If you don't want to talk about your mom, then I'm not going to push it. Everyone should be able to keep some personal things, well, personal." No truer words were spoken, particularly when it came to me.

His eyes narrowed, but thankfully he left that proverbial land mine alone for now.

# CHAPTER TWENTY-FIVE

*T*he upside of having to meet with Vanessa down in Charlotte instead of up in New York was that I got to spend more time with Brian during the week. Currently, we were in his bed on a Wednesday night, and I was enjoying the feel of his strong hands caressing my back. The lull of the air conditioner trying to keep up with the unusually hot May night was making me sleepy.

"I know dealing with Vanessa isn't your favorite thing, but I really like that you're in my bed during the week," he murmured, both of us tangled up there after a bath together had made its way to the bed.

I'd given up on idea of needing space from Brian the night before seeing Vanessa. No amount of mental preparation or separation from him could change the fact that the woman was horrible to deal with. And if I was being honest, our two-week rule no longer seemed to be enough time with him as it was, so I now took all opportunities to see him. "Mm, I like that, too. I'm going downstairs to get some water. You want anything?"

"You, back in my bed."

My belly fluttered at the thought. We were insatiable even after all these months.

"You got it." I didn't know when I'd gotten over the hesitancy of walking around him naked, but I proceeded nude to the kitchen. Brian was certainly good for my sexual confidence, I mused, slugging back the water bottle and then parading sexily back into the bedroom where he was now sitting up.

I could tell instantly by his posture and pale face that something was wrong.

"What is it?" I asked, bracing myself for bad news.

"Juliette called. She's getting on a plane to Florida to stay with her sister as we speak. Things with her husband, Rob aren't good. She thinks he may be cheating on her and addicted to prescription drugs."

I was completely shocked. "Oh my God. Do you think I should I call her?"

"She's boarding any minute and until she has proof, I don't think she wants people to know. Which I guess I should've thought about before telling you."

I tried not to take it personally. Brian would move hell and earth to help Juliette and was definitely the person she should be confiding in. But she was my friend too and knowing that she was hurting and I couldn't reach out was tough. "So what's the plan?"

"Tomorrow I'm hiring a private investigator. I'd mentioned it to her a couple weeks back, so I have some candidates. It's tricky though with Rob being a police officer, but we'll sort it out."

"Let me know if I can help in any way. Do you think she's ready for a divorce if he is cheating?"

He nodded. "Yeah and I should probably call Mark too and see if he has any suggestions for divorce attorneys in case it comes to that."

Good idea, I thought. We settled down in bed needing to get some sleep.

He sat up suddenly. "Shit, Sasha. Vanessa's meeting is tomorrow. Maybe we can reschedule. I'd hate to put off doing this for Juliette. I told her I was on it first thing in the morning."

"No, you go and do whatever you need to, and I'll explain there was a family emergency to Vanessa. I'm confident she'll understand. We're only finalizing the details for phase two. This should go smoothly considering she was happy with phase one's magazine advertisements. And Juliette is more important."

He looked reluctant. "It's not that I don't think you'd do a great job, but are you sure you're up for it on your own?"

I smiled, trying to convey false confidence. "Of course. It's my job and the proposal is sound. You said so yourself."

He breathed a sigh of relief. "Okay. Good."

What was the worst that could happen?

---

IT WAS hard to concentrate on business while knowing that Brian was helping Juliette navigate her own personal hell. I found myself checking my phone, waiting for him to indicate how things were going. The best action I could take to support both Juliette and Brian at the moment was to take care of Vanessa so neither of them were impacted. That's what I set my mind to do.

Tryon Pharmaceuticals was proving to be my most challenging client in my ten years of working in advertising. Not only was Vanessa difficult to please in general, but she obviously had an issue working with me in particular. The fact that she was keen on leering at my boyfriend in front of me didn't help, either.

Huh, I'd mentally referred to him as my boyfriend.

With ten minutes to spare, I donned my headphones and blasted my music, closing myself away in my temporary office. I let today's selection of "Fight Song" by Rachel Platten take over my mind. Afterwards, I put on my best client-facing smile and went into the conference room ready to do battle. Uh, that is, ready to meet with my client.

"Nice to see you again, Vanessa," I welcomed.

Her eyes scanned the room. "Where's Brian?"

I tried not to bristle at her inability to say hello like a normal human being. "Unfortunately, he can't make it today. He had a family emergency come up last night."

I didn't know anyone who wouldn't have been sympathetic to that statement, but clearly I'd underestimated her.

"And that excuses him from missing this meeting how? I flew all the way down from New York. If this so-called emergency turned up last night, I should've received a call last night letting me know. Did someone die?"

What a callous bitch. "I'm not at liberty to discuss his personal situation except to say that it's obviously very serious. And since I'm the lead on the account, and we worked together on this proposal, we wanted to go forward with this meeting so we didn't delay phase two."

"Yes, I suppose you are the lead, technically, aren't you?" She tapped her long red nail against her lip like she was considering something and then flopped down into one of the chairs.

I swallowed down any retort I could've made. Messing up this campaign was not an option.

We settled in and went over the PowerPoint slides in depth. Vanessa was relentless with her questions.

"I don't think I care for your first proposal, Sasha. What's the alternative?"

She damned well knew there wasn't an alternative. Furthermore, the first one was perfect for the direction her company wanted to go with television ads. "We are confident that this first proposal will boost your market share, not to mention set the company up for its long-term strategy."

"In other words, you put all of your eggs in one basket. For shame not to give a client multiple options, but then again, I'm not surprised. Perhaps Brian will have more ideas."

It took all that I had in me to utter my next sentence. "This proposal was his, but I'll be certain to relay your dissatisfaction with it when I speak with him later. If you give me until tomorrow, I'd be happy to come up with some different options."

Amazing how fast she changed her tune. "You know what? It's growing on me. But it does make me wonder: if this was Brian's idea, what does he keep you on the account for?"

"We work as a team, brainstorming and coming up with ideas to keep the client's best interests at heart instead of our individual egos. Brian will be very pleased to hear that you're comfortable with the proposal." I got up out of my seat and flipped on the lights before handing her the proposal for signature. I tried to act nonchalant, as if the two-million-dollar phase two contract was a drop in the bucket.

After she finished signing, I stood with her. "I'll see you out."

"No need, I know my way. Please tell Brian that I missed him and look forward to our next meeting." She made her way to the door.

"Certainly."

I was about to breathe a sigh of relief, but she turned.

"Tell me, Sasha, are you currently fucking him, or is it in the past?"

The shock of that question floored me. I knew she glimpsed the surprise on my face before I could cover it. "I don't know what you're talking about."

"Oh, I think we both know. A man doesn't look at a woman like Brian looks at you without having had intimate knowledge of her at some point. You know what, I answered my own question. The look is definitely one of *been there, done that.* Take care, now."

She strutted out of the office in her killer four-inch stilettos and too-tight leopard-print skirt while I envisioned a scenario in which I could tell her to go to hell and not lose my job.

After going through the motions of getting the signed contract over to the accounting department, I scanned a copy for Brian, and then set up the meetings to get the ball rolling on the actual commercial shoot.

Finally, after everything was in order, I settled into the visitor's office and refused to think about Vanessa's comments. I was on the fence about whether or not to tell Brian but reasoned he didn't need my shit on top of everything else he was dealing with. I was effectively stomping my emotions down, refusing to acknowledge how they were making me feel. You'd think I'd be better at it by now. Pushing thoughts of Vanessa out of my head, I proceeded to plow through my day.

As I was driving back to Brian's house, the number from the New York office flashed up on the car's Bluetooth. I answered and heard Nancy's voice on the car speaker.

"Sasha, I know you told me to screen your calls regarding that attorney, Michael Frank. I'm really sorry to bother you, but the message he left today I thought you might want to know about."

I steeled myself, already knowing deep down it wasn't good news. "Yes, of course, Nancy."

"He wanted to let you know that she passed yesterday. He didn't give any details but did leave his number again and that of the county morgue."

My veins felt like ice water, and I didn't know what to say.

"Do you want me to email you the details?" she asked.

"Yes, please," came an automatic voice I didn't recognize. I was numb.

———

PATIENCE WASN'T my strong suit, so waiting on Brian at his place after nine o'clock that night—after not hearing from him all day —was about to drive me mad. Finally, I couldn't stand it any longer and sent him a text.

*"Everything okay? Anything I can do to help?"*

*"On my way home,"* came the reply.

I didn't like this restlessness I was feeling. I hoped a glass of whiskey would take the edge off.

Pacing until I heard the garage door open, I had to physically grab the countertop ledge to keep myself from launching at him when he came through the front door. I tried to keep my inner turmoil at bay and focus on him. It wasn't hard to make that switch when Brian entered the kitchen, looking emotionally exhausted.

"That bad, huh?"

He nodded, walking over and kissing me briefly before crossing over to his bar. He fixed himself a stiff drink to match mine. "Yeah, it was."

"Do you feel like talking about it?"

His tired eyes met mine. "Not really. Do you mind? Right now I only want to decompress a little."

It stung. But with another glance at him, I recognized that he had the weight of the world on his shoulders at the moment. "I don't mind. Come on, let's go sit on the sofa."

I snuggled up next to him, and we both sat there in the silence, sipping our whiskey.

"Tell me how things went with Vanessa."

I was surprised he hadn't checked his email, but it spoke volumes about how wrapped up he must have been today. "Good. She signed off on the proposal. I have a meeting on Tuesday afternoon with the media department to go over the commercial shoot, but if you think that you won't be able to get away, I can reschedule for next week without an issue."

He squeezed my hip and tossed me a small smile. "No,

Tuesday is good. Great job." He held up his glass, and I clinked mine to it.

"Thanks," I murmured, thinking about the train wreck of a day it had actually been. "How is Juliette?"

He kissed me on my forehead. "I had to tell her that within hours of the PI following her husband, he had proof that he was cheating. The investigator is going to dig for more, but clearly Rob is enjoying the fact that his wife is out of town. She's going to be okay though. The tricky part is the custody. She wants proof that he's using drugs as leverage to ensure she can keep Tristan safe. Mark found a reputable divorce attorney that Juliette will work with once she gets back in a couple of weeks."

"How did she take it?"

He sighed. "Better than I thought. I think she's angrier with herself for being duped. She's put up with a lot from him over the last couple years and tried to remain positive, so an affair was a slap in the face."

"I bet, but thanks to you she has a plan and is being smart about things."

"I hope so. I'd better get to my emails. I'll let you get some sleep." He kissed me quickly and made his way downstairs to his office.

I tried not to let the fact that he wanted to be alone bother me. After showering, I waited up for him in bed awhile but finally fell asleep. Feeling him crawl in beside me later, I curled into him. When he didn't make a move to touch me after a few minutes, I propped up on my elbow.

Huh. He was already fast asleep. That was a first. Lying in a bed with Brian and no sex. I was annoyed with myself for expecting it. It had been a long, emotional day. Looking over at his sleeping face, I appreciated what type of man he was to ensure his friend was well cared for.

Deciding I wasn't going to get back to sleep anytime soon, I padded into the bathroom. It seemed that I stood there frozen in front of the mirror for an eternity before I realized there were tears streaming down my face. Before I registered what it meant, the dam started to break. The terrible things Juliette had facing her. The meeting with Vanessa that had turned into a personal attack. And lastly, although I didn't want to it to hurt, the death of my biological mother.

I grabbed a hand towel, trying to muffle the sound of my sob that sounded strange even to my own ears. I didn't hear Brian come in but felt his strong arms come around me. Turning, I buried my face in his shoulder, unable to control it any longer.

He didn't say anything, only stroked my back and let me cry it out.

Finally trusting my voice, I pulled back and murmured, "I'm sorry, I shouldn't have—"

He put a finger to my lips. "You have nothing to apologize for." He fixed his mouth over mine in a gentle kiss, only pulling away to tuck my hair behind my ears.

"The last thing you need right now is to have to comfort yet another person." I took a deep breath. "I'm okay. It's only a stupid moment of weakness." I was hesitant for him to see even a glimpse of my vulnerability for fear it would expose so much more.

He frowned. "You view needing someone, even for a moment, as a weakness, whereas I see it as a privilege to be that person for you. Would it help to hear that I needed to come home to you tonight? Needed to see your face and hear your voice?"

The tears slid down my face at his confession. "I'm not used to having someone to rely on like that. It scares me."

He smiled and held my face between his hands. "Then let's be scared together because I'm not letting go."

He kissed me deeply, and I could feel his fingers hook into the side of my panties, sliding them downward. I wasn't confident my emotional state could handle alpha Brian at the moment, however, and wavered.

He picked up on my hesitation. "We don't have to if you don't want to."

I pulled back, and my eyes locked with his. "I have something to ask you."

"Okay, ask me, honey."

I swallowed hard. "Would you make love to me?"

His eyes widened and reflected surprise, followed by something I couldn't identify. "Sasha, I—"

I didn't let him finish, putting a finger to his lips. "I know your whole theory on making love and having to be in love, but for tonight could you please fake it?"

His hand stroked the side of my face, and a shiver ran through me. He wiped the last tear that had slipped down my cheek.

I held my breath when he carefully lifted the T-shirt over my head. His fingers slid my panties down the rest of the way slowly, with his face lowering with the motion, trailing kisses from my hips to my knees.

There were no orders of getting on the bed or fast fingers this time around. Instead, he lifted me gently and placed me in the middle of his sheets. I watched, transfixed, while he took off his boxers as if in slow motion. He climbed up on the mattress and covered my body with his, settling between my legs but not entering me. His heat seeped into mine, our hands linking, and when he kissed me, the tension of the day melted away instantly.

Kissing my neck with soft nibbles, he slid down to my breasts. He teased them one by one, sucking gently. Back up the curve of my shoulder and over my collarbone, he moved up, kissing my lips reverently. "You are so beautiful."

For the first time, I was raw and vulnerable and didn't mind him seeing me as such. "You make me feel that way."

"Touch me," he invited.

Eager for the rare opportunity to explore him with unhurried touches, I glided my hands down his back, squeezing him tightly to me in a lover's embrace. My fingers ran through his hair, enjoying the silken feel of it. I smiled when he captured one of my hands and set it on the side of his face after kissing my palm.

His erection settled against my thigh, but still he made no move to fill me. Reaching down, I stroked him with my hand, enjoying the long sigh of pleasure that escaped his lips when I gripped his velvety softness.

He shifted his hips allowing me more access. "That feels like heaven."

Rubbing the crown of his hard length against my swollen clit, I moved him in small circles, then between my lips, coating him with my arousal.

"Your touch feels amazing." His seductive voice lulled me into this serenity that I'd never felt with anyone. The connection was almost overwhelming, and he wasn't even inside of me yet.

I traced his biceps with my fingers and then ran my hands slowly over his shoulders and down his back. Since he complimented me so frequently, I wanted him to know how very much I was attracted to him, too. "You're so sexy, so strong."

His lips settled over mine, and he kissed me now with tender urgency, stroking my tongue with his. He sucked in my breath until we were breathing like one.

I exhaled, so unbelievably consumed by his kiss that I swear I almost could've climaxed from the power of it alone.

His hand reached out and brushed my hair from my temple. He traced my lips with his tongue, then sucked on my bottom lip.

I shifted, aligning him with my slick entrance and letting him know I needed him now.

"Look at me," he quietly demanded.

My eyes locked on his, viewing such raw emotion in the depths that I was completely lost in the moment.

He entered me one delicious inch at a time, the whole while holding my gaze, emphasizing that this was making love.

I wrapped my legs around his waist and held him there, buried deep inside of me, for what seemed like eternity.

"You were made for me, Sash—"

Shifting my hips, I felt him harden even further inside of me. "Oh, God," I gasped.

We moved rhythmically as one with his hands lifting my hips up to the perfect angle, hitting my most sensitive spot. My eyes rolled back in my head in ecstasy even while trying to maintain contact with his. His breathing became erratic and his strokes faster. My climax came swift and hard, taking him over the edge with me.

---

LYING in his arms and listening to the rain come down, I knew something had shifted, but I didn't want to analyze it. The look in his eyes while he'd tenderly made love to me convinced me that I wasn't alone in experiencing mixed emotions. I knew this went against what he was comfortable with, what we had agreed on, and what we had ever done, yet I wouldn't have taken it back.

"The meeting with Vanessa didn't go very well, did it?" he whispered in the dark.

I sighed. "It could've gone better, but she signed anyways. I had to tell her that it was your idea." It was tempting to tell him about her personal comment, but I was a big girl and didn't need to lay one more thing on him.

He stroked my hip. "I'm sorry it had to be that way. Why didn't you tell me?"

"You had enough on your plate today, and it wasn't anything new with her. Besides, it wasn't the worst thing that happened today."

"What was?"

I hesitated. "If I tell you, you need to promise not to try to fix it, not to offer advice, or analyze my feelings. I can admit to needing you tonight, but I don't want this to turn into you trying to solve my problems."

"Okay, but now you have me concerned."

I shook my head. "Nothing to worry about. I, uh, received a call today via Nancy that my birth mom died yesterday. I don't have the details, only the number of an attorney who's been calling the last couple of weeks, probably trying to get money for rehab or maybe to get me to come see her. I don't know if it would have made a difference. It was a shock, but I'm okay." I swallowed down the guilt.

Brian held me tighter. "I want to believe you."

I bit my lip. Sasha-B-Fierce was supposed to be able to handle anything. "Then do."

The next morning, I had an early flight to catch in order to get back to the New York office to meet with another client about their newest campaign vision this afternoon. Packing my bag kept me too busy to analyze what had happened with us the night before. I'd needed Brian to be tender and sweet. He'd faked it well enough, but it had only been pretend and didn't change anything. With a little separation, I knew we'd be back to our previous arrangement and rid of any weirdness.

He carried my suitcase out to my rental car. "It's strange not having you spend the weekend and not dropping you off at the airport."

"It is." Even if I'd wanted to stay, Brian was off to California for his sister's graduation this weekend.

"I'm flying to Virginia next Friday morning. You're still coming in for McKenzie's celebration, right?"

I wavered, not realizing her party was already the weekend after next. Where was the month of May going?

"Unless you've changed your mind?" His voice had an edge.

He had misinterpreted my hesitancy. "No, I haven't. I was

only thinking in my head that I couldn't believe it was already the end of May."

He reached out, cupping my face. "I'll only say this once to keep my promise, but if you need anything…"

I held a finger up to his lips, knowing he was referring to the death of my birth mother. "I'll tell you."

"Good. I'll email you the hotel information for next weekend. And don't be anxious about my mom and sister-in-law. I'll make sure they're on good behavior. Of course, I can't say the same for me."

He tilted his head down for a kiss, and I tried not to think about the irony of him telling me not to be anxious.

# CHAPTER TWENTY-SIX

*I*t was Friday afternoon when I boarded the flight to Virginia for Kenzie's graduation party. Work had been hectic, but at least tension with Vanessa was manageable for the moment. Phase two was well under way with the Tryon Pharmaceuticals commercial set for filming next Thursday.

Several times I'd attempted to pick up the phone to call the attorney about my birth mother. But I'd never gotten through dialing the full number. Was I going to plan a funeral for a woman whose only redeeming quality was to give me up for the right amount of money? Did I want to know how she died? Why should I feel guilty? Putting most of it aside, I was ready for the distraction of a weekend with Brian.

After I landed in Dulles airport, I strode toward the exit, searching for the transportation signs. I'd take a cab to the hotel and hopefully see him later.

When I walked out of the security doors, however, I heard my name and glanced over to see him standing there, looking handsome as ever. Moving faster, I felt my heart fill with emotion. Somehow everything was better just seeing him.

"Hi," I breathed.

"Hi, gorgeous," he greeted, clearly not bothered by giving a public display of affection since he lifted me off of my feet and kissed me soundly.

I giggled, and when he pulled back, my breath caught. The way the man looked at me made me feel like I was the only woman in the room. "Tell me this means you're taking me to the hotel and we have some, uh, time."

He grinned, taking my suitcase and leading me out to his parked car. "Time for what, pray tell?"

I took out my work phone, turning on the wireless. "Hmm, if you have to ask, then perhaps I've lost my touch in inspiring it."

In the car, he gave me a sideways glance. "Do you think by any chance you can put your work phone away? The hotel is twelve minutes away, and I've already checked us in, which means I plan to be deep inside of you in thirteen." His hand reached over, unzipping my slacks and sliding his fingers into my panties.

Well, then. I shifted my hips to allow for better access and dropped my phone into my purse. Work was already forgotten.

---

IT TURNED out to be fifteen minutes before we were in the room and he was inside of me, but who was counting?

"Christ, I missed you," Brian murmured.

We were fast and furious, not even bothering with our clothes being all the way off before he buried himself deep inside of me.

His eyes flashed when I didn't respond, being too caught up in the feel of him.

I wondered if he'd wanted me to say that I'd missed him, too. But that thought was lost the moment my orgasm took over.

We lay there afterward for a few minutes before he kissed my forehead and walked into the bathroom.

The sound of the shower motivated me to get up. I tracked

his movements, while leaning against the doorframe as he adjusted the temperature of the water. "Mind if I join you?"

He crossed over to take my hand. "Only if we put an adorable shower cap on you because we don't have much time before dinner. Can't get your hair wet."

Kenzie's party wasn't until tomorrow afternoon. I hadn't known we had plans tonight. "Uh, what are we doing?"

"Dinner. The two of us. I want to take you out to a restaurant that was one of my favorites while growing up."

"Oh." I smiled, relieved that I didn't have to see his mother or Rebecca this evening. I swallowed past the lump of emotion when I thought about him taking me out to a place that was meaningful to him. He tucked my hair up under the hotel shower cap and kissed me tenderly.

"Don't worry, there will be plenty of the wolves tomorrow, but for tonight, I'd like to spend it with you and forget about the rest of the world."

"That sounds nice." I noticed the look of worry on his face. "Is everything okay, Bri? Is something going on with Juliette?" It felt like there was something he wasn't telling me. If it wasn't her, there had to be something else causing his expression.

"Juliette is okay. She's heading back up on Sunday. Can I ask a favor for this weekend, though?"

"Sure, what is it?"

"Do you think we can turn off work completely until Monday, put our business phones and laptops away?"

His question was a strange one to ask. Did he think I'd be on my phone during Kenzie's party tomorrow? "Do I get to ask why?"

He sighed. "Because after working the last couple of weeks nonstop, the last thing I want to do is talk about work or even think about it. Between the big NASCAR pitch I'm doing on Monday and helping Juliette, I'm burned out. Haven't you ever needed to turn it off for a while?"

I'd needed to turn off my personal life plenty, but never work. However, in looking at his weary face, I could see the burden in his eyes. The NASCAR account was huge. Coupled with the stress of helping Juliette, that most likely put him at his max. Nancy had my personal phone number, and she'd call me if there were any emergencies.

Reaching out, I touched his cheek. "Of course, we can do that."

He instantly looked relieved and kissed my wrist. "Thank you."

We washed quickly. While he dressed, I touched up my makeup and slipped on a dress.

"You're flying to Raleigh on Sunday?" NASCAR headquarters were located there.

"Yeah, pitch on Monday morning first thing. Then I'm flying back up to New York for a meeting with Josh." The last part was said with a sigh.

I turned, knowing something was definitely off by the resigned tone he'd used about meeting with Josh. "Do you want to talk about it? You sound down and…" I was about to say it was freaking me out, but wasn't the guy allowed to have a rough day? He'd been dealing with a full plate lately. "I'm here to listen if you want to talk about it." I wanted to be there for him for a change.

His eyes softened, and he turned me back around so that he stood behind me, both of us facing the mirror. "It'll all be better hopefully after Monday. And everything that I need is here." His hands splayed on my waist, and he leaned down, inhaling the scent of my hair. "Come on, let's go before I have other ideas."

I met his eyes in the mirror. "What if I'm into the other ideas?"

For the first time since I'd seen him in the airport, a genuine smile reached his eyes. "We'd have to make it quick because I have every intention of taking you out for a romantic dinner."

I pushed back, feeling him hard already. "Then you'd better get started."

Turned out we were late for our reservation. But we'd needed the extra time to ground us back into the here and now and let the week fade into the background. Now, if only it would stay there.

———

WE HAD an amazing date last night. True to his word, Brian put our work phones away, even going so far as to lock them up in the hotel safe. We hadn't looked at them since. I didn't regret a little downtime from the job, especially since his mood lifted almost immediately. But without the distraction of the job, my mind was fully focused on the upcoming party instead.

"Are you positive you want me to go to this thing with your whole family?" We were in the shower getting ready the morning of when I voiced my worry. I didn't need a crystal ball to tell me that his mother was going to be none too happy to see me there today.

"Have you changed your mind?"

His voice sounded disappointed, and I instantly felt bad, especially after he'd come to my parents' anniversary party. "No, I want to go, but you know how I get with meeting new people. I'm just nervous."

He took my hands in his. "Don't be. We'll be there Kenzie, and everyone will be on their best behavior."

Oh, sure, *don't be*. Such a guy's response. "What will we tell everyone, though?" This was the question that I kept asking myself. Unlike the situation at my family's event, there were plenty of crossover between our personal and professional lives at the celebration today. As Brian predicted, Josh was up in New York with Haylee, not wanting to travel this close to the baby's due date. But Josh's mother would be there for certain.

He grinned. "Hmm, let's go through the scenarios, shall we?" He pooled shower gel in his hands and began to wash me intimately.

"God—not the advertising strategy again," I groaned. But with one touch, I was ready to show up naked if it meant he wouldn't stop. My resolve needed a stern talking-to if ever I could locate it again.

"Option one is that we tell them that we've been having incredible sex the last few months, and we thought we'd announce to everyone that we're friends with benefits."

I managed a swat as he pinned my hips against the wall and started massaging my breasts.

"Option two is that we tell them we're only friends while you remember how I'm caressing you and pretend not to want to touch me during the party. I should warn you, though, that I'll have an old high school flame there, so you may see someone flirting with me the entire time." He moved me away from the wall and ran his hands over my backside, squeezing before running a hand between my legs again.

My breath hissed.

He leaned back, smiling, allowing me to rinse and catch my breath.

I didn't like either scenario. "Are those my only two options?"

The amusement that sparked in his eyes told me that he'd been hoping for my question. "There's one more choice." He turned off the water, moved me against the wall, and knelt down, eye level with my quickly-becoming-wet sex. He glanced up with a wicked grin. "Option three is we tell them that you're my girlfriend." His mouth descended on me quickly, zeroing in on my clit. Then he stopped suddenly. "Which option do you choose, Sasha?" For good measure, he reached out with his tongue and stroked the length of my slit.

"Why do I feel like you're stacking the deck toward option three?" I croaked out.

He chuckled. "Because your pussy gets a vote, and right now it's telling you to be my girlfriend so that I can bury my face in it."

His hot breath blew on my pulsating center, and my knees felt weak. Was I seriously standing in a shower against a wall, letting him use sex to get his way? Uh, yes. Yes, I was. Because evidently I'd been outvoted by the power of pussy. Terrific, now he had me calling it that. "Yes, option three."

Twenty minutes and two orgasms later, we were on our way to the party with Brian looking very pleased with himself.

---

I STARTED to fidget during the short car ride, feeling my anxiety grow over attending this party as Brian's girlfriend. I hated that I couldn't control my irrational thinking especially knowing it was *irrational.*

"Stop panicking. Everything will be good," Brian reiterated. We pulled up in front of his childhood house, and he squeezed my hand.

It was a beautiful home, set back with a private drive and gate. We stepped out, Brian handed over the keys to a valet, and then we walked toward the front door.

"Maybe we should wait. Today is about Kenzie, and I don't want to take any attention off of her," I reasoned, turning toward him before we made our entrance.

His fingers threaded with mine and he tugged me over to the side of the house. Framing my face in his hands, he met my eyes. "She'll be thrilled you're here. And you already agreed."

"I didn't agree. My treacherous pussy did. I may be your girlfriend, but to tell your mom, who knows Josh's mom... Is that what we're doing now?"

"Sasha Jayne Brooks, did you just say the word *pussy*?" he drawled.

Heat flooded my face. "That would be what you picked up from that entire sentence. And you're missing—Wait, what are you doing?" My eyes shifted down where he was using me as a shield to adjust himself.

"We need to stop talking about that particular word or anything having to do with it unless you want to greet my mother with me sporting an erection."

"Mother and erection probably shouldn't go into the same sentence," I pointed out dryly.

He laughed. "You're right and, poof, the problem has taken care of itself. Now, back to you panicking. What if I tell Josh on Monday?"

My breath left me. "That idea is only increasing my anxiety, Bri. It's a big step."

His gaze locked on mine. "I know it is. And this party is a small one toward that. I'm asking you to take it with me."

My stomach knotted with trepidation. I was moving forward in a relationship for the first time with the one man who I'd always trusted. "Okay, I'll try."

His eyes lit up, and he kissed me, not caring who might witness. Pulling back, he grinned and took me by the hand into the house.

---

"You're late, Brian, and what are you wearing? I specifically requested you to wear a white shirt for family pictures," his mother griped, coming up to us the minute we entered.

He kissed her cheek. "I prefer the baby blue shirt, Mother. You remember Sasha?" Brian asked, his hand on my lower back.

Her eyes left him for a moment and recognition dawned

when they settled on me. "I do remember her. What exactly are you doing here, though?"

I was prepared to answer, but Brian beat me to it. "She's my girlfriend, and she's here with me. Now, if you'll excuse us, I have a lot of people to introduce her to, but first we need to find Kenzie."

Her brows shot up. I could tell by the firm line to her mouth she was taking the news as expected.

He whisked me away in search of his sister and whispered, "That went better than I thought it would."

I shot him an incredulous look. "Seriously?"

The look in his eyes confirmed that he wasn't kidding.

Kenzie's reaction quickly made up for it, though. "Sasha, oh, my gosh. You came." She engulfed me in a hug and then looked to where Brian's hand held mine. "Are you guys—? Oh—oh."

Crap, she was starting to squeal.

Brian chuckled. "If you cry or screech like a girl you're going to send her for the hills. Do me a favor and play it cool for me."

She calmed down immediately, still smiling broadly. "Sorry. But you know I've never met a girlfriend of his before. Matter of fact, my friends during freshman year of college asked if he might be gay."

Now it was Brian's turn to look uncomfortable.

Huh, I liked the turn of this conversation.

"Really, Kenzie, that's the story you tell her? Is it any wonder I didn't bring anyone home before now?"

She stuck her tongue out and gave him a big hug.

"Has the fact that you're now a college graduate sunk in yet?" Brian kissed her on the cheek, looking proud of his little sister.

She beamed. "No, but that's probably because grad school is right around the corner. Mom's already pissed, by the way, because I'm not wearing the dress she picked out."

He chuckled. "She's ticked because I'm not wearing the white shirt, so there you have it. Per usual, the family bonding is off the charts."

She giggled. "Seriously, my dad is around here somewhere avoiding her probably sneaking the scotch already. Mom is such a control freak. I'm so glad we're not like that."

I stole a glance at Brian. His desire to be in control in at least one aspect of his life was making a lot more sense to me.

Judging from the tight smile on his face, he wasn't thrilled with his sister giving me this insight.

An interruption from Colby, however, distracted us all. "Hello, Sasha, Brian. Nice to see you both. Hey, Kenz."

We stood around chatting until Brian's mother interjected, insisting Brian and his sister join the family on the back lawn for pictures.

I was a spectator, along with Colby, watching while Brian's mother arranged the family in several poses. So far my anxiety in being here had been manageable. Maybe I could do this after all. I tried unsuccessfully not to laugh at the funny looks both Kenzie and Brian were giving me when my cell phone vibrated in my clutch.

I ignored it, figuring it would go to voicemail, only to hear it vibrate again. Pulling it out, I saw my assistant Nancy's number flash up. It was Saturday, and since she'd never called me on my personal phone before, I knew it had to be some sort of crisis.

"Excuse me, Colby, I have to take this," I said, stepping to the side. "Hello." Looking toward Brian, whose eyes were watching me closely; I smiled before focusing in on Nancy.

"I'm sorry to bother you on a Saturday, Sasha, and on your private number, but I tried to reach you yesterday on your work phone and via email…"

"I'm sorry, Nancy, I turned it off and shouldn't have. What's going on?"

"Evidently, Vanessa asked that Logan travel out instead of

you on Thursday for the shoot. She told him that she'd taken you off the account after meeting with Brian on Friday morning."

My eyes immediately flicked toward Brian.

His face looked concerned, probably from the way mine now appeared after getting this news.

"Did you say that Vanessa called Logan to tell him to come in my place because she'd told Brian I was off the account yesterday?"

"Yes. I'm sorry, Sasha. You may want to reach out to Brian to discover what might be happening. To find out from the client seems unprofessional. I would've thought—"

"Hang up." Brian's voice came from behind me, and he snatched the phone from my grasp. "Nancy, she'll have to call you back." He pressed the end call button and simply stared at me.

## CHAPTER TWENTY-SEVEN

*B*rian's expression let me know immediately that all of what I'd just heard had been true.

The blood drained from my face, and my heart rate skyrocketed.

"Sasha, it's not what you think," he began, pulling me further over to the side, out of view of everyone.

"Was I fired from the account yesterday?"

His silence and the grim set to his mouth were answer enough.

I tried to walk by him into the house. I needed to get away.

"Wait—" he said, grasping my elbow. "It's only temporary. There's a meeting on Monday that should resolve everything."

I turned and faced him. "But if I were to call her up at this very moment, what would she say? Oh, that's right, I can't because her number is in my work phone, and you made up some bullshit story about needing to put our phones away for the weekend because you were burned out. But that wasn't it, was it? It was to keep me from finding out. I thought maybe I was supporting you for a change, but no, it was all a deception."

"Look, it'll be fixed come next week, I promise. There's a plan—"

"I told you the one thing—" I started to have trouble talking as my heart rate and breathing began to spiral out of control. "— not to hide anything from me," I managed to get out some fragments.

He grimaced. "I wasn't hiding it. I was merely delaying it until I could..."

I wasn't listening any longer. I'd been removed from the Tryon Pharmaceuticals account on Friday morning, and my boyfriend, the one man I'd come to trust the most, had not only known about it, but had also kept it from me. He'd hidden it after I'd specifically told him how I felt about lies of omission.

Suddenly I was in a tunnel with everything becoming blurry. My heart raced, the pain of it beating so fast, it nearly doubled me over. I rushed into the house while feeling everyone's eyes on me and not being able to do a thing about it. I could hear them whispering, see them judging. And suddenly I was brought back to sixteen years old.

---

MY VERY FIRST panic attack had taken me completely off guard when I was a teenager. My mind hadn't known how to process the shock of finding out this homeless beggar woman was my birth mother and I'd been adopted. My body had shut down. I'd thought I was dying right there on the ground that day, clutching my heart and gasping for breath. Evidently, when the paramedics had arrived, they'd suspected I was experiencing a seizure. It wasn't until twenty-four hours later and a battery of tests that the doctors had determined I'd had a panic attack.

It's ironic that, to my parents, that had been a relief to hear. It meant I didn't have anything medically wrong with me. But for me, personally, it had been terrible news. I would've welcomed a diagnosis of seizures or something else that didn't have the same stigma. A panic attack meant I was weak. A panic attack meant I couldn't control things.

My parents had thought by hiding the fact that I'd been adopted, they were protecting me. But in fact they'd been shielding themselves, and so was Brian. It was only fitting that my second worst panic attack in history would start with his betrayal.

But unlike the first one, on this occasion my body knew what to expect, and I could use some of the techniques I'd learned over the years to manage it. Both Brian's and Colby's voices came into focus, and I found myself in a bedroom. I vaguely remembered someone taking my hand and leading me upstairs.

"I'm calling nine-one-one," Brian said, dialing his cell phone.

I shook my head adamantly and tried to speak. "No, it's a—" Breathe, Sasha "—panic attack."

He looked like he didn't believe me, and then Mark was there, too. Brian's college friend must have arrived at the party after we had. Then Brian's mom came in, and somewhere I could hear muffled tones arguing.

Terrific, now my anxiety was rising again. "Please—need—people—to—leave." For sixteen years I'd been able to keep this secret and now it was on display for everyone. It was my worst nightmare.

Brian knelt in front of me, grasping my hands. "Honey, how do you know it's a panic attack? What if it's something more serious?"

I shook my head and looked imploringly at Colby and Mark, who were hovering.

Finally, Colby, bless his heart, started telling everyone to get out. I could only hope one of them hadn't been McKenzie. I was sure I'd already ruined her party.

"I've—had—them—before."

Brian looked confused. "What are you talking about? When?"

I couldn't begin to go into it with him, especially since he'd been partially responsible for this one. "Please go, Brian." At least that had been a full sentence.

"I'm not leaving. Tell me what I can do."

I shook my head, wanting to be left alone. I couldn't have him, of all people, see me like this. Climbing off the bed quickly, I bolted for the bathroom and emptied the contents of my stomach.

Brian's hands held my hair back gently. After I was done, he offered me a cool wash cloth.

My head was pounding, but my breathing had started to level out. It was amazing how slowly time crawled when you wished it to go quickly, but I'd learned there was no rushing an attack, else you brought on a second one.

Brian's eyes looked concerned. "How about I drive you to the hospital?"

"No—I need to go lie—" Breathe. "—down at the hotel."

"Okay, I'll take you."

"No." I met his eyes, and that word hung between us. "I can't." The tears were starting to come now. If I didn't get out of here soon I'd be a complete hysterical mess and Brian would want to comfort me. If that happened, God only knew what else I'd reveal.

"Sasha, please—" His handsome face looked absolutely devastated.

But there was nothing I could do to soothe him or tell him it would be okay right now. I had to concentrate on myself for the moment. I walked out to the bedroom, unsteady on my feet, to see both Colby and Mark looking for direction. "I need a taxi."

Both of them glanced toward Brian.

"Why don't you lie down here for a few minutes?" Mark suggested.

I shook my head, feeling the panic start up again. "Please—I need—to go."

Brian put his arm around me, but I stepped back, not wanting his touch.

"You're making it worse—please—" The shame had started to settle in and I couldn't meet his eyes. I was no longer the Sasha he thought he knew. Instead I'd humiliated him in front of his friends and family, not to mention myself. Yes, his betrayal had been the catalyst, but a normal person could have stormed off or cursed him out. My over-reaction highlighted my inability to deal with anything challenging.

"I can drive her," Colby offered.

"No, you've been drinking. I'll take her," Mark stepped in. "Colby, you get the car brought around. Here's my tag for the valet."

I didn't know the man very well, but at that moment I was eternally grateful.

Brian's mouth fell into a hard line and both men moved to the corner of the room to have a heated debate. Finally, Mark prevailed and took my arm to lead me out.

Thank goodness Colby had the lay of the house. He bounded up the stairs and took us down the back way.

Brian didn't follow.

By the time we got in the car, my breathing had steadied and my heart rate had calmed. Absolute exhaustion battled the adrenaline needed to get the hell away from this place. I couldn't handle answering any questions about my history or revealing any more than I already had. The gig was up, and it was a matter of time before Brian wanted answers.

During the drive, Mark gratefully hadn't said anything, only chancing a few glances toward me, mostly likely to ensure he didn't have to GPS it to the nearest hospital. After pulling up at the hotel, he put the car in park, apparently intending to get out with me.

I held up my hand. "I'm better now, thank you."

He hesitated. "I realize we don't know one another very well, Sasha, but Brian insisted I see you up to your room."

"Then he'll have to get over it," I snapped. Wincing at my tone, I felt the tears threaten again. "I'm sorry, Mark. Look, I have to do this by myself. You can tell him I wouldn't let you up." I couldn't handle one more sympathetic look today.

He sighed. "No need to apologize. And I know this isn't my place, but I have to say it. Brian may have screwed up, but he's one of the best guys I know."

Yes, he was. Even in messing up, he'd managed to be tender and kind, wanting nothing more than an opportunity to explain himself. My panic attack had only confirmed that my reaction had been out of proportion to the problem. The Sasha he knew would've read him the riot act and left with her head held high. Instead, I'd hit rock bottom with plenty of witnesses to my shame. And on top of everything else, I'd ruined Kenzie's graduation party.

I turned toward Mark before getting out of the car. "Then the issue is obviously me."

---

PACKING QUICKLY, I knew I was on borrowed time. When Brian came back to the room, I intended to be gone. My pounding head made it challenging, however, and I had no choice but to move slower than usual. After glancing around the room one last time, I wheeled my suitcase toward the door. Briefly, I thought about my work phone in the safe and dismissed it. I didn't have the combination anyhow.

Opening the door, I came face to face with Brian. He was about to swipe his card.

His eyes glanced down to my suitcase and back up to my face. "I thought you were going to lie down."

"I changed my mind. You should be back at Kenzie's party. I already ruined some of it. She doesn't need her favorite brother leaving to spoil the rest." My voice was thick with emotion. It was one more thing I hated about myself at this moment.

He frowned. "She doesn't even know it happened. Everyone else there thinks I screwed up and you needed a minute. It's not as bad as you think it was."

Yeah, right. "I need to go. I have a plane to catch."

"Sasha, please give me a few minutes."

I shook my head, feeling the tears. "I can't."

He stepped into the room, forcing me to move back. The door closed behind him. "I know I screwed up, but if you'll give me until Monday to fix—"

Needing some distance, I moved toward the window, holding up my hand when he tried to come closer. "It doesn't matter."

"Don't say that. It does matter. I didn't want to keep it from you, but there are a lot of variables at the moment we're working through. It's bigger than just you or me."

The explanation didn't matter at this point. The only thing that did was getting out of here before he asked more questions. "I have to leave." My voice cracked on the last word.

"Tell me about the panic attacks."

"No." My eyes met his, and I took a deep breath, willing myself not to go into another one.

"So you can feel betrayed with my omission about Vanessa, but the fact that you've never mentioned your panic attacks before isn't the same thing?" He ran a hand through his hair, frustrated.

I sucked in my breath. "It's not the same thing, and you know it."

"How is it not when I'm ready to call an ambulance because I don't know what the hell is going on today, only to find out that it wasn't the first time—Oh, shit—did you have one that day after Jamie came by? Is that what that was?"

The air left my lungs. My secret had not only been on display at Kenzie's party, but now Brian was putting together the entire truth. Now he'd know that I was incapable of handling any stressors without collapsing into a panic attack. I'd spent the last sixteen years building up an image that had taken less than thirty minutes to implode completely. I moved toward the door.

He grabbed my arm. "You could've told me, Sash—"

I truly was on the verge of having another attack. His sympathy was only making it worse. I couldn't let him see me needing him. "I can't do this right now. I'm sorry, it's too much."

His eyes flashed with pain, and his voice rose. "So when would it be the best time?"

"What?" Why the hell was he getting angry?

"You agreed to be my girlfriend. Agreed to take the next step, and yet you can't even tell me that you fucking miss me. You can't tell me for a second that you might have feelings, too."

"I agreed because you pressured me and—" I immediately regretted my words when I saw the shattered look on his face.

"Right. I've pressured you into this whole thing. Into the rules, into sex, into a relationship. All of it." His voice was thick, and I could see the hurt in his eyes.

Although I didn't mean it and knew I was making a complete mess of this in the process, I reasoned it might be for the best if he believed that. By his own admission, I couldn't give him what he wanted. I stood quiet.

"You know what, maybe I did deliberately push you out of your comfort zone and into a relationship. In my defense, though, I did it because I'm in love with you. I'd hoped I could convince you to feel the same."

"You love me?" I asked incredulously.

He nodded. "For the last eight years."

My heart sank when I realized what that meant. "You don't love me, Brian. You don't even know me."

He looked like I was talking crazy. "How can you say that?"

"Take a good look at me. I'm not the girl you think you know." I took a deep breath. It was best he knew all of it to save him the energy of thinking he could love someone like me. "I have an anxiety disorder. I've had it all my life, but the attacks started when I was sixteen, and I found out I was adopted by having my crack-addict mother come to school during lunch to ask me for money. My parents kept it from me my whole life. Three years ago in Miami when I received that call, and we had our almost-night: panic attack. Puking my guts up after Jamie left—You guessed it correctly, another one." I paused, taking in his wide eyes and shocked expression. I was fire hosing him with my confession, but I couldn't stop now that the seal was broken.

"I throw up before each and every pitch like clockwork and shake so badly afterwards that I'm absolutely exhausted. I wear a black hair tie on my wrist to snap whenever I'm anxious, which is All. Of. The. Fucking. Time." I showed him my wrist since I'd worn one to the party. "And the truth is: Maybe I've never told you that I miss you or shared my feelings because I realize now that it doesn't matter how I feel, this relationship could never work. As much as I wish I was, I'm not the girl that you respect or that you thought you knew. I promise if you did know me, you wouldn't miss me at all."

"That's not true." Scrubbing a hand over his face, he looked completely overwhelmed with the barrage of information. "If you'd give me a chance, we can figure this out. Have you seen a therapist about your anxiety? Maybe we could go together."

I squeezed my eyes shut and fought the tears. Just when I thought I'd hit my lowest point, having him feel sorry for me was so much worse. "Stop, please."

"Sorry, I know I'm getting ahead of myself. We can take it slower. But I can even ask Mark for his therapist's name. He's up in Connecticut, and I hear he's really good. I only want to help you—"

And there it was. The unmistakable sound of what I'd tried to avoid my whole life. Someone seeing me as broken. My utter humiliation was complete. I was officially at rock bottom and Brian, someone I respected and who had once respected me had a front row seat. "I know that you'd like nothing better than to help. Part of it is because you're a good guy, the other part may have something to do with trying to control the circumstances. But I can't do this." My heart was breaking, but a happily ever after wasn't in my future. So I said the only thing I could to get him to let me go: "This isn't working for me any longer. I'm sorry."

"You don't mean that." His voice shook with emotion.

I took an unsteady breath and walked through the door. I needed to leave before I became selfish and clung to him.

"Sasha, wait—"

I turned, desperately wishing I could be the girl he thought he loved. "I'm not Sasha-B-Fierce. I never was."

# CHAPTER TWENTY-EIGHT

*A*fter the cab dropped me off at the airport, I made a beeline for the car rental counter. The last place I wanted to go was back up to New York and ironically, the one place that did appeal to me was home. The drive would be therapeutic, and I'd return to New York when I was ready.

I called my mother briefly, telling her I was on my way home. She didn't ask why, only told me to drive safely and that she'd see me soon. The tears didn't start until the halfway point into the six-hour drive from Virginia to coastal Carolina. Eight years. How could he have thought he'd been in love with me that long?

The sound of my phone coming over the car's Bluetooth startled me. Brian's number flashed, and it was tempting to answer, but I knew I'd break down if I talked to him again right now.

Giving up after a couple of attempts, he left me a text message.

*"Let me know that you're okay when you get home. Please."*

Unfortunately, it was one more reminder about what a great guy he was and launched me into a fresh round of tears over the fact that I'd never be good enough. I typed back that I was okay and left it at that.

Grateful to have the long drive behind me, I stepped through my parents' front door, and my mom greeted me immediately with a hug. When her arms came around me, I lost it.

My father, bless his heart, took over while my mom went to go fix some tea. It was her answer for anything troubling.

The big wall of a man took a seat next to me and let me cry it all out on his shoulder. Some fathers might have left a sobbing daughter to her mother, but not my dad. He knew I needed both of them.

Finally, when it subsided, I met the concerned eyes of both my parents and took a deep breath. "I don't know where to begin."

My dad patted my hand. "You start wherever you need to, baby girl."

Over the course of the next twenty minutes, I confessed to the couple dozen panic attacks I'd had over the years, the continued therapy, and my need to avoid confiding in anyone about it. I finished with my humiliation at Kenzie's graduation party today.

The tears in both their eyes showed me how they felt about not having known any of it.

"Also, you should know that my birth mother died." I sipped my tea feeling marginally better after telling them everything.

The look that they shared made it obvious they'd already heard the news. More secrets, and yet at this point, it didn't matter. How hypocritical for me to ask that they confide in me when I'd spent years hiding the shame of my anxiety attacks from the world.

My father cleared his voice and got up to pace the floor. "I'm sorry, Sasha. If we'd known that attorney had a way of contacting you, we would've told you sooner that he'd informed us as well. We didn't want to tell you over the phone."

I wasn't even angry at this omission. Considering the way I handled stress, was it any wonder people kept things from me? Sighing, I confided what had happened three years ago with paying for failed rehab and not returning the calls recently.

"Maybe if I'd called him back and had given them money for rehab, she would be getting better instead of—" Another sob broke free as the guilt slammed into me. As much as I'd tried to tell myself she didn't deserve my money, time, or love, the thought of her dying alone left me devastated.

My big bear of a dad held me like he had when I'd been sixteen and had fallen apart the first time.

Finally, when my eyes had gone dry, my father spoke softly. "She was in a state-run rehab when she passed. She was getting help, but it was too late. It was her heart from years of drug abuse. And you should know, your mother and I, we paid for a private burial. It's not much, but there's a headstone in a local cemetery outside of Raleigh."

I pulled back and searched their faces. "Why did you do that?"

My mom sat beside me and stroked my hair. "We did it in case you ever wanted to go there. Your birth mother had a troubled life that none of us could have ever saved her from, but without her, we wouldn't have you. She deserved that much from us."

I hugged her tight. Where on this earth could I have ever found better people? "Thank you." I sat back and wiped my eyes, slowly getting back to even ground.

My mom hesitated but then got up and walked into the kitchen. She came back with an envelope in her hand. "Her attorney, he gave us this to give to you. When you're ready."

"I'll take it with me, read it when I am. I don't think I've ever felt this lost. I'm not sure where to go from here."

My father patted my knee. "From the moment I laid eyes on you, I saw a survivor. There's nothing you can't conquer if you put your mind to it. You've been doing it your whole life. So you take one day at a time."

I shook my head. "I'm not strong, Daddy. Look at me."

"You know, you keep telling yourself that, and you may even start to believe it. Do you think people who are strong get there because they've never had to handle adversity?"

"I suppose not."

"I'd argue the toughest people got there the hard way. You, baby girl, have always pushed yourself. You could've chosen a lot easier path, but you didn't. And no matter what happened today with Brian, I could tell when that boy came here for our party that he loves you. It was written all of his face when he looked at you."

I smiled at the fact that he called Brian a boy. In my Daddy's eyes, we were both still kids. I took a deep breath. "He thinks he does."

"And why do you say it like he couldn't possibly?"

"Because he didn't know about any of this." I motioned to myself. Here I was, a thirty-two-year-old woman, sitting on the couch and crying my eyes out in front of my parents.

"Seems like he does now," my mother whispered.

"I fire hosed him with it all, and I know he feels bad—" My sentence was interrupted.

"Do you think he loves you because he feels sorry for you?" my dad asked, indignant at the very thought.

I cracked a smile at his disapproving tone. "No, but he saw only what I wanted him to over the last eight years. Now he sees all of it. I can't stand to have him look at me like I'm broken. He deserves better than a crack-addict's daughter who has an anxiety disorder and the inability to handle stress."

I was unprepared for my mother's anger when she shot up from her seat.

"You listen here, Sasha Jayne Brooks. You're not some crack-addict's daughter, you hear me? You're my daughter and that of your father. We raised you, and you're as much a part of us as if I'd given birth to you. I don't ever want to hear you demean yourself like that again. You should be damn proud of yourself, because I know we sure are."

My brows shot up in shock. In thirty-two years, I'd never heard my mother swear. A giggle escaped my lips. "Did you just curse, momma?"

My dad laughed, and then my mom cracked a smile. "Damn straight I did. Should tell you how passionate I feel about the subject."

For once, coming home had been the best decision.

---

WHILE THE MOONLIGHT still shone in the windows of my childhood bedroom early Sunday morning, I got up and took a walk on the beach. It was deserted at this early hour and it gave me peace. Sitting down in my favorite spot, I waited until dawn started to color the sky before I took the folded envelope out of my pocket.

There was no letter like I'd expected, but instead was a photograph that had seen better days. It showed a beautiful teenage girl with a baby tucked into her arms, smiling tiredly into the camera. On the back it simply said.

*"I always loved you, Sasha."*

The tears flowed freely and I wiped my nose on my sleeve. I'd always assumed I'd been given up because my birth mother hadn't loved me. But I'd never considered the kind of unselfish love it took to give your child up in order to give them a better life. My parents as I'd always known them provided me the life my birth mother never could have.

Looking up, I saw my sister approaching. She was the last person I'd have expected. She settled beside me, putting her arm around me.

I broke the silence after a couple of minutes. "How did you know I'd be here?"

"We came over to the house to meet for church, and Dad told me about your birth mom passing. I figured you'd be here. I'm really sorry by the way."

"Thanks, but how did you know it was here in this spot?" I was hidden away from anyone driving by and I hadn't parked a car.

She sighed. "After you'd found out about being adopted, I used to follow you, back in the day, when you'd come here. You would sit for hours, sometimes staring, sometimes crying. I've always regretted that I didn't try to comfort you."

I swallowed hard at that image. "You were only twelve, Addison, hardly able to know what to do. And I didn't know how to let anyone in at the time. Hell, I'm still working on it." But it seemed I was getting better by the minute.

"I was always so in awe of you," she whispered.

"You mean until that day."

She shook her head. "No, even more so after, actually. You were so strong and so independent. I was always intimidated by it."

I raised an incredulous brow. "I was barely holding it together."

She sighed. "I wish I would've known."

We sat there in silence as the sun came up.

Finally, I spoke. It was the first time I'd ever confided in my sister. "Brian had a nickname for me. It was Sasha-B-Fierce. That image came crashing down yesterday in the form of a panic attack."

She regarded me for a moment before answering. "The fall always seems further when viewed with your own eyes than it actually is. After I had Kassandra, I suffered from postpartum depression. I was much harder on myself than everyone else combined."

I looked at her, stunned.

She drew a shaky breath before continuing. "Here I was with an amazing husband and three beautiful children already. I should've been a pro. Instead, I could barely get out of bed and would cry for no reason. Mom and Dad knew and, of course, Ryan, but I was humiliated. I'd worked so hard to be the perfect mother and show I could do it all, and yet I couldn't seem to function."

I could hardly believe she'd been through this, and I'd been clueless. She always seemed to have it together. "What did you do?"

"Well, I started out telling Ryan he needed to leave me, because he was better off without someone like me. He of course told me to shut up and that he couldn't afford the child support even if he wanted to."

I grinned. "I can see him saying that."

She laughed. "I got counseling. When I told my therapist he'd said that, she was appalled, but after meeting him, she realized it's his personality. And it's what I'd needed, a little laughter, instead of sympathy all of the time. I still go to a group thing once a week and meet with other women who are going through it now. Ironically, helping others is how I got through the feeling of inadequacy. Once you realize everyone struggles, you stop beating yourself up so much. I guess what I'm attempting to say is trying to be perfect is exhausting. Trying to keep up the perception when you know you're not is even worse. It's like you're lying to yourself every day in the hopes that no one will catch on. I don't want my kids to grow up having this unrealistic expectation of themselves or others. I want them to know it's okay to make mistakes and have problems. The best way I could do that is to be honest with my own."

I'd never thought about it from that perspective, and wondered if that was why Juliette hadn't wanted to confide in me. Had I alienated people from confiding in me because I'd always gone out of my way to project this image that I didn't struggle? Clearly the answer was yes considering this was the first time Addison had ever admitted something in her life was less than perfect.

Ironic that admitting our faults was making me feel closer to my sister than I ever had. "I'm sorry. I wish I would've known, but in saying that realize I've never given you a reason to confide in me like this."

"I wish I would've known about you, too. But now that we do, we could be there for one another."

I swallowed hard. "I'd like that. I love you, Addison."

Her shocked eyes met mine. Sadly I wasn't sure I'd ever said those words to her.

"I love you too, Sasha."

We returned to the house and enjoyed a family brunch. There were no snipes, no passive-aggressive comments, and I realized the vulnerable Sasha I'd worked so hard to hide turned out to be more likeable than the defensive version. After my sister and family left, I went upstairs to pack, intending to return to New York tonight.

My dad knocked lightly and came in the already-open door. He took a seat on my bed. "What's the plan?"

I shrugged. "Back to work. As far as Brian and the personal stuff—I'm petrified and don't know what to do." I'd had a lot of self-reflection upon coming home and was beginning to get past the humiliation of what had happened, but how could I be certain Brian loved the real me?

"Darlin', you're the quarterback in the red zone on fourth down with inches to go. Do you want the ball, or will you settle for the field goal?"

I grinned. "I want the ball."

"You always have. But what you need to remember is that you've got an entire team behind you, blocking, cheering, what have you. There's nothing wrong with relying on those who love you to support you, Sasha Jayne. No one can do everything alone."

"You're right." I already felt lighter having confided in my family.

"Good. And remember, nothing says if you don't like the play, that you can't revise and call an audible. You're in control, baby girl, and don't let anyone ever tell you differently."

How could I possibly argue with a man who could spin a football metaphor into a life lesson?

---

WAITING in the airport for the last flight, I winced when Josh's number came up on my cell phone. I wondered immediately if Brian had confided the personal details of our relationship to him, but then realized, it didn't bother me if he had.

"Sasha Brooks here."

"Sasha, it's Josh. I hope I'm not calling too late." Was it my imagination or did he sound off?

"No, I'm at the airport waiting on my flight back up to New York. Everything okay?"

"Actually, no. I'm in a predicament. Brian had a conflict come up for tomorrow morning's NASCAR pitch, and I need someone to step in."

"That pitch is huge. What could possibly conflict with it?"

He exhaled. "NASCAR is big, but this is bigger. Will you do it?"

Clearly, he wasn't going to tell me the reason.

"Yes, of course. I, uh, need the pitch deck and any notes. I'm at the airport now. Raleigh is a three-hour drive, but I'd prefer to fly, so I can use the time to prepare."

"I can have my plane there within the hour. I'm forwarding all of the information as we speak. The two other members presenting with you have been advised of the change. I'll send you their details and you can plan to meet with them in the morning. I owe you."

It might be inappropriate on a professional level to ask, but I had to. "Tell me the conflict isn't a meeting with Tryon Pharmaceuticals on my behalf."

"Not directly, no. Good luck tomorrow, Sasha."

After hanging up the phone, I texted Brian.

**"What's going on tomorrow that you're not able to do the NASCAR pitch?"**

By the time the company's private plane flew me to Raleigh, North Carolina, and I arrived at my hotel, it was around midnight. In that time I'd studied everything I could about the NASCAR pitch. The good news is that, having grown up in the South, I'd had the damn sport—or in my opinion, non-sport because unless I could see an ass in tight pants and there was a ball, it didn't qualify—shoved down my throat. My father was a fan, with racing a close second to football. It didn't take long for me to brush up on the key drivers, standings, and races. It was going to be an all-nighter, but I would absolutely be ready. I wouldn't have been able to sleep tonight anyhow, knowing Brian still hadn't responded to my text message.

I met my team of two others before the pitch at the local diner first thing in the morning, and we went over our cues. At least I knew both of them, and they were grateful I was stepping in last minute.

Ninety minutes later, we were in the corporate offices, and I was tossing up my pancake breakfast right on cue in the ladies' room. I put my lack of sleep, Brian's non-response, and all anxiety out of my head. It was game time, or was it start-your-engine time? Maybe it was a good omen I was thinking in NASCAR terms.

I LEFT for New York directly after the presentation and arrived in the early afternoon. I was tempted to call Josh but knew if he'd wanted to answer the question as to why Brian had missed the pitch, he would've told me already. Or Brian himself would have. Unfortunately, he still hadn't responded.

My eyes were heavy, but I managed to go into the office and work a couple of hours before Nancy buzzed in. "Ms. Brooks, I have Mr. Singer here to see you."

"Uh, of course, send him in." Josh had never once come to my office unannounced.

Nancy gave me a look that reflected her surprise as well while she showed him in.

I stood up to greet him. "I could've saved you the trouble and come to your office."

"You're operating on no sleep after giving a killer pitch. The least I could do was to come over here."

"How do you know it was killer?"

"The client called. They were very pleased and we got the account. Plus Brian received an email today from one of the managers you presented with, saying how you slayed it. Do you know that there isn't one other vice president who could've pulled that off this morning like you did? Especially operating on no sleep with only ten hours of lead time."

"Thank you." It was high praise indeed coming from Josh.

"No, it's you I should be thanking."

"You're welcome. Are you going to tell me why Brian missed it?"

He sighed. "I promised him I wouldn't speak to you about it." He handed me a paper over my desk. "But I didn't say anything about showing you."

I scanned it briefly, and my heart sank. It was Brian's resignation. "Because of me?"

Josh looked like he wanted to say something. "The only thing

I can tell you is there was a meeting with Michael Dobson, the Chairman for Tryon, this morning. He was appalled that Vanessa had removed you. As of now, you're back on the account, and all decisions going forward need to be approved by him. Vanessa is no longer an employee of Tryon Pharmaceuticals."

"Holy crap. She was fired?"

"Yes, she was."

"But how did Brian's resignation come into play?"

"Michael said to convey his apology to you because, unfortunately, he's leaving on a two-week vacation to Australia this afternoon and can't do so in person. We were lucky enough to get the meeting with him this morning."

Why was he speaking so cryptically? Then I finally saw it. "Oh shit. Brian took the meeting with Dobson this morning instead of doing the NASCAR pitch?"

Josh nodded.

I stood up and paced. "I'm going to kill him. He could've waited, or I would've dealt with being off the account. Why did he need to be there? Wait, you didn't demand his resignation, did you?"

He looked insulted. "Of course not."

"I know you made a promise, but you're going to have to spell it out for me Josh."

He hesitated, and then decided to spill it. "Brian was upset that Vanessa took you off the account on Friday. I told him to wait until Monday for me to address it with Michael and not to say anything to anyone until then. But he called her Saturday demanding that you be reinstated. He told her he was going to take it up to the chairman and unfortunately Vanessa escalated things."

"Escalated how?" Something told me things got ugly fast.

"Brian will have to explain those details. Unfortunately this morning was the only time we could meet with Michael and with what transpired, Brian's presence became required, which is why you had to do the pitch down in Raleigh."

"But why the resignation if everything was taken care of?"

Josh sighed. "Because he feels like his personal decision to contact Vanessa Saturday night instead of following my direction is what made it go to hell in a hand basket. I don't disagree, however I never would've fired him for it."

There was only one reason he would've called her Saturday night. Because he'd wanted to fix things for me after I'd left that hotel room. "Shit."

"I told him I wouldn't accept it, but I'm not quite sure how I go about enforcing that."

I swallowed hard at the fact that he would go against his best friend and boss in an attempt to fix things for me. "Where's he now?"

"Stuck on a tarmac, waiting to fly back down to Charlotte. I guess there's a delay with my private plane." His smirk made it obvious what the real interruption was.

I didn't even think. I dialed his number on speaker.

"Brian Carpenter," he answered.

I froze the moment I heard his voice. Sasha-B-Fierce had dialed that phone without hesitation and was ready to give him hell. But if I wasn't really her, what would I have to say to him?

"Hello?" his voice came again.

Swallowing hard, I stopped over-thinking and went with my gut. "It's me. What the hell's going on?"

"Sasha, I heard you did an amazing job with the NASCAR pitch. I'm hoping you had a chance to speak with Josh to find out you're back on the Tryon account." His voice sounded flat.

"I did. Matter of fact, he's here with me. And your presence is required."

He sighed. "That's not happening."

The panic from his response started to fuel my temper. "We can either do it the easy or the hard way, Brian Carpenter. Either you get your ass in here right now, or I hand in my resignation this very minute." I met Josh's shocked expression.

"You don't mean that."

"The hell I don't. If you think you're the only one who would sacrifice your job for someone you love, think again."

He inhaled audibly. "What did you say?"

"If you want me to repeat it, then I suggest you figure out a way to get here quickly." I hung up before he had the chance to respond.

I turned toward Josh. "I guess now might be a good time to tell you I probably need a new supervisor. Hopefully, you're not too shocked to learn that I happen to be in love with the one I have now."

He chuckled, amusement showing in his expression. "Sasha, in the interest of full disclosure, you should know that eight years ago Brian told me that someday he hoped to have a conversation by which he informed me that his relationship with you had changed. He's been my best friend since we were five years old. Whether he wanted to hide it or not, I've always known that you've been *the one* for him from the moment he met you. Regardless of that, though, your career here has always been separate from his feelings for you. I value your talent and I hope you know me well enough to know you've always earned your position."

I bit my lip at the fact that I'd needed that confirmation. "I appreciate you telling me that."

"By the way, I've been entertaining the idea of creating a new VP position for someone who does nothing but client presentations. It would take the pressure off the VP's who are better suited toward the client care aspect and allow our very best people to win the business. This person would have to travel a lot, but could relocate to any office of their choosing. Do you know of anyone who might be interested?"

I smiled. "I can definitely think of someone who would

consider it a dream job. That is if I don't have to resign to prove a point to Brian first."

He chuckled. "Let's hope it doesn't come to that."

Nancy's voice interrupted via the intercom. "Josh, I have Haylee on the line. She said she only wants me to interrupt if you're done speaking with Sasha. But considering she admitted her water just broke, I told her that you were finished."

We both looked at each other wide-eyed until Josh finally recovered. "Okay, uh, yes, put her through. Shit."

He picked up my desk phone and swallowed hard, his eyes going wide. "Yes, I'll be right there. Okay. Are you having contractions? Okay, I'm on my way. I love you."

He hung up with a panicked look. "She's early." His hands were white-knuckling the desk.

How ironic that I was the one attempting to calm someone else down. "Each of my nieces and nephews was early. The first one was four weeks. A week or two is nothing, Josh. Get it out of your head and go get your wife. You're about to become a dad."

His face split into a grin. "Come on, you're getting in the car with me. You can help keep Haylee focused while I freak out. I'll text Brian and tell him to meet us there."

# CHAPTER TWENTY-NINE

*H*aylee was an absolute champ, getting into the town car all prepped and ready. She looked beautiful and relaxed, but when she gripped my hand, I instantly knew it was a show to keep her husband calm.

I offered her a reassuring smile.

While Josh was on the phone with his mother, she leaned over. "I'm kinda flipping out."

Huh. Clearly I wasn't the only one who'd ever faked my emotions to give a different impression from what I was actually feeling. "My go-to solution for that problem is off the table considering it would involve an alcoholic beverage."

She giggled and then was in a fit of them, finally tensing when a contraction came.

It apparently passed, and Josh squeezed her hand. "Nigel is making the remainder of the calls. I did text Brian. He'll meet us at the hospital."

Haylee sighed. "Does that mean he's retracting his resignation?"

Josh winked at me. "Oh, I think Sasha will make sure of it."

I KNEW the moment that Brian arrived in the waiting room, my body sensing his presence.

Our eyes met, and then he glanced at the clock. "What's the latest?"

"They think within the next hour," I responded quietly. "Do you have a minute?"

"Can we talk?"

Our simultaneous requests bounced off one another.

Nodding, I led him down the hall into the chapel. One look around the small room confirmed we were the only two people there.

I didn't give him a chance to speak first. "Why did you resign, Brian?"

He sighed. "I screwed up with Vanessa and instead of doing as Josh had asked, I made it a lot worse."

Blood pounded in my ears. "How did you screw up with her?"

He shifted uncomfortably which only heightened my growing anxiety about what he was going to tell me.

"Last week she kept calling, saying she was in Charlotte and wanted to get together for drinks or dinner. I blew her off, going so far as to claim I was traveling. Then she showed up at the office on Thursday night, waiting by my car. She came on to me, and I told her that I was involved with someone. She guessed it was you; I don't know how. I wouldn't confirm it, but it didn't matter. I think she saw it on my face. The next morning, she took you off the account."

I put my hands over my face. She'd known because of the way I'd reacted to her personal shots toward me.

"You have to believe nothing happened with her. The cameras proved that."

"I do believe you, unequivocally." I knew in my heart Brian

would never lie about something like this. "But why would you need cameras to prove it?"

He raked a hand through his hair. "Josh and I spoke on Friday and we both agreed that once Michael Dobson knew about you being taken off, he'd fix things. He told me to have no contact with her and leave it alone until he could meet with him."

"But you called her Saturday?"

His jaw clenched obviously unhappy that Josh revealed that much. "Unfortunately I did. I told her that she could make it right and if she didn't we'd go to Dobson. I made it personal wanting so badly to be able to call you that night and tell you I'd made things right. Instead I tipped our hand and on Sunday all hell broke loose. She told the chairman that I'd come on to her. That we'd slept together the night we met for drinks in New York and that once you'd found out, you had a personal issue with her which is why she couldn't work with you any longer."

"Jesus." I was shaking with rage.

"Josh was able to do some serious damage control before Monday to get both the hotel footage and the recording from outside the office building to show Michael that Vanessa had been lying."

"But why did you resign?"

"Because I screwed up everything. I not only went against Josh's advice, but I put the company in jeopardy. And let's not forget the NASCAR pitch that got punted to you last minute because I had to be in New York first thing instead. Lucky for me, Josh resolved the first problem and you stepped in and fixed the second one."

"He doesn't want you to quit."

"I know, but that's because he's my best friend, not because he's thinking as a boss."

I was absolutely shocked that Brian would believe this. "You can't be serious."

"I am. Take our friendship out of the picture, and I would've been fired. Hell, I might not have been given this job to begin with."

"You're crazy if you think the only reason Josh hired you or wants to keep you on is because you're his best friend. You've helped him build this company. There isn't one person who knows you or works for you who believes you have the job because you're the friend of the owner. You earned it."

"That's not what my mother thinks."

How could I never have picked up on his vulnerability when it came to his career? Had I been so selfish in my own insecurities that I'd never supported him through his? It would appear so. "Your mother would also like nothing more than for you to drop me. Are you going to listen?"

"I don't have to. You dumped me, remember?"

I exhaled heavily. "I was kind of a sucky girlfriend for the couple hours I wore that title in public, wasn't I?"

His lips curved into a small smile. "I wasn't going to win any awards, either, keeping the truth about Tryon and Vanessa from you. You should know, I really did want the break from work. I didn't think that Vanessa would actually say anything over the weekend to let you know. That's part of what set me off too. I still can't believe she made it so personal toward you."

"Yeah, well in the spirit of that, I should tell you that the last time we met one-on-one, she asked me if I was fucking you either now or in the past. I denied it, but I'm pretty sure, like you, she could see it on my face."

"And you're only now telling me this?" His frustration was evident.

"It was a personal attack, and you had a lot going on with Juliette at the time, but I'm sorry. I shouldn't have kept it from you. And obviously you should've told me about her coming to see you."

He regarded me for the longest time. "Apology accepted and given right back to you."

How could I stay mad when we had both been picking and choosing what to tell one another at some point? "You're going to have to withdraw your resignation, you know."

He arched a brow. "Are you really going to quit a job you've worked your ass off for if I don't? Your career makes you happy."

"You make me happier, Bri. And if that means we're both in the unemployment line because you don't realize how great you are at your job, then so be it. I'm pretty stubborn when I want to be."

His eyes widened with my admission. "You realize that for someone who professed not to be Sasha-B-Fierce, you're doing a damn good impression of her at the moment."

"Turns out she may have rubbed off on the real me over the years." I hadn't given myself enough credit that she was part of my personality all along.

He stepped closer. "Tell me what you said on the phone earlier."

"Before I do, you should know what you're in for. I'm serious when I say there's a lot you don't know—"

He cut me off with a kiss. "I need to hear that you love me."

"I love you, Brian." I watched a shudder run through him. "But—"

He put his thumb to my bottom lip. "No buts. Do you really think I don't know you, Sasha Jayne Brooks?"

My breath caught with the seriousness of his voice.

"I may not have known that you had anxiety attacks or what initially triggered them, but I do know that it makes you even fiercer. The fact that you've battled an anxiety disorder your whole life is remarkable. You think that I don't know what that must've cost you, how many times you must've fought it, and how lonely that must have been. But now that I do know, it only makes me more in awe of you."

His hands held my face so that our gazes were locked. "Bri—"

"I know *you*. How you listen to Titanium or other chick empowerment music before your pitches. That you go home on Friday nights after the gym and become a hermit until Saturday with some sort of chocolate indulgence. How you like to hear the bad news before the good because it's easier for you to trust the bad. I know that you love the beach when it's winter or early in the morning because it's where you can clear your head. And I know you told me you don't believe in fairy tales or happily ever after, but fuck if I'll accept that."

A tear slipped down my face. "You don't see anxiety disorders or panic attacks in fairy tales."

His mouth twitched in amusement. "You could dissect Cinderella or any of those other princess chicks. They all have flaws."

My brow arched. "Did you just call Cinderella a chick?"

He chuckled. "Yes. And I'd argue, in my completely unqualified opinion, that her being a grown-ass woman and letting her stepmother and stepsisters abuse her speaks of a deep issue with self-worth. Think about it. Why didn't she move out and get a job that paid?"

"Are you really psychoanalyzing Cinderella?" I smiled through the tears.

"If it makes you feel better, I'll go through all of them. Sleeping Beauty couldn't stay away from a simple needle on a spinning wheel? Seriously?"

I burst out laughing.

He kissed my nose playfully. "I love hearing that sound. My point isn't that I'm trying to bash princesses but that we all have flaws, and finding out that you have some is frankly a relief."

"That's the second time I've heard that in the last twenty-four hours. My sister said the same thing. It dawned on me that may be the reason Juliette hasn't reached out to me."

He shrugged. "You'd have to ask her, but I do know it's hard to admit faults to someone who doesn't appear to have any."

"That's my line for you. By the way I've had a therapist since I was sixteen. I only see her about twice a year, but I do have someone." Suddenly I didn't mind telling him all of it.

He winced. "I shouldn't have suggested that you needed to see someone. It wasn't my place."

"I blindsided you with a lot of information on Saturday, and you were only trying to help. I felt like, with all of my issues, I didn't deserve you." Admitting this out loud was the hardest thing I'd ever done.

"Honey, I almost hate to burst this misconception that I don't have my own issues, but in addition to never admitting my insecurity about working for my best friend, it's pretty damn clear that I'm the one who's screwed up the most in this relationship. If there is anyone who doesn't deserve someone, it's me not deserving you or a second chance for the fourth time."

It was a tremendous relief that he didn't see me as less for having an anxiety disorder. "It bothers me that I made you feel like you had to call Vanessa on Saturday."

"That's not your fault. My calling her on Saturday is more attributable to the fact that I can't stand it when issues are left unresolved. Another flaw in case you're counting. And it's the reason I couldn't be reminded about work over the weekend. I was already on edge, wanting to repair it."

"I'd resent you if you tried to fix me." My voice was barely a whisper. There was so much hanging on his response.

"I've never seen you as broken, honey. I may not know everything about your history, but anything you could tell me is something I'd accept because I already love you. All of you, unconditionally. What you may consider an imperfection only makes you more perfect for me."

His hands skimmed down my back, and he captured my lips in a consuming kiss.

Suddenly, a thought occurred to me. "That girl who moved away that you said you may have loved."

He grinned sheepishly. "It was you. It's always been you." He buried his face in my neck and inhaled my scent deeply.

"We're in the chapel," I reluctantly protested, feeling his lips run behind my ear, halfway tempted to continue this despite that fact.

He groaned in objection but leaned back. "Come on, our friends are having a baby. We'll continue this later, though."

I nodded, taking his hand and going with him back into the waiting room.

---

ABIGAIL MARIE SINGER made her way into the world approximately one hour later. Friends and family were on their way from all over the country, but for now only Brian and I were going into the room to see the happy couple and their new baby.

"We won't stay long," Brian said softly, peeking at the tiny little face cradled currently in Josh's arms.

I walked over to the hospital bed and hugged Haylee. She looked absolutely beautiful despite only just giving birth. Considering that most women ended up with hours upon hours of labor, I couldn't believe it had happened so quickly. "She didn't waste any time coming into the world, did she?"

Haylee blushed, and Josh gave her a half attempt at a disapproving look. "Seeing as her mother had been in labor since this morning and didn't say anything for hours, it's a wonder we made it to the hospital in time."

My eyes widened, and Haylee shrugged. "Josh had a lot of critical things happening today and was under enough stress already. She was content to wait until everything was resolved."

Oh, shit. Brian and I shared a look that conveyed our mutual horror that we were partially to blame.

But Josh played it off. "I think it's only appropriate, considering we'd like to ask you two to be the godparents of our little angel. Later we can tell her this story of the last twenty-four hours. I'd like to leave out the fact that on the day she was born both of you resigned, however."

Shocked at the request, I looked toward Haylee, who was smiling.

Josh handed the baby over to an equally stunned Brian.

I swallowed past the lump of emotion in my throat. "I don't know what to say."

Josh chuckled. "It would help if you both said yes."

Brian looked down into Abigail's face and in a baby-soft voice that had us all grinning said, "You drive a hard bargain, little Abby. Of course the answer is yes, and I officially withdraw my letter of resignation."

I nodded. "Yes, I'm honored." I brushed my fingertips over her downy hair. "And since Brian isn't resigning, I guess I'm not, either."

Josh was all smiles. "We may be setting a serious precedent in Abby getting her way, but I think it's worth it."

Abigail started to fuss, and Brian was quick to hand her back to Haylee.

He turned toward me, taking my hand. "You ready?"

I nodded, and we both offered our congratulations one last time.

Josh patted his friend on the back and walked us out. "Hopefully, you guys are ordering pizza tonight?"

I was totally lost as to why he'd ask this random question, but Brian chuckled.

"Uh, yeah, definitely," he replied, grinning.

IN THE CAB I looked at him. "What was with the pizza thing?"

He laughed. "It's code from college that was basically asking if we'd worked things out."

"You had a code in college for *working things out*?'"

"Uh, well it was more for getting lucky, but times have changed."

"You've got to be kidding." I covered my face with my hands, embarrassed.

He peeled them down into his own hands. "Come on. It was his way of making sure we're good."

I shook my head. "He's my boss's boss."

He kissed my hand. "And you're the godmother of his daughter and friends with his wife. Welcome to the world of personal and professional blurred lines. Plus if you were choosing something to be self-conscious about, I'd think it would be the fact that now he knows you were the girl he provided me period advice for."

I wanted to die a thousand deaths in that moment. Words failed me.

In front of my condo building, he helped me out of the car and quipped, "Honey, I did warn you I'm terribly flawed."

I giggled and realized I was undeniably in love with this man. "Are there any more faults I should know about? Maybe we can declare this *Amnesty Monday* and get them all out of the way."

We walked onto the elevator, and he pulled me into his embrace. Searching my face, he wore a thoughtful expression. "In the spirit of full disclosure, you should know that I've been trying to get you to fall in love with me this whole time."

"For eight years?"

He looked a little nervous to tell me. "I dreamed about it for eight, but you should know the rules were only for us."

"But you said you've done other arrangements like this."

"Sort of, but the rules were like, 'no sex at my actual house'

or hard limits for sex. Yours were to get you to stay with me."
We went through my front door, and he seemed to be bracing
himself for my reaction.

"What else?" I kept my expression neutral.

He hesitated. "I may have used sex a time or two to get my
way."

I smiled. "Oh, I'm quite aware of your methods, Brian
Carpenter. But realizing you went to all that trouble to get me to
fall in love with you only makes me love you more." I kicked off
my heels while watching him slip out of his shoes.

"I love hearing those words from you. And in the spirit of
this *Amnesty Monday*, you should probably know my dirty little
secret: I like hockey more than football."

"You can't possibly mean that." I clutched my chest as
though it hurt my heart. Then my hands moved to the buttons on
his shirt, impatient to touch him.

"I'm afraid it's true, but I've recently had incentive to pay
more attention to football. I need to ask you something about
what you told me on Saturday."

"Ask me anything." For the first time, I sincerely meant it.
There wasn't a part of me, either good or bad that I didn't want
to share with this man. It was such a relief to be honest about
it all.

"Do you really throw up before every pitch?"

My hands held his face. "I do, but please don't ever ask me if
I'm anxious. Think of it as my pre-game ritual before I take the
field and get into the zone." I slid the shirt down his arms and
lifted his T-shirt over his head.

His fingers reached around and unzipped my skirt, allowing
it to pool at my feet. He paused while unbuttoning my blouse.
"Oh, I thought of something else. You should know I have a mild
aversion to spiders."

I helped him with the last button. "I already knew that. Juliette made fun of you one day. Said you screamed like a girl, and she had to get it from your office."

He lifted me up in his arms and lay me on the bed. "It was humiliating," he muttered.

I could hardly concentrate when he unfastened my bra and lowered his head, taking a nipple between his teeth. My back arched in response. "Don't worry, I'll kill the spiders for you. But since we're disclosing all, you should know I'm a little tone-deaf. So don't expect karaoke ever."

He met my eyes, and I wondered how I could've missed the way his adoration was reflected in them. "I love you, Sasha, but I've heard you humming along to a song and know without a doubt you are not a little tone-deaf, you are completely tone-deaf." His fingers hooked in my panties and tugged them down.

I laughed. "Oh, and I don't know if you've noticed, but I'm kind of high maintenance."

"I wouldn't want it any other way. I love that you're high maintenance."

"Ha, you say that now, but no judging when in a few years I start getting Botox or some kind of Asian mud mask to keep wrinkles at bay." My hands worked his boxers off while his fingers found my slick entrance.

"You're already perfect in my eyes. I'm good with whatever you want, although I'm not a fan of you going under the knife. By the way, I tell people I'm allergic to caviar, but really I can't stand it."

I gasped when he replaced his fingers with his hardened length, feeding it into me slowly until he filled me completely. "I like ketchup on my tacos."

He completely froze and looked down into my face. "That is absolutely the most disgusting thing I've ever heard," he deadpanned.

Giggling in response, I arched my hips, wanting him to

move. "What? It's made with tomatoes and is practically like salsa."

He shook his head. "Nice try, but it is so-o-o not like salsa. I think I may have lost my erection, honey."

"Ha, you definitely did not." He was hard as ever. "That's the deal breaker out of everything?" I gripped his muscled backside and welcomed him deeper into me.

He grunted his pleasure and then moved with long, slow strokes. "There is no deal breaker, Sasha. I'm in this for the long run even if that means I will never eat Mexican food with you."

He sealed his declaration with a scorching kiss, bringing me to orgasm quickly.

"I have a request," I murmured, coming down off the high of my climax.

"I would expect nothing less, being as high maintenance as you are, but hold that thought for a few minutes."

Vocalizing my displeasure in him pulling out with a groan, I was pleased he wasn't done yet. He moved me to the edge of the bed, threw my ankles over his shoulders and took me deep on one stroke. He moved hard and fast, hitting the very end of me. After his orgasm hit, he brought me to another one of my own. Moving us both to the center of the bed, we lay there, panting for breath, naked, and entwined with one another.

"What's your request?" he asked, snuggling me into him.

"I think we need to see one another more often than once every two weeks."

"How do you propose we do that?"

I trailed a finger down his chest. "Josh is going to create a position for someone to head a client presentation team. I'm going to take the job and move down to Charlotte. Did I forget to mention that?"

His expression was priceless. "You're serious?"

"Very. I need to work out the details, but he did say I could pick which office I'd work out of. But you do know the more time we spend together, the more we may need to invoke rule number one."

"I may start picking fights on purpose just to ensure that." He pinched my backside mischievously. "Can I ask you something?"

"Anything."

"What do you think about being my girlfriend again? I promise I'll wait at least forty-eight hours before screwing something up this time."

I didn't hesitate. "No."

He sat up, looking surprised. "I was kidding about the last part. I think I could go at least a week."

My lips twitched. "I said no because I don't need to think about it. You're my best friend and make me happier than I've ever been. And when we're apart, I don't just miss you. I physically ache for you, can't stop thinking about you, and count the minutes until I get to see you again."

"Wow, you, uh win for the best *I miss you*—that was definitely worth the wait." He kissed me deeply, pulling me into him.

I put my hands on either side of his face. "I'm finding out that the best things often are."

# EPILOGUE

*W*atching the woman I'd been in love with for the last eight years moving toward me across the upscale Manhattan bar, with her eyes only for me, provided me a thrill that I'd never get used to. I absolutely loved the seductive way her hips swayed while her pencil skirt and heels made me want to throw her over my shoulder and take her some place private. We'd only been apart for five days while she made a short trip to Raleigh and then took care of selling her condo up here in New York City, but it felt like forever.

"Hi," she greeted in that breathless little way that did a number on a man's senses.

"Hi, yourself." I kissed her fully and smiled internally when she gave the little sigh of pleasure I adored so much. I'd have lipstick on me for the effort, but since her full lips were the sexiest thing on the planet, it was well worth the sacrifice.

"How did the closing on your condo go?" I was chomping at the bit to get her back to my hotel room but needed to stall in order to give Haylee and Catherine some time to set up.

"All right, but I missed you a lot."

My heart felt like it would explode out of my chest. I'd never get used to hearing her say those words and how they made me feel. "The sentiment is quite mutual. How was Raleigh?" Sasha had insisted on going by herself to visit her birth mother's gravesite. Watching her be brave alone was one of the hardest things I'd ever done. But it was also a testament to how far I'd come in working out my issues about wanting to fix everything. I'd both given her the space she needed and hadn't pushed her to talk about it directly afterward.

Her hand took mine. "It was difficult, but I needed to do it." She took a deep breath with tears in her eyes. "I was thinking the next time, maybe you could come with me?"

"I'd be honored." I cleared my emotion-clogged voice. She was so much stronger than she'd ever give herself credit for. Knowing she needed a change of subject I asked, "Do you think you'll miss living up here in New York?"

She smiled appreciatively. "I'll miss seeing my friends, but I'll travel up here every so often. North Carolina feels more like home anyhow. Now the only thing left is to look for a place down in Charlotte."

I didn't like the sound of that one bit. "You know you can stay with me."

"I love your place, but I need my own office and a space that I can put some of my things."

She'd been transitioning into her new role over the last few months and spending half her time in the Charlotte office, but I couldn't wait for her to move down permanently. "I like you staying with me."

"Then ask me something," she challenged.

I grinned. Oh, I was going to ask her something, but not right now and not what was on her mind. "Ask you what?" I decided to play dumb.

She blew out a breath, looking nervous. "Do you want to

move in together? We could get a bigger place, which I know sounds greedy considering I'm coming from a one-bedroom condo, but we could get something a little more his and hers. I'm not pushing too fast, am I?"

It was ironic that she was worried about moving too quickly when she was the one who normally panicked. It was also amusing that on the same night I was about to propose, she was asking me to move in with her. My beautiful, impatient, overanalyzing girl.

"Well, it's a big step," I hedged and then quickly reassured her when I saw the hurt flash in her eyes. "Sorry, bad joke. Of course I do. These five days apart have been torture."

She instantly smiled and leaned over, whispering in my ear, "How about we get out of here and celebrate?"

"Okay. Let me finish my drink." I needed to buy some more time. I shot a text to Haylee to make it quick as we'd be leaving the bar in fifteen minutes.

Ten minutes later, Sasha narrowed her eyes at me. "Are you are nursing your drink?"

"Impatient, are we?"

I watched while she snagged my martini glass and threw back the rest of the contents. I could add that to the long list of ways she turned me on.

"Yes, I am." She ran her hand over my bicep and leaned in for another kiss.

This woman was absolutely perfect for me. "Let me pay the tab, and then we'll go."

She smiled with satisfaction, and I prayed the waitress would take her time. Hoping to kill a few more minutes, I went to the men's room and sent another message, this time to Josh to call me and pretend it was work related. I still needed to stall.

I went to meet her in front, frowning on cue at the call coming through. "Hey, Josh. Um, no, we were about to head back to the hotel." I held up a finger for her to wait a moment. Being the professional woman she was, she pinched me on the butt and gave me some space to take the call from our boss.

"Yeah, no problem. I can get those to you. Huh, that is some interesting news." I was having a hard time keeping a straight face while Josh read me a book for his baby girl.

"Then the cow went moo and the horse went neigh—" Josh used a voice that I'd never heard before. Fatherhood definitely agreed with him.

I breathed a sigh of relief. "She went outside. Thanks, man. I owe you."

"No problem. Are you ready?"

I patted the box in my pants pocket and smiled. "I am. Oh, your wife's text came through. I'll talk to you tomorrow."

"Sounds good and Brian? Congratulations."

"Thanks, and give my goddaughter a kiss from me." Josh had been my best friend since we were five years old. It felt only right that he would be the first one to congratulate us.

---

"I THOUGHT we'd never get here," Sasha said, taking my hand in the elevator. A hum reverberated through my entire body in anticipation of what I was about to ask her.

Opening the door to the hotel suite, I let her go first and followed, pleased with what her friends had managed to do. Rose petals covered the king-sized bed, candles adorned every surface, and champagne on ice was by the small bar.

She faced me, smiling. "Wow, you went all out. This is very romantic."

Funny how she didn't assume this was a proposal at all. I leaned down and kissed her breathless, taking my time with her delectable lips.

"I'm ready to ask you something now, but only if you promise not to answer me for thirty minutes. Do you think you can be patient?"

She gave me the little "mm-hmm" that made me smile.

I dropped to one knee and watched her eyes register surprise.

"Sasha Jayne Brooks. You're my best friend and I fall in love with you more every day. You challenge me in all the right ways and make me incredibly happy. Would you do the honor of becoming my wife?"

"Oh, my God," was her response.

I took the box from my pants pocket and opened it. I hoped she liked the vintage solitaire diamond that her girlfriends had helped me pick out.

"Wait, I don't get to answer you for how long?" Her eyes were wide and her beautiful face confused.

"Thirty minutes, starting now," I said, putting the ring on the nightstand and pointing toward the alarm clock. I tugged her hand and pulled her toward the bed, kissing her neck. I took immense enjoyment from the fact that her eyes kept flicking back to the ring.

"Why are you making me wait?" The frustration was evident in her voice.

"Because I've received a hundred percent yes rate thus far when I talk you into things using sex."

She shook her head, trying not to laugh while looking annoyed. "Can I ask questions, though?"

The motivation behind delaying her answer to my question was for this reason. I knew her mind was processing the negative before the positive. That she'd need to voice her doubts and work through her anxiety before coming to what was in her heart. "Of course, but only if you get naked."

She rolled her eyes playfully at my bargaining methods but complied. "What about kids?"

The sight of her beautiful body on display had me almost distracted from her question. But it was an important one, so I made sure I locked my eyes on hers. "I could take them or leave them. Honestly. We could even adopt if you wanted to."

Her face softened at the thought. "And my last name?"

"Keep it, change it, hyphenate the crap out of it. It doesn't matter to me."

"Okay. But living together is a huge step," she barely got out, moaning when my fingers parted the lips of her pussy. She was hot, wet, and ready for me.

"Agreed, and we can have a long engagement if you'd like." I trailed kisses down the column of her throat. I had to use every ounce of willpower not to rush this. She did this to me. Made me feel like I could never get enough of her incredible body, her sassy mouth, and an inner strength that had attracted me to her in the first place. As if I'd ever been the one actually in control of this relationship.

I made love to her slowly, the way I'd always wanted to from the beginning but was afraid to, lest she see the way I'd actually felt about her for so many years. Now there were no more pretenses, no more walls.

We lay there after amongst the rose petals, catching our breath. I tried not to smile at her glance toward the clock.

She propped up on my chest. "What about the rules?"

Ah, yes, the rules. The best decision I'd ever made to ease her into a relationship with me in the hopes she'd fall in love with me. Considering how lucky they'd been for us, I was all for keeping them.

She traced a pattern on my chest with her finger and I was hard pressed not to flip her back onto the mattress for another round.

"Did you want to keep them?" I asked.

"I do, but I think we need to revise some of them. Especially since some of them would be moot after becoming engaged."

My heart beat faster at the fact that she was already thinking along those lines. "What would you like to change?"

"Namely, we need to negotiate some Sasha time."

"And here I thought all the time was Sasha time," I quipped, traveling south in order to prove my point.

"Let me rephrase then: I want some Mary Beth time."

I laughed at the memory of our time in Aruba. "Oh, I think Austin would like that, but it won't be tonight."

"You're right. Tonight you're going to, uh, ensure I forget my name and then do it again."

I cracked up at her inability to talk dirty, which turned me on more than if she'd been really good at it. "Your wish is my command."

She wasn't having it. "Not so fast. What time is it?"

I wasn't offended that she was looking at the clock again, considering I wanted her answer more than anything. "You have four more minutes."

She huffed and then lifted that indignant brow of hers. Reaching across me, she snagged the ring out of the box and slipped it on her finger, meeting my eyes. "I did warn you that I'm not very good at being told what to do all of the time, didn't I?"

I chuckled. Then a peace settled over me that I imagined would only be trumped by our actual wedding day. There had been no one else from the day I'd met Sasha eight years ago. She was my best friend, colleague, and now, finally, she'd become my wife. I kissed her deeply and hugged her tight, never wanting to let go. "I love you."

"I love you, too. I'll warn you, though, you'll need to ask my daddy for my hand. He's kind of old-fashioned that way."

I smiled smugly. "I already asked your father and invited him to the next Super Bowl."

She sat up, completely taken aback. "You got my father tickets to the Super Bowl?"

"Yes, and I asked for your hand in marriage, in case you missed that part, too." My girl loved her football.

Her cheeks heated. "I didn't mean it to sound that way."

"I know you didn't. But the best part is that I did get an extra ticket for you to accompany him."

She sat there quiet.

I'd expected a squeal or some sort of excitement. "Honey, you're kind of freaking me out with the non-reaction here. I did say the words *Super Bowl*. Plus, technically, you haven't said yes to me yet on the proposal."

"Ask me again," she whispered.

I arched a brow in surprise. Sitting up so that we were eye to eye, I took both of her hands. "Will you marry me, Sash?"

She threw her arms around me with tears in her eyes. "Yes. A thousand times yes. But don't you think for one moment there is anything else better about tonight than you asking me to become your wife. Not the ring, not the romance, and not the Super Bowl tickets."

I kissed her softly, not realizing until this moment how much I'd needed that confirmation from her. She recognized that underneath my pleasing nature was an insecurity that had silently needed to know she wanted to be with me despite all of the rest. "You must really love me."

She smirked. "I do. And thank you."

"For what?"

She pulled me down onto the bed and snuggled in close, putting her newly-adorned hand on my chest so that we could both survey the sparkle of her ring. "You think I don't know how you've managed around my anxiety with this proposal and kept me from panicking, but I do."

I swallowed past the lump in my throat. "You're okay with that?"

She scooted up and kissed me soundly. "To have someone

love and know me the way you do is better than okay. It's the freaking fairy tale."

I grinned at that sentiment. "Agreed, although our happily ever after will be a little bit naughtier."

She gave me a wicked grin. "Oh, I'm counting on it."

---

**Read the next book in the Something Series! Kenzie and Colby's story is up next in Bet Me Something.**

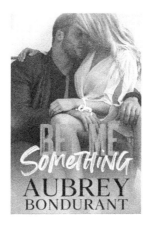

# ACKNOWLEDGMENTS

Since I published my first book, Tell Me Something at the end of June 2015, I've been on a remarkable journey. I've been fortunate enough to meet some incredible people all over the world who have taken the time to lift me up and give me the encouragement to continue.

To Karen, Donna and Sam: I have no words to tell you how much I've appreciated your advice, support and laughter. In a world where it is sometimes easier to believe the negative, your positive words, generosity and support have inspired me. And to all of the other book bloggers who continue to take chances on a new author: thank you. You are the unsung heroes for an Indie author with your tireless reading, reviewing, promoting and oh yeah, doing your day job and managing your families as well. Your efforts do not go unnoticed!

To my husband and children who continue to respect "mommy's laptop time" I love you and appreciate your patience with my "hobby."

To my friends and family who will read this book and know exactly how I came up with *ketchup on tacos*-I figured you might like that. (I swear it gives a taco that extra tang that makes it delicious! You know you want to try it now :-) A huge thanks to those who have been genuinely thrilled to not only read my book and support me, but share it with the world (even with your 90 year old grandmothers-I'm still blushing) I can't tell you how much it means to me!

And last but not least, to my editor, Alyssa Kress. You've been invaluable in this process since day one. You encourage me to push myself towards my very best work and keep it on the rails. I couldn't do it without you! www.alyssakressbookediting.com

Made in United States
Orlando, FL
10 June 2022